Praise for Clive Barker's

IN THE
FLESH

"Barker...gives his stories the certainty of bad dreams.... The first and last tales in this collection stand out as horror classics, meriting frequent glimpses into dark corners for a good while after they are done....BARKER DELVES INTO ADULT NIGHTMARES WITH THE SAME BLOODTHIRSTY GLEE AS STEPHEN KING...."
—*Boston Herald*

"With elegant, terrifying strokes, Barker draws a universe of fear underlying the commonplace.... Behind every mirror, under every carpet and in the heart of dirty streets is an elemental evil, a raw and hungry power.... This is good, scary stuff.... The pacing is inexorable, the settings chilling, and the fates remorseless. *IN THE FLESH* MAKES YOU WONDER WHAT HORROR LIES AROUND THE CORNER...."
—*Detroit News*

"BRILLIANT HORRORS BY CLIVE BARKER: A FINE NEW BRITISH WRITER..."
—*Kirkus Reviews*

"CLIVE BARKER PLAYS UPON OUR UNCONSCIOUS TERRORS....WHAT A BREATH OF FRESH, IF CHILLING, AIR."
—*The New York Times Book Review*

(more...)

Books by Clive Barker

The Inhuman Condition
In the Flesh

Published by POCKET BOOKS

Most Pocket Books are available at special quantity discounts for bulk purchases for sales promotions, premiums or fund raising. Special books or book excerpts can also be created to fit specific needs.

For details write the office of the Vice President of Special Markets, Pocket Books, 1230 Avenue of the Americas, New York, New York 10020.

CLIVE BARKER

IN THE FLESH

PUBLISHED BY POCKET BOOKS NEW YORK

POCKET BOOKS, a division of Simon & Schuster, Inc.
1230 Avenue of the Americas, New York, N.Y. 10020

Copyright © 1986 by Clive Barker
Cover artwork copyright © 1988 Jim Warren

Published by arrangement with the author
Library of Congress Catalog Card Number: 86-20450

ISBN: 0-671-61270-0

First Pocket Books printing January 1988

10 9 8 7 6 5 4 3 2 1

POCKET and colophon are trademarks of
Simon & Schuster, Inc.

Printed in the U.S.A.

To Julie

Contents

In
the
Flesh

WHEN Cleveland Smith returned to his cell after the interview with the Landing Officer, his new bunk-mate was already in residence, staring at the dust-infested sunlight through the reinforced glass window. It was a short display; for less than half an hour each afternoon (clouds permitting) the sun found its way between the wall and the administration building and edged its way along the side of B Wing, not to appear again until the following day.

"You're Tait?" Cleve said.

The prisoner looked away from the sun. Mayflower had said the new boy was twenty-two, but Tait looked five years younger. He had the face of a lost dog. An ugly dog, at that—a dog left by its owners to play in traffic. Eyes too wide, mouth too soft, arms too slender: a born victim. Cleve was irritated to have been encumbered with the boy. Tait was dead weight, and Cleve had no energies to expend on the boy's protection, despite Mayflower's pep talk about extending a welcoming hand.

"Yes," the dog replied. "William."

"People call you William?"

"No," the boy said. "They call me Billy."

"Billy." Cleve nodded, and stepped into the cell. The regime at Pentonville was relatively enlightened; cells were left open for two hours in the mornings, and often two in the afternoon, allowing the cons some freedom of movement. The arrangement had its disadvantages, however, which was where Mayflower's talk came in.

"I've been told to give you some advice."

"Oh?" the boy replied.

"You've not done time before?"

"No."

"Not even Borstal?"

Tait's eyes flickered. "A little."

"So you know what the score is. You know you're easy meat."

"Sure."

"Seems I've been volunteered," Cleve said without appetite, "to keep you from getting mauled."

Tait stared at Cleve with eyes the blue of which was milky, as though the sun were still in them. "Don't put yourself out," the boy said. "You don't owe me anything."

"Damn right I don't. But it seems I got a social responsibility," Cleve said sourly. "And you're it."

Cleve was two months into his sentence for handling marijuana, his third visit to Pentonville. At thirty years of age he was far from obsolete. His body was solid, his face lean and refined; in his court suit he could have passed for a lawyer at ten yards. A little closer, and the viewer might catch the scar on his neck, the result of an attack by a penniless addict, and a certain wariness in his gait, as if with every step forward he was keeping the option of a speedy retreat.

You're still a young man, the last judge had told him; you still have time to change your spots. He hadn't disagreed out loud, but Cleve knew in his heart he was a leopard born and bred. Crime was easy, work was not. Until somebody proved otherwise he would do what he did best, and take the consequences if caught. Doing time wasn't so unpalatable if you had the right attitude toward it. The food was edible, the company select; as long as he had something to keep his mind occupied he was content enough. At present he was reading about sin. Now *there* was a subject. In his time he'd heard so many explanations of how it had come into the world, from probation officers and lawyers and priests. Theories sociological, theological, ideological. Some were worthy of a few minutes' consideration. Most were so absurd (sin from the womb, sin from the state) he laughed in their apologists' faces. None held water for long.

It was a good bone to chew over, though. He needed a problem to occupy the days. And nights; he slept badly in prison. It wasn't *his* guilt that kept him awake but that of others. He was, after all, just a hash pusher, supplying wherever there was a demand: a minor cog in the consumerist machine, he had nothing to feel guilty about. But there were others here, *many* others, it seemed, whose dreams were not so benevolent, nor nights so peaceful. They would cry, they would complain, they would curse judges local and celestial. Their din would have kept the dead awake.

"Is it always like this?" Billy asked Cleve after a week

or so. A new inmate was making a ruckus down the landing: one moment tears, the next obscenities.

"Yes. Most of the time," said Cleve. "Some of them need to yell a bit. It keeps their minds from curdling."

"Not you," observed the unmusical voice from the bunk below, "you just read your books and keep out of harm's way. I've watched you. It doesn't bother you, does it?"

"I can live with it," Cleve replied. "I got no wife to come here every week and remind me what I'm missing."

"You been in before?"

"Twice."

The boy hesitated an instant before saying, "I suppose you know your way around the place, do you?"

"Well, I'm not writing a guidebook, but I got the general layout by now." It seemed an odd comment for the boy to make. "Why?"

"I just wondered," said Billy.

"You got a question?"

Tait didn't answer for several seconds, then said: "I heard they used to . . . used to *hang* people here."

Whatever Cleve had been expecting the boy to come out with, that wasn't it. But then he had decided several days back that Billy Tait was a strange one. Sly, sidelong glances from those milky-blue eyes; a way he had of staring at the wall or at the window like a detective at a murder scene, desperate for clues.

Cleve said, "There used to be a hanging shed, I think."

Again silence, and then another inquiry, dropped as lightly as the boy could contrive. "Is it still standing?"

"The shed? I don't know. They don't hang people anymore, Billy, or hadn't you heard?" There was no reply from below. "What's it to you, anyhow?"

"Just curious."

Billy was right; curious he was. So odd, with his vacant stares and his solitary manner, that most of the men kept clear of him. Only Lowell took any interest in him, and his motives for that were unequivocal.

"You want to lend me your lady for the afternoon?" he asked Cleve while they waited in line for breakfast. Tait, who stood within earshot, said nothing; neither did Cleve.

"You hear me? I asked you a question."

"I heard. You leave him alone."

"Share and share alike," Lowell said. "I can do you some favors. We can work something out."

"He's not available."

"Well, why don't I ask *him?*" Lowell said, grinning through his beard. "What do you say, baby?"

Tait looked around at Lowell.

"I say no thank you."

"No *thank you,*" Lowell said, and gave Cleve a second smile, this quite without humor. "You've got him well trained. Does he sit up and beg, too?"

"Take a walk, Lowell," Cleve replied. "He's not available and that's all there is to it."

"You can't keep your eyes on him every minute of the day," Lowell pointed out. "Sooner or later he's going to have to stand on his own two feet. Unless he's better kneeling."

The innuendo won a guffaw from Lowell's cell-mate, Nayler. Neither were men Cleve would have willingly faced in a free-for-all, but his skills as a bluffer were honed razor-sharp, and he used them now.

"You don't want to trouble yourself," he told Lowell. "You can only cover so many scars with a beard."

Lowell looked at Cleve, all humor fled. He clearly couldn't distinguish the truth from bluff, and equally clearly wasn't willing to put his neck on the line.

"Just don't look the other way," he said, and said no more.

The encounter at breakfast wasn't mentioned until that night when the lights had been extinguished. It was Billy who brought it up.

"You shouldn't have done that," he said. "Lowell's a bad bastard. I've heard the talk."

"You want to get raped then, do you?"

"No," he said quickly, "Christ no. I got to be fit."

"You'll be fit for nothing if Lowell gets his hands on you."

Billy slipped out from his bunk and stood in the middle of the cell, barely visible in the gloom. "I suppose you want something in return," he said.

Cleve turned on his pillow and looked at the uncertain silhouette standing a yard from him. "What have you got that I'd want, Billy Boy?" he said.

"What Lowell wanted."

"Is that what you think that bluster was all about? Me staking a claim?"

"Yeah."

"Like you said: no thank you." Cleve rolled over again to face the wall.

"I didn't mean—"

"I don't care what you meant. I just don't want to hear about it, all right? You stay out of Lowell's way, and don't give me shit."

"Hey," Billy murmured, "don't get like that, please. *Please*. You're the only one friend I've got."

"I'm nobody's friend," Cleve said to the wall. "I just don't want any inconvenience. Understand me?"

"No inconvenience," the boy repeated, dull-tongued.

"Right. Now . . . I need my beauty sleep."

Tait said no more but returned to the bottom bunk and lay down, the springs creaking as he did so. Cleve lay in silence, turning the exchange over in his head. He had no wish to lay hands on the boy, but perhaps he had made his point too harshly. Well, it was done.

From below he could hear Billy murmuring to himself, almost inaudibly. He strained to eavesdrop on what the boy was saying. It took several seconds of ear-pricking attention before Cleve realized that Billy Boy was saying his prayers.

Cleve dreamed that night. What of, he couldn't remember in the morning, though as he showered and shaved tantalizing grains of the dream sifted through his head. Scarcely ten minutes went by that morning without something—salt overturned on the breakfast table, the sound of shouts in the exercise yard—promising to break his dream, but the revelation did not come. It left him uncharacteristically edgy and short-tempered. When Wesley, a small-time forger whom he knew from his previous vacation here, approached him in the library and started to talk as though they were bosom pals, Cleve told the runt to shut up. But Wesley insisted on speaking.

"You got trouble."

"Oh. How so?"

"That boy of yours. Billy."

"What about him?"

"He's asking questions. He's getting pushy. People don't like it. They're saying you should take him in hand."

"I'm not his keeper."

Wesley pulled a face. "I'm telling you, as a friend."

"Spare me."

"Don't be stupid, Cleveland. You're making enemies."

"Oh?" said Cleve. "Name one."

"Lowell," Wesley said, quick as a flash. "Nayler for another. All kinds of people. They don't like the way Tait is."

"And how is he?" Cleve snapped back.

Wesley made a small grunt of protest. "I'm just trying to tell you," he said. "He's sly. Like a fucking rat. There'll be trouble."

"Spare me the prophecies."

The law of averages demands the worst prophet be right some of the time: this was Wesley's moment, it seemed. The day after, coming back from the workshop, where he'd exercised his intellect putting wheels on plastic cars, Cleve found Mayflower waiting for him on the landing.

"I asked you to look after William Tait, Smith," the officer said. "Don't you give a damn?"

"What's happened?"

"No, I suppose you don't."

"I asked what happened. Sir."

"Nothing much. Not this time. He's been roughed up, that's all. Seems Lowell has a hankering after him. Am I right?" Mayflower peered at Cleve, and when he got no response went on: "I made an error with you, Smith. I thought there was something worth appealing to under the hard man. My mistake."

Billy was lying on the bunk, his face bruised, his eyes closed. He didn't open them when Cleve came in.

"You O.K.?"

"Sure," the boy said softly.

"No bones broken?"

"I'll survive."

"You've got to understand—"

"Listen." Billy opened his eyes. The pupils had darkened somehow, or that was the trick the light performed with them. "I'm alive, O.K.? I'm not an idiot, you know. I knew what I was letting myself in for, coming here." He spoke as if he'd had a choice in the matter. "I can take Lowell," he went on, "so don't fret." He paused, then said, "You were right."

"About what?"

"About not having friends. I'm on my own, you're on your own. Right? I'm just a slow learner, but I'm getting the hang of it." He smiled to himself.

"You've been asking questions," Cleve said.

"Oh, yeah?" Billy replied off-handedly. "Who says?"

"If you've got questions, ask me. People don't like snoopers. They get suspicious. And then they turn their backs when Lowell and his like get heavy."

Naming the man brought a painful frown to Billy's face. He touched his bruised cheek. "He's dead," the boy murmured, almost to himself.

"Some chance," Cleve commented.

The look that Tait returned could have sliced steel. "I

mean it," he said, without a trace of doubt in his voice. "Lowell won't get out alive."

Cleve didn't comment; the boy needed this show of bravado, laughable as it was.

"What do you want to know that you go snooping around?"

"Nothing much," Billy replied. He was no longer looking at Cleve but staring at the bunk above. Quietly, he said, "I just wanted to know where the graves were, that was all."

"The graves?"

"Where they buried the men they'd hanged. Somebody told me there's a rose bush where Crippen's buried. You ever hear that?"

Cleve shook his head. Only now did he remember the boy asking about the hanging shed, and now the graves. Billy looked up at him. The bruise was ripening by the minute.

"You know where they are, Cleve?" he asked. Again, that feigned nonchalance.

"I could find out, if you do me the courtesy of telling me why you want to know."

Billy looked out from the shelter of the bunk. The afternoon sun was describing its short arc on the painted brick of the cell wall. It was weak today. The boy slid his legs off the bunk and sat on the edge of the mattress, staring at the light as he had on that first day.

"My grandfather—that is, my mother's father—was hanged here," he said, his voice raw. "In 1937. Edgar Tait. Edgar Saint Clair Tait."

"I thought you said your *mother's* father?"

"I took his name. I didn't want my father's name. I never belonged to him."

"Nobody belongs to anybody," Cleve replied. "You're your own man."

"But that's not true," Billy said with a tiny shrug, still staring at the light on the wall. His certainty was immovable; the gentility with which he spoke did not undercut the authority of the statement. "I *belong* to my grandfather. I always have."

"You weren't even born when he—"

"That doesn't matter. Coming and going; that's nothing."

Coming and going, Cleve puzzled. Did Tait mean life and death? He had no chance to ask. Billy was talking again, the same subdued but insistent flow.

"He was guilty, of course. Not the way they thought he was, but *guilty*. He knew what he was and what he was capable of; that's guilt, isn't it? He killed four people. Or at least that's what they hanged him for."

"You mean he killed more?"

Billy made another small shrug: numbers didn't matter apparently. "But nobody came to see where they'd laid him to rest. That's not right, is it? They didn't care, I suppose. All the family were glad he was gone, probably. Thought he was wrong in the head from the beginning. But he wasn't. I know he *wasn't*. I've got his hands, and his eyes. So Mama said. She told me all about him, you see, just before she died. Told me things she'd never told anybody, and only told me because of my eyes . . ." He faltered, and put his hand to his lip, as if the fluctuating light on the brick had already mesmerized him into saying too much.

"What did your mother tell you?" Cleve pressed him.

Billy seemed to weigh up alternative responses before offering one. "Just that he and I were *alike* in some ways," he said.

"Crazy, you mean?" Cleve said, only half-joking.

"Something like that," Billy replied, eyes still on the wall. He sighed, then allowed himself a further confession. "That's why I came here. So my grandfather would know he hadn't been forgotten."

"Came here?" said Cleve. "What are you talking about? You were caught and sentenced. You had no choice."

The light on the wall was extinguished as a cloud passed over the sun. Billy looked up at Cleve. The light was there, in his eyes.

"I committed a crime to get here," the boy replied. "It was a deliberate act."

Cleve shook his head. The claim was preposterous.

"I tried before—twice. It's taken time. But I got here, didn't I?"

"Don't take me for a fool, Billy," Cleve warned.

"I don't," the other replied. He stood up now. He seemed somehow lighter for the story he'd told; he even smiled, if tentatively, as he said: "You've been good to me. Don't think I don't know that. I'm grateful. Now"—He faced Cleve before saying—"I want to know where the graves are. Find that out and you won't hear another peep from me, I promise."

Cleve knew next to nothing about the prison or its history, but he knew somebody who did. There was a man by the name of Bishop—so familiar with the inmates that his name had acquired the definite article—who was often at the workshop at the same time as Cleve. The Bishop had been in and out of prison for much of his forty-odd years, mostly for misdemeanors, and, with all the fatalism of a one legged man who makes a life study of monopedia, had become an expert on prisons and the penal system. Little of his information came from books. He had gleaned the bulk of his knowledge from old lags and screws who wanted to talk the hours away, and by degrees he had turned himself into a walking encyclopedia on crime and punishment. He had made it his trade, and he sold his carefully accrued knowledge by the sentence; sometimes as geographical information to the would-be escapee, sometimes as prison mythology to the godless con in search of a local divinity. Now Cleve sought him out and laid down his payment in tobacco and IOUs.

"What can I do for you?" The Bishop asked. He was heavy but not unhealthily so. The needle-thin cigarettes he was perpetually rolling and smoking were dwarfed by his butcher's fingers, stained sepia by nicotine.

"I want to know about the hangings here."

The Bishop smiled. "Such good stories," he said, and began to tell.

On the plain details, Billy had been substantially correct. There had been hangings in Pentonville up until the middle of the century, but the shed had long since been demolished. On the spot now stood the Probation Office in B Wing. As to the story of Crippen's roses, there was truth in that too. In front of a hut on the grounds, which, The Bishop informed Cleve, was a store for gardening equipment, was a small patch of grass, in the center of which a bush flourished, planted (and at this point The Bishop confessed that he could not tell fact from fiction) in memory of Doctor Crippen, hanged in 1910.

"That's where the graves are?" Cleve asked.

"No, no," The Bishop said, reducing half of one of his skinny cigarettes to ash with a single inhalation. "The graves are alongside the wall, to the left behind the hut. There's a long lawn; you must have seen it."

"No stones?"

"Absolutely not. The plots have always been left unmarked. Only the governor knows who's buried where, and he's probably lost the plans." The Bishop ferreted for his tobacco tin in the breast pocket of his prison-issue shirt and began to roll another cigarette with such familiarity he scarcely glanced down at what he was doing. "Nobody's allowed to come and mourn, you see. Out of sight, out of mind: that's the idea. Of course, that's not the way it works, is it? People forget prime ministers, but they remember murderers. You walk on that lawn, and just six feet under are some of the most notorious men who ever graced this green and pleasant land. And not even a cross to mark the spot. Criminal, isn't it?"

"You know who's buried there?"

"Some very wicked gentlemen," The Bishop replied, as if fondly admonishing them for their mischief mongering.

"You heard of a man called Edgar Tait?"

Bishop raised his eyebrows; the fat of his brow furrowed. "Saint Tait? Oh certainly. He's not easily forgotten."

"What do you know about him?"

"He killed his wife, and then his children. Took a knife to them all, as I live and breathe."

"All?"

The Bishop put the freshly rolled cigarette to his thick lips. "Maybe not all," he said, narrowing his eyes as he tried to recall the specific details. "Maybe one of them survived. I think perhaps a daughter." He shrugged dismissively. "I'm not very good at remembering the victims. But then, who is?" He fixed his bland gaze on Cleve. "Why are you so interested in Tait? He was hanged before the war."

"Nineteen thirty-seven. He'll be well gone, eh?"

The Bishop raised a cautionary forefinger. "Not so," he said. "You see, the land this prison is built upon has special properties. Bodies buried here don't rot the way they do elsewhere." Cleve shot The Bishop an incredulous glance. "It's true," the fat man protested mildly. "I have it on unimpeachable authority. Take it from me, whenever they've had to exhume a body from the plot it's always been found in almost perfect condition." He paused to light his cigarette and drew upon it, exhaling the smoke through his mouth with his next words. "When the end of the world is upon us, the good men of Marylebone and Camden Town will rise up as rot and bone. But the wicked? They'll dance to Judgment as fresh as the day they dropped. Imagine that." This perverse notion clearly delighted him. His pudgy face puckered and dimpled with pleasure at it. "Ah," he mused, "and who'll be calling who corrupt on *that* fine morning?"

Cleve never worked out precisely how Billy talked his way on to the gardening detail, but he managed it. Perhaps he had appealed directly to Mayflower, who'd persuaded his superiors that the boy could be trusted out in the fresh air. However he worked the maneuver, in the middle of the week following Cleve's discovery of the graves' whereabouts, Billy was out in the cold April morning cutting grass.

What happened that day filtered back down the grape-vine around recreation time. Cleve had the story from three independent sources, none of whom had been on the spot. The accounts had a variety of colorations, but were clearly of the same species. The bare bones went as follows:

The gardening detail, made up of four men watched over by a single prison guard, were moving around the blocks, trimming grass and weeding beds in preparation for the spring planting. Custody had been lax, apparently. It was two or three minutes before the guard even noticed that one of his charges had edged to the periphery of the party and slipped away. The alarm was raised. The guards did not have to look far, however. Tait had made no attempt to escape, or if he had he'd been stymied in his bid by a fit of some kind, which had crippled him. He was found (and here the stories parted company considerably) on a large patch of lawn beside the wall, lying on the grass. Some reports claimed he was black in the face, his body knotted up and his tongue all but bitten through; others that he was found facedown, talking to the earth, weeping and cajoling. The consensus was that the boy had lost his mind.

The rumors made Cleve the center of attention, a situation he did not relish. For the next day he was scarcely left alone, men wanting to know what it was like to share a cell with a lunatic. He had nothing to tell, he insisted. Tait had been the perfect cell-mate— quiet, undemanding and un-questionably sane. He told the same story to Mayflower when he was grilled the following day, and later, to the prison doctor. He let not a breath of Tait's interest in the graves be known and made it his business to see The Bishop and request a similar silence of him. The man was willing to oblige only if vouchsafed the full story in due course. This Cleve promised. The Bishop, as befitted his assumed clerisy, was as good as his word.

Billy was gone for two days. In the interim Mayflower disappeared from his duties as Landing Officer. No explanation was given. In his place a man called Devlin was transferred from D Wing. His reputation went before him. He was not, it seemed, a man of rare compassion. The impression was confirmed when, the day of Billy Tait's return, Cleve was summoned into Devlin's office.

"I'm told you and Tait are close," Devlin said. He had a face as giving as granite.

"Not really, sir."

"I'm not going to make Mayflower's mistake, Smith. As far as I'm concerned, Tait is trouble. I'm going to watch him like a hawk, and when I'm not here you're going to do it for me, understand? If he so much as crosses his eyes it's the ghost train. I'll have him out of here and into a special unit before he can fart. Do I make myself clear?"

"Paying your respects, were you?"

Billy had lost weight in the hospital, pounds his scrawny frame could scarcely afford. His shirt hung off his shoulders; his belt was on its tightest notch. The thinning more than ever emphasized his physical vulnerability; a featherweight blow would floor him, Cleve thought. But it lent his face a new, almost desperate, intensity. He seemed all eyes, and those had lost all trace of captured sunlight. Gone, too, was the pretense of vacuity, replaced with an eerie purposefulness.

"I asked a question."

"I heard you," Billy said. There was no sun today, but

he looked at the wall anyway. "Yes, if you must know, I was paying my respects."

"I've been told to watch you, by Devlin. He wants you off the Landing. Transferred entirely, maybe."

"Out?" The panicked look Billy gave Cleve was too naked to be met for more than a few seconds. "Away from here, you mean?"

"I would think so."

"They can't!"

"Oh, they can. They call it the ghost train. One minute you're here; the next—"

"No," the boy said, hands suddenly fists. He had begun to shake, and for a moment Cleve feared a second fit. But he seemed, by act of will, to control the tremors, and turned his look back to his cell-mate. The bruises he'd received from Lowell had dulled to yellow-gray, but far from disappeared; his unshaven cheeks were dusted with pale-ginger hair. Looking at him Cleve felt an unwelcome twinge of concern.

"Tell me," Cleve said.

"Tell you what?" Billy asked.

"What happened at the graves."

"I felt dizzy. I fell over. The next thing I knew I was in hospital."

"That's what you told *them*, isn't it?"

"It's the truth."

"Not the way I heard it. Why don't you explain what really happened? I want you to trust me."

"I do," the boy said. "But I have to keep this to myself, see. It's between me and him."

"You and Edgar?" Cleve asked, and Billy nodded. "A man who killed all his family but your mother?"

Billy was clearly startled that Cleve possessed this information. "Yes," he said after consideration. "Yes, he killed them all. He would have killed Mama too if she hadn't escaped. He wanted to wipe the whole family out. So there'd be no heirs to carry the bad blood."

"Your blood's bad, is it?"

Billy allowed himself the slenderest of smiles. "No," he said. "I don't think so. Grandfather was wrong. Times have changed, haven't they?"

He *is* mad, Cleve thought. Lightning-swift, Billy caught the judgment.

"I'm not insane," he said. "You tell them that. Tell Devlin and whoever else asks. Tell them I'm a lamb." The fierceness was back in his eyes. There was nothing lamb-like there, though Cleve forbore saying so. "They mustn't move me out, Cleve. Not after getting so close. I've got business here. Important business."

"With a dead man?"

"With a dead man."

Whatever new purpose he displayed for Cleve, the shutters went up when Billy got back among the rest of the cons. He responded neither to the questions nor the insults bandied about; his facade of empty-eyed indifference was flawless. Cleve was impressed. The boy had a future as an actor, if he decided to forsake professional lunacy.

But the strain of concealing the newfound urgency in him rapidly began to tell. In a hollowness about the eyes and a jitteriness in his movements; in brooding and unshakable silences. The physical deterioration was apparent to the doctor to whom Billy continued to report; he pronounced the boy suffering from depression and acute insomnia and prescribed sedatives to aid sleep. These pills Billy gave to Cleve, insisting he had no need of them himself. Cleve was grateful. For the first time in many months he began to sleep well, unperturbed by the tears and shouts of his fellow inmates.

By day, the relationship between him and the boy, which had always been vestigial, dwindled down to mere courtesy. Cleve sensed that Billy was closing up entirely, removing himself from merely physical concerns.

It was not the first time he had witnessed such a premeditated withdrawal. His sister-in-law, Rosanna, had died of stomach cancer three years earlier: a protracted and, until the last weeks, steady decline. Cleve had not been close to her, but perhaps that very distance had lent him a perspective on the woman's behavior that the rest of his family had lacked. He had been startled at the systematic way she had prepared herself for death, drawing in her affections until they touched only the most vital figures in her life—her children and her priest—and exiling all others, including her husband of fourteen years.

Now he saw the same dispassion and frugality in Billy. Like a man in training to cross a waterless wasteland and too possessive of his energies to squander them in a single fruitless gesture, the boy was sinking into himself. It was eerie; Cleve became increasingly uncomfortable sharing the twelve feet by eight of the cell with Billy. It was like living with a man on Death Row.

The only consolation was the tranquilizers, which Billy readily charmed the doctor into continuing to supply. They guaranteed Cleve sleep that was restful, and, for several days at least, dreamless.

And then he dreamed the city.

Not the city first; first the desert. An empty expanse of blue-black sand, which stung the soles of his feet as he walked, and was blown up by a cool wind into his nose and eyes and hair. He had been here before, he knew. His dream-self recognized the vista of barren dunes, with neither tree nor habitation to break the monotony. But on previous visits he had come with guides (or such was his half-formed belief); now he was alone, and the clouds above his head were heavy and slate-gray, promising no sun. For what seemed hours he walked the dunes, his feet turned bloody by the sharp sand, his body, dusted by the grains, tinged blue. As exhaustion came close to defeating him, he saw ruins and approached them.

It was no oasis. There was nothing in those empty streets of health or sustenance; no fruitful trees nor sparkling fountains. The city was a conglomeration of houses, or parts of same—sometimes entire floors, sometimes single rooms—thrown down side by side in parodies of urban order. The styles were a hopeless mishmash: fine Georgian establishments standing beside mean tenement buildings with rooms burned out; a house plucked from a terraced row, perfect down to the glazed dog on the windowsill, back to back with a penthouse suite. All were scarred by a rough removal from their context: walls were cracked, offering sly glimpses into private interiors; staircases beetled cloudward without destination; doors flapped open and closed in the wind, letting on to nowhere.

There was life here, Cleve knew. Not just the lizards, rats and butterflies—albinos all—that fluttered and skipped in front of him as he walked the forsaken streets—but *human* life. He sensed that every step he took was

watched over, though he saw no sign of human presence—
not on his first visit, at least.

On the second, his dream-self forsook the trudge across
the wilderness and was delivered directly into the ne-
cropolis, his feet, easily tutored, following the same route
as he had on his first visit. The constant wind was stronger
tonight. It caught the lace curtains in this window, and a
tinkling Chinese trinket hanging in that. It carried voices
too; horrid and outlandish sounds that came from some
distant place far beyond the city. Hearing that whirring and
whittering, as of insane children, he was grateful for the
streets and the rooms, for their familiarity if not for any
comfort they might offer. He had no desire to step into
those interiors, voices or no; he did not want to discover
what marked out these snatches of architecture that they
should have been ripped from their roots and flung down in
this whining desolation.

Yet once he had visited the site, his sleeping mind went
back there, night upon night; always walking, bloody-
footed, seeing only the lizards and the rats and the butterflies, and the black sand on each threshold, blowing into
rooms and hallways that never changed from visit to visit;
that seemed, from what he could glimpse between the curtains or through a shattered wall, to have been *fixed* somehow at some pivotal moment, with a meal left uneaten on a
table set for three (the capon uncarved, the sauces steaming), or a shower left running in a bathroom in which the
lamp perpetually swung; and, in a room that might have
been a lawyer's study, a lapdog, or else a wig torn off and
flung to the floor, lying discarded on a fine carpet whose
intricacies were half devoured by sand.

Only once did he see another human being in the city,

and that was Billy. It happened strangely. One night, as he dreamed the streets, he half stirred from sleep. Billy was awake, and standing in the middle of the cell, staring up at the light through the window. It was not moonlight, but the boy bathed in it as if it were. His face was turned up to the window, mouth open and eyes closed. Cleve barely had time to register the trance the boy seemed to be in before the tranquilizers drew him back into his dream. He took a fragment of reality with him however, folding the boy into his sleeping vision. When he reached the city again, there was Billy Tait: standing on the street, his face turned up to the lowering clouds, his mouth open, his eyes closed.

The image lingered only a moment. The next, the boy was away, his heels kicking up black fans of sand. Cleve called after him. Billy ran on however, heedless; and with that inexplicable foreknowledge that dreams bring, Cleve knew where the boy was going. Off to the edge of the city, where the houses petered out and the desert began. Off to meet some friend coming in on that terrible wind, perhaps. Nothing would induce him into pursuit; yet he didn't want to lose contact with the one fellow human he had seen in these destitute streets. He called Billy's name again, more loudly.

This time he felt a hand on his arm, and started up in terror to find himself being jostled awake in his cell.

"It's all right," Billy said. "You're dreaming."

Cleve tried to shake the city out of his head, but for several perilous seconds the dream bled into the waking world, and looking down at the boy he saw Billy's hair lifted by a wind that did not, *could* not, belong in the confines of the cell. "You're dreaming," Billy said again. "Wake up."

Shuddering, Cleve sat fully up on his bunk. The city was receding—was almost gone—but before he lost sight of it entirely he felt the indisputable conviction that Billy *knew* what he was waking Cleve from; that they had been together for a few fragile moments.

"You know, don't you?" he accused the pallid face at his side.

The boy looked bewildered. "What are you talking about?"

Cleve shook his head. The suspicion became more incredible with each step he took from sleep. Even so, when he looked down at Billy's bony hand, which still clung to his arm, he half expected to see flecks of that obsidian grit beneath his fingernails. There was only dirt.

The doubts lingered however, long after reason should have bullied them into surrender. Cleve found himself watching the boy more closely from that night on, waiting for some slip of tongue or eye which would reveal the nature of his game. Such scrutiny was a lost cause. The last traces of accessibility disappeared that night; the boy became—like Rosanna—an indecipherable book, letting no clue as to the nature of his secret world out from beneath his lids. As to the dream—it was not even mentioned again. The only roundabout allusion to that night was Billy's redoubled insistence that Cleve continue to take the sedatives.

"You need your sleep," he said after coming back from the infirmary with a further supply. "Take them."

"You need sleep too," Cleve replied, curious to see how far the boy would push the issue. "I don't need the stuff any more."

"But you do," Billy insisted, proffering the vial of capsules. "You know how bad the noise is."

"Someone said they're addictive," Cleve replied, not taking the pills. "I'll do without."

"*No*," said Billy, and now Cleve sensed a level of insistence which confirmed his deepest suspicions. The boy *wanted* him drugged, and had all along. "I sleep like a babe," Billy said. "Please take them. They'll only be wasted otherwise."

Cleve shrugged. "If you're sure," he said, content—fears confirmed—to make a show of relenting.

"I'm sure."

"Then thanks." He took the vial.

Billy beamed. With that smile, in a sense, the bad times really began.

That night, Cleve answered the boy's performance with one of his own, appearing to take the tranquilizers as he usually did but failing to swallow them. Once lying on his bunk, face to the wall, he slipped them from his mouth and under his pillow. Then he pretended sleep.

Prison days both began and finished early; by eight forty-five or nine most of the cells in the four wings were in darkness, the inmates locked up until dawn and left to their own devices. Tonight was quieter than most. The weeper in the next cell but one had been transferred to D Wing; there were few other disturbances along the landing. Even without the pill Cleve felt sleep tempting him. From the bunk below he heard practically no sound, except for the occasional sigh. It was impossible to guess if Billy was actually asleep or not. Cleve kept his silence, occasionally stealing a moment-long glance at the luminous face of his watch. The minutes were leaden, and he feared, as the first hours crept by, that all too soon his imitation of sleep would become the real thing. Indeed he was turning this very possibility around in his mind when unconsciousness overcame him.

He woke much later. His sleep position seemed not to have altered. The wall was in front of him, the peeled paint like a dim map of some nameless territory. It took him a minute or two to orient himself. There was no sound from the bunk below. Disguising the gesture as one made in sleep, he drew his arm up within eye range, and looked at the pale green dial of his watch. It was one fifty-one. Several hours yet until dawn. He lay in the position he'd awakened in for a full quarter of an hour, listening for every sound in the cell, trying to locate Billy. He was loath to roll over and look for himself, for fear that the boy was standing in the middle of the cell as he had been the night of the visit to the city.

The world, though benighted, was far from silent. He could hear dull footsteps as somebody paced back and forth in the corresponding cell on the landing above; could hear water rushing in the pipes and the sound of a siren on Caledonian Road. What he couldn't hear was Billy. Not a breath of the boy.

Another quarter of an hour passed, and Cleve could feel the familiar torpor closing in to reclaim him; if he lay still much longer he would fall asleep again, and the next thing he'd know it would be morning. If he was going to learn anything, he had to roll over and *look*. Wisest, he decided, not to attempt to move surreptitiously but to turn over as naturally as possible. This he did, muttering to himself, as if in sleep, to add weight to the illusion. Once he had turned completely, and positioned his hand beside his face to shield his spying, he cautiously opened his eyes.

The cell seemed darker than it had the night he had seen Billy with his face up to the window. As to the boy, he was not visible. Cleve opened his eyes a little wider and scanned the cell as best he could from between his fingers. There was something amiss, but he couldn't quite work out what it was. He lay there for several minutes, waiting for his eyes to become accustomed to the murk. They didn't. The scene in front of him remained unclear, like a painting so encrusted with dirt and varnish its depths refuse the investigating eye. Yet he knew — *knew* — that the shadows in the corners of the cell, and on the opposite wall, were not empty. He wanted to end the anticipation that was making his heart thump, wanted to raise his head from the pebble-filled pillow and call Billy out of hiding. But good sense counseled otherwise. Instead he lay still, and sweated, and watched.

And now he began to realize what was wrong with the scene before him. The concealing shadows fell where no shadows belonged; they spread across the floor where the feeble light from the window should have been falling. Somehow, between window and wall, that light had been choked and devoured. Cleve closed his eyes to give his befuddled mind a chance to rationalize and reject this conclusion. When he opened them again his heart lurched. The shadow, far from losing potency, had grown a little.

He had never been afraid like this before, never felt a coldness in his innards akin to the chill that found him now. It was all he could do to keep his breath even and his hands where they lay. His instinct was to wrap himself up and hide his face like a child. Two thoughts kept him from doing so. One was that the slightest movement might draw unwelcome attention to him. The other, that Billy was somewhere in the cell, and perhaps as threatened by this living darkness as he.

And then, from the bunk below, the boy spoke. His voice was soft, presumably so as not to wake his sleeping cell-mate. It was also eerily intimate. Cleve entertained no thought that Billy was talking in his sleep; the time for willful self-deception was long past. The boy was addressing the darkness; of that unpalatable fact there could be no doubt.

". . . it hurts . . ." he said, with a faint note of accusation. ". . . You didn't tell me how much it hurts. . . ."

Was it Cleve's imagination, or did the wraith of shadows bloom a little in response, like a squid's ink in water? He was horribly afraid.

The boy was speaking again. His voice was so low Cleve could barely catch the words.

". . . it must be soon . . ." he said with quiet urgency. ". . . I'm not afraid. Not afraid."

Again the shadow shifted. This time, when Cleve looked into its heart, he made some sense of the chimerical form it embraced. His throat shook; a cry lodged behind his tongue, hot to be shouted.

". . . all you can teach me . . ." Billy was saying, ". . . quickly . . ." The words came and went, but Cleve barely heard them. His attention was on the curtain of shadow, and the figure—stitched from darkness—that moved in its folds. It was not an illusion. There was a man there: or rather a crude copy of one, its substance tenuous, its outline deteriorating all the time and being hauled back into some semblance of humanity again only with the greatest effort. Of the visitor's features Cleve could see little, but enough to sense deformities paraded like virtues: a face resembling a plate of rotted fruit, pulpy and peeling, swelling here with a nest of flies, and there suddenly fallen away to a pestilent core. How could the boy bring himself to converse so easily with such a *thing?* And yet, putrescence notwithstanding, there was a bitter dignity in the bearing of the creature, in the anguish of its eyes, and the toothless O of its maw.

Suddenly, Billy stood up. The abrupt movement, after so many hushed words, almost unleashed the cry from Cleve's throat. He swallowed it, with difficulty, and closed his eyes down to a slit, staring through the bars of his lashes at what happened next.

Billy was talking again, but now the voice was too low to allow for eavesdropping. He stepped toward the shadow, his body blocking much of the figure on the opposite wall. The cell was no more than two or three strides wide, but by some mellowing of physics, the boy seemed to take five, six, seven steps away from the bunk. Cleve's eyes widened: he knew he was not being watched. The shadow and its acolyte had business between them: it occupied their attention utterly.

Billy's figure was smaller than seemed possible within the confines of the cell, as if he had stepped through the wall and into some other province. And only now, with his eyes wide, did Cleve recognize that place. The darkness from which Billy's visitor was made was cloud-shadow and dust; behind him, barely visible in the bewitched murk, but recognizable to any who had been there, was the city of Cleve's dreams.

Billy had reached his master. The creature towered

above him, tattered and spindly, but aching with power. Cleve didn't know how or why the boy had gone to it, and he feared for Billy's safety now that he had, but fear for his own safety shackled him to the bunk. He realized in that moment that he had never loved anyone, man or woman, sufficiently to pursue them into the shadow of that shadow. The thought brought a terrible isolation, knowing that same instant that none, seeing *him* walk to his damnation, would take a single step to claim him from the brink. Lost souls both, he and the boy.

Now Billy's lord was lifting his swollen head, and the incessant wind in those blue streets was rousing his horse mane into furious life. On the wind, the same voices Cleve had heard carried before, the cries of mad children, somewhere between tears and howls. As if encouraged by these voices, the entity reached out toward Billy and embraced him, wrapping the boy round in vapor. Billy did not struggle in his embrace but rather returned it. Cleve, unable to watch this horrid intimacy, closed his eyes against it, and when—seconds? minutes?, later—he opened them again, the encounter seemed to be over. The shadow thing was blowing apart, relinquishing its slender claim to coherence. It fragmented, pieces of its tattered anatomy flying off into the streets like litter before wind. Its departure seemed to signal the dispersal of the entire scene; the streets and houses were already being devoured by dust and distance. Even before the last of the shadow's scraps had been wafted out of sight the city was lost to sight. Cleve was pleased to be rid of it. Reality, grim as it was, was preferable to that desolation. Brick by painted brick the wall was asserting itself again, and Billy, delivered from his master's arms, was back in the solid geometry of the cell, staring up at the light through the window.

Cleve did not sleep again that night. Indeed he wondered, lying on his unyielding mattress and staring up at the stalactites of paint depending from the ceiling, whether he could ever again find safety in sleep.

Sunlight was a showman. It threw its brightness down with such flamboyance, eager as any tinsel-merchant to dazzle and distract. But beneath the gleaming surface it illuminated was another state; one that sunlight—ever the crowd pleaser—conspired to conceal. It was vile and desperate, that condition. Most, blinded by sight, never even glimpsed it. But Cleve knew the state of sunlessness now; had even walked it, in dreams; and though he mourned the loss of his innocence, he knew he could never retrace his steps back into light's hall of mirrors.

He tried his damnedest to keep this change in him from Billy; the last thing he wanted was for the boy to suspect his eavesdropping. But concealment was well nigh impossible. Though the following day Cleve made every show of normality he could contrive, he could not quite cover his unease. It slipped out without his being able to control it, like sweat from his pores. And the boy knew, no doubt of it, he *knew*. Nor was he slow to give voice to his suspicions. When, following the afternoon's workshop, they returned to their cell, Billy was quick to come to the point.

"What's wrong with you today?"

Cleve busied himself with remaking his bed, afraid even to glance at Billy. "Nothing's wrong," he said. "I don't feel particularly well, that's all."

"You have a bad night?" the boy inquired. Cleve could feel Billy's eyes boring into his back.

"No," he said, pacing his denial so that it didn't come too quickly. "I took your pills, like always."

"Good."

The exchange faltered, and Cleve was allowed to finish his bed making in silence. The business could only be extended so long, however. When he turned from the bunk, job done, he found Billy sitting at the small table, with one of Cleve's books open in his lap. He casually flicked through the volume, all sign of his previous suspicion vanished. Cleve knew better than to trust to mere appearances, however.

"Why'd you read these things?" the boy asked.

"Passes the time," Cleve replied, undoing all his labors by clambering up on to the top bunk and stretching out there.

"No. I don't mean why do you read books? I mean, why read *these* books? All this stuff about sin."

Cleve only half heard the question. Lying there on the bunk reminded him all too acutely of how the night had been. Reminded him too that darkness was even now crawling up the side of the world again. At that thought his stomach seemed to aspire to his throat.

"Did you hear me?" the boy asked.

Cleve murmured that he had.

"Well, why then; why the books? About damnation and all?"

"Nobody else takes them out of the library," Cleve replied, having difficulty shaping thoughts to speak when the others, unspoken, were so much more demanding.

"You don't believe it then?"

"No," he replied. "No, I don't believe a word of it."

The boy kept his silence for a while. Though Cleve wasn't looking at him, he could hear Billy turning pages. Then, another question, but spoken more quietly; a confession.

"Do you ever get *afraid?*"

The inquiry startled Cleve from his trance. The conversation had changed back from talk of reading matter to something altogether more pertinent. Why did Billy ask about fear unless he too was afraid?

"What have I got to be scared of?" Cleve asked.

From the corner of his eye he caught the boy shrugging slightly before replying. "Things that happen," he said, his voice soulless. "Things you can't control."

"Yes," Cleve replied, not certain of where this exchange was leading. "Yes, of course. Sometimes I'm scared."

"What do you do then?" Billy asked.

"Nothing *to* do, is there?" Cleve said. His voice was as hushed as Billy's. "I gave up praying the morning my father died."

He heard the soft pat as Billy closed the book, and inclined his head sufficiently to catch sight of the boy. Billy could not entirely conceal his agitation. He *is* afraid, Cleve saw; he doesn't want the night to come any more than I do. He found the thought of their shared fear reassuring. Perhaps the boy didn't entirely belong to the shadow; perhaps he could even cajole Billy into pointing their route out of this spiraling nightmare.

He sat upright, his head within inches of the cell ceiling. Billy looked up from his meditations, his face a pallid oval of twitching muscle. Now was the time to speak, Cleve knew; *now,* before the lights were switched out along the landings, and all the cells consigned to shadows. There would be no time then for explanations. The boy would already be half lost to the city and beyond persuasion.

"I have dreams," Cleve said. Billy said nothing but simply stared back, hollow-eyed. "I dream a city."

The boy didn't flinch. He clearly wasn't going to volunteer elucidation; he would have to be bullied into it.

"Do you know what I'm talking about?"

Billy shook his head. "No," he said lightly, "I never dream."

"Everybody dreams."

"Then I just don't remember them."

"I remember mine," Cleve said. He was determined, now that he'd broached the subject, not to let Billy squirm free. "And you're there. You're in that city."

Now the boy flinched; only a treacherous lash but enough to reassure Cleve that he wasn't wasting his breath.

"What is that place, Billy?" he asked.

"How should I know?" the boy returned, about to laugh, then discarding the attempt. "I don't know, do I? They're your dreams."

Before Cleve could reply he heard the voice of one of the guards as he moved along the row of cells, telling the men to bed down for the night. Very soon, the lights would be extinguished and he would be locked up in this narrow cell for ten hours. With Billy; and phantoms.

"Last night," he said, fearful of mentioning what he'd heard and seen without due preparation, but more fearful still of facing another night on the borders of the city, alone in darkness. "Last night I saw . . ." He faltered. Why wouldn't the words come? "Saw . . ."

"Saw what?" the boy demanded, his face inscrutable;

whatever sign of apprehension there had been in it had now vanished. Perhaps he too had heard the guard's advance and known that there was nothing to be done; no way of staying the night's advance.

"*What did you see?*" Billy insisted.

Cleve sighed. "My mother," he replied.

The boy betrayed his relief only in the tenuous smile that crept across his lips.

"Yes . . . I saw my mother. Large as life."

"And it upset you, did it?" Billy asked.

"Sometimes dreams do."

The guard had reached B. 3. 20. "Lights out in two minutes," he said as he passed.

"You should take some more of those pills," Billy advised, putting down the book and crossing to his bunk. "Then you'd be like me. No dreams."

Cleve had lost. He, the arch bluffer, had been outbluffed by the boy, and now had to take the consequences. He lay, facing the ceiling, counting off the seconds until the light went out, while below the boy undressed and slipped between the sheets.

There was still time to jump up and call the guard back; time to beat his head against the door until somebody came. But what would he say to justify his histrionics? That he had bad dreams? *Who didn't?* That he was afraid of the dark? *Who wasn't?* They would laugh in his face and tell him to go back to bed, leaving him with all camouflage blown, and the boy and his master waiting at the wall. There was no safety in such tactics.

Nor in prayer either. He had told Billy the truth, about his giving up God when his prayers for his father's life had gone unanswered. Of such divine neglect was atheism made; belief could not be rekindled now, however profound his terror.

Thoughts of his father led inevitably to thoughts of childhood; few other subjects, if any, could have engrossed his mind sufficiently to steal him from his fears but this. When the lights were finally extinguished, his frightened mind took refuge in memories. His heart rate slowed; his fingers ceased to tremble, and eventually, without his being the least aware of it, sleep stole him.

The distractions available to his conscious mind were not available to his unconscious. Once asleep, fond recollection was banished; childhood memories became a thing of the past, and he was back, bloody-footed, in that terrible city.

Or rather, on its borders. For tonight he did not follow the familiar route past the Georgian house and its attendant tenements, but walked instead to the outskirts of the city, where the wind was stronger than ever, and the voices it carried clear. Though he expected with every step he took to see Billy and his dark companion, he saw nobody. Only butterflies accompanied him along the path, luminous as his watch face. They settled on his shoulders and his hair like confetti, then fluttered off again.

He reached the edge of the city without incident and stood, scanning the desert. The clouds, solid as ever, moved overhead with the majesty of juggernauts. The voices seemed closer tonight, he thought, and the passions they expressed less distressing than he had found them previously. Whether the mellowing was in them or in his response to them he couldn't be certain.

And then, as he watched the dunes and the sky, mesmerized by their blankness, he heard a sound and glanced over his shoulder to see a smiling man, dressed in what was surely his Sunday finery, walking out of the city toward him. He was carrying a knife, the blood on it, and on his hand and shirt front, was wet. Even in his dream state, and immune, Cleve was intimidated by the sight and stepped back—a word of self-defense on his lips. The smiling man seemed not to see him however, but advanced past Cleve and out into the desert, dropping the blade as he crossed some invisible boundary. Only now did Cleve see that others had done the same, and that the ground at the city limit was littered with lethal keepsakes—knives, ropes (even a human hand, lopped off at the wrist)—most of which were all but buried.

The wind was bringing the voices again: tatters of senseless songs and half-finished laughter. He looked up from the sand. The exiled man had gone out a hundred yards from the city and was now standing on top of one of the dunes, apparently waiting. The voices were becoming louder all the time. Cleve was suddenly nervous. Whenever he had been here in the city, and heard this cacophony, the picture he had conjured of its originators had made his blood run cold. Could he now stand and wait for the banshees to appear? Curiosity was discretion's better. He glued his eyes to the ridge over which they would come, his heart thumping, unable to look away. The man in the Sunday suit had begun to take his jacket off. He discarded it and began to loosen his tie.

And now Cleve thought he saw something in the dunes, and the noise rose to an ecstatic howl of welcome. He stared, defying his nerves to betray him, determined to look this horror in its many faces.

Suddenly, above the din of their music, somebody was

screaming; a man's voice, but high-pitched, gelded with terror. It did not come from here in the dream-city, but from that other fiction he occupied, the name of which he couldn't quite remember. He pressed his attention back to the dunes, determined not to be denied the sight of the reunion about to take place in front of him. The scream in that nameless elsewhere mounted to a throat-breaking height, and stopped. But now an alarm bell was ringing in its place, more insistent than ever. Cleve could feel his dream slipping.

"No . . ." he murmured, ". . . let me see. . . ."

The dunes were moving. But so was his consciousness —out of the city and back toward his cell. His protests brought him no concession. The desert faded, the city too. He opened his eyes. The lights in the cell were still off: the alarm bell was ringing. There were shouts in cells on the landings above and below, and the sound of guards' voices, raised in a confusion of inquiries and demands.

He lay on his bunk a moment, hoping, even now, to be returned into the enclave of his dream. But no; the alarm was too shrill, the mounting hysteria in the cells around too compelling. He conceded defeat and sat up, wide awake.

"What's going on?" he said to Billy.

The boy was not standing in his place by the wall. Asleep, for once, despite the din.

"Billy?"

Cleve leaned over the edge of his bunk, and peered into the space below. It was empty. The sheets and blankets had been thrown back.

Cleve jumped down from his bunk. The entire contents of the cell could be taken at two glances, there was no-where to hide. The boy was not to be seen. Had he been spirited away while Cleve slept? It was not unheard of; this was the ghost train of which Devlin had warned: the unexplained removal of difficult prisoners to other establishments. Cleve had never heard of this happening at night, but there was a first time for everything.

He crossed to the door to see if he could make some sense of the shouting outside, but it defied interpretation. The likeliest explanation was a fight, he suspected: two cons who could no longer bear the idea of another hour in the same space. He tried to work out where the initial scream had come from, to his right or left, above or below; but the dream had confounded all direction.

As he stood at the door, hoping a guard might pass by, he felt a change in the air. It was so subtle he scarcely registered it at first. Only when he raised his hand to wipe sleep from his eyes did he realize that his arms were solid gooseflesh.

From behind him he now heard the sound of breathing, or a ragged parody of same.

He mouthed the word "Billy" but didn't speak it. The gooseflesh had found his spine; now he began to shake. The cell *wasn't* empty after all; there was somebody in the tiny space with him.

He screwed his courage tight and forced himself to turn around. The cell was darker than it had been when he awoke; the air was a teasing veil. But Billy was not in the cell; nobody was.

And then the noise came again and drew Cleve's attention to the bottom bunk. The space was pitch black, a shadow—like that on the wall—too profound and too volatile to have natural origins. Out of it, a croaking attempt at breath that might have been the last moments of an asthmatic. He realized that the murk in the cell had its source there—in the narrow space of Billy's bed; the shadow bled onto the floor and curled up like fog on to the top of the bunk.

Cleve's supply of fear was not inexhaustible. In the past several days he had used it up in dreams and waking dreams; he'd sweated, he'd frozen, he'd lived on the edge of sane experience and survived. Now, though his body still insisted on gooseflesh, his mind was not moved to panic. He felt cooler than he ever had, whipped by recent events into a new impartiality. He would *not* cower. He would *not* cover his eyes and pray for morning, because if he did one day he would wake to find himself dead and he'd never know the nature of this mystery.

He took a deep breath and approached the bunk. It had begun to shake. The shrouded occupant in the lower tier was moving about violently.

"Billy," Cleve said.

The shadow moved. It pooled around his feet; it rolled up into his face, smelling of rain on stone, cold and comfortless.

He was standing no more than a yard from the bunk, and still he could make nothing out; the shadow defied him. Not to be denied sight, he reached toward the bed. At his solicitation the veil divided like smoke, and the shape that thrashed on the mattress made itself apparent.

It was Billy, of course; and yet not. A lost Billy, perhaps, or one to come. If so, Cleve wanted no part of a future that could breed such trauma. There, on the lower bunk, lay a dark, wretched shape, still solidifying as Cleve watched, knitting itself together from the shadows. There was something of a rabid fox in its incandescent eyes, in its arsenal of needle-teeth; something of an upturned insect in the way it was half curled upon itself, its back more shell than flesh and more nightmare than either. No part of it was fixed. Whatever figuration it had (perhaps it had many) Cleve was watching the status dissolve. The teeth were growing yet longer and, in so doing, more insubstantial, their matter extruded to the point of frailty, then dispersed like mist; its hooked limbs, pedaling the air, were also growing paltry. Beneath the chaos he saw the ghost of Billy Tait, mouth open and babbling agonies, striving to make itself known. He wanted to reach into the maelstrom and snatch the boy out, but he sensed that the process he was watching had its own momentum and it might be fatal to intervene. All he could do was stand and watch as Billy's thin white limbs and heaving abdomen writhed to slough off this dire anatomy. The luminous eyes were almost the last to go, spilling out from their sockets on myriad threads and flying off into black vapor.

At last he saw Billy's face, truant clues to its former condition still flickering across it. And then, even these were dispersed, the shadows gone, and only Billy was lying on the bunk, naked and heaving with the exertion of his anguish.

He looked at Cleve, his face innocent of expression.

Cleve remembered how the boy had complained to the creature from the city. ". . . *it hurts* . . . " he'd said, hadn't he? ". . . *You didn't tell me how much it hurts*. . . ." It was the observable truth. The boy's body was a wasteland of sweat and bone; a more unappetizing sight was scarcely imaginable. But *human;* at least that.

Billy opened his mouth. His lips were ruddy and slick, as if he were wearing lipstick.

"Now . . . ," he said, trying to speak between painful breaths. "Now what shall we do?"

The act of speaking seemed too much for him. He made a gagging sound in the back of his throat, and pressed his hand to his mouth. Cleve moved aside as Billy stood up and stumbled across to the bucket in the corner of the cell, kept there for their night wastes. He failed to reach it before nausea overtook him; fluid splashed between his fingers and hit the floor. Cleve looked away as Billy threw up, preparing himself for the stench he would have to tolerate until slopping-out time the following morning. It was not the smell of vomit that filled the cell, however, but something sweeter and more cloying.

Mystified, Cleve looked back toward the figure crouching in the corner. On the floor between his feet were splashes of dark fluid; rivulets of the same ran down his bare legs. Even in the gloom of the cell, it was unmistakably blood.

In the most well-ordered of prisons violence could—and inevitably did—erupt without warning. The relationship of two cons, incarcerated together for sixteen hours out of every twenty-four, was an unpredictable thing. But as far as had been apparent to either prisoners or guards there had been no bad blood between Lowell and Nayler; nor, until that scream began, had there been a sound from their cell: no argument, no raised voices. What had induced Nayler to spontaneously attack and slaughter his cell-mate, and then inflict devastating wounds upon himself, was a subject for debate in dining hall and exercise yard alike. The why of the problem, however, took second place to the how. The rumors describing the condition of Lowell's body when found defied the imagination; even among men inured against casual brutality the descriptions were met with shock. Lowell had not been much liked; he had been a bully and a cheat. But nothing he'd done deserved such mutilation. The man had been ripped open, his eyes put out, his genitals torn off. Nayler, the only possible antagonist, had then contrived to open up his own belly. He was now in an intensive care unit; the prognosis was not hopeful.

It was easy, with such a buzz of outrage going about the wing, for Cleve to spend the day all but unnoticed. He too had a story to tell: but who would believe it? He barely believed it himself. In fact on and off through the day, when the images came back to him afresh, he asked himself if he was entirely sane. But then sanity was a movable feast, wasn't it? One man's madness might be another's politics. All he knew for certain was that he had seen Billy Tait transform. He clung to that certainty with a tenaciousness born of near despair. If he ceased to believe the evidence of his own eyes, he had no defense left to hold the darkness at bay.

After ablutions and breakfast, the entire wing was confined to cells; workshops, recreation—any activity that required movement around the landings—was canceled while Lowell's cell was photographed and examined, then swabbed out. Following breakfast, Billy slept through the morning; a state more akin to coma than sleep, such was its profundity. When he awoke for lunch he was brighter and more outgoing than Cleve had seen him in weeks. There was no sign beneath the vacuous chatter that he knew what had happened the previous night. In the afternoon Cleve faced him with the truth.

"You killed Lowell," he said. There was no point in trying to pretend ignorance any longer; if the boy didn't remember now what he'd done, he would surely recall in time. And with that memory, how long before he remembered that Cleve had watched him transform? Better to confess it now. "I saw you," Cleve said. "I saw you change. . . ."

Billy didn't seem much disturbed by these revelations.

"Yes," he said. "I killed Lowell. Do you blame me?" The question, begging a hundred others, was put lightly, as a matter of mild interest, no more.

"What happened to you?" Cleve said. "I saw you— *there*"—he pointed, appalled at the memory, at the lower bunk—"you weren't human."

"I didn't mean you to see," the boy replied. "I gave you the pills, didn't I? You shouldn't have spied."

"And the night before . . . ," Cleve said. "I was awake then too."

The boy blinked like a bemused bird, head slightly cocked. "You really have been stupid," he said. "So stupid."

"Whether I like it or not, I'm not out of this," Cleve said. "I have dreams."

"Oh, yes." Now a frown marred the porcelain brow. "Yes. You dream the city, don't you?"

"What is that place, Billy?"

"I read somewhere: *The dead have highways*. You ever hear that? Well . . . they have cities too."

"The dead? You mean it's some kind of ghost town?"

"I never wanted you to become involved. You've been

better to me than most here. But I *told* you, I came to Pentonville to do business."

"With Tait."

"That's right."

Cleve wanted to laugh; what he was being told—*a city of the dead?*—only heaped nonsense upon nonsense. And yet his exasperated reason had not sniffed out one explanation more plausible.

"My grandfather killed his children," Billy said, "because he didn't want to pass his condition on to another generation. He learned late, you see. He didn't realize, until he had a wife and children, that he wasn't like most men. He was special. But he didn't *want* the skills he'd been given, and he didn't want his children to survive with that same power in their blood. He would have killed himself, and finished the job, but that my mother escaped. Before he could find her and kill her too, he was arrested."

"And hanged. And buried."

"Hanged and buried, but not *lost*. Nobody's lost, Cleve. Not ever."

"You came here to find him."

"More than find him: make him *help* me. I knew from the age of ten what I was capable of. Not quite consciously, but I had an inkling. And I was afraid. Of course I was afraid: it was a terrible mystery."

"This mutation: you've always done it?"

"No. Only *known* I was capable of it. I came here to make my grandfather tutor me, make him *show me how*. Even now"—he looked down at his wasted arms—"with him teaching me . . . the pain is almost unbearable."

"Why do it then?"

The boy looked at Cleve incredulously. "To be *not* my-

57

self; to be smoke and shadow. To be something terrible." He seemed genuinely puzzled by Cleve's unwillingness. "Wouldn't you do the same?"

Cleve shook his head. "What you became last night was repellent."

Billy nodded. "That's what my grandfather thought. At his trial he called himself an abomination. Not that they knew what he was talking about, of course, but that's what he said. He stood up and said: 'I am Satan's excrement'" —Billy smiled at the thought—"'for God's sake hang me and burn me.' He's changed his mind since then. The century's getting old and stale; it needs new tribes." He looked at Cleve intently. "Don't be afraid," he said. "I won't hurt you, unless you try to tell tales. You won't do that, will you?"

"What could I say that would sound like sanity?" Cleve returned mildly. "No, I won't tell tales."

"Good. And in a little while I'll be gone, and you'll be gone. And you can forget."

"I doubt it."

"Even the dreams will stop when I'm not here. You only share them because you have some mild talents as a sensitive. Trust me. There's nothing to be afraid of."

"The city—"

"What about it?"

"Where are its citizens? I never see anybody. No, that's not quite true. I saw one. A man with a knife . . . going out into the desert . . ."

"I can't help you. I go as a visitor myself. All I know is what my grandfather tells me: that it's a city occupied by dead souls. Whatever you've seen there, forget about it. You don't belong there. You're not dead yet."

* * *

Was it wise to believe always what the dead told you? Were they purged of all deceit by the act of dying, and delivered into their new state like saints? Cleve could not believe such naiveté. More likely they took their talents with them, good and bad, and used them as best they could. There would be shoemakers in paradise, wouldn't there? Foolish to think they'd forgotten how to sew leather.

So perhaps Edgar Tait *lied* about the city. There was more to that place than Billy knew. What about the voices on the wind, the man and the knife, dropping it among a litter of weapons before moving off to God alone knew where? What ritual was that?

Now—with the fear used up, and no untainted reality left to cling to, Cleve saw no reason not to go to the city willingly. What could be there, in those dusty streets, that was worse than what he had seen in the bunk below him, or what had happened to Lowell and Nayler? Beside such atrocities the city was a haven. There was a serenity in its empty thoroughfares and plazas; a sense Cleve had there that all action was over, all rage and distress finished with; that these interiors (with the bath running and the cup brimming) had seen the *worst*, and were now content to sit out the millennium. When that night brought sleep, and the city opened up in front of him, he went into it not as a frightened man astray in hostile territory but as a visitor content to relax a while in a place he knew too well to become lost in, but not well enough to be weary of.

As if in response to this newfound ease, the city opened itself to him. Wandering the streets, feet bloody as ever, he found the doors open wide, the curtains at the windows drawn back. He did not disparage the invitation they offered but went to look more closely at the houses and tenements. On closer inspection he found them not the paradigms of domestic calm he'd first taken them for. In each he discovered some sign of violence recently done. In one, perhaps no more than an overturned chair, or a mark on the floor where a heel had slid in a spot of blood; in others, the manifestations were more obvious. A hammer, its claw clotted, had been left on a table laid with newspapers. There was a room with its floorboards ripped up, and black plastic parcels, suspiciously slick, laid beside the hole. In one, a mirror had been shattered; in another, a set of false teeth left beside a hearth in which a fire flared and spat.

They were murder scenes, all of them. The victims had gone—to other cities, perhaps, full of slaughtered children and murdered friends—leaving these tableaux fixed forever in the breathless moments that followed the crime. Cleve walked down the streets, the perfect voyeur, and peered into scene after scene, reconstructing in his mind's eye the hours that had preceded the studied stillness of each room. Here a child had died: its cot was overturned; here someone had been murdered in his bed, the pillow soaked in blood; the ax on the carpet. Was this damnation then, the killers obliged to wait out some portion of eternity (all of it, perhaps) in the room they had murdered in?

Of the malefactors themselves he saw nothing, though logic implied that they must be close by. Was it that they had the power of invisibility to keep themselves from the prying eyes of touring dreamers like himself; or did a time in this nowhere transform them, so that they were no longer flesh and blood but became part of their cell—a chair, a china doll?

Then he remembered the man at the perimeter who'd come in his fine suit, bloody-handed, and walked out into the desert. *He* had not been invisible.

"Where are you?" he said, standing on the threshold of a mean room, with an open oven and utensils in the sink, water running on them. "Show yourself."

A movement caught his eye, and he glanced across to the door. There was a man standing there. He had been there all along, Cleve realized, but so still, and so perfectly a part of this room, that he had not been visible until he moved his eyes and looked Cleve's way. He felt a twinge of unease, thinking that each room he had peered into had, most likely, contained one or more killers, each similarly camouflaged by stasis. The man, knowing he'd been seen, stepped out of hiding. He was in late middle-age and had cut himself that morning as he shaved.

"Who are you?" he said. "I've seen you before. Walking by."

He spoke softly and sadly—an unlikely killer, Cleve thought.

"Just a visitor," he told the man.

"There are no visitors here," he replied, "only prospective citizens."

Cleve frowned, trying to work out what the man meant. But his dream-mind was sluggish, and before he could solve the riddle of the man's words there were others.

"Do I know you?" the man asked. "I find I forget more and more. That's no use, is it? If I forget I'll never leave, will I?"

"Leave?" Cleve repeated.

"Make an exchange," the man said, realigning his toupee.

"And go where?"

"Back. Do it over."

Now he approached Cleve across the room. He stretched out his hands, palms up; they were blistered.

"You can help me," he said. "I can make a deal with the best of them."

"I don't understand you."

The man clearly thought he was bluffing. His upper lip, which boasted a dyed black mustache, curled. "Yes you do," he said. "You understand perfectly. You just want to sell yourself, the way everybody does. Highest bidder, is it? What are you, an assassin?"

Cleve shook his head. "I'm just dreaming," he replied.

The man's fit of pique subsided. "Be a friend," he said. "I've got no influence; not like some. Some of them, you know, they come here and they're out again in a matter of hours. They're professionals. They make arrangements. But me? With me it was a crime of passion. I didn't come prepared. I'll stay here till I can make a deal. Please be a friend."

"I can't help you," Cleve said, not even certain of what the man was requesting.

The killer nodded. "Of course not," he said, "I didn't expect . . ."

He turned from Cleve and moved to the oven. Heat flared up from it and made a mirage of the hob. Casually, he put one of his blistered palms on the door and closed it; almost as soon as he had done so it creaked open again. "Do you know just how appetizing it is—the smell of cooking flesh?" he said, as he returned to the oven door and attempted to close it a second time. "Can anybody blame me? Really?"

Cleve left him to his ramblings; if there was sense there it was probably not worth his laboring over. The talk of exchanges and of escape from the city: it defied Cleve's comprehension.

He wandered on, tired now of peering into the houses. He'd seen all he wanted to see. Surely morning was close, and the bell would ring on the landing. Perhaps he should even wake himself, he thought, and be done with this tour for the night.

As the thought occurred, he saw the girl. She was no more than six or seven years old, and she was standing at the next intersection. This was no killer, surely. He started toward her. She, either out of shyness or some less benign motive, turned to her right and ran off. Cleve followed. By the time he had reached the intersection she was already a long way down the next street; again he gave chase. As dreams would have such pursuits, the laws of physics did not pertain equally to pursuer and pursued. The girl seemed to move easily, while Cleve struggled against air as thick as treacle. He did not give up, however, but pressed on wherever the girl led. He was soon a good distance from any location he recognized in a warren of yards and alleyways —all, he supposed, scenes of blood-letting. Unlike the main thoroughfares, this ghetto contained few entire spaces, only snatches of geography: a grass verge, more red than green; a piece of scaffolding, with a noose depending from it; a pile of earth. And now, simply, a wall.

The girl had led him into a cul-de-sac; she herself had disappeared however, leaving him facing a plain brick wall, much weathered, with a narrow window in it. He approached: this was clearly what he'd been led here to see. He peered through the reinforced glass, dirtied on his side by an accumulation of bird-droppings, and found himself staring into one of the cells at Pentonville. His stomach flipped over. What kind of game was this; led out of a cell and into this dream-city, only to be led back into prison? But a few seconds of study told him that it was not *his* cell. It was Lowell and Nayler's. Theirs were the pictures taped to the gray brick, theirs the blood spread over floor and wall and bunk and door. This was another murder scene.

"My God Almighty," he murmured. "Billy . . ."

He turned away from the wall. In the sand at his feet lizards were mating; the wind that found its way into this backwater brought butterflies. As he watched them dance, the bell rang in B Wing, and it was morning.

It was a trap. Its mechanism was by no means clear to Cleve—but he had no doubt of its purpose. Billy would go to the city, soon. The cell in which he had committed murder already awaited him, and of all the wretched places Cleve had seen in that assemblage of charnel houses surely the tiny, blood-drenched cell was the worst.

The boy could not know what was planned for him; his grandfather had lied about the city by exclusion, failing to tell Billy what special qualifications were required to exist there. And why? Cleve returned to the oblique conversation he'd had with the man in the kitchen. That talk of exchanges, of deal making, of *going back*. Edgar Tait had regretted his sins, hadn't he? He'd decided, as the years passed, that he was *not* the Devil's excrement, that to be returned into the world would not be so bad an idea. Billy was somehow an instrument in that return.

"My grandfather doesn't like you," the boy said when they were locked up again after lunch. For the second consecutive day all recreation and workshop activities had been canceled, while a cell-by-cell inquiry was undertaken regarding Lowell's and —as of the early hours of that day —Nayler's deaths.

"Doesn't he?" Cleve said. "And why?"

"Says you're too inquisitive. In the city."

Cleve was sitting on the top bunk; Billy on the chair against the opposite wall. The boy's eyes were bloodshot; a small but constant tremor had taken over his body.

"You're going to die," Cleve said. What other way to state that fact was there, but baldly? "I saw . . . in the city . . ."

Billy shook his head. "Sometimes you talk like a crazy man. My grandfather says I shouldn't trust you."

"He's afraid of me, that's why."

Billy laughed derisively. It was an ugly sound, learned, Cleve guessed, from Grandfather Tait. "He's afraid of no one," Billy retorted.

"Afraid of what I'll see. Of what I'll tell you."

"No," said the boy with absolute conviction.

"He told you to kill Lowell, didn't he?"

Billy's head jerked up. "Why'd you say that?"

"You never wanted to murder him. Maybe scare them both a bit, but not *kill* them. It was your loving grandfather's idea."

"Nobody tells me what to do," Billy replied, his gaze icy. "Nobody."

"All right," Cleve conceded, "maybe he *persuaded* you, eh? Told you it was a matter of family pride. Something like that?" The observation clearly touched a nerve; the tremors had increased.

"So? What if he did?"

"I've seen where you're going to go, Billy. A place just waiting for you." The boy stared at Cleve but didn't interrupt. "Only murderers occupy the city, Billy. That's why your grandfather's there. And if he can find a replacement —if he can reach out and make more murder—he can go free."

Billy stood up, face like a fury. All trace of derision had gone. "What do you mean *free?*"

"Back to the world. *Back here.*"

"You're lying."

"Ask him."

"He wouldn't cheat me. His blood's my blood."

"You think he cares? After fifty years in that place, waiting for a chance to be out and away. You think he gives a *damn* how he does it?"

"I'll tell him how you lie," Billy said. The anger was not entirely directed at Cleve; there was an undercurrent of doubt there, which Billy was trying to suppress. "You're dead," he said, "when he finds out how you're trying to poison me against him. You'll see him, then. Oh yes. You'll see him. And you'll wish to Christ you hadn't."

There seemed to be no way out. Even if Cleve could convince the authorities to move him before night fell —(a slim chance indeed; he would have to reverse all that he had claimed about the boy, tell them Billy was dangerously insane, or something similar. Certainly not the truth.)— even if he were to have himself transferred to another cell, there was no promise of safety in such a maneuver. The boy had said he was smoke and shadow. Neither door nor bars could keep such insinuations at bay; the fate of Lowell and Nayler was proof positive of that. Nor was Billy alone.

There was Edgar St. Clair Tait to be accounted for, and what powers might he possess? Yet to stay in the same cell with the boy tonight would amount to self-slaughter, wouldn't it? He would be delivering himself into the hands of the beasts.

When they left their cells for the evening meal, Cleve looked around for Devlin, located him, and asked for the opportunity of a short interview, which was granted. After the meal, Cleve reported to the officer.

"You asked me to keep an eye on Billy Tait, sir."

"What about him?"

Cleve had thought hard about what he might tell Devlin that would bring an immediate transfer: nothing had come to mind. He stumbled, hoping for inspiration, but was empty-mouthed.

"I . . . I . . . want to put in a request for a cell transfer."

"Why?"

"The boy's unbalanced," Cleve replied. "I'm afraid he's going to do me harm. Have another of his fits."

"You could lay him flat with one hand tied behind your back. He's worn to the bone." At this point, had he been talking to Mayflower, Cleve might had been able to make a direct appeal to the man. With Devlin such tactics would be doomed from the beginning.

"I don't know why you're complaining. He's been as good as gold," said Devlin, savoring the parody of fond father. "Quiet; always polite. He's no danger to you or anyone."

"You don't know him—"

"What are you trying to pull?"

"Put me in a Rule 43 cell, sir. *Anywhere*, I don't mind. Just get me out of his way. *Please.*"

Devlin didn't reply but stared at Cleve, mystified. At last, he said, "You *are* afraid of him."

"Yes."

"What's wrong with you? You've shared cells with hard men and never turned a hair."

"He's different," Cleve replied; there was little else he could say except: "He's insane. I tell you he's insane."

"All the world's crazy, save thee and me, Smith. Hadn't you heard?" Devlin laughed. "Go back to your cell and stop bellyaching. You don't want a ghost train ride, now do you?"

When Cleve returned to the cell, Billy was writing a letter. Sitting on his bunk, poring over the paper, he looked utterly vulnerable. What Devlin said was true: the boy *was* worn to the bone. It was difficult to believe, looking at the ladder of his vertebrae, visible through his T-shirt, that this frail form could survive the throes of transformation. But then, maybe it would not. Maybe the rigors of change would tear him apart with time. But not soon enough.

"Billy . . ."

The boy didn't take his eyes from his letter.

". . . what I said, about the city . . ."

He stopped writing—

". . . Maybe I *was* imagining it all. Just dreaming."

—and started again.

". . . I only told you because I was afraid for you. That was all. I want us to be friends."

Billy looked up. "It's not in my hands," he said very

simply. "Not now. It's up to Grandfather. He may be merciful; he may not."

"Why do you have to tell him?"

"He knows what's in me. He and I . . . we're like one. That's how I know he wouldn't cheat me."

Soon it would be night; the lights would go out along the wing, the shadows would come.

"So I just have to wait, do I?" Cleve said.

Billy nodded. "I'll call him, and then we'll see."

Call him? Cleve thought. Did the old man need summoning from his resting place every night? Was that what he had seen Billy doing, standing in the middle of the cell, eyes closed and face up to the window? If so, perhaps the boy could be *prevented* from putting in his call to the dead.

As the evening deepened Cleve lay on his bunk and thought his options through. Was it better to wait here and see what judgment came from Tait, or attempt to take control of the situation and block the old man's arrival? If he did so, there would be no going back; no room for pleas or apologies: his aggression would undoubtedly breed aggression. If he failed to prevent the boy from calling Tait, it would be the end.

The lights went out. In cells up and down the five landings of B Wing men would be turning their faces to their pillows. Some, perhaps, would lie awake planning their careers when this minor hiccup in their professional lives was over; others would be in the arms of invisible mistresses. Cleve listened to the sounds of the cell: the rattling progress of water in the pipes, the shallow breathing from the bunk below. Sometimes it seemed that he had lived a second lifetime on this stale pillow, marooned in darkness.

The breathing from below soon became practically inaudible; nor was there sound of movement. Perhaps Billy was waiting for Cleve to fall asleep before he made any move. If so, the boy would wait in vain. He would not close his eyes and leave them to slaughter him in his sleep. He wasn't a pig, to be taken uncomplaining to the knife.

Moving as cautiously as possible, so as to arouse no suspicion, Cleve unbuckled his belt and pulled it through the loops of his trousers. He might make a more adequate binding by tearing up his sheet and pillowcase, but he could not do so without arousing Billy's attention. Now he waited, belt in hand, and pretended sleep.

Tonight he was grateful that the noise in the Wing kept stirring him from dozing, because it was fully two hours before Billy moved out of his bunk, two hours in which— despite his fear of what would happen should he sleep— Cleve's eyelids betrayed him on three or four occasions. But others on the landings were tearful tonight; the deaths of Lowell and Nayler had made even the toughest cons jittery. Shouts—and countercalls from those awakened— punctuated the hours. Despite the fatigue in his limbs, sleep did not master him.

When Billy finally got up from the lower bunk it was well past twelve and the landing was all but quiet. Cleve could hear the boy's breath; it was no longer even but had a catch in it. He watched, eyes like slits, as Billy crossed the cell to his familiar place in front of the window. There was no doubt that he was about to call up the old man.

As Billy closed his eyes, Cleve sat up, threw off his blanket and slipped down from the bunk. The boy was slow to respond. Before he quite comprehended what was happening, Cleve had crossed the cell and thrust him back against the wall, hand clamped over Billy's mouth.

"No, you don't," Cleve growled. "I'm not going to go like Lowell." Billy struggled, but Cleve was easily his physical superior.

"He's not going to come tonight," Cleve said, staring into the boy's wide eyes, "because you're not going to call him."

Billy fought more violently to be free, biting hard against his captor's palm. Cleve instinctively removed his hand and in two strides the boy was at the window, reaching up. In his throat, a strange half-song; on his face, sudden and inexplicable tears. Cleve dragged him away.

"Shut your noise up!" he snapped. But the boy continued to make the sound. Cleve hit him, open-handed but hard, across the face. *"Shut up!"* he said. Still the boy refused to cease his singing; now the music had taken on another rhythm. Again Cleve hit him, and again. But the assault failed to silence him. There was a whisper of change in the air of the cell, a shifting in its chiaroscuro. The shadows were moving.

Panic took Cleve. Without warning he made a fist and punched the boy hard in the stomach. As Billy doubled up an upper-cut caught his jaw. It drove his head back against the wall, his skull connecting with the brick. Billy's legs gave and he collapsed. A featherweight, Cleve had once thought, and it was true. Two good punches and the boy was laid out cold.

Cleve glanced around the cell. The movement in the shadows had been arrested; they trembled though, like greyhounds awaiting release. Heart hammering, he carried Billy back to his bunk and laid him down. There was no sign of consciousness returning; the boy lay limply on the mattress while Cleve tore up his sheet and gagged him, thrusting a ball of fabric into the boy's mouth to prevent him from making a sound behind his gag. He then proceeded to tie Billy to the bunk, using both his own belt and the boy's, supplemented with further makeshift bindings of torn sheets. It took several minutes to finish the job. As Cleve was lashing the boy's legs together, Billy began to stir. His eyes flickered open, full of puzzlement. Then, realizing his situation, he began to thrash his head from side to side; there was little else he could do to signal his protest.

"No, Billy," Cleve murmured to him, throwing a blanket across his bound body to keep the fact from any guard who might look in through the peephole before morning, "tonight, you don't bring him. Everything I said was true, boy. He wants out, and he's using you to escape." Cleve took hold of Billy's head, fingers pressed against his cheeks. "He's not your friend. *I am*. Always have been." Billy tried to shake his head from Cleve's grip but couldn't. "Don't waste your energy," Cleve advised. "It's going to be a long night."

He left the boy on the bunk, crossed the cell to the wall, and slid down it to sit on his haunches and watch. He would stay awake until dawn, and then, when there was some light to think by, he'd work out his next move. For now, he was content that his crude tactics had worked.

The boy had stopped trying to fight; he had clearly realized the bonds were too expertly tied to be loosened. A kind of calm descended on the cell: Cleve sitting in the patch of light that fell through the window, the boy lying in the gloom of the lower bunk, breathing steadily through his nostrils. Cleve glanced at his watch. It was twelve fifty-four. When was morning? He didn't know. Five hours, at least. He put his head back, and stared at the light.

It mesmerized him. The minutes ticked by slowly but steadily, and the light did not change. Sometimes a guard would advance along the landing, and Billy, hearing the footsteps, would begin his struggling afresh. But nobody looked into the cell. The two prisoners were left to their thoughts; Cleve to wonder if there would ever come a time when he could be free of the shadow behind him, Billy to think whatever thoughts came to bound monsters. And still the dead-of-night minutes went, minutes that crept across the mind like dutiful schoolchildren, one upon the heels of the next, and after sixty had passed that sum was called an hour. And dawn was closer by that span, wasn't it? But then so was death, and so, presumably, the end of the world: that glorious Last Trump of which The Bishop had spoken so fondly, when the dead men under the lawn outside would rise as fresh as yesterday's bread and go out to meet their Maker. And sitting there against the wall, listening to Billy's inhalations and exhalations, and watching the light in the glass and through the glass, Cleve knew without doubt that even if he escaped this trap, it was only a temporary respite; that this long night, its minutes, its hours, were a foretaste of a longer vigil. He almost despaired then; felt his soul sink into a hole from which there seemed to be no hope of retrieval. *Here* was the real world; he wept. Not joy, not light, not looking forward; only this waiting in ignorance, without hope, even of fear, for fear came only to those with dreams to lose. The hole was deep and dim. He peered up out of it at the light through the window, and his thoughts became one wretched round. He forgot the bunk and the boy lying there. He forgot the numbness that had overtaken his legs. He might, given time, have forgotten even the simple act of taking breath but for the smell of urine that pricked him from his fugue.

He looked toward the bunk. The boy was voiding his bladder, but that act was simply a symptom of something else altogether. Beneath the blanket, Billy's body was moving in a dozen ways that his bonds should have prevented. It took Cleve a few moments to shake off lethargy, and seconds more to realize what was happening. Billy was changing.

Cleve tried to stand upright, but his lower limbs were dead from sitting still for so long. He almost fell forward across the cell, and only prevented himself by throwing out an arm to grasp the chair. His eyes were glued to the gloom of the lower bunk. The movements were increasing in scale and complexity. The blanket was pitched off. Beneath it Billy's body was already beyond recognition; the same terrible procedure as he had seen before, but in reverse. Matter gathering in buzzing clouds about the body, and congealing into atrocious forms. Limbs and organs summoned from the ineffable, teeth shaping themselves like needles and plunging into place in a head grown large and swelling still. He begged for Billy to stop, but with every drawn breath there was less of humanity to appeal to. The strength the boy had lacked was granted to the beast; it had already broken almost all its constraints, and now, as Cleve watched, it struggled free of the last, and rolled off the bunk onto the floor of the cell.

Cleve backed off toward the door, his eyes scanning Billy's mutated form. He remembered his mother's horror at earwigs and saw something of that insect in this anatomy: the way it bent its shiny back upon itself, exposing the paddling intracacies that lined its abdomen. Elsewhere, no analogy offered a hold on the sight. Its head was rife with tongues, that licked its eyes clean in place of lids, and ran back and forth across its teeth, wetting and rewetting them constantly; from seeping holes along its flanks came a sewer stench. Yet even now there was a residue of something human trapped in this foulness, its rumor only serving to heighten the filth of the whole. Seeing its hooks and its spines, Cleve remembered Lowell's rising scream and felt his own throat pulse, ready to loose a sound its equal should the beast turn on him.

But Billy had other intentions. He moved—limbs in horrible array—to the window and clambered up, pressing his head against the glass like a leech. The music he made was not like his previous song—but Cleve had no doubt it was the same summoning. He turned to the door and began to beat upon it, hoping that Billy would be too distracted with his call to turn on him before assistance came.

"Quick! For Christ's sake! Quick!" He yelled as loudly as exhaustion would allow, and glanced over his shoulder once to see if Billy was coming for him. He was not; he was still clamped to the window, though his call had all but faltered. Its purpose was achieved. Darkness was tyrant in the cell.

Panicking, Cleve turned back to the door and renewed his tattoo. There was somebody running along the landing now; he could hear shouts and imprecations from other cells. "Jesus Christ, help me!" he shouted. He could feel a chill at his back. He didn't need to turn to know what was happening behind him. The shadow growing, the wall dissolving so that the city and its occupant could come through. Tait was here. He could feel the man's presence, vast and dark. Tait the child killer, Tait the shadow-thing, Tait the transformer. Cleve beat on the door till his hands bled. The feet seemed a continent away. Were they coming? Were they coming?

The chill behind him became a blast. He saw his shadow thrown up on to the door by flickering blue light; smelled sand and blood.

And then, the voice. Not the boy, but that of his grandfather, of Edgar St. Clair Tait. This was the man who had pronounced himself the Devil's excrement, and hearing that abhorrent voice, Cleve believed both in hell and its master, believed himself already in the bowels of Satan, a witness to its wonders.

"You are too inquisitive," Edgar said. "It's time you went to bed."

Cleve didn't want to turn. The last thought in his head was that he *should* turn and look at the speaker. But he was no longer subject to his own will; Tait had fingers in his head and was dabbling there. He turned, and looked.

The hanged man was in the cell. He was not that beast Cleve had half seen, that face of pulp and eggs. He was here in the flesh; dressed for another age, and not without charm. His face was well made; his brow wide, his eyes unflinching. He still wore his wedding ring on the hand that stroked Billy's bowed head like that of a pet dog.

"Time to die, Mr. Smith," he said.

On the landing outside, Cleve heard Devlin shouting. He had no breath left to answer with. But he heard keys in the lock or was that some illusion his mind had made to placate his panic?

The tiny cell was full of wind. It threw over the chair and table, and lifted the sheets into the air like childhood ghosts. And now it took Tait, and the boy with him; sucked them back into the receding perspectives of the city.

"Come on now," Tait demanded, his face corrupting, "we need you, body and soul. Come with us, Mr. Smith. We won't be denied."

"No!" Cleve yelled back at his tormentor. The suction was plucking at his fingers, at his eyeballs. "I won't—"

Behind him, the door was rattling.

"I won't, you hear!"

Suddenly, the door was thrust open, and threw him forward into the vortex of fog and dust that was sucking Tait and his grandchild away. He almost went with them but for a hand that grabbed at his shirt and dragged him back from the brink, even as consciousness gave itself up.

Somewhere, far away, Devlin began to laugh like a hyena. He's lost his mind, Cleve decided; and the image his darkening thoughts evoked was one of the contents of Devlin's brain escaping through his mouth like a flock of flying dogs.

He awoke in dreams; and in the city. He awoke remembering his last conscious moments: Devlin's hysteria, the hand arresting his fall as the two figures were sucked away in front of him. He had followed them, it seemed, unable to prevent his comatose mind from retreading the familiar route to the murderers' metropolis. But Tait had not won yet. He was still only *dreaming* his presence here. His corporeal self was still in Pentonville; his dislocation from it informed his every step.

He listened to the wind. It was eloquent as ever: the voices coming and going with each gritty gust, but never, even when the wind died to a whisper, disappearing entirely. As he listened he heard a shout. In this mute city the sound was a shock; it startled rats from their nests and birds up from some secluded plaza.

Curious, he pursued the sound, whose echoes were almost traced on the air. As he hurried down the empty streets he heard further raised voices, and now men and women were appearing at the doors and windows of their cells. So many faces, and nothing in common between one and the next to confirm the hopes of a physiognomist. Murder had as many faces as it had occurrences. The only common quality was one of wretchedness, of minds despairing after an age at the site of their crime. He glanced at them as he went, sufficiently distracted by their looks not to notice where the shout was leading him until he found himself once more in the ghetto to which he had been led by the child.

Now he rounded a corner, and at the end of the cul-de-sac he'd seen from his previous visit here (the wall, the window, the bloody chamber beyond) he saw Billy, writhing in the sand at Tait's feet. The boy was half himself and half that beast he had become in front of Cleve's eyes. The better part was convulsing in its attempt to climb free of the other, but without success. In one moment the boy's body would surface, white and frail, only to be subsumed the next into the flux of transformation. Was that an arm forming, and being snatched away again before it could gain fingers?; was that a face pressed from the house of tongues that was the beast's head? The sight defied analysis. As soon as Cleve fixed upon some recognizable feature it was drowned again.

Edgar Tait looked up from the struggle in front of him,

and bared his teeth at Cleve. It was a display a shark might have envied.

"He doubted me, Mr. Smith," the monster said, "and came looking for his cell."

A mouth appeared from the patchwork on the sand and gave out a sharp cry, full of pain and terror.

"Now he wants to be away from me," Tait said. "You sowed the doubt. He must suffer the consequences." He pointed a trembling finger at Cleve, and in the act of pointing the limb transformed, flesh becoming bruised leather. "You came where you were not wanted, and look at the agonies you've brought."

Tait kicked the thing at his feet. It rolled over on to its back, vomiting.

"He needs me," Tait said. "Don't you have the sense to see that? Without me, he's lost."

Cleve didn't reply to the hanged man but instead addressed the beast on the sand.

"Billy?" he said, calling the boy out of the flux.

"Lost," Tait said.

"Billy," Cleve repeated. "Listen to me. . . ."

"He won't go back now," Tait said. "You're just dreaming this. But he's *here,* in the flesh.

"Billy," Cleve persevered. "Do you hear me? It's me; it's Cleve."

The boy seemed to pause in his gyrations for an instant, as if hearing the appeal. Cleve said Billy's name again, and again.

It was one of the first skills the human child learned: to call itself something. If anything could reach the boy it was surely his own name.

"Billy . . . Billy . . ." At the repeated word, the body rolled itself over.

Tait seemed to have become uneasy. The confidence he'd displayed was now silenced. His body was darkening, the head becoming bulbous. Cleve tried to keep his eyes off the subtle distortions in Edgar's anatomy and concentrate on winning Billy back. The repetition of the name was paying dividends; the beast was being subdued. Moment by moment there was more of the boy emerging. He looked pitiful; skin-and-bones on the black sand. But his face was almost reconstructed now, and his eyes were on Cleve.

"Billy . . . ?"

He nodded. His hair was plastered to his forehead with sweat; his limbs were in a spasm.

"You know where you are? *Who* you are?"

At first it seemed as though comprehension escaped the boy. And then—by degrees—recognition formed in his eyes, and with it came a terror of the man standing over him.

Cleve glanced up at Tait. In the few seconds since he had last looked all but a few human characteristics had been erased from his head and upper torso, revealing corruptions more profound than those of his grandchild. Billy gazed up over his shoulder like a whipped dog.

"You belong to me," Tait pronounced, through features barely capable of speech. Billy saw the limbs descending to snatch at him, and rose from his prone position to escape them, but he was too late. Cleve saw the spiked hook of Tait's limb wrap itself around Billy's neck, and draw him close. Blood leapt from the slit windpipe, and with it the whine of escaping air.

Cleve yelled.

"With me," Tait said, the words deteriorating into gibberish.

Suddenly the narrow cul-de-sac was filling up with brightness, and the boy and Tait and the city were being bleached out. Cleve tried to hold on to them, but they were slipping from him; and in their place another concrete reality: a light, a face (faces) and a voice calling him out of one absurdity and into another.

The doctor's hand was on his face. It felt clammy.

"What on earth were you dreaming about?" he asked, the perfect idiot.

Billy had gone.

Of all the mysteries that the governor—and Devlin and the other guards who had stepped into cell B. 3. 20 that night—had to face, the total disappearance of William Tait from an unbreached cell was the most perplexing. Of the vision that had set Devlin giggling like a loon nothing was said; easier to believe in some collective delusion than that they'd seen some objective reality. When Cleve attempted to articulate the events of that night, and of the many nights previous to that, his monologue, interrupted often by his tears and silences, was met with feigned understanding and sideways glances. He told the story over several times, however, despite their condescension, and they, looking no doubt for a clue among his lunatic fables as to the reality of Billy Tait's Houdini act, attended every word. When they found nothing among his tales to advance their investigations, they began to lose their tempers with him. Consolation was replaced with threats. They demanded, voices louder each time they asked the question, where

Billy had gone. Cleve answered the only way he knew how. "To the city," he told them. "He's a murderer, you see."

"And his body?" the governor said. "Where do you suppose his *body* is?"

Cleve didn't know, and said so. It wasn't until much later, four full days later in fact, that he was standing by the window watching the gardening detail bearing this spring's plantings cross between wings, that he remembered the lawn.

He found Mayflower, who had been returned to B Wing in lieu of Devlin, and told the officer the thought that had come to him. "He's in the grave," he said. "He's with his grandfather. Smoke and shadow."

They dug up the coffin by cover of night, an elaborate shield of poles and tarpaulins erected to keep proceedings from prying eyes, and lamps, bright as day but not so warm, trained on the labors of the men volunteered as an exhumation party. Cleve's answer to the riddle of Tait's disappearance had met with almost universal bafflement, but no explanation—however absurd—was being overlooked in a mystery so intractable. Thus they gathered at the unmarked grave to turn earth that looked not to have been disturbed in five decades: the governor, a selection of Home Office officials, a pathologist and Devlin. One of the doctors, believing that Cleve's morbid delusion would be best countered if he viewed the contents of the coffin and saw his error with his own eyes, convinced the governor that Cleve should also be numbered among the spectators.

There was little in the confines of Edgar St. Clair Tait's coffin that Cleve had not seen before. The corpse of the murderer—returned here (as smoke perhaps?) neither quite beast nor quite human, and preserved, as The Bishop had promised, as undecayed as the day of his execution— shared the coffin with Billy Tait, who lay, naked as a babe, in his grandfather's embrace. Edgar's corrupted limb was still wound around Billy's neck, and the walls of the coffin were dark with congealed blood. But Billy's face was not besmirched. *He looks like a doll,* one of the doctors observed. Cleve wanted to reply that no doll had such tear stains on its cheeks, nor such despair in its eyes, but the thought refused to become words.

Cleve was released from Pentonville three weeks later after special application to the Parole Board, with only two-thirds of his sentence completed. He returned, within half a year, to the only profession that he had ever known. Any hope he might have had of release from his dreams was short-lived. The place was with him still: neither so focused nor so easily traversed now that Billy—whose mind had opened that door—was gone, but still a potent terror, the lingering presence of which wearied Cleve.

Sometimes the dreams would almost recede completely, only to return again with terrible potency. It took Cleve several months before he began to grasp the pattern of this vacillation. *People* brought the dream to him. If he spent time with somebody who had murderous intentions, the city came back. Nor were such people so rare. As he grew more sensitive to the lethal streak in those around him he found himself scarcely able to walk the street. They were *everywhere,* these embryonic killers, people wearing smart clothes and sunny expressions were striding the pavement and imagining, as they strode, the deaths of their employers and their spouses, of soap-opera stars and incompetent tailors. The world had murder on its mind, and he could no longer bear its thoughts.

Only heroin offered some release from the burden of experience. He had never done much intravenous H, but it rapidly became heaven and earth to him. It was an expensive addiction however, and one which his increasingly truncated circle of professional contacts could scarcely hope to finance. It was a man called Grimm, a fellow addict so desperate to avoid reality he could get high on fermented milk, who suggested that Cleve might want to do some work to earn him a fee the equal of his appetite. It seemed like a wise idea. A meeting was arranged, and a proposal put. The fee for the job was so high it could not be refused by a man so in need of money. The job, of course, was murder.

"There are no visitors here, only prospective citizens." He had been told that once, though he no longer quite remembered by whom, and he believed in prophecies. If he didn't commit murder now, it would only be a matter of time until he did.

But though the details of the assassination that he undertook had a terrible familiarity to him, he had not anticipated the collision of circumstances by which he ended fleeing from the scene of his crime barefoot, and running so hard on pavement and tarmac that by the time the police cornered him and shot him down his feet were bloody, and ready at last to tread the streets of the city—just as he had in dreams. ·

The room he'd killed in was waiting for him, and he lived there, hiding his head from any who appeared in the street outside, for several months. (He assumed time passed here, by the beard he'd grown; though sleep came seldom, and day never.) After a while, however, he braved the cool wind and the butterflies and took himself off to the city perimeters, where the houses petered out and the desert took over. He went, not to see the dunes, but to listen to the voices that came always, rising and falling, like the howls of jackals or children.

He stayed there a long while, and the wind conspired with the desert to bury him. But he was not disappointed with the fruit of his vigil. For one day (or year), he saw a man come to the place and drop a gun in the sand, then wander out into the desert, where, after a while, the makers of the voices came to meet him, loping and wild, dancing on their crutches. They surrounded him, laughing. He went with them, laughing. And though distance and the wind smudged the sight, Cleve was certain he saw the man picked up by one of the celebrants, and taken on to its shoulders as a boy, thence snatched into another's arms as a baby, until, at the limit of his senses, he heard the man bawl as he was delivered back into life. He went away content, knowing at last how sin (and he) had come into the world.

The
Forbidden

LIKE a flawless tragedy, the elegance of which structure is lost upon those suffering in it, the perfect geometry of the Spector Street Estate was visible only from the air. Walking in its drear canyons, passing through its grimy corridors from one gray concrete rectangle to the next, there was little to seduce the eye or stimulate the imagination. What few saplings had been planted in the quadrangles had long since been mutilated or uprooted; the grass, though tall, resolutely refused a healthy green.

No doubt the estate and its two companion developments had once been an architect's dream. No doubt the city planners had wept with pleasure at a design that housed three and thirty-six persons per hectare, and still boasted space for a children's playground. Doubtless fortunes and reputations had been built upon Spector Street, and at its opening fine words had been spoken of its being a yardstick by which all future developments would be measured.

But the planners—tears wept, words spoken—had left the estate to its own devices; the architects occupied restored Georgian houses at the other end of the city, and probably never set foot here.

They would not have been shamed by the deterioration of the estate even if they had. Their brainchild (they would doubtless argue) was as brilliant as ever: its geometries as precise, its ratios as calculated; it was *people* who had spoiled Spector Street. Nor would they have been wrong in such an accusation. Helen had seldom seen an inner city environment so comprehensively vandalized. Lamps had been shattered and backyard fences overthrown; cars whose wheels and engines had been removed and chassis then burned, blocked garage facilities. In one courtyard three or four ground-floor maisonettes had been entirely gutted by fire, their windows and doors boarded up with planks and corrugated metal shutters.

More startling still were the graffiti. That was what she had come here to see, encouraged by Archie's talk of the place, and she was not disappointed. It was difficult to believe, staring at the multiple layers of designs, names, obscenities and dogmas that were scrawled and sprayed on every available brick, that Spector Street was barely three and a half years old. The walls, so recently virgin, were now so profoundly defaced that the Council Cleaning Department could never hope to return them to their former condition. A layer of whitewash to cancel this visual cacophony would only offer the scribes a fresh and yet more tempting surface on which to make their mark.

Helen was in seventh heaven. Every corner she turned offered some fresh material for her thesis: "Graffiti: The Semiotics of Urban Despair." It was a subject that married her two favorite disciplines—sociology and esthetics—and as she wandered around the estate she began to wonder if there wasn't a book, in addition to her thesis, in the subject. She walked from courtyard to courtyard, copying down a large number of the more interesting scrawlings and noting their location. Then she went back to the car for her camera and tripod and returned to the most fertile of the areas, to make a thorough visual record of the walls.

It was a chilly business. She was not an expert photographer, and the late October sky was in full flight, shifting the light on the bricks from one moment to the next. As she adjusted and readjusted the exposure to compensate for the light changes, her fingers steadily became clumsier, her temper correspondingly thinner. But she struggled on, the idle curiosity of passersby notwithstanding. There were so many designs to document. She reminded herself that her present discomfort would be amply repaid when she showed the slides to Trevor, whose doubt of the project's validity had been perfectly apparent from the beginning.

"The writing on the wall?" he'd said, half smiling in that irritating fashion of his. "It's been done a hundred times."

This was true, of course; and yet not. There certainly were learned works on graffiti, chock full of sociological jargon: *cultural disenfranchisement; urban alienation*. But she flattered herself that *she* might find something among this litter of scrawlings that previous analysts had not: some unifying convention perhaps, that she could use as the lynchpin of her thesis. Only a vigorous cataloguing and cross-referencing of the phrases and images before her would reveal such a correspondence; hence the importance of this photographic study. So many hands had worked here; so many minds left their mark, however casually: if she could find some pattern, some predominant motive, or *motif,* the thesis would be guaranteed some serious attention, and so, in turn, would she.

"What are you doing?" a voice from behind her asked.

She turned from her calculations to see a young woman with a stroller on the pavement behind her. She looked weary, Helen thought, and pinched by the cold. The child in the stroller was mewling, his grimy fingers clutching an orange lollipop and the wrapping from a chocolate bar. The bulk of the chocolate, and the remains of previous Jujubes, were displayed down the front of his coat.

Helen offered a thin smile to the woman; she looked in need of it.

"I'm photographing the walls," she said in answer to the initial inquiry, though surely this was perfectly apparent.

The woman—she could barely be twenty, Helen judged —said, "You mean the filth?"

"The writing and the pictures," Helen said. Then: "Yes. The filth."

"You from the council?"

"No, the university."

"It's bloody disgusting," the woman said. "The way they do that. It's not just kids, either."

"No?"

"Grown men. Grown men, too. They don't give a damn. Do it in broad daylight. You see 'em . . . broad daylight." She glanced down at the child, who was sharpening his lollipop on the ground. "Kerry!" she snapped, but the boy took no notice. "Are they going to wipe it off?" she asked Helen.

"I don't know," Helen said, and reiterated: "I'm from the university."

"Oh," the woman replied, as if this were new information, "so you're nothing to do with the council?"

"No."

"Some of it's obscene, isn't it. Really dirty. Makes me
embarrassed to see some of the things they draw."

Helen nodded, casting an eye at the boy in the stroller.
Kerry had decided to put his lollipop in his ear for safe-
keeping.

"Don't do that!" his mother told him, and leaned over to
slap the child's hand. The blow, which was negligible,
started the child bawling. Helen took the opportunity to
return to her camera. But the woman still desired to talk.
"It's not just on the outside, neither," she commented.

"I beg your pardon?" Helen said.

"They break into the flats when they get vacant. The
council tried to board them up, but it does no good. They
break in anyway. Use them as toilets, and write more filth
on the walls. They light fires too. Then nobody can move
back in."

The description piqued Helen's curiosity. Would the
graffiti on the *inside* walls be substantially different from
the public displays? It was certainly worth an investigation.

"Are there any places you know of around here like
that?"

"Empty flats, you mean?"

"With graffiti."

"Just by us, there's one or two," the woman volunteered.
"I'm in Butts's Court."

"Maybe you could show me?" Helen asked.

The woman shrugged.

"By the way, my name's Helen Buchanan."

"Anne-Marie," the mother replied.

"I'd be very grateful if you could point me to one of those empty flats."

Anne-Marie was baffled by Helen's enthusiasm and made no attempt to disguise it, but she shrugged again and said, "There's nothing much to see. Only more of the same stuff."

Helen gathered up her equipment and they walked side by side through the intersecting corridors between one square and the next. Though the estate was low-rise, each court only five stories high, the effect of each quadrangle was horribly claustrophobic. The walkways and staircases were a thief's dream, rife with blind corners and ill-lit tunnels. The rubbish-dumping facilities—chutes from the upper floors down which bags of refuse could be pitched —had long since been sealed up, thanks to their efficiency as fire traps. Now plastic bags of refuse were piled high in the corridors, many torn open by roaming dogs, their contents strewn across the ground. The smell, even in the cold weather, was unpleasant. In high summer it must have been overpowering.

"I'm over the other side," Anne-Marie said, pointing across the quadrangle. "The one with the yellow door." She then pointed along the opposite side of the court. "Five or six maisonettes from the far end," she said. "There's two of them been emptied out. Few weeks now. One of the family's moved into Ruskin Court; the other did a bunk in the middle of the night."

With that, she turned her back on Helen and wheeled Kerry, who had taken to trailing spittle from the side of his stroller, around the side of the square.

"Thank you," Helen called after her. Anne-Marie glanced over her shoulder briefly but did not reply. Appetite whetted, Helen made her way along the row of ground floor maisonettes, many of which, though inhabited, showed little sign of being so. Their curtains were closely drawn; there were no milk bottles on the doorsteps, or children's toys left where they had been played with. Nothing, in fact, of *life* here. There *were* more graffiti however, sprayed, shockingly, on the doors of occupied houses. She granted the scrawlings only a casual perusal, in part because she feared that one of the doors might open as she examined a choice obscenity sprayed upon it, but more because she was eager to see what revelations the empty flats ahead might offer.

The malign scent of urine, both fresh and stale, welcomed her at the threshold of number 14, and beneath that the smell of burned paint and plastic. She hesitated for fully ten seconds, wondering if stepping into the maisonette was a wise move. The territory of the estate behind her was indisputably foreign, sealed off in its own misery, but the rooms in front of her were more intimidating still: a dark maze which her eyes could barely penetrate. But when her courage faltered she thought of Trevor, and how badly she wanted to silence his condescension. So thinking, she advanced into the place, deliberately kicking a piece of charred timber aside as she did so, in the hope that she would alert any tenant into showing himself.

There was no sound of occupancy however. Gaining confidence, she began to explore the front room of the maisonette which had been—to judge by the remains of a disemboweled sofa in one corner and the sodden carpet underfoot—a living room. The pale green walls were, as Anne-Marie had promised, extensively defaced, both by minor scribblers—content to work in pen, or even more crudely in soft charcoal—and by those with aspirations to public works, who had sprayed the walls in half a dozen colors.

Some of the comments were of interest, though many she had already seen on the walls outside. Familiar names and couplings repeated themselves. Though she had never set eyes on these individuals she knew how badly Fabian J. (A OK!) wanted to deflower Michelle; and that Michelle, in her turn, had the hots for somebody called Mr. Sheen. Here, as elsewhere, a man called White Rat boasted of his endowment, and the return of the Syllabub Brothers was promised in red paint. One or two of the pictures accompanying, or at least adjacent to, these phrases were of particular interest. An almost emblematic simplicity informed them. Beside the word *Christos* was a stick man with his hair radiating from his head like spines, and other heads impaled on each spine. Close by was an image of intercourse so brutally reduced that at first Helen took it to illustrate a knife plunging into a sightless eye. But fascinating as the images were, the room was too gloomy for her film and she had neglected to bring a flash. If she wanted a reliable record of these discoveries she would have to come again and for now be content with a simple exploration of the premises.

The maisonette wasn't that large, but the windows had been boarded up throughout, and as she moved farther from the front door the dubious light petered out altogether. The smell of urine, which had been strong at the door, intensified too, until by the time she reached the back of the living room and stepped along a short corridor into another room beyond, it was as cloying as incense. This room, being farthest from the front door, was also the darkest, and she had to wait a few moments in the cluttered gloom to allow her eyes to become useful. This, she guessed, had been the bedroom. What little furniture the residents had left behind them had been smashed to smithereens. Only the mattress had been left relatively untouched, dumped in the corner of the room among a wretched litter of blankets, newspapers and pieces of crockery.

Outside, the sun found its way between the clouds, and two or three shafts of sunlight slipped between the boards nailed across the bedroom window and pierced the room like annunciations, scoring the opposite wall with bright lines. Here, the graffitists had been busy once more: the usual clamor of love letters and threats. She scanned the wall quickly, and as she did so her eye was led by the beams of light across the room to the wall that contained the door she had stepped through.

Here, the artists had also been at work, but had produced an image the like of which she had not seen anywhere else. Using the door, which was centrally placed in the wall like a mouth, the artists had sprayed a single, vast head onto the stripped plaster. The painting was more adroit than most she had seen, rife with detail that lent the image an unsettling veracity. The cheekbones jutting through skin the color of buttermilk; the teeth, sharpened to irregular points, all converging on the door. The sitter's eyes were, owing to the room's low ceiling, set mere inches above the upper lip, but this physical adjustment only lent force to the image, giving the impression that he had thrown his head back. Knotted strands of his hair snaked from his scalp across the ceiling.

Was it a portrait? There was something naggingly *spe-*

cific in the details of the brows and the lines around the wide mouth; in the careful picturing of those vicious teeth. A nightmare certainly: a facsimile, perhaps, of something from a heroin fugue. Whatever its origins, it was potent. Even the illusion of door-as-mouth worked. The short passageway between living room and bedroom offered a passable throat, with a tattered lamp in lieu of tonsils. Beyond the gullet, the day burned white in the nightmare's belly. The whole effect brought to mind a ghost train painting. The same heroic deformity, the same unashamed intention to scare. And it worked; she stood in the bedroom almost stupefied by the picture, its red-rimmed eyes fixing her mercilessly. Tomorrow, she determined, she would come here again, this time with high-speed film and a flash to illuminate the masterwork.

As she prepared to leave the sun went in, and the bands of light faded. She glanced over her shoulder at the boarded windows, and saw for the first time that one four-word slogan had been sprayed on the wall beneath them.

"Sweets to the sweet," it read. She was familiar with the quote, but not with its source. Was it a profession of love? If so, it was an odd location for such an avowal. Despite the mattress in the corner, and the relative privacy of this room, she could not imagine the intended reader of such words ever stepping in here to receive her bouquet. No adolescent lovers, however heated, would lie down here to play at mothers and fathers; not under the gaze of the terror on the wall. She crossed to examine the writing. The paint looked to be the same shade of pink as had been used to color the gums of the screaming man; perhaps the same hand?

Behind her, a noise. She turned so quickly she almost tripped over the blanket-strewn mattress.

"Who——?"

At the other end of the gullet, in the living room, was a scab-kneed boy of six or seven. He stared at Helen, eyes glittering in the half-light, as if waiting for a cue.

"Yes?" she said.

"Anne-Marie says do you want a cup of tea?" he declared without pause or intonation.

Her conversation with the woman seemed hours past. She was grateful for the invitation however. The damp in the maisonette had chilled her.

"Yes . . ." she said to the boy. "Yes please."

The child didn't move but simply stared at her.

"Are you going to lead the way?" she asked him.

"If you want," he replied, unable to raise a trace of enthusiasm.

"I'd like that."

"You taking photographs?" he asked.

"Yes. Yes, I am. But not in here."

"Why not?"

"It's too dark," she told him.

"Don't it work in the dark?" he wanted to know.

"No."

The boy nodded at this, as if the information somehow fitted well into his scheme of things, and about-turned without another word, clearly expecting Helen to follow.

If she had been taciturn in the street, Anne-Marie was anything but in the privacy of her own kitchen. Gone was the guarded curiosity, to be replaced by a stream of lively chatter and a constant scurrying between half a dozen minor domestic tasks, like a juggler keeping several plates spinning simultaneously. Helen watched this balancing act with some admiration; her own domestic skills were negligible. At last, the meandering conversation turned back to the subject that had brought Helen here.

"Them photographs," Anne-Marie said, "why'd you want to take them?"

"I'm writing about graffiti. The photos will illustrate my thesis."

"It's not very pretty."

"No, you're right, it isn't. But I find it interesting."

Anne-Marie shook her head. "I hate the whole estate," she said. "It's not safe here. People getting robbed on their own doorsteps. Kids setting fire to the rubbish day in, day out. Last summer we had the fire brigade here two, three times a day, till they sealed them chutes off. Now people just dump the bags in the passageways, and that attracts rats."

"Do you live here alone?"

"Yes," she said, "since Davey walked out."

"That your husband?"

"He was Kerry's father, but we weren't never married. We lived together two years, you know. We had some good times. Then he just upped and went off one day when I was at me Mam's with Kerry." She peered into her tea cup. "I'm better off without him," she said. "But you get scared sometimes. Want some more tea?"

"I don't think I've got time."

"Just a cup," Anne-Marie said, already up and unplugging the electric kettle to take it to the sink for a refill. As she was about to turn on the tap she saw something on the draining board and drove her thumb down, grinding it out.

"Got you, you bugger," she said, then turned to Helen. "We got these bloody ants."

"Ants?"

"Whole estate's infected. From Egypt, they are: pharaoh ants, they're called. Little brown sods. They breed in the central heating ducts, you see; that way they get into all the flats. Place is plagued with them."

This unlikely exoticism (ants from Egypt?) struck Helen as comical, but she said nothing. Anne-Marie was staring out of the kitchen window and into the backyard.

"You should tell them," she said, though Helen wasn't certain whom she was being instructed to tell. "Tell them that ordinary people can't even walk the streets any longer—"

"Is it really so bad?" Helen said, frankly tiring of this catalogue of misfortunes.

Anne-Marie turned from the sink and looked at her hard.

"We've had murders here," she said.

"Really?"

"We had one in the summer. An old man he was, from Ruskin. That's just next door. I didn't know him, but he was a friend of the sister of the woman next door. I forget his name."

"And he was murdered?"

"Cut to ribbons in his own front room. They didn't find him for almost a week."

"What about his neighbors? Didn't they notice his absence?"

Anne-Marie shrugged, as if the most important pieces of information—the murder and the man's isolation—had been divulged and any further inquiries into the problem were irrelevant. But Helen pressed the point.

"Seems strange to me," she said.

Anne-Marie plugged in the filled kettle. "Well, it happened," she replied, unmoved.

"I'm not saying it didn't, I just—"

"His eyes had been taken out," she said, before Helen could voice any further doubts.

Helen winced. "No," she said under her breath.

"That's the truth," Anne-Marie said. "And that wasn't all that'd been done to him." She paused for effect, then went on: "You wonder what kind of person's capable of doing things like that, don't you? You wonder." Helen nodded. She was thinking precisely the same thing.

"Did they ever find the man responsible?"

Anne-Marie snorted her disparagement: "Police don't give a damn what happens here. They keep off the estate as much as possible. When they do patrol all they do is pick up kids for getting drunk and that. They're afraid, you see. That's why they keep clear."

"Of this killer?"

"Maybe," Anne-Marie replied. Then: "He had a hook."

"A hook?"

"The man what done it. He had a hook, like Jack the Ripper."

Helen was no expert on murder, but she felt certain that the Ripper hadn't boasted a hook. It seemed churlish to question the truth of Anne-Marie's story, however; though she silently wondered how much of this—the eyes taken out, the body rotting in the flat, the hook—was elaboration. The most scrupulous of reporters was surely tempted to embellish a story once in a while.

Anne-Marie had poured herself another cup of tea and was about to do the same for her guest.

"No thank you," Helen said. "I really should go."

"You married?" Anne-Marie asked, out of the blue.

"Yes. To a lecturer from the university."

"What's his name?"

"Trevor."

Anne-Marie put two heaped spoonfuls of sugar into her cup of tea. "Will you be coming back?" she asked.

"Yes, I hope to. Later in the week. I want to take some photographs of the pictures in the maisonette across the court."

"Well, call in."

"I shall. And thank you for your help."

"That's all right," Anne-Marie replied. "You've got to tell somebody, haven't you?"

"The man apparently had a hook instead of a hand."

Trevor looked up from his plate of *tagliatelle con prosciutto*. "Beg your pardon?"

Helen had been at pains to keep her recounting of this story as uncolored by her own response as she could. She was interested to know what Trevor would make of it, and she knew that if she once signaled her own stance he would instinctively take an opposing view out of plain bloody-mindedness.

"He had a hook," she repeated, without inflection.

Trevor put down his fork and plucked at his nose, sniffing. "I didn't read anything about this," he said.

"You don't read the local papers," Helen returned. "Neither of us do. Maybe it never made any of the nationals."

"'Geriatric Murdered by Hook-Handed Maniac'?" Trevor said, savoring the hyperbole. "I would have thought it very newsworthy. When was all of this supposed to have happened?"

"Sometime last summer. Maybe we were in Ireland."

"Maybe," said Trevor, taking up his fork again. Bending to his food, the polished lens of his spectacles reflected only the plate of pasta and chopped ham in front of him, not his eyes.

"Why do you say *maybe?*" Helen prodded.

"It doesn't sound quite right," he said. "In fact it sounds bloody preposterous."

"You don't believe it?" Helen said.

Trevor looked up from his food, tongue rescuing a speck of *tagliatelle* from the corner of his mouth. His face had relaxed into that noncommittal expression of his—the same face he wore, no doubt, when listening to his students. "Do *you* believe it?" he asked Helen. It was a favorite time-gaining device of his, another seminar trick, to question the questioner.

"I'm not certain," Helen replied, too concerned with finding some solid ground in this sea of doubts to waste energy scoring points.

"All right, forget the tale," Trevor said, deserting his food for another glass of red wine. "What about the teller? Did you trust her?"

Helen pictured Anne-Marie's earnest expression as she told the story of the old man's murder. "Yes," she said. "Yes, I think I would have known if she'd been lying to me."

"So why's it so important, anyhow? I mean, whether she's lying or not, what the fuck does it matter?"

It was a reasonable question, if irritatingly put. Why *did* it matter? Was it that she wanted to have her worst feelings about Spector Street proved false? That such an estate be filthy, be hopeless, be a dump where the undesirable and the disadvantaged were tucked out of public view—all that was a liberal commonplace, and she accepted it as an unpalatable social reality. But the story of the old man's murder and mutilation was something other. An image of violent death that, once with her, refused to part from her company.

She realized, to her chagrin, that this confusion was plain on her face, and that Trevor, watching her across the table, was not a little entertained by it.

"If it bothers you so much," he said, "why don't you go back there and ask around, instead of playing believe-it-or-not over dinner?"

She couldn't help but rise to his remark. "I thought you liked guessing games," she said.

He threw her a sullen look. "Wrong again," he said.

The suggestion that she investigate was not a bad one, though doubtless he had ulterior motives for offering it. She viewed Trevor less charitably day by day. What she had once thought in him a fierce commitment to debate she now recognized as mere power-play. He argued, not for the thrill of dialectic, but because he was pathologically competitive. She had seen him, time and again, take up attitudes she knew he did not espouse, simply to spill blood. Nor, more's the pity, was he alone in this sport. Academe was one of the last strongholds of the professional timewaster. On occasion their circle seemed entirely dominated by educated fools, lost in a wasteland of stale rhetoric and hollow commitment.

From one wasteland to another. She returned to Spector

Street the following day, armed with a flashgun in addition
to her tripod and high-sensitivity film. The wind was up
today, and it was Arctic, more furious still for being
trapped in the maze of passageways and courts. She made
her way to number 14 and spent the next hour in its be-
fouled confines, meticulously photographing both the bedroom and living-room walls. She had half expected the
impact of the head in the bedroom to be dulled by reac-
quaintance. It was not. Though she struggled to capture its
scale and detail as best she could, she knew the photographs would be at best a dim echo of its perpetual howl.

Much of its power lay in its context, of course. That
such an image might be stumbled upon in surroundings so
drab, so conspicuously lacking in mystery, was akin to
finding an icon on a rubbish heap: a gleaming symbol of
transcendence from a world of toil and decay into some
darker but more tremendous realm. She was painfully
aware that the intensity of her response probably defied her
articulation. Her vocabulary was analytic, replete with
buzz-words and academic terminology, but woefully impoverished when it came to evocation. The photographs,
pale as they would be, would, she hoped, at least hint at
the potency of this picture, even if they couldn't conjure up
the way it froze the bowels.

When she emerged from the maisonette the wind was as
uncharitable as ever, but the boy waiting outside—the
same child as had attended upon her yesterday—was
dressed as if for spring weather. He grimaced in his effort
to keep the shudders at bay.

"Hello," Helen said.

"I waited," the child announced.

"Waited?"

"Anne-Marie said you'd come back."

"I wasn't planning to come until later in the week," Helen said. "You might have waited a long time."

The boy's grimace relaxed a notch. "It's all right," he said. "I've got nothing to do."

"What about school?"

"Don't like it," the boy replied, as if not obliged to be educated if it wasn't to his taste.

"I see," said Helen, and began to walk down the side of the quadrangle. The boy followed. On the patch of grass at the center of the quadrangle several chairs and two or three dead saplings had been piled.

"What's this?" she said, half to herself.

"Bonfire Night," the boy informed her. "Next week."

"Of course."

"You going to see Anne-Marie?" he asked.

"Yes."

"She's not in."

"Oh. Are you sure?"

"Yeah."

"Well, perhaps *you* can help me. . . ." She stopped and turned to face the child; smooth sacs of fatigue hung beneath his eyes. "I heard about an old man who was murdered near here," she said to him. "In the summer. Do you know anything about that?"

"No."

"Nothing at all? You don't remember anybody getting killed?"

"No," the boy said again, with impressive finality. "I don't remember."

"Well; thank you anyway."

This time, when she retraced her steps back to the car,

the boy didn't follow. But as she turned the corner out of the quadrangle she glanced back to see him standing on the spot where she'd left him, staring after her as if she were a madwoman.

By the time she had reached the car and packed the photographic equipment into the trunk there were specks of rain in the wind, and she was sorely tempted to forget she'd ever heard Anne-Marie's story and make her way home, where the coffee would be warm even if the welcome wasn't. But she needed an answer to the question Trevor had put the previous night. Do *you* believe it? he'd asked when she'd told him the story. She hadn't known how to answer then, and she still didn't. Perhaps (why did she sense this?) the terminology of verifiable truth was redundant here; perhaps the final answer to his question was not an answer at all, only another question. If so, so. She had to find out.

Ruskin Court was as forlorn as its fellows, if not more so. It didn't even boast a bonfire. On the third floor balcony a woman was taking washing in before the rain broke; on the grass in the center of the quadrangle two dogs were absent-mindedly rutting, the fuckee staring up at the blank sky. As she walked along the empty pavement she set her face determinedly; a purposeful look, Bernadette had once said, deterred attack. When she caught sight of two women talking at the far end of the court she crossed over to them hurriedly, grateful for their presence.

"Excuse me?"

The women, both middle-aged, ceased their animated exchange and looked her over.

"I wonder if you can help me?"

She could feel their appraisal, and their distrust; they

went undisguised. One of the pair, her face florid, said plainly, "What do you want?"

Helen suddenly felt bereft of the least power to charm. What was she to say to these two that wouldn't make her motives appear ghoulish? "I was told . . . ," she began, and then stumbled, aware that she would get no assistance from either woman. ". . . I was told there'd been a murder near here. Is that right?"

The florid woman raised eyebrows so plucked they were barely visible. "Murder?" she said.

"Are you from the press?" the other woman inquired. The years had soured her features beyond sweetening. Her small mouth was deeply lined; her hair, which had been dyed brunette, showed a half-inch of gray at the roots.

"No, I'm not from the press," Helen said. "I'm a friend of Anne-Marie's, in Butts's Court." This claim of *friend* stretched the truth, but it seemed to mellow the women somewhat.

"Visiting, are you?" the florid woman asked.

"In a manner of speaking—"

"You missed the warm spell—"

"Anne-Marie was telling me about somebody who'd been murdered here, during the summer. I was curious about it."

"Is that right?"

"Do you know anything about it?"

"Lots of things go on around here," said the second woman. "You don't know the half of it."

"So it's true," Helen said.

"They had to close the toilets," the first woman put in.

"That's right. They did," the other said.

"The toilets?" Helen said. What had this to do with the old man's death?

"It was terrible," the first said. "Was it your Frank, Josie, who told you about it?"

"No, not Frank," Josie replied. "Frank was still at sea. It was Mrs. Tyzack."

The witness established, Josie relinquished the story to her companion, and turned her gaze back upon Helen. The suspicion had not yet died from her eyes.

"This was only the month before last," Josie said. "Just about the end of August. It was August, wasn't it?" She looked to the other woman for verification. "You've got the head for dates, Maureen."

Maureen looked uncomfortable. "I forget," she said, clearly unwilling to offer testimony.

"I'd like to know," Helen said. Josie, despite her companion's reluctance, was eager to oblige.

"There's some lavatories," she said, "outside the shops —you know, public lavatories. I'm not quite sure how it all happened exactly, but there used to be a boy . . . well, he wasn't a boy really. I mean he was a man of twenty or more, but he was"—she fished for the words—"mentally subnormal, I suppose you'd say. His mother used to have to take him around like he was a four-year-old. Anyhow, she let him go into the lavatories while she went to that little supermarket, what's it called?" She turned to Maureen for prompting, but the other woman just looked back, her disapproval plain. Josie was ungovernable, however. "Broad daylight, this was," she said to Helen. "Middle of the day. Anyhow, the boy went to the toilet, and the mother was in the shop. And after a while, you know how you do, she's busy shopping, she forgets about him, and then she thinks he's been gone a long time . . ."

At this juncture Maureen couldn't prevent herself from butting in: the accuracy of the story apparently took precedence over her wariness.

"She got into an argument," she corrected Josie, "with the manager. About some bad bacon she'd had from him. That was why she was such a time."

"I see," said Helen.

"Anyway," said Josie, picking up the tale, "she finished her shopping and when she came out he still wasn't there—"

"So she asked someone from the supermarket—" Maureen began, but Josie wasn't about to have her narrative snatched away at this vital juncture.

"She asked one of the men from the supermarket," she repeated over Maureen's interjection, "to go down into the lavatory and find him."

"It was terrible," said Maureen, clearly picturing the atrocity in her mind's eye.

"He was lying on the floor, in a pool of blood."

"Murdered?"

Josie shook her head. "He'd have been better off dead. He'd been attacked with a razor"—she let this piece of information sink in before delivering the *coup de grâce*—"and they'd cut off his private parts. Just cut them off and flushed them down a toilet. No reason on earth to do it."

"Oh my God."

"Better off dead," Josie repeated. "I mean, they can't mend something like that, can they?"

The appalling tale was rendered worse still by the *sang-*

froid of the teller, and by the casual repetition of "Better off dead."

"The boy," Helen said. "Was he able to describe his attackers?"

"No," said Josie, "he's practically an imbecile. He can't string more than two words together."

"And nobody saw anyone go into the lavatory? Or leaving it?"

"People come and go all the time," Maureen said. This, though it sounded like an adequate explanation, had not been Helen's experience. There was not a great bustle in the quadrangle and passageways; far from it. Perhaps the shopping mall was busier, she reasoned, and might offer adequate cover for such a crime.

"So they haven't found the culprit," she said.

"No," Josie replied, her eyes losing their fervor. The crime and its immediate consequences were the nub of this story; she had little or no interest in either the culprit or his capture.

"We're not safe in our own bed," Maureen observed. "You ask anyone."

"Anne-Marie said the same," Helen replied. "That's how she came to tell me about the old man. Said he was murdered during the summer, here in Ruskin Court."

"I do remember something," Josie said. "There *was* some talk I heard. An old man, and his dog. He was battered to death, and the dog ended up . . . I don't know. It certainly wasn't here. It must have been one of the other estates."

"Are you sure?"

The woman looked offended by this slur on her memory.

The Forbidden

"Oh yes," she said, "I mean if it had been here, we'd have known the story, wouldn't we?"

Helen thanked the pair for their help and decided to take a stroll around the quadrangle anyway, just to see how many more maisonettes were unoccupied. As in Butts's Court, many of the curtains were drawn and all the doors locked. But then if Spector Street *was* under siege from a maniac capable of the murder and mutilation such as she'd heard described, she was not surprised that the residents took to their homes and stayed there. There was nothing much to see around the court. All the unoccupied maisonettes and flats had been recently sealed, to judge by a litter of nails left on a doorstep by the council workmen. One sight *did* catch her attention however. Scrawled on the paving stones she was walking over—and all but erased by rain and the passage of feet—the same phrase she'd seen in the bedroom of number 14: "Sweets to the sweet." The words were so benign; why did she seem to sense menace in them? Was it in their excess, perhaps, in the sheer over-abundance of sugar upon sugar, honey upon honey?

She walked on, though the rain persisted, away from the quadrangles and into a concrete no-man's-land through which she had not previously passed. This was—or had been—the site of the estate's amenities. Here was the children's playground, its metal-framed rides overturned, its sandpit fouled by dogs, its paddling pool empty. And here too were the shops. Several had been boarded up; those that hadn't were dingy and unattractive, their windows protected by heavy wire mesh.

She walked along the row, and rounded a corner, and there in front of her was a squat brick building. The public

113

lavatory, she guessed, though the signs designating it as such had gone. The iron gates were closed and padlocked. Standing in front of the charmless building, the wind gusting around her legs, she couldn't help but think of what had happened here. Of the man-child, bleeding on the floor, helpless to cry out. It made her queasy even to contemplate it. She turned her thoughts instead to the felon. What would he look like, she wondered, a man capable of such a depravity? She tried to make an image of him, but no detail she could conjure up carried sufficient force. But then monsters were seldom very terrible once hauled into the plain light of day. As long as this man was known only by his deeds he held untold power over the imagination; but the human truth beneath the terrors would, she knew, be bitterly disappointing. No monster he, just a whey-faced apology for a man more needful of pity than awe.

The next gust of wind brought the rain on more heavily. It was time, she decided, to be done with adventures for the day. Turning her back on the public lavatories, she hurried back through the quadrangles to the refuge of the car, the icy rain needling her face to numbness.

The dinner guests looked gratifyingly appalled at the story, and Trevor, to judge by the expression on his face, was furious. It was done now, however; there was no taking it back. Nor could she deny the satisfaction she took in having silenced the interdepartmental babble about the table. It was Bernadette, Trevor's assistant in the history department, who broke the agonizing hush.

"When was this?"

"During the summer," Helen told her.

"I don't recall reading about it," said Archie, much the

better for two hours of drinking; it mellowed a tongue that was otherwise fulsome in its self-coruscation.

"Perhaps the police are suppressing it," Daniel commented.

"Conspiracy?" said Trevor, plainly cynical.

"It's happening all the time," Daniel shot back.

"Why should they suppress something like this?" Helen said. "It doesn't make sense."

"Since when has police procedure made sense?" Daniel replied.

Bernadette cut in before Helen could answer. "We don't even bother to read about these things any longer," she said.

"Speak for yourself," somebody piped up, but she ignored them and went on:

"We're punch-drunk with violence. We don't see it any longer, even when it's in front of our noses."

"On the screen every night," Archie put in. "Death and disaster in full color."

"There's nothing very modern about that," Trevor said. "An Elizabethan would have seen death all the time. Public executions were a very popular form of entertainment."

The table broke up into a cacophony of opinions. After two hours of polite gossip the dinner party had suddenly caught fire. Listening to the debate rage, Helen was sorry she hadn't had time to have the photographs processed and printed; the graffiti would have added further fuel to this exhilarating row. It was Purcell, as usual, who was the last to weigh in with his point of view; and—again, as usual—it was devastating.

"Of course, Helen, my sweet," he began, that affected weariness in his voice edged with the anticipation of controversy, "your witnesses could all be lying, couldn't they?"

The talking around the table dwindled, and all heads turned in Purcell's direction. Perversely, he ignored the attention he'd garnered and turned to whisper in the ear of the boy he'd brought—a new passion who would, as in the past, be discarded in a matter of weeks for another pretty urchin.

"Lying?" Helen said. She could already feel herself bristling at the observation, and Purcell had spoken only a dozen words.

"Why not?" the other replied, lifting his glass of wine to his lips. "Perhaps they're all weaving some elaborate fiction or other. The story of the spastic's mutilation in the public toilet. The murder of the old man. Even that hook. All quite familiar elements. You must be aware that there's something *traditional* about these atrocity stories. One used to exchange them all the time; there was a certain *frisson* in them. Something competitive maybe, in attempting to find a new detail to add to the collective fiction; a fresh twist that would render the tale that little bit more appalling when you passed it on."

"It may be familiar to you—" Helen said defensively. Purcell was always so *poised;* it irritated her. Even if there were validity in his argument, which she doubted, she was damned if she'd concede it. "—I've never heard this kind of story before."

"Haven't you?" said Purcell, as though she were admitting to illiteracy. "What about the lovers and the escaped lunatic, have you heard that one?"

"I've heard that," Daniel said.

"The lover is disemboweled—usually by a hook-handed

man—and the body left on the top of the car, while the fiancé cowers inside. It's a cautionary tale, warning of the evils of rampant heterosexuality." The joke won a round of laughter from everyone but Helen. "These stories are very common."

"So you're saying that they're telling me lies," she protested.

"Not lies, exactly—"

"You said *lies.*"

"I was being provocative," Purcell returned, his placatory tone more enraging than ever. "I don't mean to imply there's any serious mischief in it. But you must concede that so far you haven't met a single *witness.* All these events have happened at some unspecified date to some unspecified person. They are reported at several removes. They occurred at best to the brothers of friends of distant relations. Please consider the possibility that perhaps these events do not exist in the real world at all, but are merely titillation for bored housewives."

Helen didn't make an argument in return, for the simple reason that she lacked one. Purcell's point about the conspicuous absence of witnesses was perfectly sound; she herself had wondered about it. It was strange, too, the way the women in Ruskin Court had speedily consigned the old man's murder to another estate, as though these atrocities always occurred just out of sight—around the next corner, down the next passageway—but never *here.*

"So why?" said Bernadette.

"Why what?" Archie puzzled.

"The stories. Why tell these horrible stories if they're not true?"

"Yes," said Helen, throwing the controversy back into Purcell's ample lap. *"Why?"*

Purcell preened himself, aware that his entry into the debate had changed the basic assumption at a stroke. "I don't know," he said, happy to be done with the game now that he'd shown his arm. "You really mustn't take me too seriously, Helen. *I* try not to." The boy at Purcell's side tittered.

"Maybe it's simply taboo material," Archie said.

"Suppressed—" Daniel prompted.

"Not the way you mean it," Archie retorted. "The whole world isn't politics, Daniel."

"Such naiveté."

"What's so taboo about death?" Trevor said. "Bernadette already pointed out: it's in front of us all the time. Television, newspapers."

"Maybe that's not close enough," Bernadette suggested.

"Does anyone mind if I smoke?" Purcell broke in. "Dessert seems to have been indefinitely postponed."

Helen ignored the remark and asked Bernadette what she meant by "not close enough."

Bernadette shrugged. "I don't know precisely," she confessed, "maybe just that death has to be *near;* we have to *know* it's just around the corner. The television's not intimate enough."

Helen frowned. The observation made some sense to her, but in the clutter of the moment she couldn't root out its significance.

"Do you think they're stories too?" she asked.

"Andrew has a point—" Bernadette replied.

"Most kind," said Purcell. "Has somebody got a match? The boy's pawned my lighter."

"—about the absence of witnesses."

"All that proves is that I haven't met anybody who's actually *seen* anything," Helen encountered, "not that witnesses don't exist."

"All right," said Purcell. "Find me one. If you can prove to me that your atrocity monger actually lives and breathes, I'll stand everyone dinner at Apollinaire's. How's that? Am I generous to a fault, or do I just know when I can't lose?" He laughed, knocking on the table with his knuckles by way of applause.

"Sounds good to me," said Trevor. "What do you say, Helen?"

She didn't go back to Spector Street until the following Monday, but all weekend she was there in thought: standing outside the locked toilet, with the wind bringing rain; or in the bedroom, the portrait looming. Thoughts of the estate claimed all her concern. When, late on Saturday afternoon, Trevor found some petty reason for an argument, she let the insults pass, watching him perform the familiar ritual of self-martyrdom without being touched by it in the least. Her indifference only enraged him further. He stormed out in high dudgeon, to visit whichever of his women was in favor this month. She was glad to see the back of him. When he failed to return that night she didn't even think of weeping about it. He was foolish and vacuous. She despaired of ever seeing a haunted look in his dull eyes; and what worth was a man who could not be haunted?

He did not return Sunday night either, and it crossed her mind the following morning, as she parked the car in the heart of the estate, that nobody even knew she had come, and that she might lose herself for days here and nobody would be any the wiser. Like the old man Anne-Marie had told her about: lying forgotten in his favorite armchair with his eyes hooked out, while the flies feasted and the butter went rancid on the table.

It was almost Bonfire Night, and over the weekend the small heap of combustibles in Butts's Court had grown to a substantial size. The construction looked unsound, but that didn't prevent a number of boys from clambering over and into it. Much of its bulk was made up of furniture, filched, no doubt, from boarded-up properties. She doubted if it could burn for any time: if it did, it would be chokingly smoky. Four times, on her way across to Anne-Marie's house, she was waylaid by children begging for money to buy fireworks.

"Penny for the guy," they'd say, though none had a guy to display. She had emptied her pockets of change by the time she reached the front door.

Anne-Marie was in today, though there was no welcoming smile. She simply stared at her visitor as if mesmerized.

"I hope you don't mind me calling . . ."

Anne-Marie made no reply.

". . . I just wanted a word."

"I'm busy," the woman finally announced. There was no invitation inside, no offer of tea.

"Oh. Well . . . it won't take more than a moment."

The back door was open and a draft blew through the house. Papers were flying about in the backyard. Helen could see them lifting into the air like vast white moths.

"What do you want?" Anne-Marie asked.

"Just to ask you about the old man."

The woman frowned minutely. She looked as if she might be sick. Helen thought her face had the color and texture of stale dough. Her hair was lank and greasy.

"What old man?"

"Last time I was here, you told me about an old man who'd been murdered, do you remember?"

"No."

"You said he lived in the next court."

"I don't remember," Anne-Marie said.

"But you *distinctly* told me—"

Something fell to the floor in the kitchen and smashed. Anne-Marie flinched but did not move from the doorstep, her arm barring Helen's way into the house. The hallway was littered with the child's toys, gnawed and battered.

"Are you all right?"

Anne-Marie nodded. "I've got work to do," she said.

"And you don't remember telling me about the old man?"

"You must have misunderstood," Anne-Marie replied, and then, her voice hushed: "You shouldn't have come. Everybody *knows*."

"Knows what?"

The girl had begun to tremble. "You don't understand, do you? You think people aren't watching?"

"What does it matter? All I asked was—"

"I don't know *anything*," Anne-Marie reiterated. "Whatever I said to you, I lied about it."

"Well, thank you anyway," Helen said, too perplexed by the confusion of signals from Anne-Marie to press the point any further. Almost as soon as she had turned from the door she heard the lock snap closed behind her.

* * *

That conversation was only one of several disappointments that morning brought. Helen went back to the row of shops and visited the supermarket that Josie had spoken of. There she inquired about the lavatories and their recent history. The supermarket had changed hands only in the last month, and the new owner, a taciturn Pakistani, insisted that he knew nothing of when or why the lavatories had been closed. She was aware, as she made her inquiries, of being scrutinized by the other customers in the store; she felt like a pariah. That feeling deepened when, after leaving the supermarket, she saw Josie emerging from the launderette and called after her, only to have the woman pick up her pace and duck away into the maze of corridors. Helen followed but rapidly lost both her quarry and her way.

Frustrated to the verge of tears, she stood among the overturned rubbish bags and felt a surge of contempt for her foolishness. She didn't belong here, did she? How many times had she criticized others for their presumption in claiming to understand societies they had merely viewed from afar? And here was she, committing the same crime, coming here with her camera and her questions, using the lives (and deaths) of these people as fodder for party conversation. She didn't blame Anne-Marie for turning her back; had she deserved better?

Tired and chilled, she decided it was time to concede Purcell's point. It *was* all fiction she had been told. They had played with her—sensing her desire to be fed some horrors—and she, the perfect fool, had fallen for every ridiculous word. It was time to pack up her credulity and go home.

One call demanded to be made before she returned to the car however: she wanted to look a final time at the painted head. Not as an anthropologist among an alien tribe, but as a confessed ghost train rider: for the thrill of it. Arriving at number 14, however, she faced the last and most crushing disappointment. The maisonette had been sealed up by conscientious council workmen. The door was locked; the front window boarded over.

She was determined not to be so easily defeated however. She made her way around the back of Butts's Court and located the yard of number 14 by simple mathematics. The gate was wedged closed from the inside, but she pushed hard against it, and with the effort, it opened. A heap of rubbish—rotted carpets, a box of rain-sodden magazines, a denuded Christmas tree—had blocked it.

She crossed the yard to the boarded-up windows and peered through the slats of wood. It wasn't bright outside, but it was darker still within; it was difficult to catch more than the vaguest hint of the painting on the bedroom wall. She pressed her face close to the wood, eager for a final glimpse.

A shadow moved across the room, momentarily blocking her view. She stepped back from the window, startled, not certain of what she'd seen. Perhaps merely her own shadow, cast through the window? But then *she* hadn't moved; it had.

She approached the window again, more cautiously. The air vibrated; she could hear a muted whine from somewhere, though she couldn't be certain whether it came from inside or out. Again, she put her face to the rough boards, and suddenly, something leaped at the window.

This time she let out a cry. There was a scrabbling sound from within as nails raked the wood.

A dog! And a big one to have jumped so high.

"Stupid," she told herself aloud. A sudden sweat bathed her.

The scrabbling had stopped almost as soon as it had started, but she couldn't bring herself to go back to the window. Clearly the workmen who had sealed up the maisonette had failed to check it properly and incarcerated the animal by mistake. It was ravenous, to judge by the slavering she'd heard; she was grateful she hadn't attempted to break in. The dog—hungry, maybe half-mad in the stinking darkness—could have taken out her throat.

She stared at the boarded-up window. The slits between the boards were barely a half-inch wide, but she sensed that the animal was up on its hind legs on the other side, watching her through the gap. She could hear its panting now that her own breath was regularizing; she could hear its claws raking the sill.

"Bloody thing . . . ," she said. "Damn well stay in there."

She backed off toward the gate. Hosts of wood lice and spiders, disturbed from their nests by the moving of the carpets behind the gate, were scurrying underfoot, looking for a fresh darkness to call home.

She closed the gate behind her and was making her way around the front of the block when she heard the sirens; two ugly spirals of sound that made the hair on the back of her neck tingle. They were approaching. She picked up her speed, and came around into Butts's Court in time to see several policemen crossing the grass behind the bonfire and an ambulance mounting the pavement and driving around to the other side of the quadrangle. People had emerged from their flats and were standing on their balconies, staring down. Others were walking around the court, nakedly curious, to join a gathering congregation. Helen's stomach seemed to drop to her bowels when she realized *where* the hub of interest lay: at Anne-Marie's doorstep. The police were clearing a path through the throng for the ambulance men. A second police car had followed the route of the ambulance onto the pavement; two plainclothes officers were getting out.

She walked to the periphery of the crowd. What little talk there was among the onlookers was conducted in low voices; one or two of the older women were crying. Though she peered over the heads of the spectators she could see nothing. Turning to a bearded man, whose child was perched on his shoulders, she asked what was going on. He didn't know. Somebody dead, he'd heard, but he wasn't certain.

"Anne-Marie?" she asked.

A woman in front of her turned and said: "You know her?" almost awed, as if speaking of a loved one.

"A little," Helen replied hesitantly. "Can you tell me what's happened?"

The woman involuntarily put her hand to her mouth, as if to stop the words before they came. But here they were nevertheless: "The child—" she said.

"Kerry?"

"Somebody got into the house around the back. Slit his throat."

Helen felt the sweat come again. In her mind's eye the newspapers rose and fell in Anne-Marie's yard.

"No," she said.

"Just like that."

She looked at the tragedienne who was trying to sell her this obscenity, and said "No" again. It defied belief; yet her denials could not silence the horrid comprehension she felt.

She turned her back on the woman and jostled her way out of the crowd. There would be nothing to see, she knew, and even if there had been she had no desire to look. These people—still emerging from their homes as the story spread—were exhibiting an appetite she was disgusted by. She was not one of them; would never *be* one of them. She wanted to slap every eager face into sense; wanted to say: "It's pain and grief you're going to spy on. Why? Why?" But she had no courage left. Revulsion had drained her of all but the energy to wander away, leaving the crowd to its sport.

Trevor had come home. He did not attempt an explanation of his absence but waited for her to cross-question him. When she failed to do so he sank into an easy *bonhomie* that was worse than his expectant silence. She was dimly aware that her lack of interest was probably more unsettling for him than the histrionics he had been anticipating. She couldn't have cared less.

She tuned the radio to the local station and listened for news. It came surely enough, confirming what the woman in the crowd had told her. Kerry Latimer was dead. Person or persons unknown had gained access to the house via the backyard and murdered the child while he played on the kitchen floor. A police spokesman mouthed the usual platitudes, describing Kerry's death as an "unspeakable crime," and the miscreant as "a dangerous and deeply disturbed individual." For once, the rhetoric seemed justified, and the man's voice shook discernibly when he spoke of the scene that had confronted the officers in the kitchen of Anne-Marie's house.

"Why the radio?" Trevor casually inquired, when Helen had listened for news through three consecutive bulletins. She saw no point in withholding her experience at Spector Street from him; he would find out sooner or later. Coolly, she gave him a bald outline of what had happened at Butts's Court.

"This Anne-Marie is the woman you first met when you went to the estate. Am I right?"

She nodded, hoping he wouldn't ask her too many questions. Tears were close, and she had no intention of breaking down in front of him.

"So you were right," he said.

"Right?"

"About the place having a maniac."

"No," she said. "No."

"But the kid—"

She got up and stood at the window, looking down two stories into the darkened street below. Why did she feel the need to reject the conspiracy theory so urgently? Why was she now praying that Purcell had been right, and that all she'd been told had been lies? She went back to the way Anne-Marie had been when she'd visited her that morning: pale, jittery; *expectant*. She had been like a woman anticipating some arrival, hadn't she, eager to shoo unwanted visitors away so that she could turn back to the business of waiting? But waiting for what, or *whom?* Was it possible that Anne-Marie actually knew the murderer? Had perhaps invited him into the house?

"I hope they find the bastard," she said, still watching the street.

"They will," Trevor replied. "A baby murderer, for Christ's sake. They'll make it a high priority."

A man appeared at the corner of the street, turned, and whistled. A large Alsatian came to heel, and the two set off down toward the cathedral.

"The dog," Helen murmured.

"What?"

She had forgotten the dog in all that had followed. Now the shock she'd felt as it had leaped at the window shook her again.

"What dog?" Trevor pressed her.

"I went back to the flat today—where I took the pictures of the graffiti. There was a dog in there. Locked in."

"So?"

"It'll starve. Nobody knows it's there."

"How do you know it wasn't locked in to kennel it?"

"It was making such a noise," she said.

"Dogs bark," Trevor replied. "That's all they're good for."

"No," she said very quietly, remembering the noises through the boarded window. "It didn't bark."

"Forget the dog," Trevor said. "And the child. There's nothing you can do about it. You were just passing through."

His words only echoed her own thoughts of earlier in the day, but somehow, for reasons that she could find no words to convey, that conviction had decayed in the last hours. She was not just passing through. Nobody ever just *passed through;* experience always left its mark. Sometimes it merely scratched; on occasion it took off limbs. She did not know the extent of her present wounding, but she knew it was more profound than she yet understood, and it made her afraid.

"We're out of booze," she said, emptying the last dribble of whiskey into her tumbler.

Trevor seemed pleased to have a reason to be accommodating. "I'll go out, shall I?" he said. "Get a bottle or two?"

"Sure," she replied. "If you like."

He was gone only half an hour; she would have liked him to be longer. She didn't want to talk, only to sit and think through the unease in her belly. Though Trevor had dismissed her concern for the dog—and perhaps justifiably so—she couldn't help but go back to the locked maisonette in her mind's eye: to picture again the raging face on the bedroom wall, and hear the animal's muffled growl as it pawed the boards over the window. Whatever Trevor had said, she didn't believe the place was being used as a makeshift kennel. No, the dog was *imprisoned* in there, no doubt of it, running round and round, driven, in its desperation, to eat its own feces, growing more insane with every hour that passed. She became afraid that somebody—kids maybe, looking for more tinder for their bonfire—would break into the place, ignorant of what it contained. It wasn't that she feared for the intruders' safety, but that the dog, once liberated, would come for her. It would know where she was (so her drunken head construed) and come sniffing her out.

Trevor returned with the whiskey, and they drank together until the early hours, when her stomach revolted. She took refuge in the toilet—Trevor outside asking her if she needed anything, her telling him weakly to leave her alone. When, an hour later, she emerged, he had gone to bed. She did not join him but lay down on the sofa and dozed through until dawn.

The murder was news. The next morning it made all the tabloids as a front-page splash, and found prominent positions in the heavyweights too. There were photographs of the stricken mother being led from the house, and others, blurred but potent, taken over the backyard wall and through the open kitchen door. Was that blood on the floor, or shadow?

Helen did not bother to read the articles—her aching head rebelled at the thought—but Trevor, who had brought the newspapers in, was eager to talk. She couldn't work out if this was further peacemaking on his part or a genuine interest in the issue.

"The woman's in custody," he said, poring over the *Daily Telegraph*. It was a paper he was politically averse to, but its coverage of violent crime was notoriously detailed.

The observation demanded Helen's attention, unwilling or not. "Custody?" she said. "Anne-Marie?"

"Yes."

"Let me see."

He relinquished the paper, and she glanced over the page.

"Third column," Trevor prompted.

She found the place, and there it was in black and white. Anne-Marie had been taken into custody for questioning to justify the time lapse between the estimated hour of the child's death, and the time that it had been reported. Helen read the relevant sentences over again, to be certain that she'd understood properly. Yes, she had. The police pathologist estimated Kerry to have died between six and six-thirty that morning; the murder had not been reported until twelve.

She read the report over a third and fourth time, but repetition did not change the horrid facts. The child had been murdered before dawn. When she had gone to the house that morning Kerry had already been dead four hours. The body had been in the kitchen, a few yards down the hallway from where she had stood, and Anne-Marie had said *nothing*. That air of expectancy she had had about her—what had it signified? That she awaited some cue to lift the receiver and call the police?

"My Christ . . . ," Helen said, and let the paper drop.

"What?"

"I have to go to the police."

"Why?"

"To tell them I went to the house," she replied. Trevor looked mystified. "The baby was dead, Trevor. When I saw Anne-Marie yesterday morning, Kerry was already dead."

She rang the number given in the paper for any persons offering information, and half an hour later a police car came to pick her up. There was much that startled her in the two hours of interrogation that followed, not least the fact that nobody had reported her presence on the estate to the police, though she had surely been noticed.

"They don't want to know," the detective told her. "You'd think a place like that would be swarming with witnesses. If it is, they're not coming forward. A crime like this—"

"Is it the first?" she said.

He looked at her across a chaotic desk. "First?"

"I was told some stories about the estate. Murders. This summer."

The detective shook his head. "Not to my knowledge. There's been a spate of muggings; one woman was put in hospital for a week or so. But no; no murders."

She liked the detective. His eyes flattered her with their lingering, and his face with its frankness. Past caring whether she sounded foolish or not, she said: "Why do they tell lies like that? About people having their eyes cut out. Terrible things."

The detective scratched his long nose. "We get it too," he said. "People come in here, they confess to all kinds of crap. Talk all night, some of them, about things they've done, or *think* they've done. Give you it all in the minutest detail. And when you make a few calls, it's all invented. Out of their minds."

"Maybe if they didn't tell you the stories . . . they'd actually go out and do it."

The detective nodded. "Yes," he said. "God help us. You might be right at that."

And the stories *she'd* been told, were they confessions of uncommitted crimes, accounts of the worst imaginable, imagined to keep fiction from becoming fact? The thought chased its own tail: these terrible stories still needed a *first cause*, a well-spring from which they leaped. As she walked home through the busy streets she wondered how many of her fellow citizens knew such stories. Were these inventions common currency, as Purcell had claimed? Was there a place, however small, reserved in every heart for the monstrous?

"Purcell rang," Trevor told her when she got home. "To invite us out to dinner."

The invitation wasn't welcome, and she made a face.

"Apollinaire's, remember?" he reminded her. "He said he'd take us all to dinner if you proved him wrong."

The thought of getting a dinner out of the death of Anne-Marie's infant was grotesque, and she said so.

"He'll be offended if you turn him down."

"I don't give a damn. I don't want dinner with Purcell."

"Please," he said softly. "He can get difficult, and I want to keep him smiling just at the moment."

She glanced across at him. The look he'd put on made him resemble a drenched spaniel. Manipulative bastard, she thought; but said, "All right, I'll go. But don't expect any dancing on the tables."

"We'll leave that to Archie," he said. "I told Purcell we were free tomorrow night. Is that all right with you?"

"Whenever."

"He's booking a table for eight o'clock."

The evening papers had relegated The Tragedy of Baby Kerry to a few column inches on an inside page. In lieu of much fresh news they simply described the house-to-house inquiries that were now going on at Spector Street. Some of the later editions mentioned that Anne-Marie had been released from custody after an extended period of questioning and was now residing with friends. They also mentioned, in passing, that the funeral was to be the following day.

Helen had not entertained any thoughts of going back to Spector Street for the funeral when she went to bed that night, but sleep seemed to change her mind, and she woke with the decision made for her.

* * *

Death had brought the estate to life. Walking through to Ruskin Court from the street, she had never seen such numbers out and about. Many were already lining the curb to watch the funeral cortège pass, and looked to have claimed their niche early, despite the wind and the ever-present threat of rain. Some were wearing items of black clothing—a coat, a scarf—but the overall impression, despite the lowered voices and the studied frowns, was one of celebration. Children running around, untouched by reverence; occasional laughter escaping from between gossiping adults—Helen could feel an air of anticipation that made her spirits, despite the occasion, almost buoyant.

Nor was it simply the presence of so many people that reassured her; she was, she conceded to herself, happy to be back here in Spector Street. The quadrangles, with their stunted saplings and their gray grass, were more real to her than the carpeted corridors she was used to walking; the anonymous faces on the balconies and streets meant more than her colleagues at the university. In a word, she felt *home*.

Finally, the cars appeared, moving at a snail's pace through the narrow streets. As the hearse came into view —its tiny white casket decked with flowers—a number of women in the crowd gave quiet voice to their grief. One onlooker fainted; a knot of anxious people gathered around her. Even the children were stilled now.

Helen watched, dry-eyed. Tears did not come very easily to her, especially in company. As the second car, containing Anne-Marie and two other women, drew level with her, Helen saw that the bereaved mother was also eschewing any public display of grief. She seemed, indeed, to be almost elevated by the proceedings, sitting upright in the back of the car, her pallid features the source of much admiration. It was a sour thought, but Helen felt as though she was seeing Anne-Marie's finest hour; the one day in an otherwise anonymous life in which she was the center of attention. Slowly, the cortège passed by and disappeared from view.

The crowd around Helen was already dispersing. She detached herself from the few mourners who still lingered at the curb and wandered through from the street into Butts's Court. It was her intention to go back to the locked maisonette, to see if the dog was still there. If it was, she would put her mind at rest by finding one of the estate caretakers and informing him of the fact.

The quadrangle was, unlike the other courts, practically empty. Perhaps the residents, being neighbors of Anne-Marie's, had gone on to the crematorium for the service. Whatever the reason, the place was eerily deserted. Only children remained, playing around the pyramid bonfire, their voices echoing across the empty expanse of the square.

She reached the maisonette and was surprised to find the door open again, as it had been the first time she'd come here. The sight of the interior made her light-headed. How often in the past several days had she imagined standing here, gazing into that darkness. There was no sound from inside. The dog had surely run off—either that, or died. There could be no harm, could there, in stepping into the place one final time, just to look at the face on the wall, and its attendant slogan?

"Sweets to the sweet." She had never looked up the origins of that phrase. No matter, she thought. Whatever it had stood for once, it was transformed here, as everything was; herself included. She stood in the front room for a few moments, to allow herself time to savor the confrontation ahead. Far away behind her the children were screeching like mad birds.

She stepped over a clutter of furniture and toward the short corridor that joined living room to bedroom, still delaying the moment. Her heart was quick in her: a smile played on her lips.

And there! At last! The portrait loomed, compelling as ever. She stepped back in the murky room to admire it more fully and her heel caught on the mattress that still lay in the corner. She glanced down. The squalid bedding had been turned over, to present its untorn face. Some blankets and a rag-wrapped pillow had been tossed over it. Something glistened among the folds of the uppermost blanket. She bent down to look more closely and found there a handful of sweets—chocolates and caramels—wrapped in bright paper. And littered among them, neither so attractive nor so sweet, a dozen razor-blades. There was blood on several. She stood up again and backed away from the mattress, and as she did so a buzzing sound reached her ears from the next room. She turned, and the light in the bedroom diminished as a figure stepped into the gullet between her and the outside world. Silhouetted against the light, she could scarcely see the man in the doorway, but she smelled him. He smelled like cotton candy, and the buzzing was with him or in him.

"I just came to look," she said, ". . . at the picture."

The buzzing went on—the sound of a sleepy afternoon, far from here. The man in the doorway did not move.

"Well," she said, "I've seen what I wanted to see." She

hoped against hope that her words would prompt him to stand aside and let her past, but he didn't move, and she couldn't find the courage to challenge him by stepping toward the door.

"I have to go," she said, knowing that despite her best efforts fear seeped between every syllable. "I'm expected . . ."

That was not entirely untrue. Tonight they were all invited to Apollinaire's for dinner. But that wasn't until eight, which was four hours away. She would not be missed for a long while yet.

"If you'll excuse me," she said.

The buzzing had quieted a little, and in the hush the man in the doorway spoke. His unaccented voice was almost as sweet as his scent.

"No need to leave yet," he breathed.

"I'm due . . . due . . ."

Though she couldn't see his eyes, she felt them on her, and they made her feel drowsy, like that summer that sang in her head.

"I came for you," he said.

She repeated the four words in her head. *I came for you.* If they were meant as a threat, they certainly weren't spoken as one.

"I don't . . . know you," she said.

"No," the man murmured. "But you doubted me."

"Doubted?"

"You weren't content with the stories, with what they wrote on the walls. So I was obliged to come."

The drowsiness slowed her mind to a crawl, but she grasped the essentials of what the man was saying. That he was legend, and she, in disbelieving him, had obliged him to show his hand. She looked, now, down at those hands. One of them was missing. In its place, a hook.

"There will be some blame," he told her. "They will say your doubts shed innocent blood. But I say what's blood for, if not for shedding? And in time the scrutiny will pass. The police will leave, the cameras will be pointed at some fresh horror, and they will be left alone, to tell stories of the Candyman again."

"Candyman?" she said. Her tongue could barely shape that blameless word.

"I came for you," he murmured so softly that seduction might have been in the air. And so saying, he moved through the passageway and into the light.

She knew him, without doubt. She had known him all along, in that place kept for terrors. It was the man on the wall. His portrait painter had not been a fantasist: the picture that howled over her was matched in each extraordinary particular by the man she now set eyes upon. He was bright to the point of gaudiness: his flesh a waxy yellow, his thin lips pale blue, his wild eyes glittering as if their irises were set with rubies. His jacket was a patchwork, his trousers the same. He looked, she thought, almost ridiculous, with his blood-stained motley, and the hint of rouge on his jaundiced cheeks. But people were facile. They needed these shows and shams to keep their interest. Miracles; murders; demons driven out and stones rolled from tombs. The cheap glamour did not taint the sense beneath. It was only, in the natural history of the mind, the bright feathers that drew the species to mate with its secret self.

And she was almost enchanted. By his voice, by his colors, by the buzz from his body. She fought to resist the rapture, though. There was a *monster* here, beneath this fetching display; its nest of razors was at her feet, still drenched in blood. Would it hesitate to slit her own throat if it once laid hands on her?

As the Candyman reached for her she dropped down and snatched the blanket up, flinging it at him. A rain of razors and candy fell around his shoulders. The blanket followed, blinding him. But before she could snatch the moment to slip past him, the pillow that had lain on the blanket rolled in front of her.

It was not a pillow at all. Whatever the forlorn white casket she had seen in the hearse had contained, it was not the body of Baby Kerry. That was *here*, at her feet, its blood-drained face turned up to her. He was naked. His body showed everywhere signs of the fiend's attentions.

In the two heartbeats she took to register this last horror, the Candyman threw off the blanket. In his struggle to escape from its folds, his jacket had come unbuttoned, and she saw—though her senses protested—that the contents of his torso had rotted away, and the hollow was now occupied by a nest of bees. They swarmed in the vault of his chest, and encrusted in a seething mass the remnants of flesh that hung there. He smiled at her plain repugnance.

"Sweets to the sweet," he murmured, and stretched his hooked hand toward her face. She could no longer see light from the outside world or hear the children playing in Butts's Court. There was no escape into a saner world than this. The Candyman filled her sight; her drained limbs had no strength to hold him at bay.

"Don't kill me," she breathed.

"Do you believe in me?" he said.

She nodded minutely. "How can I not?" she said.

"Then why do you want to live?"

She didn't understand, and was afraid her ignorance would prove fatal, so she said nothing.

"If you would learn," the fiend said, "just a *little* from me . . . you would not beg to live." His voice had dropped to a whisper. "I am rumor," he sang in her ear. "It's a blessed condition, believe me. To live in people's dreams; to be whispered at street corners, but not have to *be*. Do you understand?"

Her weary body understood. Her nerves, tired of jangling, understood. The sweetness he offered was life without living: was to be dead, but remembered everywhere; immortal in gossip and graffiti.

"Be my victim," he said.

"No . . ." she murmured.

"I won't force it upon you," he replied, the perfect gentleman. "I won't oblige you to die. But think; *think*. If I kill you here—if I unhook you"—he traced the path of the promised wound with his hook; it ran from groin to neck—"think how they would mark this place with their talk . . . point it out as they passed by and say, '*She* died there, the woman with the green eyes.' Your death would be a parable to frighten children with. Lovers would use it as an excuse to cling closer together."

She had been right: this *was* a seduction.

"Was fame ever so easy?" he asked.

She shook her head. "I'd prefer to be forgotten," she replied, "than be remembered like that."

He made a tiny shrug. "What do the good know?" he said. "Except what the bad teach them by their excesses?" He raised his hooked hand. "I said I would not oblige you to die and I'm true to my word. Allow me, though, a kiss at least. . . ."

He moved toward her. She murmured some nonsensical threat, which he ignored. The buzzing in his body had risen in volume. The thought of touching his body, of the proximity of the insects, was horrid. She forced her lead-heavy arms up to keep him at bay.

His lurid face eclipsed the portrait on the wall. She couldn't bring herself to touch him, and instead stepped back. The sound of the bees rose; some, in their excitement, had crawled up his throat and were flying from his mouth. They climbed about his lips; in his hair.

She begged him over and over to leave her alone, but he would not be placated. At last she had nowhere left to retreat to; the wall was at her back. Steeling herself against the stings, she put her hands on his crawling chest and pushed. As she did so his hand shot out and around the back of her neck, the hook nicking the flushed skin of her throat. She felt blood come; felt certain he would open her jugular in one terrible slash. But he had given his word, and he was true to it.

Aroused by this sudden activity, the bees were everywhere. She felt them moving on her, searching for morsels of wax in her ears, and sugar at her lips. She made no attempt to swat them away. The hook was at her neck. If she so much as moved it would wound her. She was trapped, as in her childhood nightmares, with every chance of escape stymied. When sleep had brought her to such hopelessness—the demons on every side, waiting to tear her limb from limb—one trick remained. To let go; to give up all ambition to life, and leave her body to the dark. Now, as the Candyman's face pressed to hers, and the sound of bees blotted out even her own breath, she played that hidden hand. And, as surely as in dreams, the room and the fiend were painted out and gone.

She woke from brightness into dark. There were several panicked moments when she couldn't think of where she was, then several more when she remembered. But there was no pain about her body. She put her hand to her neck; it was, barring the nick of the hook, untouched. She was lying on the mattress she realized. Had she been assaulted as she lay in a faint? Gingerly, she investigated her body. She was not bleeding; her clothes were not disturbed. The Candyman had, it seemed, simply claimed his kiss.

She sat up. There was precious little light through the boarded window—and none from the front door. Perhaps it was closed, she reasoned. But no; even now she heard somebody whispering on the threshold. A woman's voice.

She didn't move. They were crazy, these people. They had known all along what her presence in Butts's Court had summoned, and they had *protected* him—this honeyed psychopath; given him a bed and an offering of bonbons, hidden him away from prying eyes, and kept their silence when he brought blood to their doorsteps. Even Anne-Marie, dry-eyed in the hallway of her house, knowing that her child was dead a few yards away.

The child! That was the evidence she needed. Somehow they had conspired to get the body from the casket (what had they substituted; a dead dog?) and brought it here to the Candyman's tabernacle as a toy, or a lover. She would take Baby Kerry with her—to the police—and tell the whole story. Whatever they believed of it, and that would probably be very little, the fact of the child's body was incontestable. That way at least some of the crazies would suffer for their conspiracy. Suffer for *her* suffering.

The whispering at the door had stopped. Now somebody was moving toward the bedroom. Whoever it was hadn't brought a light. Helen made herself small, hoping she might escape detection.

A figure appeared in the doorway. The gloom was too impenetrable for her to make out more than a slim figure, who bent down and picked up a bundle on the floor. A fall of blond hair identified the newcomer as Anne-Marie: the bundle she was picking up was undoubtedly Kerry's corpse. Without looking in Helen's direction, the mother about-faced and made her way out of the bedroom.

Helen listened as the footsteps receded across the living room. Swiftly, she got to her feet and crossed to the passageway. From there she could vaguely see Anne-Marie's outline in the doorway of the maisonette. No lights burned in the quadrangle beyond. The woman disappeared, and Helen followed as speedily as she could, eyes fixed on the door ahead. She stumbled once, and once again, but reached the door in time to see Anne-Marie's vague form in the night ahead.

She stepped out of the maisonette and into the open air. It was chilly; there were no stars. All the lights on the balconies and corridors were out, nor did any burn in the flats; not even the glow of a television. Butts's Court was deserted.

She hesitated before going in pursuit of the girl. Why didn't she slip away now, cowardice coaxed her, and find her way back to the car? But if she did that the conspirators would have time to conceal the child's body. When she got back here with the police there would be sealed lips and shrugs and she would be told she had imagined the corpse and the Candyman. All the terrors she had tasted would recede into rumor again. Into words on a wall. And every day she lived from now on she would loathe herself for not going in pursuit of sanity.

She followed. Anne-Marie was not making her way around the quadrangle but moving toward the center of the lawn in the middle of the court. To the bonfire! Yes; to the bonfire! It loomed in front of Helen now, blacker than the night sky. She could just make out Anne-Marie's figure, moving to the edge of the piled timbers and furniture, and ducking to climb into its heart. This was how they planned to remove the evidence. To bury the child was not certain enough; but to cremate it, and pulverize the bones—who would ever know?

She stood a dozen yards from the pyramid and watched as Anne-Marie climbed out again and moved away, folding her figure into the darkness.

Quickly, Helen moved through the long grass and located the narrow space in among the piled timbers into which Anne-Marie had put the body. She thought she could see the pale form; it had been laid in a hollow. She couldn't reach it however. Thanking God that she was as slim as the mother, she squeezed through the narrow aperture. Her dress snagged on a nail as she did so. She turned round to disengage it, fingers trembling. When she turned back she had lost sight of the corpse.

She fumbled blindly ahead of her, her hands finding wood and rags and what felt like the back of an old arm-chair, but not the cold skin of the child. She had hardened herself against contact with the body; she had endured worse in the last hours than picking up a dead baby. Determined not to be defeated, she advanced a little farther, her shins scraped and her fingers spiked with splinters. Flashes of light were appearing at the corners of her aching eyes; her blood whined in her ears. But there, *there!*—the body was no more than a yard and a half ahead of her. She ducked down to reach beneath a beam of wood, but her fingers missed the forlorn bundle by inches. She stretched farther, the whine in her head increasing, but still she could not reach the child. All she could do was bend double and squeeze into the hidey-hole the children had left in the center of the bonfire.

It was difficult to get through. The space was so small she could barely crawl on hands and knees, but she made it. The child lay facedown. She fought back the remnants of squeamishness and went to pick it up. As she did so, something landed on her arm. The shock startled her. She almost cried out, but swallowed the urge, and brushed the irritation away. It buzzed as it rose from her skin. The whine she had heard in her ears was not her blood but the hive.

"I knew you'd come," the voice behind her said, and a wide hand covered her face. She fell backward and the Candyman embraced her.

"We have to go," he said in her ear, as flickering light spilled between the stacked timbers. "Be on our way, you and I."

She fought to be free of him, to cry out for them not to light the bonfire, but he held her lovingly close. The light grew: warmth came with it; and through the kindling and the first flames she could see figures approaching the pyre out of the darkness of Butts's Court. They had been there all along: waiting, the lights turned out in their homes, and broken all along the corridors. Their final conspiracy.

The bonfire caught with a will, but by some trick of its construction the flames did not invade her hiding place quickly; nor did the smoke creep through the furniture to choke her. She was able to watch how the children's faces gleamed; how the parents called them from going too close, and how they disobeyed; how the old women, their blood thin, warmed their hands and smiled into the flames. Presently the roar and the crackle became deafening, and the Candyman let her scream herself hoarse in the certain knowledge that nobody could hear her, and even if they had, would not have moved to claim her from the fire.

The bees vacated the fiend's belly as the air became hotter, and mazed the air with their panicked flight. Some, attempting escape, caught fire, and fell like tiny meteors to the ground. The body of Baby Kerry, which lay close to the creeping flames, began to cook. Its downy hair smoked; its back blistered.

Soon the heat crept down Helen's throat and scorched her pleas away. She sank back, exhausted, into the Candyman's arms, resigned to his triumph. In moments they would be on their way, as he had promised, and there was no help for it.

Perhaps they would remember her, as he had said they might, finding her cracked skull in tomorrow's ashes. Perhaps she might become, in time, a story with which to frighten children. She had lied, saying she preferred death to such questionable fame. She did not. As to her seducer, he laughed as the conflagration sniffed them out. There was no permanence for him in this night's death. His deeds were on a hundred walls and ten thousand lips, and should he be doubted again his congregation could summon him with sweetness. He had reason to laugh. So, as the flames crept upon them, did she, as through the fire she caught sight of a familiar face moving between the onlookers. It was Trevor. He had forsaken his meal at Apollinaire's and come looking for her.

She watched him questioning this fire watcher and that, but they shook their heads, all the while staring at the pyre with smiles buried in their eyes. Poor dupe, she thought, following his antics. She willed him to look past the flames in the hope that he might see her burning. Not so that he could save her from death—she was long past hope of that—but because she pitied him in his bewilderment and wanted to give him, though he would not have thanked her for it, something to be haunted by. That, and a story to tell.

The
Madonna

JERRY Coloqhoun waited on the steps of the Leopold Road Swimming Pools for over thirty-five minutes before Garvey turned up. His feet were steadily losing feeling as the cold crept up through the soles of his shoes. The time would come, he reassured himself, when *he'd* be the one to keep people waiting. Indeed, such a prerogative might not be so far away, if he could persuade Ezra Garvey to invest in the Pleasure Dome. It would require an appetite for risk, and substantial assets, but his contacts had assured him that Garvey, whatever his reputation, possessed both in abundance. The source of the man's money was not an issue in the proceedings, or so Jerry had persuaded himself. Many a nicer plutocrat had turned the project down flat in the last six months; in such circumstances fineness of feeling was a luxury he could scarcely afford.

He was not all that surprised by the reluctance of investors. These were difficult times, and risks were not to be undertaken lightly. More, it took a measure of imagination, a faculty not overabundant among the moneyed he'd met, to see the Pools transformed into the gleaming amenity complex he envisaged. But his researches had convinced him that in an area like this—where houses once teetering on demolition were being bought up and refurbished by a generation of middle-class sybarites—that in such an area the facilities he had planned would scarcely fail to make money.

There was a further inducement. The Council, which owned the Pools, was eager to unload the property as speedily as possible; it had debtors aplenty. Jerry's bribee at the Directorate of Community Services—the same man who'd happily filched the keys to the property for two bottles of gin—had told him that the building could be purchased for a song if the offer was made swiftly. It was all a question of good timing.

A skill, apparently, that Garvey lacked. By the time he arrived the numbness had spread north to Jerry's knees, and his temper had worn thin. He made no show of it, however, as Garvey got out of his chauffeur-driven Rover and came up the steps. Jerry had only spoken to him by telephone and had expected a larger man, but despite the lack of stature there was no doubting Garvey's authority. It was there in the plain look of appraisal he gave Coloqhoun; in the joyless features; in the immaculate suit.

The pair shook hands.

"It's good to see you, Mr. Garvey."

The man nodded but returned no pleasantry. Jerry, eager to be out of the cold, opened the front door and led the way inside.

"I've only got ten minutes," Garvey said.

"Fine," Jerry replied. "I just wanted to show you the layout."

"You've surveyed the place?"

"Of course."

This was a lie. Jerry had been over the building the previous August, courtesy of a contact in the Architects' Department, and had, since that time, looked at the place from the outside several times. But it had been five months since he'd actually stepped into the building; he hoped accelerating decay had not taken an unshakable hold since then. They stepped into the vestibule. It smelled damp but not overpoweringly so.

"There's no electricity on," he explained. "We have to go by flashlight." He fished the heavy-duty flashlight from his pocket and trained the beam on the inner door. It was padlocked. He stared at the lock, dumbfounded. If this door had been locked last time he was here, he didn't remember. He tried the single key he'd been given, knowing before he put it to the lock that the two were hopelessly mismatched. He cursed under his breath, quickly skipping through the options available. Either he and Garvey about-faced, and left the Pools to its secrets—if mildew, creeping rot and a roof that was within an ace of surrender could be classed as secrets—or else he made an attempt to break in. He glanced at Garvey, who had taken a prodigious cigar from his inside pocket and was stroking the end with a flame; velvet smoke billowed.

"I'm sorry about the delay," he said.

"It happens," Garvey returned, clearly unperturbed.

"I think strong-arm tactics may be called for," Jerry said, feeling out the other man's response to a break-in.

"Suits me."

Jerry quickly rooted about the darkened vestibule for an implement. In the ticket booth he found a metal-legged stool. He hoisted it out of the booth and crossed back to the door, aware of Garvey's amused but benign gaze upon him, and, using one of the legs as a lever, broke the shackle of the padlock. The lock clattered to the tiled floor.

"Open sesame," he murmured with some satisfaction, and pushed the door open for Garvey.

The sound of the falling lock seemed still to linger in the deserted corridors when they stepped through, its din receding toward a sigh as it diminished. The interior looked more inhospitable than Jerry had remembered. The fitful daylight that fell through the mildewed panes of the skylights along the corridor was blue-gray—the light and that which it fell upon vying in dreariness. Once, no doubt, the Leopold Road Pools had been a showcase of Deco design —of shining tiles and cunning mosaics worked into floor and wall. But not in Jerry's adult life, certainly. The tiles underfoot had long since lifted with the damp; along the walls they had fallen in the hundreds, leaving patterns of white ceramic and dark plaster like some vast and clueless crossword puzzle. The air of destitution was so profound that Jerry had half a mind to give up his attempt at selling the project to Garvey on the spot. Surely there was no hope of a sale here, even at the ludicrously low asking price. But Garvey seemed more engaged than Jerry had allowed. He was already stalking down the corridor, puffing on his cigar and grunting to himself as he went. It could be no more than morbid curiosity, Jerry felt, that took the developer deeper into this echoing mausoleum. And yet:

"It's atmospheric. The place has possibilities," Garvey said. "I don't have much of a reputation as a philanthropist, Coloqhoun—you must know that—but I've got a taste for some of the finer things." He had paused in front of a mosaic depicting a nondescript mythological scene—fish, nymphs and sea-gods at play. He grunted appreciatively, describing the sinuous line of the design with the wet end of his cigar.

"You don't see craftsmanship like that nowadays," he commented.

Jerry thought it unremarkable but said, "It's superb."

"Show me the rest."

The complex had once boasted a host of facilities—sauna rooms, Turkish baths, thermal baths—in addition to the two pools. These various areas were connected by a warren of passageways that, unlike the main corridor, had no skylights: the flashlight had to suffice here. Dark or no, Garvey wanted to see all the public areas. The ten minutes he had warned were his limit stretched into twenty and thirty, the exploration constantly brought to a halt as he discovered some new felicity to comment upon. Jerry listened with feigned comprehension: he found the man's enthusiasm for the decor confounding.

"I'd like to see the pools now," Garvey announced when they'd made a thorough investigation of the subordinate amenities. Dutifully, Jerry led the way through the labyrinth toward the two pools. In a small corridor a little way from the Turkish baths Garvey said:

"Hush."

Jerry stopped walking. "What?"

"I heard a voice."

Jerry listened. The flashlight's beam, splashing off the tiles, threw a pale luminescence around them, which drained the blood from Garvey's features.

"I don't hear—"

"I said *hush*," Garvey snapped. He moved his head to and fro slowly. Jerry could hear nothing. Neither, now, could Garvey. He shrugged and pulled on his cigar. It had gone out, killed by the damp air.

"A trick of the corridors," Jerry said. "The echoes in the place are misleading. Sometimes you hear your own footsteps coming back to meet you."

Garvey grunted again. The grunt seemed to be his most valued part of speech. "I did hear something," he said, clearly not satisfied with Jerry's explanation. He listened again. The corridors were pin-drop hushed. It was not even possible to hear the traffic on Leopold Road. At last, Garvey seemed content.

"Lead on," he said. Jerry did just that, though the route to the pools was by no means clear to him. They took several wrong turnings, winding their way through a maze of identical corridors, before they reached their intended destination.

"It's warm," said Garvey as they stood outside the smaller of the two pools.

Jerry murmured his agreement. In his eagerness to reach the pools he had not noticed the steadily escalating temperature. But now that he stood still he could feel a film of sweat on his body. The air was humid, but it smelled not of damp and mildew, as elsewhere in the building. This was a sicklier, almost opulent, scent. He hoped Garvey, cocooned in the smoke of his relit cigar, could not share the smell; it was far from pleasant.

"The heating's on," Garvey said.

"It certainly seems like it," Jerry returned, though he couldn't think why. Perhaps the Department of Engineers warmed the heating system through once in a while, to keep it in working order. In which case, were they in the bowels of the building somewhere? Perhaps Garvey *had* heard voices? He mentally constructed a line of explanation should their paths cross.

"The pools," he said, and pulled open one of the double-doors. The skylight here was even dirtier than those in the main corridor; precious little light illuminated the scene. Garvey was not to be thwarted, however. He stepped through the door and across to the lip of the pool. There was little to see; the surfaces here were covered with several years' growth of mold. On the bottom of the pool, barely discernible beneath the algae, a design had been worked into the tiles. A bright fish-eye glanced up at them, perfectly thoughtless.

"Always had a fear of water," Garvey said ruminatively as he stared into the drained pool. "Don't know where it comes from."

"Childhood," Jerry ventured.

"I don't think so," the other replied. "My wife says it's the womb."

"The womb?"

"I didn't like swimming around in there, she says," he replied, with a smile that might have been at his own expense but was more likely at that of his wife.

A short sound came to meet them across the empty expanse of the pool, as of something falling. Garvey froze. "You hear *that?*" he said. "There's somebody in here." His voice had suddenly risen half an octave.

"Rats," Jerry replied. He wished to avoid an encounter with the engineers if possible; difficult questions might well be asked.

"Give me the torch," Garvey said, snatching it from Jerry's hand. He scanned the opposite side of the pool with the beam. It lit a series of dressing rooms, and an open door that led out of the pool. Nothing moved.

"I don't like vermin—" Garvey said.

"The place has been neglected," Jerry replied.

"—Especially the human variety." Garvey thrust the flashlight back into Jerry's hands. "I've got enemies, Mr. Coloqhoun. But then you've done your research on me, haven't you? You know I'm no lily-white." Garvey's concern about the noises he thought he'd heard now made unpalatable sense. It wasn't rats he was afraid of but grievous bodily harm. "I think I should be going," he said. "Show me the other pool and we'll be away."

"Surely." Jerry was as happy to be going as his guest. The incident had raised his temperature. The sweat came profusely now, trickling down the back of his neck. His sinuses ached. He led Garvey across the hallway to the door of the larger pool and pulled. The door refused him.

"Problem?"

"It must be locked from the inside."

"Is there another way in?"

"I think so. Do you want me to go round the back?"

Garvey glanced at his watch. "Two minutes," he said. "I've got appointments."

Garvey watched Coloqhoun disappear down the darkened corridor, the flashlight's beam running on ahead of him. He didn't like the man. He was too closely shaven; and his shoes were Italian. But—the proposer aside—the project had some merit. Garvey liked the Pools with its adjuncts, the uniformity of the design, the banality of the decorations. Unlike many, he found institutions reassuring:

hospitals, schools, even prisons. They smacked of social order; they soothed that part of him fearful of chaos. Better a world too organized than one not organized enough.

Again his cigar had gone out. He put it between his teeth and lit a match. As the first flare died, he caught an inkling sight of a naked girl in the corridor ahead, watching him. The glimpse was momentary, but when the match dropped from his fingers and the light failed, she appeared in his mind's eye, perfectly remembered. She was young—fifteen at the most—and her body full. The sweat on her skin lent her such sensuality she might have stepped from his dream-life. Dropping his stale cigar, he rummaged for another match and struck it, but in the meager seconds of darkness the child-beauty had gone, leaving only the trace of her sweet body scent on the air.

"Girl?" he said.

The sight of her nudity, and the shock in her eyes, made him eager for her.

"Girl?"

The flame of the second match failed to penetrate more than a yard or two down the corridor.

"Are you there?"

She could not be far, he reasoned. Lighting a third match, he went in search of her. He had gone only a few steps when he heard somebody behind him. He turned. The flashlight lit the fright on his face. It was only the Italian Shoes.

"There's no way in."

"There's no need to blind me," Garvey said. The beam dropped.

"I'm sorry."

"There's somebody here, Coloqhoun. A girl."

"A girl?"

"You know something about it maybe?"

"No."

"She was stark naked. Standing three or four yards from me."

Jerry looked at Garvey, mystified. Was the man suffering from sexual delusions?

"I tell you I saw a girl," Garvey protested, though no word of contradiction had been offered. "If you hadn't arrived I'd have had my hands on her." He glanced back down the corridor. "Get some light down there." Jerry trained the beam on the maze. There was no sign of life.

"Damn," said Garvey, his regret quite genuine. He looked back at Jerry. "All right," he said. "Let's get the hell out of here."

"I'm interested," he said, as they parted on the step. "The project has potential. Do you have a ground plan of the place?"

"No, but I can get my hands on one."

"Do that." Garvey was lighting a fresh cigar. "And send me your proposals in more detail. Then we'll talk again."

It took a considerable bribe to get the plans of the Pools out of his contact at the Architects' Department, but Jerry eventually secured them. On paper the complex looked like a labyrinth. And like the best labyrinths, there was no order apparent in the layout of shower rooms and bathrooms and changing rooms. It was Carole who proved that thesis to be wrong.

"What is this?" she asked him as he pored over the plans that evening. They'd had four or five hours together at his flat—hours without the bickering and the bad feeling that had soured their time together of late.

"It's the ground plan of the swimming pools on Leopold Road. Do you want another brandy?"

"No thanks." She peered at the plan while he got up to refill his glass.

"I think I've got Garvey in on the deal."

"You're going to do business with him, are you?"

"Don't make me sound like a white slaver. The man's got money."

"Dirty money."

"What's a little dirt between friends?"

She looked at him frostily, and he wished he could have played back the previous ten seconds and erased the comment.

"I *need* this project," he said, taking his drink across to the sofa and sitting opposite her, the ground plan spread on the low table between them. "I need something to go right for me for once."

Her eyes refused to grant him a reprieve.

"I just think Garvey and his like are bad news," she said. "I don't care how much money he's got. He's a villain, Jerry."

"So I should give the whole thing up, should I? Is that what you're saying?" They'd had this argument, in one guise or another, several times in the last few weeks. "I should just forget all the hard labor I've put in and add this failure to all the others?"

"There's no need to shout."

"I'm not shouting!"

She shrugged. "All right," she said quietly, "you're not shouting."

"Christ!"

She went back to perusing the ground plan. He watched her from over the rim of his whiskey tumbler; saw the parting down the middle of her head, and the fine blond hair that divided from there. They made so little sense to each other, he thought. The processes that brought them to their present impasse were perfectly obvious; yet time and again they failed to find the common ground necessary for a fruitful exchange of views. Not simply on this matter, on half a hundred others. Whatever thoughts buzzed beneath her tender scalp, they were a mystery to him. And his to her, presumably.

"It's a spiral," she said.

"What is?"

"The Pools. It's designed like a spiral. Look."

He stood up to get a bird's-eye view of the ground plan as she traced a route through the passageways with her index finger. She was right. Though the imperatives of the architects' brief had muddied the clarity of the image, there was indeed a rough spiral built into the maze of corridors and rooms. Her circling fingers drew tighter and yet tighter loops as it described the shape. At last it came to rest on the large pool, the locked pool. He stared at the plan in silence. Without her pointing it out he knew he could have looked at the design for a week and never seen the underlying structure.

Carole decided she would not stay the night. It was not, she tried to explain at the door, that things between them were over; only that she valued their intimacy too much to misuse it as bandaging. He half grasped the point; she too pictured them as wounded animals. At least they had some metaphorical life in common.

He was not unused to sleeping alone. In many ways he preferred to be solitary in his bed than to share it with someone, even Carole. But tonight he wanted her with him; not her, even, but *somebody*. He felt sourcelessly fretful, like a child. When sleep came it fled again, as if in fear of dreams.

Sometime toward dawn he got up, preferring wakefulness to that wretched sleep-hopping, wrapped his dressing gown around his shivering body, and went through to brew himself some tea. The ground plan was still spread on the coffee table where they had left it from the night before. Sipping the warm sweet Assam, he stood and pondered over it. Now that Carole had pointed it out, all he could concentrate upon—despite the clutter of marginalia that demanded his attention—was the spiral, that undisputable evidence of a hidden hand at work beneath the apparent chaos of the maze. It seized his eye and seduced it into following its unremitting route, round and round, tighter and tighter; and toward *what?* A locked swimming pool.

Tea drunk, he returned to bed; this time, fatigue got the better of his nerves and the sleep he'd been denied washed over him. He was wakened at seven-fifteen by Carole, who was phoning before she went to work to apologize for the previous night.

"I don't want everything to go wrong between us, Jerry. You do know that, don't you? You know you're precious to me."

He couldn't take love talk in the morning. What seemed romantic at midnight struck him as ridiculous at dawn. He answered her declarations of commitment as best he could, and arranged to see her the following evening. Then he returned to his pillow.

* * *

Scarcely a quarter-hour had passed since he'd visited the Pools without Ezra Garvey thinking of the girl he'd glimpsed in the corridor. Her face had come back to him during dinner with his wife and sex with his mistress. So untrammeled, that face, so bright with possibilities.

Garvey thought of himself as a woman's man. Unlike most of his fellow potentates, whose consorts were a convenience best paid to be absent when not required for some specific function, Garvey enjoyed the company of the opposite sex. Their voices, their perfume, their laughter. His greed for their proximity knew few bounds; they were precious creatures whose company he was willing to spend small fortunes to secure. His jacket was therefore weighed down with money and expensive trinkets when he returned, that morning, to Leopold Road.

The pedestrians on the street were too concerned with keeping their heads dry (a cold and steady drizzle had fallen since dawn) to notice the man on the step standing under a black umbrella while another bent to the business of undoing the padlock. Chandaman was an expert with locks. The shackle snapped open within seconds. Garvey lowered his umbrella and slipped into the vestibule.

"Wait here," he instructed Chandaman. "And close the door."

"Yes, sir."

"If I need you, I'll shout. You got the torch?"

Chandaman produced the flashlight from his jacket. Garvey took it, switched it on, and disappeared down the corridor. Either it was substantially colder outside than it had been the day before yesterday, or else the interior was hot. He unbuttoned his jacket, and loosened his tightly knotted tie. He welcomed the heat, reminding him as it did of the sheen on the dream girl's skin, of the heat-languored look In her dark eyes. He advanced down the corridor, splashing the flashlight's beam off the tiles. His sense of direction had always been good; it took him only a short time to find his way to the spot outside the large pool where he had encountered the girl. There he stood still and listened.

Garvey was a man used to looking over his shoulder. All his professional life, whether in or out of prison, he had needed to watch for the assassin at his back. Such ceaseless vigilance had made him sensitive to the least sign of human presence. Sounds another man might have ignored played a warning tattoo upon his eardrum. But here? Nothing. Silence in the corridors; silence in the sweating anterooms and the Turkish baths; silence in every tiled enclave from one end of the building to the other. And yet he knew he was not alone. When five senses failed him a sixth—belonging, perhaps, more to the beast in him than the sophisticate his expensive suit spoke of—sensed presences. This faculty had saved his hide more than once. Now, he hoped, it would guide him into the arms of beauty.

Trusting to instinct, he extinguished the light and headed off down the corridor from which the girl had first emerged, feeling his way along the walls. His quarry's presence tantalized him. He suspected she was a mere wall away, keeping pace with him along some secret passage he had no access to. The thought of this stalking pleased him. She and he, alone in this sweating maze, playing a game that both knew must end in capture. He moved stealthily, his pulse ticking off the seconds of the chase at neck and wrist and groin. His crucifix was glued to his breast bone with perspiration.

At last, the corridor divided. He halted. There was precious little light: what there was etched the tunnels deceptively. Impossible to judge distance. But trusting to his instinct, he turned left and followed his nose. Almost immediately, a door. It was open, and he walked through into a larger space; or so he guessed from the muted sound of his footsteps. Again, he stood still. This time, his straining ears were rewarded with a sound. Across the room from him, the soft pad of naked feet on the tiles. Was it his imagination, or did he even glimpse the girl, her body carved from the gloom, paler than the surrounding darkness, and smoother? Yes; it was she. He almost called out after her, and then thought better of it. Instead he went in silent pursuit, content to play her game for as long as it pleased her. Crossing the room, he stepped through another door which let on to a further tunnel. The air here was much warmer than anywhere else in the building, clammy and ingratiating as it pressed itself upon him. A moment's anxiety caught his throat: that he was neglecting every article of an autocrat's faith, putting his head so willingly into this warm noose. It could so easily be a setup: the girl, the chase. Around the next corner the breasts and the beauty might be gone, and there would be a knife at his heart. And yet he *knew* this wasn't so; *knew* that the footfall ahead was a woman's, light and lithe; that the swelter that brought new tides of sweat from him could nurture only softness and passivity here. No knife could prosper in such heat: its edge would soften, its ambition go neglected. He was safe.

Ahead, the footsteps had halted. He halted too. There was light from somewhere, though its source was not apparent. He licked his lips, tasting salt, then advanced. Beneath his fingers the tiles were glossed with water; under his heels, they were slick. Anticipation mounted in him with every step.

Now the light was brightening. It was not day. Sunlight had no route into this sanctum; this was more like moonlight—soft-edged, evasive—though that too must be exiled here, he thought. Whatever its origins, by it he finally set eyes on the girl; or rather, on *a* girl, for it was not the same he had seen two days before. Naked she was, young she was; but in all other respects different. He caught a glance from her before she fled from him down the corridor and turned a corner. Puzzlement now lent piquancy to the chase: not one but two girls, occupying this secret place. *Why?*

He looked behind him, to be certain his escape route lay open should he wish to retreat, but his memory, befuddled by the scented air, refused a clear picture of the way he'd come. A twinge of concern checked his exhilaration, but he refused to succumb to it, and pressed on, following the girl to the end of the corridor and turning left after her. The passageway ran for a short way before making another left; the girl even now was disappearing around that corner. Dimly aware that these gyrations were becoming tighter as he turned upon himself and upon himself again, he went where she led, panting now with the breath-quenching air and the insistence of the chase.

Suddenly, as he turned one final corner, the heat became smotheringly close, and the passageway delivered him out into a small, dimly lit chamber. He unbuttoned the top of his shirt; the veins on the back of his hands stood out like cord; he was aware of how his heart and lungs were laboring. But, he was relieved to see, the chase finished here. The object of his pursuit was standing with her back to him across the chamber, and at the sight of her smooth back and exquisite buttocks his claustrophobia evaporated.

"Girl . . . ," he panted. "You led me quite a chase."

She seemed not to hear him, or, more likely, was extending the game to its limits out of waywardness.

He started across the slippery tiles toward her.

"I'm talking to you."

As he came within half a dozen feet of her, she turned. It was not the girl he had just pursued through the corridor, not indeed the one he had seen two days before. This creature was another altogether. His gaze rested on her unfamiliar face a few seconds only, however, before sliding giddily down to meet the child she held in her arms. It was suckling like any newborn babe, pulling at her young breast with no little hunger. But in his four and a half decades of life Garvey's eyes had never seen a creature its like. Nausea rose in him. To see the girl giving suck was surprise enough, but to such a *thing,* such an outcast of any tribe, human or animal, was almost more than his stomach could stand. Hell itself had offspring more embraceable.

"What in Christ's name—?"

The girl stared at Garvey's alarm, and a wave of laughter broke over her face. He shook his head. The child in her arms uncurled a puckered limb and clamped it to its comforter's bosom so as to get better purchase. The gesture lashed Garvey's disgust into rage. Ignoring the girl's protests he snatched the abomination from her arms, holding it long enough to feel the glistening sac of its body squirm in his grasp, then flung it as hard as he could against the far wall of the chamber. As it struck the tiles it cried out, its complaint ending almost as soon as it began, only to be taken up instantly by the mother. She ran across the room to where the child lay, its apparently boneless body split open by the impact. One of its limbs, of which it possessed at least half a dozen, attempted to reach up to touch her sobbing face. She gathered the thing up into her arms; threads of shiny fluid ran across her belly and into her groin.

Out beyond the chamber something gave voice. Garvey had no doubt of its cue; it was answering the death-cry of the child, and the rising wail of its mother—but this sound was more distressing than either. Garvey's imagination was an impoverished faculty. Beyond his dreams of wealth and women lay a wasteland. Yet now, at the sound of that voice, the wasteland bloomed, and gave forth horrors he'd believed himself incapable of conceiving. Not portraits of monsters, which, at the best, could be no more than assemblies of experienced phenomena. What his mind created was more *feeling* than sight; belonged to his marrow, not to his mind. All certainty trembled—masculinity, power; the twin imperatives of dread and reason—all turned their collars up and denied knowledge of him. He shook, afraid as only dreams made him afraid, while the cry went on and on. Then he turned his back on the chamber, and ran, the light throwing his shadow in front of him down the dim corridor.

His sense of direction had deserted him. At the first intersection, and then at the second, he made an error. A few yards on he realized his mistake and tried to double back, but merely exacerbated the confusion. The corridors all looked alike: the same tiles, the same half-light, each fresh corner he turned either led him into a chamber he had not passed through or complete cul-de-sacs. His panic spiraled. The wailing had now ceased; he was alone with his rasping breath and half-spoken curses. Coloqhoun was responsible for this torment, and Garvey swore he would have its purpose beaten out of the man even if he had to break every bone in Coloqhoun's body personally. He clung to thoughts of that beating as he ran on; it was his only comfort. Indeed so preoccupied did he become with thought of the agonies he'd make Coloqhoun suffer he failed to realize that he had traced his way round in a circle and was running back *toward* the light until his sliding heels delivered him into a familiar chamber. The child lay on the floor, dead and discarded. Its mother was nowhere to be seen.

Garvey halted, and took stock of his situation. If he went back the way he'd come the route would only confound him again; if he went ahead, through the chamber and toward the light, he might cut the Gordian knot and be delivered back to his starting point. The swift wit of the solution pleased him. Cautiously, he crossed the chamber to the door on the other side and peered through. Another short corridor presented itself, and beyond that a door that let on to an open space. The pool! Surely the pool!

He threw caution to the wind and moved out of the chamber and along the passage.

With every step he took, the heat intensified. His head thumped with it. He pressed on to the end of the passageway, and out into the arena beyond.

The large pool had not been drained, unlike the smaller. Rather, it was full almost to brimming—not with clear water, but with a scummy broth that steamed even in the heat of the interior. *This* was the source of the light. The water in the pool gave off a phosphorescence that tinged everything—the tiles, the diving board, the changing rooms (himself, no doubt)—with the same fulvous wash.

He scanned the scene in front of him. There was no sign of the women. His route to the exit lay unchallenged; nor could he see sign of padlock or chains on the double doors. He began toward them. His heel slid on the tiles, and he glanced down briefly to see that he had crossed a trail of fluid—difficult, in the bewitched light, to make out its color—that either ended at the water's edge, or began there.

He looked back toward the water, curiosity getting the better of him. The steam swirled; an eddy toyed with the scum. And there! His eye caught sight of a dark, anonymous shape sliding beneath the skin of the water. He thought of the creature he'd killed; of its formless body and the dangling loops of its limbs. Was this another of that species? The liquid brightness lapped against the poolside at his feet; continents of scum broke into archipelagoes. Of the swimmer, there was no sign.

Irritated, he looked away from the water. He was no longer alone. Three girls appeared from somewhere and were moving down the edge of the pool toward him. One he recognized as the girl he had first seen here. She was wearing a dress, unlike her sisters. One of her breasts was bared. She looked at him gravely as she approached; by her side she trailed a rope, decorated along its length with stained ribbons tied in limp but extravagant bows.

At the arrival of these three graces the fermenting waters of the pool were stirred into a frenzy as its occupants rose to meet the women. Garvey could see three or four restless forms teasing—but not breaking—the surface. He was caught between his instinct to take flight (the rope, though prettified, was still a rope) and the desire to linger and see what the pool contained. He glanced toward the door. He was within ten yards of it. A quick dash and he'd be out into the cool air of the corridor. From there, Chandaman was within calling distance.

The girls stood a few feet from him and watched him. He returned their looks. All the desires that had brought him here had taken heel. He no longer wanted to cup the breasts of these creatures, or dabble at the intersection of their gleaming thighs. These women were not what they seemed. Their quietness wasn't docility but a drug-trance; their nakedness wasn't sensuality but a horrid indifference that offended him. Even their youth, and all it brought— the softness of their skins, the gloss of their hair—even that was somehow corrupt. When the girl in the dress reached out and touched his sweating face, Garvey made a small cry of disgust, as if he'd been licked by a snake. She was not fazed by his response but stepped closer to him still, her eyes fixed on his, smelling not of perfume like his mistress but of fleshliness. Affronted as he was, he could not turn away. He stood, meeting the slut's eyes, as she kissed his cheek, and the beribboned rope was wrapped around his neck.

Jerry called Garvey's office at half-hour intervals through the day. At first he was told that he was out of the office and would be available later that afternoon. As the day wore on, however, the message changed. Garvey was not going to be in the office at all that day, Jerry was informed. Mr. Garvey is feeling unwell, the secretary told him; he has gone home to rest. Please call again tomorrow. Jerry left with her the message that he had secured the ground plan to the Pools and would be delighted to meet and discuss their plans at Mr. Garvey's convenience.

Carole called in the late afternoon.

"Shall we go out tonight?" she said. "Maybe a film?"

"What do you want to see?" he said.

"Oh, I hadn't really thought that far. We'll talk about it this evening, shall we?"

They ended up going to a French movie, which seemed, as far as Jerry could grasp, completely lacking in plot; it was simply a series of dialogues between characters discussing their traumas and their aspirations, the former being in direct proportion to the failure of the latter. It left him feeling torpid.

"You didn't like it . . ."

"Not much. All that browbeating."

"And no shoot-out."

She smiled to herself.

"What's so funny?"

"Nothing."

"Don't say nothing."

She shrugged. "I was just smiling, that's all. Can't I smile?"

"Jesus. All this conversation needs is subtitles."

They walked along Oxford Street a little way.

"Do you want to eat?" he said as they came to the head of Poland Street. "We could go to the Red Fort."

"No thanks. I hate eating late."

"For Christ's sake, let's not argue about a bloody film."

"Who's arguing?"

"You're so infuriating—"

"That's something we've got in common, anyhow," she returned. Her neck was flushed.

"You said this morning—"

"What?"

"About us not losing each other—"

"That was this morning," she said, eyes steely. And then, suddenly: "You don't give a *fuck*, Jerry. Not about me, not about anybody."

She stared at him, almost defying him to respond. When he failed to, she seemed curiously satisfied.

"Goodnight," she said, and began to walk away from him. He watched her take five, six, seven steps from him, the deepest part of him wanting to call after her, but a dozen irrelevancies—pride, fatigue, inconvenience—blocked his doing so. What eventually uprooted him, and put her name on his lips, was the thought of an empty bed tonight; of the sheets warm only where he lay, and chilly as hell to left and right of him.

"Carole."

She didn't turn; her step didn't even falter. He had to trot to catch up with her, conscious that this scene was probably entertaining the passersby.

"Carole." He caught hold of her arm. Now she stopped. When he moved round to face her he was shocked to see that she was crying. This discomfited him; he hated her tears only marginally less than his own.

"I surrender," he said, trying a smile. "The film was a masterpiece. How's that?"

She refused to be soothed by his antics; her face was swollen with unhappiness.

"Don't," he said. "Please don't. I'm not . . ." (Very good at apologies, he wanted to say, but he was so bad at them he couldn't even manage that much.)

"Never mind," she said softly. She wasn't angry, he saw; only miserable.

"Come back to the flat."

"I don't want to."

"*I* want you to," he replied. That at least was sincerely meant. "I don't like talking in the street."

He hailed a cab, and they made their way back to Kentish Town, keeping their silence. Halfway up the stairs to the door of the flat Carole said, "Foul perfume."

There was a strong, acidic smell lingering on the stairs.

"Somebody's been up here," he said, suddenly anxious, and hurried on up the flight to the front door of his flat. It was open, the lock had been unceremoniously forced, the wood of the doorjamb splintered. He cursed.

"What's wrong?" Carole asked, following him up the stairs.

"Break-in."

He stepped into the flat and switched on the light. The interior was chaos. The whole flat had been comprehensively trashed. Everywhere, petty acts of vandalism—pictures smashed, pillows de-gutted, furniture reduced to timber. He stood in the middle of the turmoil and shook, while Carole went from room to room, finding the same thorough destruction in each.

"This is personal, Jerry."

He nodded.

"I'll call the police," she volunteered. "You find out what's missing."

He did as he was told, white-faced. The blow of this invasion numbed him. As he walked listlessly through the flat to survey the pandemonium—turning broken items over, pushing drawers back into place—he found himself imagining the intruders about their business, laughing as they worked through his clothes and keepsakes. In the corner of his bedroom he found a heap of his photographs. They had urinated on them.

"The police are on their way," Carole told him. "They said not to touch anything."

"Too late," he murmured.

"What's missing?"

"Nothing," he told her. All the valuables—the stereo and video equipment, his credit cards, his few items of jewelry—were there. Only then did he remember the ground plan. He returned to the living room and proceeded to root through the wreckage, but he knew damn well he wasn't going to find it.

"Garvey," he said.

"What about him?"

"He came for the ground plan of the Pools. Or sent someone."

"Why?" Carole replied, looking at the chaos. "You were going to give it to him anyway."

Jerry shook his head. "You were the one who warned me to stay clear—"

"I never expected anything like this."

"That makes two of us."

The police came and went, offering faint apologies for the fact that they thought an arrest unlikely. "There's a lot of vandalism around at the moment," the officer said. "There's nobody in downstairs . . ."

"No. They're away."

"Last hope, I'm afraid. We're getting calls like this all the time. You're insured?"

"Yes."

"Well, that's something."

Throughout the interview Jerry kept silent on his suspicions though he was repeatedly tempted to point the finger. There was little purpose in accusing Garvey at this juncture. For one, Garvey would have alibis prepared; for another, what would unsubstantiated accusations do but further inflame the man's unreason?

"What will you do?" Carole asked him when the police had picked up their shrugs and left.

"I don't know. I can't even be certain it *was* Garvey. One minute he's all sweetness and light; the next this. How do I deal with a mind like that?"

"You don't. You leave it alone," she replied. "Do you want to stay here, or go over to my place?"

"Stay," he said.

They made a perfunctory attempt to restore the former status quo—righting the furniture that was not too crippled to stand and clearing up the broken glass. Then they turned the slashed mattress over, located two unmutilated cushions, and went to bed.

She wanted to make love, but that reassurance, like so much of his life of late, was doomed to failure. There was no making good between the sheets what had been so badly soured out of them. His anger made him rough, and his roughness in turn angered her. She frowned beneath him, her kisses unwilling and tight. Her reluctance only spurned him on to fresh crassness.

"Stop," she said, as he was about to enter her. "I don't want this."

He did, and badly. He pushed before she could further her objections.

"I said *don't*, Jerry."

He shut out her voice. He was half as heavy again as she.

"*Stop*."

He closed his eyes. She told him again to stop, this time with real fury, but he just thrust harder—the way she'd ask him to sometimes, when the heat was really on—beg him to, even. But now she only swore at him, and threatened, and every word she said made him more intent not to be cheated of this, though he felt nothing at his groin but fullness and discomfort, and the urge to be finished.

She began to fight, raking at his back with her nails, and pulling at his hair to unclamp his face from her neck. It passed through his head as he labored that she would hate him for this, and on that, at least, they would be of one accord, but the thought was soon lost to sensation.

The poison passed, he rolled off her.

"Bastard," she said.

His back stung. When he got up from the bed he left blood on the sheets. Digging through the chaos in the living room he located an unbroken bottle of whiskey. The glasses, however, were all smashed, and out of absurd fastidiousness he didn't want to drink from the bottle. He squatted against the wall, his back chilled, feeling neither wretched nor proud. The front door opened, and was slammed. He waited, listening to Carole's feet on the stairs. Then tears came, though these too he felt utterly detached from. Finally, the bout dispatched, he went through into the kitchen, found a cup, and drank himself senseless.

Garvey's study was an impressive room; he'd had it fashioned after that of a tax lawyer he'd known, the walls lined with books purchased by the yard, the color of carpet and paint work alike muted, as though by an accrual of cigar smoke and learning. When he found sleep difficult, as he did now, he would retire to the study, sit on his leather-backed chair behind a vast desk, and dream of legitimacy. Not tonight, however; tonight his thoughts were otherwise preoccupied. Always, however much he might try to turn to another route, they went back to Leopold Road.

He remembered little of what had happened at the Pools. That in itself was distressing; he had always prided himself upon the acuteness of his memory. Indeed his recall of faces seen and favors done had in no small measure helped him to his present power. Of the hundreds in his employ he boasted that there was not a doorkeeper or a cleaner he could not address by Christian name.

But of the events at Leopold Road, barely thirty-six hours old, he had only the vaguest recollection; of the women closing upon him, and the rope tightening around his neck; of their leading him along the lip of the pool to some chamber the vileness of which had practically snatched his senses away. What had followed his arrival there moved in his memory like those forms in the filth of the pool: obscure, but horribly distressing. There had been humiliation and horrors, hadn't there? Beyond that, he remembered nothing.

He was not a man to kowtow to such ambiguities without argument, however. If there were mysteries to be uncovered here, then he would do so, and take the consequence of revelation. His first offensive had been sending Chandaman and Fryer to tear up Coloqhoun's place. If, as he suspected, this whole enterprise was some elaborate trap devised by his enemies, then Coloqhoun was involved in its setting. No more than a front man, no doubt; certainly not the mastermind. But Garvey was satisfied that the destruction of Coloqhoun's goods and chattels would warn his masters of his intent to fight. It had borne other fruit too. Chandaman had returned with the ground plan of the Pools; they were spread on Garvey's desk now. He had traced his route through the complex time and again, hoping that his memory might be jogged. He had been disappointed.

Weary, he got up and went to the study window. The garden behind the house was vast and painstakingly tended. He could see little of the immaculate borders at the moment, however; the starlight barely described the world outside. All he could see was his own reflection in the polished pane.

As he focused on it, his outline seemed to waver, and he felt a loosening in his lower belly, as if something had come unknotted there. He put his hand to his abdomen. It twitched, it trembled, and for an instant he was back in the Pools, and naked, and something lumpen moved in front of his eyes. He almost yelled, but stopped himself by turning away from the window and staring at the room; at the carpets and the books and the furniture; at sober, solid reality. Even then the images refused to leave his head entirely. The coils of his innards were still jittery.

It was several minutes before he could bring himself to look back at the reflection in the window. When at last he did all trace of the vacillation had disappeared. He would countenance no more nights like this, sleepless and haunted. With the first light of dawn came the conviction that today was the day to break Mr. Coloqhoun.

Jerry tried to call Carole at her office that morning. She was repeatedly unavailable. Eventually he simply gave up trying and turned his attentions to the Herculean task of restoring some order to the flat. He lacked the focus and the energy to do a good job, however. After a futile hour, in which he seemed not to have made more than a dent, he gave up. The chaos accurately reflected his opinion of himself. Best perhaps that it be left to lie.

Just before noon, he received a call.

"Mr. Coloqhoun? Mr. *Gerard* Coloqhoun?"

"That's right."

"My name's Fryer. I'm calling on behalf of Mr. Garvey."

"Oh?"

Was this to gloat, or threaten further mischief?

"Mr. Garvey was expecting some proposals from you," Fryer said.

"Proposals?"

"He's very enthusiastic about the Leopold Road project, Mr. Coloqhoun. He feels there's substantial monies to be made."

Jerry said nothing; this palaver confounded him.

"Mr. Garvey would like another meeting as soon as possible."

"Yes?"

"At the Pools. There's a few architectural details he'd like to show his colleagues."

"I see."

"Would you be available later on today?"

"Yes. Of course."

"Four-thirty?"

The conversation more or less ended there, leaving Jerry mystified. There had been no trace of enmity in Fryer's manner; no hint, however subtle, of bad blood between the two parties. Perhaps, as the police had suggested, the events of the previous night *had* been the work of anonymous vandals—the theft of the ground plan a whim of theirs. His depressed spirits rose. All was not lost.

He rang Carole again, buoyed up by this turn of events. This time he did not take the repeated excuses of her colleagues but insisted on speaking to her. Finally, she picked up the phone.

"I don't want to talk to you, Jerry. Just go to hell."

"Just hear me out—"

She slammed the receiver down before he said another word. He rang back immediately. When she answered and heard his voice, she seemed baffled that he was so eager to make amends.

"Why are you even trying?" she said. "Jesus Christ, what's the use?" He could hear the tears in her throat.

"I want you to understand how sick I feel. Let me make it right. *Please* let me make it right."

She didn't reply to his appeal.

"Don't put the phone down. Please don't. I know it was unforgivable. Jesus, I know . . ."

Still she kept her silence.

"Just think about it, will you? Give me a chance to put things right. Will you do that?"

Very quietly, she said, "I don't see the use."

"May I call you tomorrow?"

He heard her sigh.

"May I?"

"Yes. Yes."

The line went dead.

He set out for his meeting at Leopold Road with a full three-quarters of an hour to spare, but halfway to his destination the rain came on, great spots of it which defied the best efforts of his windshield wipers. The traffic slowed; he crawled for half a mile, with only the rear lights of the vehicle ahead visible through the deluge. The minutes ticked by, and his anxiety mounted. By the time he edged his way out of the fouled-up traffic to find another route, he was already late. There was nobody waiting on the steps of the Pools, but Garvey's powder-blue Rover was parked a little way down the road. There was no sign of the chauffeur. Jerry found a place to park on the opposite side of the road and crossed through the rain. It was a matter of fifty yards from the door of the car to that of the Pools, but by the time he reached his destination he was drenched and breathless. The door was open. Garvey had clearly manipulated the lock and slipped out of the downpour. Jerry ducked inside.

Garvey was not in the vestibule, but somebody was. A man of Jerry's height but with half again the width. He was wearing leather gloves. His face, but for the absence of seams, might have been of the same material.

"Coloqhoun?"

"Yes."

"Mr. Garvey is waiting for you inside."

"Who are you?"

"Chandaman," the man replied. "Go right in."

There was a light at the far end of the corridor. Jerry pushed open the glass-paneled vestibule doors and walked down toward it. Behind him, he heard the front door snap closed, and then the echoing tread of Garvey's lieutenant.

Garvey was talking with another man, shorter than Chandaman, who was holding a sizable flashlight. When the pair heard Jerry approach they looked his way; their conversation abruptly ceased. Garvey offered no welcoming comment or hand but merely said, "About time."

"The rain . . . ," Jerry began, then thought better of offering a self-evident explanation.

"You'll catch your death," the man with the flashlight said. Jerry immediately recognized the dulcet tones of:

"Fryer."

"The same," the man returned.

"Pleased to meet you."

They shook hands, and as they did so Jerry caught sight of Garvey, who was staring at him as though in search of a second head. The man didn't say anything for what seemed like half a minute, but simply studied the growing discomfort on Jerry's face.

"I'm not a stupid man," Garvey said eventually.

The statement, coming out of nowhere, begged response.

"I don't even believe you're the main man in all of this," Garvey went on. "I'm prepared to be charitable."

"What's this about?"

"Charitable," Garvey repeated, "because I think you're out of your depth. Isn't that right?"

Jerry just frowned.

"I think that's right," Fryer replied.

"I don't think you understand how much trouble you're in even now, do you?" Garvey said.

Jerry was suddenly uncomfortably aware of Chandaman standing behind him, and of his own utter vulnerability.

"But I don't think ignorance should ever be bliss," Garvey was saying. "I mean, even if you don't *understand*, that doesn't make you exempt, does it?"

"I haven't a clue what you're talking about," Jerry protested mildly. Garvey's face, by the light of the flashlight, was drawn and pale; he looked in need of a holiday.

"This place," Garvey returned. "I'm talking about *this place*. The women you put in here . . . for my benefit. What's it all about, Coloqhoun? That's all I want to know. *What's it all about?*"

Jerry shrugged lightly. Each word Garvey uttered merely perplexed him more, but the man had already told him ignorance would not be considered a legitimate excuse. Perhaps a question was the wisest reply.

"You saw women here?" he said.

"Whores, more like," Garvey responded. His breath smelled of last week's cigar ash. "Who are you working for, Coloqhoun?"

"For myself. The deal I offered—"

"Forget your fucking deal," Garvey said. "I'm not interested in deals."

"I see," Jerry replied. "Then I don't see any point in this conversation." He took a half-step away from Garvey, but the man's arm shot out and caught hold of his rain-sodden coat.

"I didn't tell you to go," Garvey said.

"I've got business—"

"Then it'll have to wait," the other replied, scarcely relaxing his grip. Jerry knew that if he tried to shrug off Garvey and make a dash for the front door he'd be stopped by Chandaman before he made three paces. If, on the other hand, he didn't try to escape—

"I don't much like your sort," Garvey said, removing his hand. "Smart brats with an eye to the main chance. Think you're so damn clever, just because you've got a fancy accent and a silk tie. Let me tell you something"—he jabbed his finger at Jerry's throat—"I don't give a shit about you. I just want to know who you work for. Understand?"

"I already told you—"

"Who do you work for?" Garvey insisted, punctuating each word with a fresh jab. "Or you're going to feel very sick."

"For Christ's sake—I'm not working for anybody. And I don't know anything about any women."

"Don't make it worse than it already is," Fryer advised him with feigned concern.

"I'm telling the truth."

"I think the man wants to be hurt," Fryer said. Chandaman gave a joyless laugh. "Is that what you want?"

"Just name some names," Garvey said. "Or we're going to break your legs." The threat, unequivocal as it was, did nothing for Jerry's clarity of mind. He could think of no way out of this but to continue to insist upon his innocence. If he named some fictitious employer the lie would be uncovered in moments, and the consequences could only be worse for the attempted deception.

"Check my credentials," he pleaded. "You've got the resources. Dig around. I'm not a company man, Garvey; I never have been."

Garvey's eye left Jerry's face for a moment and moved to his shoulder. Jerry grasped the significance of the sign a heartbeat too late to prepare himself for the blow to his kidneys from the man at his back. He pitched forward, but before he could collide with Garvey, Chandaman had snatched at his collar and was throwing him against the wall. He doubled up, the pain blinding him to all other thoughts. Vaguely, he heard Garvey asking him again who his boss was. He shook his head. His skull was full of ball bearings; they rattled between his ears.

"Jesus . . . Jesus . . . ," he said, groping for some word of defense to keep another beating at bay, but he was hauled upright before any presented itself. The flashlight was turned on him. He was ashamed of the tears that were rolling down his cheeks.

"*Names*," said Garvey.

The ball bearings rattled on.

"Again," said Garvey, and Chandaman was moving in to give his fists further exercise. Garvey called him off as Jerry came close to passing out. The leather face withdrew.

"Stand up when I'm talking to you," Garvey said.

Jerry attempted to oblige, but his body was less than willing to comply. It trembled, it felt fit to die.

"Stand up," Fryer reiterated, moving between Jerry and his tormentor to prod the point home. Now, in close proximity, Jerry smelled that acidic scent Carole had caught on the stairs: it was Fryer's cologne.

"Stand up!" the man insisted.

Jerry raised a feeble hand to shield his face from the blinding beam. He could not see any of the trio's faces, but he was dimly aware that Fryer was blocking Chandaman's access to him. To Jerry's right, Garvey struck a match, and applied the flame to a cigar. A moment presented itself: Garvey was occupied, the thug stymied. Jerry took it.

Ducking down beneath the beam he broke from his place against the wall, contriving to knock the flashlight from Fryer's hand as he did so. The light-source clattered across the tiles and went out.

In the sudden darkness, Jerry made a stumbling bid for freedom. Behind him, he heard Garvey curse; heard Chandaman and Fryer collide as they scrabbled for the fallen flashlight. He began to edge his way along the wall to the end of the corridor. There was evidently no safe route past his tormentors to the front door; his only hope lay in losing himself in the networks of corridors that lay ahead.

He reached a corner, and made a right, vaguely remembering that this led him off the main hallways and into the service corridors. The beating that he'd taken, though interrupted before it could incapacitate, had rendered him breathless and bruised. He felt every step he took as a sharp pain in his lower abdomen and back. When he slipped on the slimy tiles, the impact almost made him cry out.

At his back, Garvey was shouting again. The flashlight had been located. Its light bounced down the labyrinth to find him. Jerry hurried on, glad of the murky illumination, but not of its source. They would follow, and quickly. If, as Carole had said, the place was a simple spiral, the corridors describing a relentless loop with no way out of the configuration, he was lost. But he was committed. Head giddied by the mounting heat, he moved on, praying to find a fire exit that would give him passage out of this trap.

"He went this way," Fryer said. "He must have done."

Garvey nodded; it was indeed the likeliest route for Colquhoun to have taken. Away from the light and into the labyrinth.

"Shall we go after him?" Chandaman said. The man was fairly salivating to finish the beating he'd started. "He can't have got far."

"No," said Garvey. Nothing, not even the promise of knighthood, would have induced him to follow.

Fryer had already advanced down the passageway a few yards, shining the beam on the glistening walls.

"It's warm," he said.

Garvey knew all to well how warm it was. Such heat wasn't natural, not for England. This was a temperate isle; that was why he had never set foot off it. The sweltering heat of other continents bred grotesqueries he wanted no sight of.

"What do we do?" Chandaman demanded. "Wait for him to come out?"

Garvey pondered this. The smell from the corridor was beginning to distress him. His innards were churning, his skin was crawling. Instinctively, he put his hand to his groin. His manhood had shrunk in trepidation.

"No," he said suddenly.

"No?"

"We're not waiting."

"He can't stay in there forever."

"I said *no!*" He hadn't anticipated how profoundly the sweat of the place would upset him. Irritating as it was to let Coloqhoun slip away like this, he knew that if he stayed here much longer he risked losing his self-control.

"You two can wait for him at his flat," he told Chandaman. "He'll have to come home sooner or later."

"Damn shame," Fryer muttered as he emerged from the passageway. "I like a chase."

Perhaps they weren't following. It was several minutes now since Jerry had heard the voices behind him. His heart had stopped its furious pumping. Now, with the adrenaline no longer giving speed to his heels and distracting his muscles from their bruising, his pace slowed to a crawl. His body protested at even that.

When the agonies of taking another step became too much he slid down the wall and sat slumped across the passageway. His rain-drenched clothes clung to his body and about his throat; he felt both chilled and suffocated by them. He pulled at the knot of his tie, and then unbuttoned his jacket and his shirt. The air in the labyrinth was warm on his skin. Its touch was welcome.

He closed his eyes and made a studied attempt to mesmerize himself out of this pain. What was feeling but a trick of the nerve-endings? There were techniques for dislocating the mind from the body and leaving agonies behind. But no sooner had his lids closed than he heard muted sounds somewhere nearby. Footsteps; the lull of voices. It wasn't Garvey and his associates: the voices were female. Jerry raised his leaden head and opened his eyes. Either he had become used to the darkness in his few moments of meditation or else a light had crept into the passageway; it was surely the latter.

He got to his feet. His jacket was dead weight, and he

sloughed it off, leaving it to lie where he'd been squatting. Then he started in the direction of the light. The heat seemed to have risen considerably in the last few minutes: it gave him mild hallucinations. The walls seemed to have forsaken verticality, the air to have traded transparency for a shimmering aurora.

He turned a corner. The light brightened. Another corner, and he was delivered into a small tiled chamber, the heat of which took his breath away. He gasped like a stranded fish and peered across the chamber—the air thickening with every pulse-beat—at the door on the far side. The yellowish light through it was brighter still, but he could not summon the will to follow it a yard farther; the heat here had defeated him. Sensing that he was within an ace of unconsciousness, he put his hand out to support himself, but his palm slid on the slick tiles, and he fell, landing on his side. He could not prevent a shout spilling from him.

Groaning his misery, he tucked his legs up close to his body, and lay where he'd fallen. If Garvey had heard his yell, and sent his lieutenants in pursuit, then so be it. He was past caring.

The sound of movement reached him from across the chamber. Raising his head an inch from the floor he opened his eyes to a slit. A naked girl had appeared in the doorway opposite, or so his reeling senses informed him. Her skin shone as if oiled; here and there, on her breasts and thighs, were smudges of what might have been old blood. Not her blood, however. There was no wound to spoil her gleaming body.

The girl had begun to laugh at him, a light, easy laugh that made him feel foolish. Its musicality entranced him however, and he made an effort to get a better look at her. She had started to move across the chamber toward him, still laughing; and now he saw that there were others behind her. These were the women Garvey had babbled about; this the trap he had accused Jerry of setting.

"Who are you?" he murmured as the girl approached him. Her laughter faltered when she looked down at his pain-contorted features.

He attempted to sit upright, but his arms were numb, and he slid back to the tiles again. The woman had not answered his inquiry, nor did she make any attempt to help him. She simply stared down at him as a pedestrian might at a drunk in the gutter, her face unreadable. Looking up at her, Jerry felt his tenuous grip on consciousness slipping. The heat, his pain, and now this sudden eruption of beauty was too much for him. The distant women were dispersing into darkness, the entire chamber folding up like a magician's box until the sublime creature in front of him claimed his attention utterly. And now, at her silent insistence, his mind's eye seemed to be plucked from his head, and suddenly he was speeding over her skin, her flesh a landscape, each pore a pit, each hair a pylon. He was hers, utterly. She drowned him in her eyes, and flayed him with her lashes; she rolled him across her abdomen, and down the soft channel of her spine. She took him between her buttocks, and then up into her heat, and out again just as he thought he must burn alive. The velocity exhilarated him. He was aware that his body, somewhere below, was hyperventilating in its terror; but his imagination—careless of breath—went willingly where she sent him, looping like a bird, until he was thrown, ragged and dizzy, back into the cup of his skull. Before he could apply the fragile tool of reason to the phenomena he had just experienced, his eyes fluttered closed and he passed out.

The body does not need the mind. It has procedures aplenty—lungs to be filled and emptied, blood to be pumped and food profited from—none of which require the authority of thought. Only when one or more of these procedures falters does the mind become aware of the intricacy of the mechanism it inhabits. Coloqhoun's faint lasted only a few minutes, but when he came to he was aware of his body as he had seldom been before: as a trap. Its fragility was a trap; its shape, its size, its very gender was a trap. And there was no flying out of it; he was shackled to, or *in*, this wretchedness.

These thoughts came and went. In between them there were brief sights through which he fell giddily, and still briefer moments in which he glimpsed the world outside himself.

The women had picked him up. His head lolled; his hair dragged on the floor. I am a trophy, he thought in a more coherent instant. Then the darkness came again. And again he struggled to the surface, and now they were carrying him along the edge of the large pool. His nostrils were filled with contradictory scents, both delectable and fetid. From the corner of his lazy eye he could see water so bright it seemed to burn as it lapped the shores of the pool: and something else too—shadows moving in the brightness.

They mean to drown me, he thought. And then: I'm already drowning. He imagined water filling his mouth: imagined the forms he had glimpsed in the pool invading his throat and slipping into his belly. He struggled to vomit them back up, his body convulsing.

A hand was laid on his face. The palm was blissfully cool. *"Hush,"* somebody murmured to him, and at the words his delusions melted away. He felt himself coaxed out of his terrors and into consciousness.

The hand had evaporated from his brow. He looked around the gloomy room for his savior, but his eyes didn't travel far. On the other side of this chamber—which looked to have been a communal shower-room—several pipes, set high in the wall, delivered solid arcs of water onto the tiles, where gutters channeled it away. A fine spray and the gushing of the fountains filled the air. Jerry sat up. There was movement behind the cascading veil of water: a shape too vast by far to be human. He peered through the drizzle to try to make sense of the folds of flesh. Was it an animal? There was a pungent smell in here that had something of the menagerie about it.

Moving with considerable caution so as not to arouse the beast's attention, Jerry attempted to stand up. His legs, however, were not the equal of his intention. All he could do was crawl a little way across the room on his hands and knees, and peer—one beast at another—through the veil.

He sensed that he was sensed; that the dark, recumbent creature had turned its eyes in his direction. Beneath its gaze, he felt his skin creep with gooseflesh, but he couldn't take his eyes off it. And then, as he squinted to scrutinize it better, a spark of phosphorescence began in its substance, and spread—fluttering waves of jaundiced light—up and across its tremendous form, revealing itself to Coloqhoun.

Not it; *she*. He knew indisputably that this creature was female, though it resembled no species or genus he knew of. As the ripples of luminescence moved through the creature's physique, it revealed with every fresh pulsation some new and phenomenal configuration. Watching her, Jerry thought of something slow and molten—glass, perhaps; or stone—its flesh extruded into elaborate forms and recalled again into the furnace to be remade. She had neither head nor limbs recognizable as such, but her contours were ripe with clusters of bright bubbles that might have been eyes, and she threw out here and there iridescent ribbons—slow, pastel flames—that seemed momentarily to ignite the very air.

Now the body issued a series of soft noises: scuttlings and sighs. He wondered if he was being addressed, and if so, how he was expected to respond. Hearing footfalls behind him, he glanced around at one of the women for guidance.

"Don't be afraid," she said.

"I'm not," he replied. It was the truth. The prodigy in front of him was electrifying but woke no fear in him.

"What is she?" he asked.

The woman stood close to him. Her skin, bathed by the shimmering light off the creature, was golden. Despite the circumstances—or perhaps because of them—he felt a tremor of desire.

"She is the Madonna. The Virgin Mother."

Mother? Jerry mouthed, swiveling his head back to look at the creature again. The waves of phosphorescence had ceased to break across her body. Now the light pulsed in one part of her anatomy only, and at this region, in rhythm with the pulse, the Madonna's substance was swelling and splitting. Behind him he heard further footsteps; and now whispers echoed about the chamber, and chiming laughter, and applause.

The Madonna was giving birth. The swollen flesh was opening; liquid light gushing; the smell of smoke and blood filled the shower room. A girl gave a cry, as if in sympathy with the Madonna. The applause mounted, and suddenly the slit spasmed and delivered the child—something between a squid and a shorn lamb—onto the tiles. The water from the pipes slapped it into consciousness immediately, and it threw back its head to look about it; its single eye vast and perfectly lucid. It squirmed on the tiles for a few moments before the girl at Jerry's side stepped forward into the veil of water and picked it up. Its toothless mouth sought out her breast immediately. The girl delivered it to her tit.

"Not human . . . ," Jerry murmured. He had not prepared himself for a child so strange, and yet so unequivocally intelligent. "Are all . . . all the children like that?"

The surrogate mother gazed down at the sac of life in her arms. "No one is like another," she replied. "We feed them. Some die. Others live, and go their ways."

"Where, for God's sake?"

"To the water. To the sea. Into dreams."

She cooed to it. A fluted limb, in which light ran as it had in its parent, paddled the air with pleasure.

"And the father?"

"She needs no husband," the reply came. "She could make children from a shower of rain if she so desired."

Jerry looked back at the Madonna. All but the last vestige of light had been extinguished in her. The vast body threw out a tendril of saffron flame, which caught the cascade of water, and threw dancing patterns on the wall.

Then it was still. When Jerry looked back for the mother and child, they had gone. Indeed all the women had gone but one. It was the girl who had first appeared to him. The smile she'd worn was on her face again as she sat across the room from him, her legs splayed. He gazed at the place between them, and then back at her face.

"What are you afraid of?" she asked.

"I'm not afraid."

"Then why don't you come to me?"

He stood up, and crossed the chamber to where she sat. Behind him, the water still slapped and ran on the tiles, and behind the fountains the Madonna murmured in her flesh. He was not intimidated by her presence. The likes of him was surely beneath the notice of such a creature. If she saw him at all she doubtless thought him ridiculous. Jesus! he was ridiculous even to himself. He had neither hope nor dignity to lose.

Tomorrow, all this would be a dream: the water, the children, the beauty who even now stood up to embrace him. Tomorrow he would think he had died for a day and visited a shower room for angels. For now, he would make what he could of the opportunity.

After they had made love, he and the smiling girl, when he tried to recall the specifics of the act, he could not be certain that he had performed at all. Only the vaguest memories remained to him, and they were not of her kisses, or of how they coupled, but of a dribble of milk from her breast and the way she murmured, "Never . . . never . . ." as they had entwined. When they were done, she was indifferent. There were no more words, no more smiles. She just left him alone in the drizzle of the chamber. He buttoned up his soiled trousers, and left the Madonna to her fecundity.

A short corridor led out of the shower room and into the large pool. It was, as he had vaguely registered when they had brought him into the presence of the Madonna, brimming. Her children played in the radiant water, their forms multitudinous. The women were nowhere to be seen, but the door to the outer corridor stood open. He walked through it, and had taken no more than half a dozen steps before it slid closed behind him.

Now, all too late, Ezra Garvey knew that returning to the Pools (even for an act of intimidation, which he had traditionally enjoyed) had been an error. It had reopened a wound in him that he had hoped was near to healing; and it had brought memories of his second visit there, of the women and what they had displayed to him closer to the surface (memories which he had sought to clarify until he began to grasp their true nature). They had drugged him somehow, hadn't they?; and then, when he was weak and had lost all sense of propriety, they had exploited him for their entertainment. They had suckled him like a child, and made him their plaything. The memories of that merely perplexed him; but there were others, too deep to be distinguished quite, that *appalled*. Of some inner chamber, and of water falling in a curtain; of a darkness that was terrible, and a luminescence that was more terrible still.

The time had come, he knew, to trample these dreams underfoot and be done with such bafflement. He was a man who forgot neither favors done nor favors owed. A little before eleven he had two telephone conversations, to call some of those favors in. Whatever lived at Leopold Road

Pools would prosper there no longer. Satisfied with his night's maneuvers, he went upstairs to bed.

He had drunk the best part of a bottle of schnapps since returning from the incident with Coloqhoun, chilled and uneasy. Now the spirit in his system caught up with him. His limbs felt heavy, his head heavier still. He did not even concern himself to undress, but lay down on his double bed for a few minutes to allow his senses to clear. When he next woke, it was 1:30 A.M.

He sat up. His belly was cavorting again; indeed his whole body seemed to be traumatized. He had seldom been ill in his forty-odd years: success had kept ailments at bay. But now he felt terrible. He had a headache which was near to blinding—he stumbled from his bedroom down to the kitchen more by aid of touch than sight. There he poured himself a glass of milk, sat down at the table, and put it to his lips. He did not drink however. His gaze had alighted on the hand that held his glass. He stared at it through a fog of pain. It didn't seem to be *his* hand: it was too fine, too smooth. He put the glass down, trembling, but it tipped over, the milk pooling on the teak tabletop and running off onto the floor.

He got to his feet, the sound of the milk dribbling onto the kitchen tiles awaking curious thoughts, and moved unsteadily through to his study. He needed to be with somebody: *anybody* would do. He picked up his telephone book and tried to make sense of the scrawlings on each page, but the numbers would not come clear. His panic was growing. Was this insanity? The delusion of his transformed hand, the unnatural sensations that were running through his body. He reached to unbutton his shirt, and in doing so his hand brushed another delusion, more absurd than the first.

Fingers unwilling, he tore at the shirt, telling himself over and over that none of this was possible.

But the evidence was plain. He touched a body which was no longer his. There were still signs that the flesh and bone belonged to him—an appendix scar on his lower abdomen, a birthmark beneath his arm—but the substance of his body had been teased (was *being* teased still, even as he watched) into shapes that shamed him. He clawed at the forms that disfigured his torso, as if they might dissolve beneath his assault, but they merely bled.

In his time, Ezra Garvey had suffered much, almost all his sufferings self-inflicted. He had undergone periods of imprisonment; come close to serious physical wounding; had endured the deceptions of beautiful women. But those torments were nothing beside the anguish he felt now. He was not himself! His body had been taken from him while he slept and this changeling left in its place. The horror of it shattered his self-esteem, and left his sanity teetering.

Unable to hold back the tears, he began to pull at the belt of his trousers. Please God, he babbled, please God let me be whole still. He could barely see for the tears. He wiped them away, and peered at his groin. Seeing what deformities were in progress there, he roared until the windows rattled.

Garvey was not a man for prevarication. Deeds, he knew, were not best served by debate. He wasn't sure how this treatise on transformation had been written into his system, and he didn't much care. All he could think of was how many deaths of shame he would die if this vile condition ever saw the light of day. He returned to the kitchen, selected a large meat-knife from the drawer, then adjusted his clothing and left the house.

His tears had dried. They were wasted now, and he was not a wasteful man. He drove through the empty city down to the river and across Blackfriars Bridge. There he parked and walked down to the water's edge. The Thames was high and fast tonight, the tops of the waters were whipped white.

Only now, having come so far without examining his intentions too closely, did fear of extinction give him pause. He was a wealthy and influential man; were there not other routes out of this ordeal other than the one he had come headlong to? Pill peddlars who could reverse the lunacy that had seized his cells; surgeons who might slice off the offending parts and knit his lost self back together again? But how long would such solutions last? Sooner or later, the process would begin again: he knew it. He was beyond help.

A gust of wind blew spume up off the water. It rained against his face, and the sensation finally broke the seal on his forgetfulness. At last he remembered it all: the shower room, the spouts from the severed pipes beating on the floor, the heat, the women laughing and applauding. And finally, the thing that lived behind the water wall, a creature that was worse than any nightmare of womanhood his grieving mind had dredged up. He had fucked there, in the presence of that behemoth, and in the fury of the act— when he had momentarily forgotten himself—the bitches had worked this rapture upon him. No use for regrets. What was done, was done. At least he had made provision for the destruction of their lair. Now he would undo by self-surgery what they had contrived by magic, and so at last deny them sight of their handiwork.

The wind was cold, but his blood was hot. It came

gushingly as he slashed at his body. The Thames received the libation with enthusiasm. It lapped at his feet; it whipped itself into eddies. He had not finished the job, however, when the loss of blood overcame him. No matter, he thought, as his knees buckled and he toppled into the water, no one will know me now but fishes. The prayer he offered up as the river closed over him was that death not be a woman.

Long before Garvey had awakened in the night, and discovered his body in rebellion, Jerry had left the Pools, got into his car, and attempted to drive home. He had not been the equal of that simple task, however. His eyes were bleary, his sense of direction confused. After a near accident at an intersection he parked the car and began to walk back to the flat. His memories of what had just happened to him were by no means clear, though the events were mere hours old. His head was full of strange associations. He walked in the solid world, but half dreaming. It was the sight of Chandaman and Fryer, waiting for him in the bedroom of his flat, that slapped him back into reality. He did not wait for them to greet him, but turned and ran. They had emptied his stock of spirits as they lay in ambush, and were slow to respond. He was down the stairs and gone from the house before they could give chase.

He walked to Carole's; she was not in. He didn't mind waiting. He sat on the front steps of her home for half an hour, and when the tenant of the top floor flat arrived talked his way into the comparative warmth of the house itself and kept vigil on the stairs. There he fell to dozing, and retraced his steps over the route he'd come, back to the intersection where he'd abandoned the car. A crowd of people were passing the place. *"Where are you going?"* he asked them. *"To see the yatches,"* they replied. *"What yatches are those?"* he wanted to know, but they were already drifting away, chattering. He walked on a while. The sky was dark, but the streets were illuminated nevertheless by a wash of blue and shadowless light. Just as he was about to come within sight of the Pools, he heard a splashing sound, and, turning a corner, discovered that the tide was coming in up Leopold Street. What sea was this? he inquired of the gulls overhead, for the salt tang in the air declared these waters as ocean, not river. Did it matter what sea it was, they returned? Weren't all seas *one* sea, finally? He stood and watched the wavelets creeping across the tarmac. Their advance, though gentle, overturned lamp posts, and so swiftly eroded the foundations of the buildings that they fell, silently, beneath the glacial tide. Soon the waves were around his feet. Fishes, tiny darts of silver, moved in the water.

"Jerry?"

Carole was on the stairs, staring at him.

"What the hell's happened to you?"

"I could have drowned," he said.

He told her about the trap Garvey had set at Leopold Road, and how he'd been beaten up; then of the thugs' presence at his own house. She offered cool sympathy. He said nothing about the chase through the spiral, or the women, or the something that he'd seen in the shower room. He couldn't have articulated it even if he'd wanted to: every hour that passed since he'd left the Pools he was less certain of having seen anything at all.

"Do you want to stay here?" she asked him when he'd finished his account.

"I thought you'd never ask."

"You'd better have a bath. Are you sure they didn't break any bones?"

"I think I'd feel it by now if they had."

No broken bones, perhaps; but he had not escaped unmarked. His torso was a patchwork of ripening bruises, and he ached from head to foot. When, after half an hour of soaking, he got out of the bath and surveyed himself in the mirror, his body seemed to be puffed up by the beating, the skin of his chest tender and tight. He was not a pretty sight.

"Tomorrow, you must go to the police," Carole told him later as they lay side by side. "And have this bastard Garvey arrested."

"I suppose so . . . ," he said.

She leaned over him. His face was bland with fatigue. She kissed him lightly.

"I'd like to love you," she said. He did not look at her. "Why do you make it so difficult?"

"Do I?" he said, his eyelids drooping. She wanted to slide her hand beneath the bathrobe he was still wearing—she had never quite understood his coyness, but it charmed her—and caress him. But there was a certain insularity in the way he lay that signaled his wish to be left untouched, and she respected it.

"I'll turn out the light," she said, but he was already asleep.

* * *

The tide was not kind to Ezra Garvey. It picked up his body and played it back and forth awhile, picking at it like a replete diner toying with food he had no appetite for. It carried the corpse a mile downstream, and then tired of its burden. The current relegated it to the slower water near the banks, and there—abreast of Battersea—it became snagged in a mooring rope. The tide went out; Garvey did not. As the water level dropped he remained depending from the rope, his bloodless bulk revealed inch by inch as the tide left him, and the dawn came looking. By eight o'clock he had gained more than morning as an audience.

Jerry woke to the sound of the shower running in the adjacent bathroom. The bedroom curtains were still drawn. Only a fine dart of light found its way down to where he lay. He rolled over to bury his head in the pillow where the light couldn't disturb him, but his brain, once stirred, began to whirl. He had a difficult day ahead, in which he would have to make some account of recent events to the police. There would be questions asked and some of them might prove uncomfortable. The sooner he thought his story through, the more watertight it would be. He rolled over, and threw off the sheet.

His first thought as he looked down at himself was that he had not yet truly awakened but still had his face buried in the pillow and was merely dreaming this waking. Dreaming too the body he inhabited—with its budding breasts and its soft belly. This was not his body; his was of the other sex.

He tried to shake himself awake, but there was nowhere to wake to. He was here. This transformed anatomy was his—its slit, its smoothness, its strange weight—all *his*. In the hours since midnight he had been unknitted and re-made in another image.

From next door the sound of the shower brought the Madonna back into his head. Brought the woman too, who had coaxed him into her and whispered, as he frowned and thrust, "Never . . . never . . . ," telling him, though he couldn't know it, that this coupling was his last as a man. They had conspired—woman and Madonna—to work this wonder upon him, and wasn't it the finest failure of his life that he would not even hold on to his own sex; that maleness itself, like wealth and influence, was promised, then snatched away again?

He got up off the bed, turning his hands over to admire their newfound fineness, running his palms across his breasts. He was not afraid, nor was he jubilant. He accepted this *fait accompli* as a baby accepts its condition, having no sense of what good or bad it might bring.

Perhaps there were more enchantments where this had come from. If so, he would go back to the Pools and find them for himself; follow the spiral into its hot heart, and debate mysteries with the Madonna. There were miracles in the world! Forces that could turn flesh inside out without drawing blood; that could topple the tyranny of the real and make play in its rubble.

Next door, the shower continued to run. He went to the bathroom door, which was slightly ajar, and peered in. Though the shower was on, Carole was not under it. She was sitting on the side of the bath, her hands pressed over her face. She heard him at the door. Her body shook. She did not look up.

"I saw . . . ," she said. Her voice was guttural; thick with barely suppressed abhorrence. "Am I going mad?"

"No."

"Then what's happening?"

"I don't know," he replied simply. "Is it so terrible?"

"Vile," she said. "Revolting. I don't want to look at you. You hear me? *I don't want to see.*"

He didn't attempt to argue. She didn't want to know him, and that was her prerogative.

He slipped through into the bedroom, dressed in his stale and dirty clothes, and headed back to the Pools.

He went unnoticed; or rather, if anybody along his route noted a strangeness in their fellow pedestrian—a disparity between the clothes worn and the body that wore them— they looked the other way, unwilling to tackle such a problem at such an hour, and sober.

When he arrived at Leopold Road there were several men on the steps. They were talking, though he didn't know it, of imminent demolition. Jerry lingered in the doorway of a shop across the road from the Pools until the trio departed, and then made his way to the front door. He feared that they might have changed the lock, but they hadn't. He got in easily, and closed the door behind him.

He had not brought a flashlight, but when he plunged into the labyrinth he trusted to his instinct, and it did not forsake him. After a few minutes of exploration in the benighted corridors he stumbled across the jacket which he had discarded the previous day; a few turns beyond he came into the chamber where the laughing girl had found him. There was a hint of daylight here, from the pool beyond. All but the last vestiges of that luminescence that had first led him here had gone.

He hurried on through the chamber, his hopes sinking. The water still brimmed in the pool, but almost all its light had flickered out. He studied the broth: there was no movement in the depths. *They had gone.* The mothers; the children. And, no doubt, the first cause. The Madonna.

He walked through to the shower room. She had indeed left. Furthermore, the chamber had been destroyed, as if in a fit of pique. The tiles had been torn from the walls; the pipes ripped from the plasterwork and melted in the Madonna's heat. Here and there he saw splashes of blood.

Turning his back on the wreckage, he returned to the pool, wondering if it had been his invasion that had frightened them from this makeshift temple. Whatever the reason, the witches had gone, and he, their creature, was left to fend for himself, deprived of their mysteries.

He wandered along the edge of the pool, despairing. The surface of the water was not quite calm: a circle of ripples had awakened in it and was growing by the heartbeat. He stared at the eddy as it gained momentum, flinging its arms out across the pool. The water level had suddenly begun to drop. The eddy was rapidly becoming a whirlpool, the water foaming about it. Some trap had been opened in the bottom of the pool, and the waters were draining away. Was this where the Madonna had fled? He rushed back to the far end of the pool and examined the tiles. Yes! She had left a trail of fluid behind her as she crept out of her shrine to the safety of the pool. And if this was where *she* had gone, would they not all have followed?

Where the waters were draining to he had no way of

knowing. To the sewers maybe, and then to the river, and finally out to sea. To death by drowning; to the extinction of magic. Or by some secret channel down into the earth, to some sanctuary safe from inquiry where rapture was not forbidden.

The water was rapidly becoming frenzied as suction called it away. The vortex whirled and foamed and spat. He studied the shape it described. A spiral, of course, elegant and inevitable. The waters were sinking fast now; the splashing had mounted to a roar. Very soon it would all be gone, the door to another world sealed up and lost.

He had no choice: he leaped. The circling undertow snatched at him immediately. He barely had time to draw breath before he was sucked beneath the surface and dragged round and round, down and down. He felt himself buffeted against the floor of the pool, then somersaulted as he was pulled inexorably closer to the exit. He opened his eyes. Even as he did so the current dragged him to the brink, and over. The stream took him in its custody and flung him back and forth in its fury.

There was light ahead. How far it lay, he couldn't calculate, but what did it matter? If he drowned before he reached that place, and ended his journey dead, so what? Death was no more certain than the dream of masculinity he'd lived these years. Terms of description fit only to be turned up and over and inside out. The earth was bright, wasn't it, and probably full of stars. He opened his mouth and shouted into the whirlpool, as the light grew and grew, an anthem in praise of paradox.

Babel's
Children

WHY could Vanessa never resist the road that had no signpost marking it, the track that led to God alone know where? Her enthusiasm for following her nose had got her into trouble often enough in the past. A near-fatal night spent lost in the Alps; that episode in Marrakech that had almost ended in rape; the adventure with the sword-swallower's apprentice in the wilds of Lower Manhattan. And yet despite what bitter experience should have taught her, when the choice lay between the marked route and the unmarked, she would always, without question, take the latter.

Here, for instance. This road that meandered toward the coast of Kithnos: what could it possibly offer her but an uneventful drive through the scrubland hereabouts—a chance encounter with a goat along the way—and a view from the cliffs of the blue Aegean. She could enjoy such a view from her hotel at Merikha Bay, and scarcely get out of bed to do so. But the other highways that led from this crossroads were so clearly *marked:* one to Loutra, with its ruined Venetian fort, the other to Driopis. She had visited neither village, and had heard that both were charming, but the fact that they were so clearly named seriously marred their attraction for her. This other road, however, though it might—indeed probably *did*—lead nowhere, at least led to an *unnamed* nowhere. That was no small recommendation. Thus fueled by sheer perversity, she set off along it.

The landscape to either side of the road (or, as it rapidly became, *track)* was at best undistinguished. Even the goats she had anticipated were not in evidence here, but then the sparse vegetation looked less than nourishing. The island was no paradise. Unlike Santorini, with its picturesque volcano, or Mykonos—the Sodom of the Cyclades—with its plush beaches and plusher hotels, Kithnos could boast nothing that might draw the tourist. That, in short, was why she was here: as far from the crowd as she could conspire to get. This track, no doubt, would take her farther still.

The cry she heard from the hillocks off to her left was not meant to be ignored. It was a cry of naked alarm, and it was perfectly audible above the grumbling of her rented car. She brought the ancient vehicle to a halt and turned off the engine. The cry came again, but this time it was followed by a shot, and a space, then a second shot. Without thinking, she opened the car door and stepped out onto the track. The air was fragrant with sand lilies and wild thyme —scents that the petrol stench inside the car had effectively masked. Even as she breathed the perfume she heard a third shot, and this time she saw a figure—too far from where she stood to be recognizable, even if it had been her husband—mounting the crown of one of the hillocks, only to disappear into a trough again. Three or four beats later, and his pursuers appeared. Another shot was fired but, she was relieved to see, into the air rather than at the man. They were warning him to stop rather than aiming to kill. The details of the pursuers were as indistinct as those of the escapee except that—an ominous touch—they were dressed from head to foot in billowing black garb.

She hesitated at the side of the car, not certain of whether she should get back in and drive away or go and find out what this hide-and-seek was all about. The sound of guns was not particularly pleasant, but could she possibly turn her back on such a mystery? The men in black had disappeared after their quarry, but she pinned her eyes to the spot they had left, and started off toward it, keeping her head down as best she could.

Distances were deceptive in such unremarkable terrain; one sandy hillock looked much like the next. She picked her way among the squirting cucumber for fully ten minutes before she became certain that she had missed the spot from which pursued and pursuer had vanished—and by that time she was lost in a sea of grass-crested knolls. The cries had long since ceased, the shots too. She was left only with the sound of gulls, and the rasping debate of cicadas around her feet.

"Damn," she said. "Why do I do these things?"

She selected the largest hillock in the vicinity and trudged up its flank, her feet uncertain in the sandy soil, to see if the vantage point offered a view of the track she'd left, or even of the sea. If she could locate the cliffs, she could orient herself relative to the spot on which she'd left the car, and head off in that approximate direction, knowing that sooner or later she'd be bound to reach the track. But the hummock was too puny; all that was revealed from its summit was the extent of her isolation. In every direction, the same indistinguishable hills, raising their backs to the afternoon sun. In desperation, she licked her finger and put it up to the wind, reasoning that the breeze would most likely be off the sea, and that she might use that slender information to base her mental cartography upon. The breeze was negligible, but it was the only guide she had, and she set off in the direction she hoped the track lay.

After five increasingly breathless minutes of tramping up and down the hillocks, she scaled one of the slopes and found herself looking not upon her car but at a cluster of whitewashed buildings—dominated by a squat tower and ringed like a garrison with a high wall—which her previous perches had given her no glimpse of. It immediately occurred to her that the running man and his three overattentive admirers had originated here, and that wisdom probably counseled against approaching the place. But then without directions from somebody might she not wander around forever in this wasteland and never find her way back to the car? Besides, the buildings looked reassuringly unpretentious. There was even a hint of foliage peeping above the bright walls that suggested a sequestered garden within, where she might at least get some shade. Changing direction, she headed toward the entrance.

She arrived at the wrought-iron gates exhausted. Only when in sight of comfort would she concede the weight of her weariness to herself: the trudge across the hillocks had reduced her thighs and shins to quivering incompetence.

One of the large gates was ajar, and she stepped through. The yard beyond was paved, and mottled with doves' droppings: several of the culprits sat in a myrtle tree and cooed at her appearance. From the yard several covered walkways led off into a maze of buildings. Her perversity unchastened by adventure, she followed the one that looked least promising and it led her out of the sun and into a balmy passage, lined with plain benches, and out the other side into a smaller enclosure. Here the sun fell upon one of the walls, in a niche of which stood a statue of the Virgin Mary—her notorious child, fingers raised in blessing, perched upon her arm. And now, seeing the statue, the pieces of this mystery fell into place: the secluded location, the silence, the plainness of the yards and walkways—this was surely a religious establishment.

She had been godless since early adolescence and had seldom stepped over the threshold of a church in the intervening twenty-five years. Now, at forty-one, she was past recall, and so felt doubly a trespasser here. But then she wasn't seeking sanctuary, was she? Merely directions. She could ask them and get gone.

As she advanced across the sunlit stone she had that curious sensation of self-consciousness which she associated with being spied upon. It was a sensitivity her life with Ronald had sophisticated into a sixth sense. His ridiculous jealousies, which had, only three months earlier, ended their marriage, had led him to spying strategies that would not have shamed the agencies of Whitehall or Washington. Now she felt not one but several pairs of eyes upon her. Though she squinted up at the narrow windows that overlooked the courtyard, and seemed to see movement at one of them, nobody made any effort to call down to her, however. A mute order, perhaps, their vow of silence so profoundly observed that she would have to communicate in sign-language? Well, so be it.

Somewhere behind her, she heard running feet; several pairs, rushing toward her. And from down the walkway, the sound of the iron gates clanging closed. For some reason her heartbeat tripped over itself, and alarmed her blood. Startled, it leaped to her face. Her weakened legs began to quiver again.

She turned to face the owners of those urgent footsteps and as she did so caught sight of the stone Virgin's head moving a fraction. Its blue eyes had followed her across the yard and now were unmistakably following her back. She stood stock still; best not to run, she thought, with Our Lady at your back. It would have done no good to have taken flight anyway, because even now three nuns were appearing from out of the shadow of the cloisters, their habits billowing. Only their beards, and the gleaming automatic rifles they carried, fractured the illusion of their being Christ's brides. She might have laughed at this incongruity, but that they were pointing their weapons straight at her heart.

There was no word of explanation offered, but then in a place that harbored armed men dressed as nuns a glimpse of sweet reason was doubtless as rare as feathered frogs.

She was bundled out of the courtyard by the three holy sisters, who summarily searched her high and low, as though she had just razed the Vatican. She took this invasion without more than a cursory objection. Not for a moment did they take their rifle sights off her, and in such circumstances obedience seemed best. Search concluded, one of them invited her to re-dress, and she was escorted to a small room and locked in. A little while later, one of the nuns brought her a bottle of palatable retsina, and, to complete this catalogue of incongruities, the best deep-dish pizza she'd had this side of Chicago. Alice, lost in Wonderland, could not have thought it curiouser.

"There may have been an error," the man with the waxed mustache conceded after several hours of interrogation. She was relieved to discover he had no desire to pass as an abbess, despite the garb of the garrison. His office— if such it was—was sparsely furnished, its only remarkable artifact a human skull, its bottom jaw missing, which sat on the desk and peered vacuously at her. He himself was better dressed; his bow-tie immaculately tied, his trousers holding a lethal crease. Beneath his calculated English, Vanessa thought she sniffed the hint of an accent. French? German? It was only when he produced some chocolate from his desk that she decided he was Swiss. His name, he claimed, was Mr. Klein.

"An error?" she said. "You're damn right there's been an error!"

"We've located your car. We have also checked with your hotel. So far, your story has been verified."

"I'm not a liar," she said. She was well past the point of courtesy with Mr. Klein, despite his bribes with the confectionery. By now it must be late at night, she guessed, though as she wore no watch and the bald little room, which was in the bowels of one of the buildings, had no windows, it was difficult to be certain. Time had been telescoped with only Mr. Klein, and his undernourished Number Two, to hold her wearied attention. "Well, I'm glad you're satisfied," she said. "Now will you let me get back to my hotel? I'm tired."

Klein shook his head. "No," he said. "I'm afraid that won't be possible."

Vanessa stood up quickly, and the violence of her movement overturned the chair. Within a second of the sound the door had opened and one of the bearded sisters appeared, pistol at the ready.

"It's all right, Stanislaus," Mr. Klein purred. "Mrs. Jape hasn't slit my throat."

Sister Stanislaus withdrew and closed the door behind him.

"Why?" said Vanessa, her anger distracted by the appearance of the guard.

"Why what?" Mr. Klein asked.

"The nuns."

Klein sighed heavily and put his hand on the coffeepot that had been brought a full hour earlier, to see if it was still warm. He poured himself half a cup before replying. "In my own opinion, much of this is redundant, Mrs. Jape, and you have my *personal* assurance that I will see you released as rapidly as is humanly possible. In the meanwhile I beg your indulgence. Think of it as a game." His face soured slightly. "They like games."

"Who do?"

Klein frowned. "Never mind," he said. "The less you know, the less we'll have to make you forget."

Vanessa gave the skull a beady eye. "None of this makes any sense," she said.

"Nor should it," Mr. Klein replied. He paused to sip his stale coffee. "You made a regrettable error in coming here, Mrs. Jape. And indeed, we made an error letting you in. Normally, our defenses are stricter than you found them.

But you caught us off-guard . . . and the next thing we knew—"

"Look," said Vanessa, "I don't know what's going on here. I don't *want* to know. All I want is to be allowed to go back to my hotel and finish my holiday in peace." Judging by the expression on her interrogator's face, her appeal was not proving persuasive. "Is that so much to ask?" she said. "I haven't *done* anything, I haven't *seen* anything. What's the problem?"

Mr. Klein stood up.

"The problem," he repeated quietly to himself. "Now there's a question." He didn't attempt to answer, however. Merely called: "Stanislaus?"

The door opened, and the nun was there.

"Return Mrs. Jape to her room, will you?"

"I shall protest to my embassy!" Vanessa said, her resentment flaring. "I have rights!"

"Please," said Mr. Klein, looking pained. "Shouting will help none of us."

The nun took hold of Vanessa's arm. She felt the proximity of his pistol.

"Shall we go?" he asked politely.

"Do I have any choice?" she replied.

"No."

The trick of good farce, she had once been informed by her brother-in-law, a sometime actor, was that it be played with deadly seriousness. There should be no sly winks to the gallery, signaling the farceur's comic intention; no business that was so outrageous it would undermine the reality of the piece. By these stringent standards she was surrounded by a cast of experts: all willing—habits, wimples and spying Madonnas notwithstanding—to perform as though this ridiculous situation was in no way out of the ordinary. Try as she might, she could not call their bluff; not break their po-faces, not win a single sign of self-consciousness from them. Clearly she lacked the requisite skills for this kind of comedy. The sooner they realized this error and discharged her from the company, the happier she'd be.

She slept well, helped on her way by half the contents of a bottle of whiskey that some thoughtful person had left in her little room when she returned to it. She had seldom drunk so much in such a short period of time, and when—just about dawn—she was awakened by a light tapping on her door, her head felt swollen and her tongue like a suede glove. It took her a moment to orient herself, during which time the rapping was repeated, and the small window in the door opened from the other side. An urgent face was pressed to it: that of an old man, with a fungal beard and wild eyes.

"Mrs. Jape," he hissed. *"Mrs. Jape.* May we have words?"

She crossed to the door and looked through the window. The old man's breath was two parts stale ouzo to one of fresh air. It kept her from pressing too close to the window, though he beckoned her.

"Who are you?" Vanessa asked, not simply out of abstract curiosity, but because the features, sunburned and leathery, reminded her of somebody.

The man gave her a fluttering look. "An admirer," he said.

"Do I know you?"

He shook his head. "You're much too young," he said.

"But I know *you*. I watched you come in. I wanted to warn you, but I didn't have time."

"Are you a prisoner here too?"

"In a manner of speaking. Tell me . . . did you see Floyd?"

"Who?"

"He escaped. The day before yesterday."

"Oh," Vanessa said, beginning to thread these dropped pearls together. "Floyd was the man they were chasing?"

"Yes. He slipped out, you see. They went after him—the clods—and left the gate open. The security is *shocking* these days"—he sounded genuinely outraged by the situation—"not that I'm not pleased you're here." There was some desperation in his eyes, she thought; some sorrow he fought to keep submerged. "We heard shots," he said. "They didn't get him, did they?"

"Not that I saw," Vanessa replied. "I went to look. But there was no sign—"

"Ha!" said the old man, brightening. "Maybe he did get away then."

It had already occurred to Vanessa that this conversation might be a trap; that the old man was her captors' dupe, and this was just another way to squeeze information from her. But her instincts instructed her otherwise. He looked at her with such affection, and his face, which was that of a master clown, seemed incapable of forged feeling. For better or worse, she *trusted* him. She had little choice.

"Help me get out," she said. "I have to get out."

He looked crestfallen. "So soon?" he said. "You only just arrived."

"I'm not a *thief*. I don't like being locked up."

He nodded. "Of course you don't," he replied, silently

admonishing himself for his selfishness. "I'm sorry. It's just that a beautiful woman . . ." He stopped himself, then began again, on a fresh tack. "I never had much of a way with words."

"Are you *sure* I don't know you from somewhere?" Vanessa inquired. "Your face is somehow familiar."

"Really?" he said. "That's very nice. We all think we're forgotten here, you see."

"All?"

"We were snatched away such a time ago. Many of us were only beginning our researches. That's why Floyd made a run for it. He wanted to do a few month's decent work before the end. I feel the same sometimes." His melancholy train halted, and he returned to her question. "My name is Harvey Gomm; Professor Harvey Gomm. Though these days I forget what I was professor *of*."

Gomm. It was a singular name, and it rang bells, but she could at present find no tune in the chimes.

"You *don't* remember, do you?" he said, looking straight into her eyes.

She wished she could lie, but that might alienate the man—the only voice of sanity she'd discovered here—more than the truth; which was:

"No . . . I don't exactly remember. Maybe a clue?"

But before he could offer her another piece of his mystery, he heard voices.

"Can't talk now, Mrs. Jape."

"Call me Vanessa."

"May I?" His face bloomed in the warmth of her beneficence. "*Vanessa.*"

"You *will* help me?" she said.

"As best I may," he replied. "But if you see me in company—"

"—We never met."

"Precisely. *Au revoir*." He closed the panel in the door, and she heard his footsteps vanish down the corridor. When her custodian, an amiable thug called Guillemot, arrived several minutes later bearing a tray of tea, she was all smiles.

Her outburst of the previous day seemed to have borne some fruit. That morning, after breakfast, Mr. Klein called in briefly and told her that she would be allowed out onto the grounds of the place (with Guillemot in attendance), so that she might enjoy the sun. She was further supplied with a new set of clothes—a little large for her, but a welcome relief from the sweaty garments she had now worn for over twenty-four hours. This last concession to her comfort was a curate's egg, however. Pleased as she was to be wearing clean underwear, the fact that the clothes had been supplied at all suggested that Mr. Klein was not anticipating a prompt release.

How long would it be, she tried to calculate, before the rather obtuse manager of her tiny hotel realized that she wasn't coming back; and in that event, what would he do? Perhaps he had already alerted the authorities; perhaps they would find the abandoned car and trace her to this curious fortress. On this last point her hopes were dashed that very morning, during her constitutional. The car was parked in the laurel-tree enclosure beside the gate, and to judge by the copious blessings rained upon it by the doves had been there overnight. Her captors were not fools. She might have to wait until somebody back in England became concerned and attempted to trace her whereabouts, during which time she might well die of boredom.

Others in the place had found diversions to keep them from insanity's door. As she and Guillemot wandered around the grounds that morning she could distinctly hear voices—one of them Gomm's—from a nearby courtyard. They were raised in excitement.

"What's going on?"

"They're playing games," Guillemot replied.

"Can we go and watch?" she asked casually.

"No."

"I like games."

"Do you?" he said. "We'll play then, eh?"

This wasn't the response she'd wanted, but pressing the point might have aroused suspicion.

"Why not?" she said. Winning the man's trust could only be to her advantage.

"Poker?" he said.

"I've never played."

"I'll teach you," he replied. The thought clearly pleased him. In the adjacent courtyard the players now sent up a din of shouts. It sounded to be some kind of race, to judge by the mingled calls of encouragement, and the subsequent deflation as the winning post was achieved. Guillemot caught her listening.

"Frogs," he said. "They're racing frogs."

"I wondered."

Guillemot looked at her almost fondly, and said, "Better not."

Despite Guillemot's advice, once her attention focused on the sound of the games she could not drive the din from her head. It continued through the afternoon, rising and falling. Sometimes laughter would erupt; as often, there would be arguments. They were like children, Gomm and his friends, the way they fought over such an inconsequential pursuit as racing frogs. But in lieu of more nourishing diversions, could she blame them? When Gomm's face appeared at the door later that evening, almost the first thing she said was: "I heard you this morning, in one of the courtyards. And then this afternoon, too. You seemed to be having a good deal of fun."

"Oh, the games," Gomm replied. "It was a busy day. So much to be sorted out."

"Do you think you could persuade them to let me join you? I'm getting so bored in here."

"Poor Vanessa. I wish I could help. But it's practically impossible. We're so overworked at the moment, especially with Floyd's escape."

Overworked, she thought, *racing frogs?* Fearing to offend, she didn't voice the doubt. "What's going on here?" she said. "You're not criminals, are you?"

Gomm looked outraged. *"Criminals?"*

"I'm sorry . . ."

"No. I understand why you asked. I suppose it must strike you as odd . . . our being locked up here. But no, we're not criminals."

"What then? What's the big secret?"

Gomm took a deep breath before replying. "If I tell you," he said, "will you help us to get out of here?"

"How?"

"Your car. It's at the front."

"Yes, I saw it."

"If we could get to it, would you drive us?"

"How many of you?"

"Four. There's me, there's Ireniya, there's Mottershead, and Goldberg. Of course Floyd's probably out there somewhere, but he'll just have to look after himself, won't he?"

"It's a small car," she warned.

"We're small people," Gomm returned. "You shrink with age, you know, like dried fruit. And we're *old*. With Floyd we had three hundred and ninety-eight years between us. All that bitter experience," he said, "and not one of us *wise*."

In the yard outside Vanessa's room shouting suddenly erupted. Gomm disappeared from the door, and reappeared again briefly to murmur: "They found him. Oh my God, they found him." Then he fled.

Vanessa crossed to the window and peered through. She could not see much of the yard below, but what she could see was full of frenzied activity, sisters hithering and thithering. At the center of this commotion she could see a small figure—the runaway Floyd, no doubt—struggling in the grip of two guards. He looked to be much the worse for his days and nights of living rough, his drooping features dirtied, his balding pate peeling from an excess of sun. Vanessa heard the voice of Mr. Klein rise above the babble, and he stepped into the scene. He approached Floyd and proceeded to berate him mercilessly. Vanessa could not catch more than one in every ten words, but the verbal assault rapidly reduced the old man to tears. She turned away from the window, silently praying that Klein would choke on his next piece of chocolate.

So far, her time here had brought a curious collection of experiences: one moment pleasant (Gomm's smile, the pizza, the sound of games played in a similar courtyard), the next (the interrogation, the bullying she'd just wit-

nessed) unpalatable. And still she was no nearer understanding what the function of this prison was: why it only
had five inmates (six, if she included herself) and all so
old—shrunk by age, Gomm had said. But after Klein's
humiliation of Floyd she was now certain that no secret,
however pressing, would keep her from aiding Gomm in
his bid for freedom.

The professor did not come back that evening, which
disappointed her. Perhaps Floyd's recapture had meant
stricter regulations about the place, she reasoned, though
that principle scarcely applied to her. She, it seemed, was
practically forgotten. Though Guillemot brought her food
and drink he did not stay to teach her poker as they had
arranged, nor was she escorted out to take the air. Left in
the stuffy room without company, her mind undisturbed by
any entertainment but counting her toes, she rapidly became listless and sleepy.

Indeed, she was dozing through the middle of the afternoon when something hit the wall outside the window. She
got up and was crossing to see what the sound was when an
object was hurled through the window. It landed with a
clunk on the floor. She went to snatch a glimpse of the
sender, but he'd gone.

The tiny parcel was a key wrapped in a note. "Vanessa,"
it read, "Be ready. Yours, in *saecula saeculorum*. H.G."

Latin was not her forte; she hoped the final words were
an endearment, not an instruction. She tried the key in the
door of her cell. It worked. Clearly Gomm didn't intend
her to use it *now*, however, but to wait for some signal. *Be
ready*, he'd written. Easier said than done, of course. It
was so tempting, with the door open and the passageway

out to the sun clear, to forget Gomm and the others and make a break for it. But H.G. had doubtless taken some risk acquiring the key. She owed him her allegiance.

After that, there was no more dozing. Every time she heard a footstep in the cloisters, or a shout in the yard, she was up and ready. But Gomm's call didn't come. The afternoon dragged on into evening. Guillemot appeared with another pizza and a bottle of Coca-Cola for dinner, and before she knew it night had fallen and another day was gone.

Perhaps they would come by cover of darkness, she thought, but they didn't. The moon rose, its seas smirking, and there was still no sign of H.G. or this promised exodus. She began to suspect the worst: that their plan had been discovered and they were all being punished for it. If so, would not Mr. Klein sooner or later root out *her* involvement? Though her part had been minimal, what sanctions might the chocolate man take out against her? Sometime after midnight she decided that waiting here for the ax to fall was not her style at all, and she would be wise to do as Floyd had done, and run for it.

She let herself out of the cell, and locked it behind her, then hurried along the cloisters, cleaving to the shadows as best she could. There was no sign of human presence—but she remembered the watchful Virgin, who'd first spied on her. Nothing was to be trusted here. By stealth and sheer good fortune she eventually found her way out into the yard in which Floyd had faced Mr. Klein. There she paused to work out which way the exit lay from here. But clouds had moved across the face of the moon, and in darkness her fitful sense of direction deserted her completely. Trusting to the luck that had got her thus far unarrested, she chose one of the exits from the yard, and slipped through it, following her nose along a covered walkway which twisted and turned before leading out into yet another courtyard, larger than the first. A light breeze teased the leaves of two entwined laurel-trees in the center of the yard; night insects tuned up in the walls. Peaceable as it was, the square offered no promising route that she could see, and she was about to go back the way she'd come when the moon shook off its veils and lit the yard from wall to wall.

It was empty but for the laurel trees and their shadow, but that shadow fell across an elaborate design that had been painted onto the pavement of the yard. She stared at it, too curious to retreat, though she could make no sense of the thing at first; the pattern seemed to be just that: a pattern. She stalked it along one edge, trying to fathom its significance. Then it dawned on her that she was viewing the entire picture upside down. She moved to the other side of the courtyard and the design came clear. It was a map of the world, reproduced down to the most insignificant isle. All the great cities were marked and the oceans and continents crisscrossed with hundreds of fine lines that marked latitudes, longitudes and much else besides. Though many of the symbols were idiosyncratic, it was clear that the map was rife with political detail. Contested borders; territorial waters; exclusion zones. Many of these had been drawn and redrawn in chalk, as if in response to daily intelligence. In some regions, where events were particularly fraught, the land mass was all but obscured by scribblings.

Fascination came between her and her safety. She didn't hear the footsteps at the North Pole until their owner was stepping out of hiding and into the moonlight. She was about to make a run for it, when she recognized Gomm.

"Don't move," he murmured across the world.

She did as she was instructed. Glancing around him like a besieged rabbit until he was certain the yard was deserted, H.G. crossed to where Vanessa stood.

"What are you doing here?" he demanded of her.

"You didn't come," she accused him. "I thought you'd forgotten me."

"Things got difficult. They watch us all the time."

"I couldn't go on waiting, Harvey. This is no place to take a holiday."

"You're right, of course," he said, a picture of dejection. "It's hopeless. *Hopeless*. You should make your getaway on your own. Forget about us. They'll never let us out. The truth's too terrible."

"What truth?"

He shook his head. "Forget about it. Forget we ever met."

Vanessa took hold of his spindly arm. "I will *not*," she said. "I have to know what's happening here."

Gomm shrugged. "Perhaps you should know. Perhaps the whole world should know." He took her hand, and they retreated into the relative safety of the cloisters.

"What's the map for?" was her first question.

"This is where we play," he replied, staring at the turmoil of scrawlings on the courtyard floor. He sighed. "Of course it wasn't always games. But systems decay, you know. It's an irrefutable condition common to both matter and ideas. You start off with fine intentions and in two decades . . . *two decades* . . . ," he repeated, as if the fact appalled him afresh, ". . . we're playing with frogs."

"You're not making much sense, Harvey," Vanessa said. "Are you being deliberately obtuse or is this senility?"

He prickled at the accusation, but it did the trick. Gaze still fixed on the map of the world, he delivered the next words crisply as if he'd rehearsed this confession.

"There was a day of sanity, back in 1962, in which it occurred to the potentates that they were on the verge of destroying the world. Even to potentates the idea of an earth only fit for cockroaches was not particularly beguiling. If annihilation was to be prevented, they decided, our better instincts had to prevail. The mighty gathered behind locked doors at a symposium in Geneva. There had never been such a meeting of minds. The leaders of Politburos and Parliaments, Congresses, Senates—the lords of the earth—in one colossal debate. And it was decided that in the future world affairs should be overseen by a special committee, made up of great and influential minds like my own—men and women who were not subject to the whims of political favor, who could offer some guiding principles to keep the species from mass suicide. This committee was to be made up of people in many areas of human endeavor —the best of the best—an intellectual and moral elite, whose collective wisdom would bring a new golden age. That was the theory anyway."

Vanessa listened, without voicing the hundred questions his short speech had so far brought to mind. Gomm went on.

"And for a while, it worked. It really worked. There were only thirteen of us—to keep some consensus. A Russian, a few of us Europeans, dear Yoniyoko, of course, a New Zealander, a couple of Americans . . . We were a high-powered bunch. Two Nobel Prize winners, myself included—"

Now she remembered Gomm, or at least where she'd once seen that face. They had both been much younger. She a schoolgirl, taught *his* theories by rote.

"—Our brief was to encourage mutual understanding between the powers-that-be, help shape compassionate economic structures and develop the cultural identity of emergent nations. All platitudes, of course, but they sounded fine at the time. As it was, almost from the beginning our concerns were *territorial*."

"Territorial?"

Gomm made an expansive gesture, taking in the map in front of him. "Helping to divide the world up," he said. "Regulating little wars so they didn't become big wars, keeping dictatorships from getting too full of themselves. We became the world's domestics, cleaning up wherever the dirt got too thick. It was a great responsibility, but we shouldered it quite happily. It rather pleased us, at the beginning, to think that we thirteen were shaping the world, and that nobody but the highest echelons of government knew that we even existed."

This, thought Vanessa, was the Napoleon syndrome writ large. Gomm was indisputably insane, but what a heroic insanity! And it was essentially harmless. Why did they have to lock him up? He surely wasn't capable of doing damage.

"It seems unfair," she said, "that you're locked away in here."

"Well, that's for our own security, of course," Gomm replied. "Imagine the chaos if some anarchist group found out where we operated from, and did away with us. *We run the world*. It wasn't meant to be that way, but as I said, systems decay. As time went by the potentates—knowing they had us to make critical decisions for them—concerned themselves more and more with the pleasures of high office and less and less with *thinking*. Within five years we were no longer advisers but surrogate overlords, juggling nations."

"What fun," Vanessa said.

"For a while, perhaps," Gomm replied. "But the glamour faded very quickly. And after a decade or so, the pressure began to tell. Half of the committee are already dead. Golovatenko threw himself out of a window. Buchanan— the New Zealander—had syphilis and didn't know it. Old age caught up with dear Yoniyoko, and Bernheimer and Sourbutts. It'll catch up with all of us sooner or later, and Klein keeps promising to provide people to take over when we've gone, but they don't *care*. They don't give a damn! We're functionaries, that's all." He was getting quite agitated. "As long as we provide them with judgments, they're happy. Well"—his voice dropped to a whisper— "we're giving it up."

Was this a moment of self-realization, Vanessa wondered. Was the sane man in Gomm's head attempting to throw off the fiction of world domination? If so, perhaps she could aid the process.

"You want to get away?" she said.

Gomm nodded. "I'd like to see my home once more before I die. I've given up so much, Vanessa, for the committee, and it almost drove me mad." *Ah*, she thought, *he knows*. "Does it sound selfish if I say that my life seems too great a sacrifice to make for global peace?" She smiled at his pretensions to power, but said nothing. "If it does, it does! I'm unrepentant. I want out! I want—"

"Keep your voice down," she advised him.

Gomm remembered himself and nodded.

"I want a little freedom before I die. We all do. And we thought you could help us, you see." He looked at her. "What's wrong?" he said.

"Wrong?"

"Why are you looking at me like that?"

"You're not well, Harvey. I don't think you're dangerous, but—"

"Wait a minute," Gomm said. "What do you think I've been telling you? I go to all this trouble—"

"Harvey. It's a fine story."

"*Story?* What do you mean, *story?*" he said, petulantly. "Oh . . . I see. You don't believe me, do you? That's it! I just told you the greatest secret in the world, and you don't believe me!"

"I'm not saying you're lying—"

"Is that it? You think I'm a lunatic!" Gomm exploded. His voice echoed around the rectangular world. Almost immediately there were voices from several of the buildings, and fast upon those the thunder of feet.

"Now look what you've done," Gomm said.

"*I've* done?"

"We're in trouble."

"Look, H.G., this doesn't mean—"

"Too late for retractions. You stay where you are—I'm going to make a run for it. Distract them."

He was about to depart when he turned back to her, caught hold of her hand, and put it to his lips.

"If I'm mad," he said, "you made me that way."

Then he was off, his short legs carrying him at a fair speed across the yard. He did not even reach the laurel trees however, before the guards arrived. They shouted for him to stop. When he failed to do so one of the men fired. Bullets ploughed the ocean around Gomm's feet.

"All right," he yelled, coming to a halt and putting his hands in the air. *"Mea culpa!"*

The firing stopped. The guards parted as their commander stepped through.

"Oh, it's you, Sidney," H.G. said to the captain. The man visibly flinched to be so addressed in front of inferior ranks.

"What are you doing out at this time of night?" Sidney demanded.

"Star gazing," Gomm replied.

"You weren't alone," the captain said. Vanessa's heart sank. There was no route back to her room without crossing the open courtyard; and even now, with the alarm raised, Guillemot would probably be checking on her.

"That's true," said Gomm. "I wasn't alone." Had she offended the old man so much he was now going to betray her? "I saw the woman you brought in—"

"Where?"

"Climbing over the wall," he said.

"Jesus wept!" the captain said, and swung around to order his men in pursuit.

"I said to her," Gomm was prattling, "I said, you'll break your neck climbing over the wall. You'd be better waiting until they open the gate—"

Open the gate. He wasn't such a lunatic, after all. "Phillipenko," the captain said, "escort Harvey back to his dormitory."

Gomm protested. "I don't need a bedtime story, thank you."

"Go with him."

The guard crossed to H.G. and escorted him away. The captain lingered long enough to murmur, "Who's a clever boy, Sidney?" under his breath, then followed. The courtyard was empty again, but for the moonlight, and the map of the world.

Vanessa waited until every last sound had died, and then slipped out of hiding, taking the route the dispatched guards had followed. It led her, eventually, into an area she vaguely recognized from her walk with Guillemot. Encouraged, she hurried on along a passageway which let out into the yard with Our Lady of the Electric Eyes. She crept along the wall, and ducked beneath the statue's gaze and out, finally, to meet the gates. They were indeed open. As the old man had protested when they'd first met, security *was* woefully inadequate, and she thanked God for it.

As she ran toward the gates she heard the sound of boots on the gravel, and glanced over her shoulder to see the captain, rifle in hand, stepping from behind the tree.

"Some chocolate, Mrs. Jape?" said Mr. Klein.

"This is a lunatic asylum," she told him when they had escorted her back to the interrogation room. "Nothing more nor less. You've no right to hold me here."

He ignored her complaints.

"You spoke to Gomm," he said, "and he to you."

"What if he did?"

"What did he tell you?"

"I said, What if he did?"

"And *I* said: *What did he tell you?*" Klein roared. She

would not have guessed him capable of such apoplexy. "I want to know, Mrs. Jape."

Much against her will she found herself shaking at his outburst.

"He told me nonsense," she replied. "He's insane. I think you're *all* insane."

"*What* nonsense did he tell you?"

"It was rubbish."

"I'd like to know, Mrs. Jape," Klein said, his fury abating. "Humor me."

"He said there was some kind of committee at work here that made decisions about world politics and that he was one of them. That was it, for what it's worth."

"And?"

"And I gently told him he was out of his mind."

Mr. Klein forged a smile. "Of course, this is a complete fiction," he said.

"Of course," said Vanessa. "Jesus Christ, don't treat me like an imbecile, Mr. Klein. I'm a grown woman—"

"Mr. Gomm—"

"He said he was a professor."

"Another delusion. *Mr.* Gomm is a paranoid schizophrenic. He can be extremely dangerous, given half a chance. You were pretty lucky."

"And the others?"

"Others?"

"He's not alone. I've heard them. Are they all schizophrenics?"

Klein sighed. "They're all deranged, though their conditions vary. And in their time, unlikely as it may seem, they've all been killers." He paused to allow this information to sink in. "Some of them multiple killers. That's why they have this place to themselves, hidden away. That's why the officers are armed."

Vanessa opened her mouth to ask why they were required to masquerade as nuns, but Klein was not about to give her an opportunity.

"Believe me, it's as inconvenient for me as it is irritating for you to be here," he said.

"Then let me go."

"When my investigations are complete," he said. "In the meanwhile, your cooperation would be appreciated. If Mr. Gomm or any of the other patients tries to co-opt you into some plan or other, please report them to me *immediately*. Will you do that?"

"I suppose—"

"And *please* refrain from any further escape attempts. The next one could prove fatal."

"I wanted to ask—"

"Tomorrow, maybe," Mr. Klein said, glancing at his watch as he stood up. "For now, sleep."

Which, she debated with herself when that sleep refused to come, of all the routes to the truth that lay before her, was the *unlikeliest* path? She had been given several alternatives: by Gomm, by Klein, by her own common sense. All of them were temptingly improbable. All, like the path that had brought her here, unmarked as to their final destination. She had suffered the consequence of her perversity in following that track of course; here she was, weary and battered, locked up with little hope of escape. But that perversity was her nature—perhaps, as Ronald had once said, the one indisputable fact about her. If she disregarded that instinct now, despite all it had brought her to, she was lost. She lay awake, turning the available alternatives over in her head. By morning she had made up her mind.

She waited all day, hoping Gomm would come, but she wasn't surprised when he failed to show. It was possible that events of the previous evening had landed him in deeper trouble than even he could talk his way out of. She was not left entirely to herself however. Guillemot came and went, with food, with drink—and in the middle of the afternoon—with playing cards. She picked up the gist of five-card poker quite rapidly, and they passed a contented hour or two playing, while the air carried shouts from the courtyard where the bedlamites were racing frogs.

"Do you think you could arrange for me to have a bath, or at least a shower?" she asked him when he came for her dinner tray that evening. "It's getting so that I don't like my own company."

He actually smiled as he responded. "I'll find out for you."

"Would you?" she gushed. "That's very kind."

He returned an hour later to tell her that dispensation had been sought and granted; would she like to accompany him to the showers?

"Are you going to scrub my back?" she casually inquired.

Guillemot's eyes flickered with panic at the remark, and his ears flushed beetroot red. "Please follow me," he said. Obediently, she followed, trying to keep a mental picture of their route should she want to retrace it later without her custodian.

The facilities he brought her to were far from primitive, and she regretted, walking into the mirrored bathroom, that actually washing was not high on her list of priorities. Never mind; cleanliness was for another day.

"I'll be outside the door," Guillemot said.

"That's reassuring," she replied, offering him a look she trusted he would interpret as promising, and closed the door. Then she ran the shower as hot as it would go, until steam began to cloud the room, and went down on her hands and knees to soap the floor. When the bathroom was sufficiently veiled and the floor sufficiently slick, she called Guillemot. She might have been flattered by the speed of his response, but she was too busy stepping behind him as he fumbled in the steam, and giving him a hefty push. He slid on the floor, and stumbled against the shower, yelping as scalding water met his scalp. His automatic rifle clattered to the floor, and by the time he was righting himself she had it in her hand, and pointed at his torso, a substantial target. Though she was no sharpshooter and her hands were trembling, a blind woman couldn't have missed at such a range; she knew it, and so did Guillemot. He put his hands up.

"Don't shoot."

"If you move a muscle—"

"Please . . . don't shoot."

"Now . . . you're going to take me to Mr. Gomm and the others. Quickly and quietly."

"Why?"

"Just take me," she said, gesturing with the rifle that he should lead the way out of the bathroom. "And if you try to do anything clever, I'll shoot you in the back," she said. "I know it's not very manly, but then I'm not a man. I'm just an unpredictable woman. So treat me very carefully."

"Yes."

He did as he was told, meekly, leading her out of the building and through a series of passageways that took them—or so she guessed—toward the bell tower and the complex that clustered about it. She had always assumed this, the heart of the fortress, to be a chapel. She could not have been more wrong. The outer shell might be tiled roof and whitewashed walls, but that was merely a facade; they stepped over the threshold into a concrete maze more reminiscent of a bunker than a place of worship. It briefly occurred to her that the place had been built to withstand a nuclear attack, an impression reinforced by the fact that the corridors all led *down*. If this was an asylum, it was built to house some rare lunatics.

"What is this place?" she asked Guillemot.

"We call it the Boudoir," he said. "It's where everything happens."

There was little happening at present; most of the offices off the corridors were in darkness. In one room a computer calculated its chances of independent thought, unattended; in another a telex machine wrote love letters to itself. They descended into the bowels of the place unchallenged, until, rounding a corner, they came face to face with a woman on her hands and knees, scrubbing the linoleum. The encounter startled both parties, and Guillemot was swift to take the initiative. He knocked Vanessa sideways against the wall and ran for it. Before she had time to get him in her sights, he was gone.

She cursed herself. It would be moments only before alarm bells started to ring and guards came running. She was lost if she stayed where she was. The three exits from this hallway looked equally uncompromising, so she simply made for the nearest, leaving the cleaner to stare after her. The route she took proved to be another adventure. It led her through a series of rooms, one of which was lined with dozens of clocks, all showing different times; the next of which contained upward of fifty black telephones; the third and largest was lined on every side with television screens. They rose, one upon another, from floor to ceiling. All but one was blank. The exception was showing what she first took to be a mud-wrestling contest but was in fact a poorly reproduced pornographic film. Sitting watching it, sprawled on a chair with a beer can balanced on his stomach, was a mustachioed nun. He stood up as she entered: caught in the act. She pointed the rifle at him.

"I'm going to shoot you dead," she told him.

"Shit."

"Where's Gomm and the others?"

"What?"

"Where are they?" she demanded. *"Quickly!"*

"Down the hall. Turn left and left again," he said. Then added, "I don't want to die."

"Then sit down and shut up," she replied.

"Thank God," he said.

"Why don't you?" she told him. As she backed out of the room he fell down on his knees, while the mud wrestlers cavorted behind him.

Left and left again. The directions were fruitful: they led her to a series of rooms. She was just about to knock on one of the doors when the alarm sounded. Throwing caution to the wind, she pushed all the doors open. Voices from within complained at being awakened and asked what the alarm was ringing for. In the third room she found Gomm. He grinned at her.

"Vanessa," he said, bounding out into the corridor. He

was wearing a long vest and nothing else. "You came, eh? *You came!*"

The others were appearing from their rooms, bleary with sleep. Ireniya, Floyd, Mottershead, Goldberg. She could believe, looking at their raddled faces, that they indeed had four hundred years between them.

"Wake up, you old buggers," Gomm said. He had found a pair of trousers and was pulling them on.

"The alarm's ringing," one commented. His hair, which was bright white, was almost at his shoulders.

"They'll be here soon," Ireniya said.

"No matter," Gomm replied.

Floyd was already dressed. "I'm ready," he announced.

"But we're outnumbered," Vanessa protested. "We'll never get out alive."

"She's right," said one, squinting at her. "It's no use."

"Shut up, Goldberg," Gomm snapped. "She's got a gun, hasn't she?"

"One," said the white-haired individual. This must be Mottershead. "One gun against all of them."

"I'm going back to bed," Goldberg said.

"This is a chance to escape," Gomm said. "Probably the only chance we'll ever get."

"He's right," the woman said.

"And what about the games?" Goldberg reminded them.

"Forget the games," Floyd told the other. "Let them stew awhile."

"It's too late," said Vanessa. "They're coming." There were shouts from both ends of the corridor. "We're trapped."

"Good," said Gomm.

"You *are* insane," she told him plainly.

"You can still shoot us," he replied, grinning.

Floyd grunted. "I don't want to get out of here *that* much," he said.

"*Threaten* it! *Threaten* it!" Gomm said. "Tell them if they try anything you'll shoot us all!"

Ireniya smiled. She had left her teeth in her bedroom. "You're not just a pretty face," she said to Gomm.

"He's right," said Floyd, beaming now. "They wouldn't dare risk us. They'll have to let us go."

"You're out of your minds," Goldberg muttered. "There's nothing out there for us." He returned to his room and slammed the door. Even as he did so the corridor was blocked off at either end by a mass of guards. Gomm took hold of Vanessa's rifle and raised it to point at his heart.

"Be gentle," he said, and threw her a kiss.

"Put down the weapon, Mrs. Jape," said a familiar voice. Mr. Klein had appeared among the throng of guards. "Take it from me, you are completely surrounded."

"I'll kill them all," Vanessa said, a little hesitantly. Then again, this time with more feeling: "I'm warning you. I'm desperate. I'll kill them *all* before you shoot me."

"I see," said Klein quietly. "And why should you assume that I give a damn whether you kill them or not? They're insane. I told you that: all lunatics, killers . . ."

"We both know that isn't true," said Vanessa, gaining confidence from the anxiety on Klein's face. "I want the front gates opened and the key in the ignition of my car. If you try anything stupid, Mr. Klein, I will systematically shoot these hostages. Now dismiss your bully-boys and do as I say."

Mr. Klein hesitated, then signaled a general withdrawal.

Gomm's eyes glittered. "Nicely done," he whispered.

"Why don't you lead the way?" Vanessa suggested. Gomm did as he was instructed, and her small party snaked their way out past the massed clocks and telephones and video screens. Every step they took Vanessa expected a bullet to find her, but Mr. Klein was clearly too concerned for the health of the ancients to risk calling her bluff. They reached the open air without incident.

The guards were in evidence outside, though attempting to stay out of sight. Vanessa kept the rifle trained on the four captives as they headed through the yards to where her car was parked. The gates had been opened.

"Gomm," she whispered. "Open the car doors."

Gomm did so. He had said that age had shrunk them all, and perhaps it was true, but there were five of them to fit into the small vehicle, and it was tightly packed. Vanessa was the last to get in. As she ducked to slide into the driving seat a shot rang out, and she felt a blow to her shoulder. She dropped the rifle.

"Bastards," said Gomm.

"Leave her," somebody piped up in the back, but Gomm was already out of the car and bundling her into the back beside Floyd. He then slid into the driving seat himself and started the engine.

"Can you drive?" Ireniya demanded.

"Of course I can bloody drive!" he retorted, and the car jerked forward through the gates, the gears grating.

Vanessa had never been shot before, and hoped—if she survived this episode—to avoid its happening again. The wound in her shoulder was bleeding badly. Floyd did his best to stanch the wound, but Gomm's driving made any really constructive help practically impossible.

"There's a track," she managed to tell him, "off that way."

"*Which way's that way?*" Gomm yelled.

"*Right! Right!*" she yelled back.

Gomm took both hands off the wheel and looked at them.

"*Which is right?*"

"*For Christ's sake—*"

Ireniya, in the seat beside him, pressed his hands back onto the wheel. The car performed a tarantella. Vanessa groaned with every bump.

"I see it!" said Gomm. "I see the track!" He revved the car up, his foot slammed down on the accelerator.

One of the back doors, which had been inadequately secured, flipped open and Vanessa almost fell out. Mottershead, reaching over Floyd, yanked her back to safety, but before they could close the door it met the boulder that marked the convergence of the two tracks. The car bucked as the door was torn off its hinges.

"We needed more air in here," said Gomm, and drove on.

Theirs was not the only engine disturbing the Aegean night. There were lights behind them, and the sound of hectic pursuit. With Guillemot's rifle left in the convent, they had no sudden death to bargain with, and Klein knew it.

"Step on it!" Floyd said, grinning from ear to ear. "They're coming after us."

"I'm going as fast as I can," Gomm insisted.

"Turn off the lights," Ireniya suggested. "It'll make us less of a target."

"Then I won't be able to see the track," Gomm complained over the roar of the engine.

"So what? You're not driving on it anyhow."

Mottershead laughed, and so—against her better instincts—did Vanessa. Maybe the loss of blood was making her irresponsible, but she couldn't help herself. Four Methuselahs and herself in a three-door car driving around in the dark: only a madman would have taken this seriously. And *there* was the final and incontestable proof that these people weren't the lunatics Klein had marked them as, for they saw the humor in it too. Gomm had even taken to singing as he drove: snatches of Verdi, and a falsetto rendering of "Over the Rainbow."

And if—as her dizzied mind had concluded—these were creatures as sane as herself, then what of the tale that Gomm had told? Was that true too? Was it possible that Armageddon had been kept at bay by these few giggling geriatrics?

"They're gaining on us!" Floyd said. He was on his knees on the back seat, peering out of the window.

"We're not going to make it," Mottershead observed, his laughter barely abating. "We're all going to die."

"There!" Ireniya yelled. "There's another track! Try that! Try that!"

Gomm swung the wheel, and the car almost tipped over as it swung off the main track and followed this new route. With the lights extinguished it was impossible to see more than a glimmer of the road ahead, but Gomm's style was not about to be cramped by such minor considerations. He revved the car until the engine fairly screeched. Dust was flung up and through the gap where the door had been; a goat fled from the path ahead, avoiding death by seconds.

"Where are we going?" Vanessa yelled.

"Haven't a clue," Gomm returned. "Have you?"

Wherever they were heading, they were going at a fair speed. This track was flatter than the one they'd left, and Gomm was taking full advantage of the fact. Again, he'd taken to singing.

Mottershead was leaning out of the window on the far side of the car, his hair streaming, watching for their pursuers.

"We're losing them!" he howled triumphantly. "We're losing them!"

A common exhilaration seized all the travelers now, and they began to sing along with H.G. They were singing so loudly that Gomm couldn't hear Mottershead inform him that the road ahead seemed to disappear. Indeed H.G. was not aware that he had driven the car over the cliff until the vehicle took a nosedive and the sea came up to meet them.

"Mrs. Jape? Mrs. Jape?"

Vanessa woke unwillingly. Her head hurt, her arm hurt. There had been some terrible times recently, though it took her a while to remember the substance of them. Then the memories came back. The car pitching over the cliff; the cold sea rushing in through the open door; the frantic cries around her as the vehicle sank. She had struggled free, only half conscious, vaguely aware that Floyd was floating up beside her. She had said his name, but he had not answered. She said it again, now.

"Dead," said Mr. Klein. "They're all dead."

"Oh my God," she murmured. She was looking not at his face but at a chocolate stain on his waistcoat.

"Never mind them now," he insisted.

"Never mind?"

"There's more important business, Mrs. Jape. You must get up, and quickly."

The urgency in Klein's voice brought Vanessa to her feet. "Is it morning?" she said. There were no windows in the room they occupied. This was the Boudoir, to judge by its concrete walls.

"Yes, it's morning," Klein replied impatiently. "Now, will you come with me? I have something to show you." He opened the door and they stepped out into the grim corridor. A little way ahead it sounded as if a major argument was going on; dozens of raised voices, imprecations and pleadings.

"What's happening?"

"They're warming up for the Apocalypse," he replied, and led the way into the room where Vanessa had last seen the mud wrestlers. Now all the video screens were buzzing and each displayed a different interior. There were war rooms and presidential suites, cabinet offices and halls of congress. In every one of them, somebody was shouting.

"You've been unconscious two full days," Klein told her, as if this went some way to explaining the cacophony. Her head ached. She looked from screen to screen: from Washington to Hamburg to Sydney to Rio de Janeiro. Everywhere around the globe the mighty were waiting for news. But the oracles were dead.

"They're just performers," Klein said, gesturing at the shouting screens. "They couldn't run a three-legged race, never mind the world. They're getting hysterical, and their button fingers are starting to itch."

"What am I supposed to do about it?" Vanessa returned. This tower of Babel depressed her. "I'm no strategist."

"Neither were Gomm and the others. They might have been, once upon a time, but things soon fell apart."

"Systems decay," she said.

"Isn't *that* the truth. By the time I came here half the committee were already dead. And the rest had lost all interest in their duties—"

"But they still provided judgments, as H.G. said?"

"Oh yes."

"They ruled the world?"

"After a fashion," Klein replied.

"What do you mean: after a fashion?"

Klein looked at the screens. His eyes seemed to be on the verge of spilling tears.

"Didn't he explain? They played *games*, Mrs. Jape. When they became bored with sweet reason and the sound of their own voices, they gave up debate and took to flipping coins."

"No."

"And racing frogs of course. That was always a favorite."

"But the governments—" she protested, "—surely they didn't just accept . . . "

"You think they care?" Klein said, "As long as they're in the public eye what does it matter to them what verbiage they're spouting, or how it was arrived at?"

Her head spun. "All *chance?*" she said.

"Why not? It has a very respectable tradition. Nations have fallen on decisions divined from the entrails of sheep."

"It's preposterous."

"I agree. But I ask you, in all honesty, is it any more terrifying than leaving the power in *their* hands?" He pointed to the rows of irate faces. Democrats sweating that the morrow would find them without causes to espouse or applause to win; despots in terror that without instruction their cruelties would lose favor and be overturned. One premier seemed to have suffered a bronchial attack and was being supported by two of his aides; another clutched a revolver and was pointing it at the screen, demanding satisfaction. A third was chewing his toupee. Were these the finest fruit of the political tree, babbling, bullying, cajoling idiots, driven to apoplexy because nobody would tell them which way to jump? There wasn't a man or woman among them Vanessa would have trusted to guide her across the road.

"Better the frogs," she murmured, bitter thought that it was.

The light in the courtyard, after the dead illumination of the bunker, was dazzlingly bright, but Vanessa was pleased to be out of earshot of the stridency within. They would find a new committee very soon, Klein had told her as they made their way out into the open air: it would be a matter of weeks only before equilibrium was restored. In the meanwhile, the earth could be blown to smithereens by the desperate creatures she had just seen. They needed *judgments,* and quickly.

"Goldberg is still alive," Klein said. "And he will go on with the games; but it takes two to play."

"Why not you?"

"Because he hates me. Hates all of us. He says that he'll only play with you."

Goldberg was sitting under the laurel trees, playing patience. It was a slow business. His shortsightedness required him to bring each card to within three inches of his nose to read it, and by the time he had got to the end of the line he had forgotten those cards at the beginning.

"She's agreed," said Klein. Goldberg didn't look up from his game. "I said, *'she's agreed.'* "

"I'm blind, not deaf," Goldberg told Klein, still perusing the cards. When he eventually looked up it was to squint at Vanessa. "I told them it would end badly," he said softly, and Vanessa knew that beneath this show of fatalism he felt the loss of his companions acutely. "I said from the beginning, we were here to stay. No use to escape." He shrugged, and returned to the cards. "What's to escape *to?* The world's changed. I know. We changed it."

"It wasn't so bad," Vanessa said.

"The world?"

"The way they died."

"Ah."

"We were enjoying ourselves, until the last minute."

"Gomm was such a sentimentalist," Goldberg said. "We never much liked each other."

A large frog jumped into Vanessa's path. The movement caught Goldberg's eye.

"Who is it?" he said.

"Who is it?"

The creature regarded Vanessa's foot balefully. "Just a frog," she replied.

"What does it look like?"

"It's fat," she said. "With three dots on its back."

"That's Israel," he told her. "Don't tread on him."

"Could we have some decisions by noon?" Klein butted in. "Particularly the Gulf situation, and the Mexican dispute, and—"

"Yes, yes, yes," said Goldberg. "Now go away."

"We could have another Bay of Pigs—"

"You're telling me nothing I don't know. Go! You're disturbing the nations." He peered at Vanessa. "Well, are you going to sit down or not?"

She sat.

"I'll leave you to it," Klein said, and retreated.

Goldberg had begun to make a sound in his throat— *"kek-kek-kek"*—imitating the voice of a frog. In response, there came a croaking from every corner of the courtyard. Hearing the sound, Vanessa stifled a smile. Farce, she had told herself once before, had to be played with a straight face, as though you believed every outrageous word. Only tragedy demanded laughter; and that, with the aid of the frogs, they might yet prevent.

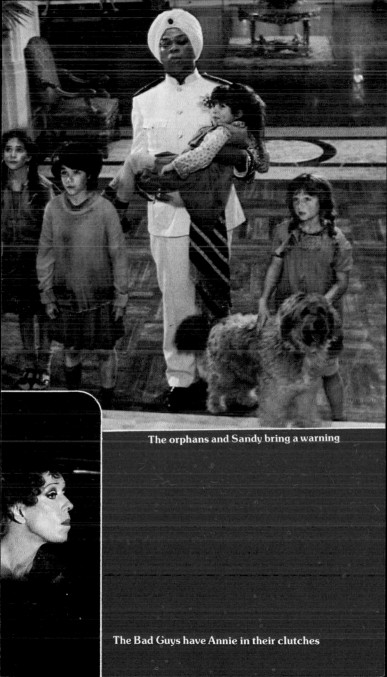

The orphans and Sandy bring a warning

The Bad Guys have Annie in their clutches

Leapin' Lizards!
Annie and
her rescuer

Together Forever,
Annie and her 'Daddy'

His energies flowed strongly during those hours, and Miss Farrell, being young, had learned to conquer her own weariness and keep pace with his output.

Slipping quietly down the corridor, Annie opened the door only wide enough for Sandy and her to wriggle inside. If Warbucks saw them come in, he gave no sign, but Grace raised her head and placed one admonishing finger on her lips. Annie nodded; she hadn't come for conversation, only to be near other human beings and hear the sound of voices. She didn't mind being invisible, and she kept a low profile as she and Sandy edged their way to the big leather chair in the corner, and crept into it, snuggling down together, Annie feeling safe at last, although Sandy still appeared nervous.

Oliver Warbucks was dictating at a rapid pace, and Grace Farrell's pencil was fairly flying over the pages of her steno book.

". . . In conclusion, because your country has raised its voice loud and clear for freedom and democracy," he was saying, "I will extend to you a credit line for the acquisition of thirty-five fighter planes. They come with a year's supply of spare parts, ammunition and advisers . . . What's this?"

Annie opened her eyes to find Warbucks glaring at her and Sandy, Grace looking apologetic.

"Sandy's not used to sleeping in a room all by himself," explained Annie almost truthfully.

As if to corroborate her statement, Sandy gave a low whine and a growl. The hairs on his spine and the back of his neck were quite stiff.

"Makes him nervous," said Annie, stroking him, feeling the tension in the muscles of his shoulders and neck.

At this, Sandy leaped from the chair, still growling. His eyes were fixed on the windows, the tall French windows of Warbucks' study, which opened onto a stone balcony outside. Now he broke into a series of short, loud barks.

Warbucks glared at Grace in exasperation. These interruptions were all her fault! "Where were we?"

"Ammunition and advisers, sir," read Grace Farrell from her notes.

"Are you getting a lot done?" inquired Annie in a friendly voice. Despite Warbucks' gruffness, despite his preoccupations with business and power, there was something about him she liked very much, something she couldn't put a name to, but which made her sorry to be leaving him in the morning.

Oliver Warbucks turned to the little girl with the freckled face who would insist on talking while he was dictating. At the same time, that scruffy little dog of hers broke into furious barks, all of them noisily directed at the French windows, which were, of course, closed.

"I'd get more done if some people . . ." he began, then saw the look in Annie's eyes and softened his voice and his words, ". . . if Roosevelt would leave me alone. Six phone calls since I got home."

"What's he want?" asked Annie, thrilled.

"My support for the New Deal. It's laughable," scoffed Warbucks.

"He *is* the president," Annie pointed out.

Great jumping Jehoshaphat! Was the child a Democrat on top of everything else? How could Miss Farrell have . . . ?

Now Sandy's barking was incessant and frantic, and Warbucks gave up. "Punjab!" he roared, wanting the dog taken away at once.

What happened next was too fast and too furious and too confusing to sort out right away. At his command, Punjab and the Asp rushed into the room, but instead of grabbing at Sandy, they flew past him, toward the French windows. There was a smashing sound and the tinkle of glass as a round black bomb, its fuse lit, flew through the window, hit the floor and began to roll toward Warbucks. The Asp made a dive for the bomb, snatched it up and threw it in a lateral pass to Punjab, who nearly fumbled it but recovered and dashed with it out of the room. The Asp threw open the French windows to catch a departing glimpse of the wild-eyed bearded anarchist disappearing over the balcony. At once, Sandy leaped through the windows and after the radical.

Through all of this commotion, Oliver Warbucks didn't miss a beat. Although Annie and Grace ran to the door after Punjab, Warbucks didn't stir. With a sigh of exasperation at all the commotion, he picked up the microphone to his dictating machine and switched it on.

"A letter on my personal stationery to Miss Emmeline Bush, Smith College, Northampton, Mass. Dear Emmy . . ."

Outside the door, an unmuffled boom as the bomb exploded harmlessly. Punjab came back, dusting his hands, followed by Annie and Grace. Outside, on the balcony, Sandy and the Asp had their paws and hands full. Sandy had dragged the Red Menace back up the balcony by the cuffs of his pants, but the man was armed to the teeth and putting up quite a fight. Sandy kept his teeth buried in the man's leg, but the Asp couldn't get close enough for a karate chop. However, as soon as Punjab joined them on the balcony, the fight was over, and the glowering, cursing anarchist was marched into the office, subdued.

"It has come to my attention," continued Warbucks into the Dictaphone, "that you have spent the five thousand dollars I gave you to purchase a horse for Madison Square Garden. Emmy, dear, that money was for schoolbooks and next year's tuition. Only my affection for your mother prevents me from being very angry. It is not enough in this uncertain age for a young woman to know nothing but how to set a table and sit a horse. I am willing to subsidize your studies in anthropology, but only if you're willing to study anthropology. Your mother and I lunch regularly every other Saturday at the Plaza. Meet us there. We need to sort this out. Your exasperated Uncle Oliver."

Annie watched wide-eyed as Punjab and the Asp marched Warbucks' would-be assassin through the office, and out to the police. She glanced at Grace, whose face was pale and who was breathing hard, now that the excitement was over. Grace was staring at Warbucks with mingled fear and relief showing strongly on her usually placid features. It suddenly became apparent to Annie that Miss Farrell's constant solicitude for her employer might have little to do with the salary she was paid. Annie looked at Warbucks, but he was still busy with his dictating.

"P.S. I assume you are riding some embarrassing saddle held together with baling wire and safety pins. This is not acceptable equipment for Madison Square Garden. This too must be discussed."

He hung the microphone back on its rack and turned his attention to the pile of letters that needed his signature. Annie, who was just beginning to recover from the ninety seconds of peak excitement, moved slowly to the desk. She was still puzzled.

"What was that all about?"

Warbucks glanced up casually, as though nothing had happened, but one hand dropped below and patted Sandy on the head.

"Not bad, Taffy," he acknowledged, which from Warbucks was the highest possible praise.

"Sandy," corrected Annie automatically. "Was that man trying to kill you?"

Grace came and took Annie by the hand, leading her gently out of the room.

"Who'd want to kill Mr. Warbucks?" asked Annie again. She was completely bewildered; everything had happened so fast, and without a word being spoken in explanation.

"The Bolsheviks," Grace told her. "Mr. Warbucks is the living proof that the American system works."

"The Bolsheviks," whispered Annie, shuddering. The little she had gleaned about them from Miss Hannigan's radio had led the orphans to imagine them with gleaming fangs, horns, and tails. Not to mention bombs. Well, she'd seen the bomb, all right, and she was willing to bet there was a tail under those ragged black clothes. "Leapin' lizards!" she whistled. Then, turning back to him, she asked the billionaire, "You want Sandy to sleep with you, Mr. Warbucks?"

Warbucks' eyes popped open in dismay. "Good Lord, no!" he gasped, showing more anxiety than he had when the bomb came through the window. "I never sleep with a dog if I can avoid it."

Annie nodded and went off to bed, where she curled up with the heroic Sandy and went promptly to sleep, tuckered out from the excitement.

In his office, Oliver Warbucks turned to Grace Farrell and asked quietly, "Shall we resume?"

"Of course, sir," and she took her place at the other side of the desk, her pencil poised over her note pad. She was her usual calm, efficient self again, but there was something unspoken between them. Both of them knew that Annie would not be going back to the Hudson Street Home in the morning, or be traded in for some boy orphan. She'd be finishing out her week.

When Oliver Warbucks did anything, he never did it by halves. The next morning Annie was awakened by a small parade into her bedroom, led by Miss Farrell, and made up of Cecille and Annette carrying large boxes from Best and Company and De Pinna. In them were more clothes than Annie had seen in all of her ten years. Dresses for daytime, crisp with pleats and sailor collars, with smocking and puffed sleeves. Dresses for dinnertime, of rich blue or maroon velvet with lace-edged collars and tiny pearl buttons. And Annie's special favorite, a plain tailored red dress with a set-in belt and a white piqué pilgrim collar. It was the exact color of her old red sweater, and Annie knew she'd be wearing it a lot. There were outfits for riding, snappy little jodhpurs and a velvet-collared jacket of hunting pink. There were tennis dresses for her lessons with Don Budge, short white skirts and sweaters with little white socks to match. There was even a golfing costume, with tiny plus fours, an argyle sweater and a fuzzy cap. There was dainty underwear of cotton batiste, nightgowns with rosebuds embroidered on them, and, for later in the year, a darling little brown tweed coat trimmed in brown velvet, with velvet-trimmed leggings to match, and a little velvet bonnet and muff so dear that Annie gave a squeak of joy when they were unpacked. And there was more, much more.

Annie thought she'd never come to the bottoms of the boxes, so jammed with wonderful things were they. Grace Farrell sat on the edge of Annie's bed as the child went through the mounds of tissue paper. She was enjoying Annie's pleasure almost as much as the little girl was enjoying her new possessions.

"Gee, Miss Farrell, I never seen so many beautiful things in my life!" Then the tiny face clouded. "I hope Miss Hannigan will let me keep some of them. At least the red dress."

Miss Hannigan's name threw a momentary chill over both their hearts. Even though both of them knew this visit was to be short, they'd pushed that knowledge as far away as they could.

"Oh, I'm certain she will, dear," said Miss Farrell comfortingly. *She will if I have anything to say about it,* she thought to herself grimly. Yet, she knew how absurd these luxurious outfits would be in an orphanage, how impractical. She hoped with all her heart that they weren't doing Annie any harm by taking her out of her old life for a week. But just to see the child so happy! Although they'd known each other for only a day, Miss Farrell felt a deep fondness for Annie beginning to grow.

As for Annie, she had never met anybody as sweet or as warm as Grace Farrell. It wouldn't be only the luxury she'd miss, going back to the Hudson Street Home for Girls, it would be the kindly presence of Miss Farrell. And, yes, she'd miss Oliver Warbucks, too. He wasn't quite as scary as she'd been led to picture. Not at all. She remembered the gentle pat and the quiet word of praise he'd given Sandy last night, and she knew there was more of the same buried in him somewhere, just waiting to come out.

Sandy, of course, would miss the luxury. He'd been shampooed and de-flead and was basking in his new cleanliness, a warm breakfast making a comforting lump in his stomach. Who said it was a dog's life?

Breakfast was the first thing on Annie's agenda for today, but when she'd been led down the stairs to the imposing dining room that seated forty, with its sixty-foot-long table set for one, her heart quailed. Mr. Warbucks and Miss Farrell had had their breakfast hours ago, and Annie faced a solitary meal, if you didn't count the footmen waiting on her. She slipped away from the table and ran down the service steps to the huge, warm, bright kitchen, and begged Mrs. Pugh to let her eat there, at the scrubbed pine kitchen table. The kitchen was bustling with activity and good smells—fresh bread baking for lunch, onions being fried. How could Mrs. Pugh refuse her?

So Annie ate her bacon and eggs and whole-wheat toast with orange marmalade and drank her fresh-squeezed grapefruit juice and a tall glass of milk with the best appetite she'd ever had. And even Sandy, after a hairy moment or two with Mrs. Pugh's cat, who wasn't about to share her kitchen with this loutish beast, settled under

Annie's chair, contentedly gnawing a bone. This would set the pattern for her future breakfasts. Lunch she'd take with Miss Farrell, and dinner was served early in her room, but breakfasts were eaten in the kitchen, just as they should always be.

After she finished her meal and had mopped the last bit of egg yolk off her plate with the last bite of toast, Annie wandered through the ground floor of the mansion, marveling at everything she looked at. Of course, she wasn't educated to appreciate art, her eye had never been trained nor her taste formed by experts, but Annie was quick to learn, quick to appreciate, and had a warm feeling for beauty. She stopped to gaze at landscapes by Turner, portraits by Gainsborough, religious paintings by El Greco and Memling, without knowing the first thing about them. Yet she recognized them as unique and special. But the picture that caught her eye and her heart was a soft study of a lovely woman and her little daughter, dressed in matching bonnets and the styles of forty years ago. Their faces were plump and very pretty, and their lips were very red, their eyes a velvet black; they looked alike. The painter, a man named Auguste Renoir, had captured the affection between the two in the casual depiction of the child's arm around her mother's neck, and the mother's caressing glance at her little girl. The picture brought a surprising lump to Annie's throat, she wanted to reach into it and touch them both, even to join them for a few minutes and learn their names. What she wanted most was to have a share in that affection, to feel a mother's arms. She tore herself away from the painting with a promise to come back to it tomorrow.

The library of Oliver Warbucks was like nothing she had ever imagined. It seemed to be two stories high, and books were shelved so close to the ceiling that a little ladder on wheels had to be used to fetch them from the topmost shelves. There must have been twelve or thirteen thousand books in that room with its painted pilasters and marble facings, and all of them were bound in green leather, their titles and authors and the initials O.W. stamped on their spines in gold. Annie was afraid to touch one, much as she longed to.

A long table in the library was covered with newspapers

in twenty-three foreign languages, and picture magazines from all over the world. Annie leafed through these, and the events of the day leaped out at her in pictures. A lot of the photographs had to do with Germany, where a new chancellor had been elected, a man named Adolf Hitler, who dressed his followers in paramilitary style, with brown shirts and armbands. The pictures of Hitler gave Annie a creepy feeling; she couldn't tell why. But she sure didn't like his face.

She put the magazines back on the table and turned her attention to a globe nearly as big as she was, a map of the world that was entirely up to date, with little colored pins stuck in it all over, representing Oliver Warbucks' farflung business empire. His interests spanned the huge globe—oil, rubber, manganese, diamonds, uranium ore, gold, silver, copper, tin, coal, iron, sugar, cocoa, tea, coffee, saffron, silk—there was nothing grown, dug, mined, drilled anywhere in the world that Oliver Warbucks didn't have a share in. The black pins represented his factories, and Annie saw to her astonishment that he had mills and manufactories as far away as Alaska, Hong Kong, Fiji, Rumania, Scotland, and India. Wow! There was so much to see and do, so much to learn, how was she ever going to cram it in, with only a week?

A footman appeared silently in the doorway, asking if Annie would care to join Mr. Warbucks in the swimming pool. Would she! She was up in her room in ten seconds, had changed into her bathing suit in thirty more, and was at poolside fastening on her rubber bathing cap before two minutes had gone by.

Oliver Warbucks was swimming underwater when Annie arrived. Sandy took one horrified look and dived in head-first without hesitation, swimming toward Warbucks and seizing the billionaire's backside in his teeth, hauling him up to the surface in another daring rescue.

"Get your damn dog out of my damn pool!" shouted the billionaire indignantly. The humiliation of being dragged to the surface by a dog!

"He thought you were drowning," called Annie. "Like my suit?" She was very proud of her first bathing suit; it was a bright yellow that set off the color of her hair and her pale skin.

"What? Oh, yes."

"Miss Farrell picked it out," said Annie, sticking one toe into the water.

"That's nice," said Warbucks without much interest. He was concentrating on his backstroke, which needed a little work.

Annie slid into the water and paddled toward the billionaire. "She's got a really good eye, don'tcha think? She really knows what looks good on a person, don'tcha think?" She watched for Warbucks' reaction to her praise of Miss Farrell, but not much was forthcoming. "I mean this looks just about perfect on me, don'tcha think?" It was evident that this line of conversation wasn't getting them anywhere.

But, while Warbucks wasn't actually listening to what Annie was saying, he *was* in fact paying attention to her. To her liveliness, her quick smile, her lack of fear, her obvious intelligence. He swam over next to her, and gave her rubber-capped head an awkward pat, much the same kind as the one he'd given Sandy.

"I never thought I'd get used to a girl," he said in mild astonishment.

"Girls are easier to get used to than boys," replied Annie with some complacence. She was reveling in the pat. "Look how used to Miss Farrell you are. She does all the work around here and you don't even know her first name."

Warbucks uttered a short, barking laugh. "I do. It's Grace," he said, as he swam toward the pool steps. He climbed up and shook the excess water off him, while Annie floated on her back and admired him. He was a man in splendid physical condition, with a barrel chest and a strong pair of legs. He wore an old-fashioned two-piece tank suit of black wool, mixed with something new he was developing, a synthetic called "nylon," which he was certain would revolutionize fabric technology. Nylon dried quickly, due to its molecular construction, and someday every bathing suit in the world would be entirely or partially made of it. Now he reached for his long terrycloth robe.

"She thinks you're the greatest thing since sliced bread," called Annie.

Annie

Warbucks' head jerked around to stare at the child in astonishment. What the devil was she talking about? Miss Farrell? Sliced bread? "I beg your pardon?" he asked, somewhat stiffly.

"I know it's none of my business," Annie went on cheerfully, "but you never notice anything." If she only had a week here, she was going to have to work fast and never mind the consequences.

Warbucks was dazed; he could barely comprehend the significance of what Annie was saying. But he had work to do; there was no time to stand around discussing sliced bread with a ten-year-old. It was with no little relief that he tied the belt of his robe and hurried out of there.

Annie's visit progressed. It even fell into something of a routine. Tennis lessons, a riding lesson, regular meals. Toys and games and books arrived from the stores in profusion, and Annie enjoyed them all. She was enjoying everything, what orphan wouldn't? Sandy was putting on weight and was losing some of that hangdog look. Even his bark was more authoritative.

Annie was making friends. The maids and the footmen loved her. Mrs. Pugh adored her, especially the way she cleaned her plate and asked for more. She took to preparing special goodies for Annie. Poor Annie! She would have preferred a steak or a turkey leg any day, but Mrs. Pugh took to stuffing her with Lobster Thermidor, Frog's Legs Provençale, Sweetbreads in Madeira. But Annie drew the line at Calves' Brains with Caper Sauce, and Mrs. Pugh fried her a hamburger instead.

Even Drake, who relied upon his dignity as head butler to see him through life's crises—and there is no dignity in the world, not a king's or even a pope's, as complete and unassailable as the dignity of a head butler—unbent a little now in Annie's presence, and was once seen to—almost—smile. Sandy, of course, was still beyond the pale as far as Drake was concerned, but at least he didn't make Drake sneeze anymore, now that he was bathed daily.

Although one could never tell what the Asp was thinking, Annie felt that he liked her. In between his duties as chauffeur and bodyguard to Oliver Warbucks, he managed

68

to sandwich sessions with Annie, during which he taught her, swiftly and silently, certain centuries-old secrets of self-defense. How to deliver a deadly blow with the back of one's hand; where the vital points on an enemy's body were; how to come and go so silently as to almost become invisible—all very useful information for a ten-year-old girl.

With Punjab, however, Annie had a very special relationship. They adored each other. He called her Princess. From the very first minute, when he'd taken her hand in his and looked deeply into her eyes, they'd had a very special friendship, this nine-foot-tall Indian and the four-foot-high orphan. It was as though they had been linked together in an earlier life, and knew each other very well. Punjab seemed to know everything in the world—ahead of time—and sometimes, with a magical pass of his huge hands, he did Indian fakir tricks for Annie's delight. The immense power of his huge body turned to gentleness whenever he was with Annie. Sandy, who was still the tiniest bit wary of the Asp, was melted butter where Punjab was concerned.

Annie's affection for Grace, and Grace's for Annie, grew day by day. But that was hardly surprising, since there was a deep maternal streak in Miss Farrell, and a deep need for mothering in Annie. Besides, loving Miss Farrell was no great trick. Who couldn't love a young woman as beautiful and kind as she was? But caring for Oliver Warbucks was an entirely different matter—now *there* was a challenge. Powerful, arrogant, busy all the time, Warbucks scarcely exchanged a word with Annie. The world made heavy demands on his time and energies. Yet, despite all of this, Annie felt closer to Warbucks with every passing day. His second-floor office was the nerve center of the house; sometimes Annie thought it was the nerve center of the entire world. It was Warbucks' command post, and he ran it like a five-star general.

In addition to the latest in office equipment, Warbucks' office boasted a Wall Street ticker-tape machine, and two teletype machines, one connected to the Associated Press and the other for overseas dispatches. News from around the world arrived at once in that office, and Warbucks absorbed it all. It wasn't looking too good for the world these days, and he sometimes wondered how long he'd have to shoulder the burden of failing national economies.

There was a short-wave radio that received marine band signals as well as all the major cities of Europe, and on the wall behind Warbucks' massive walnut desk was a finely detailed map of the world with more of his pins stuck in it. Warbucks worked long, long hours in this room, making decisions that affected history.

Annie loved being with him, in his office, watching him work, and he'd grown accustomed, even in so short a time, to being with her. Something about this orphan child struck a note in the area under his watch chain in the region of the heart. Her independence and fearlessness reminded him of himself, and he had finally gotten over wishing she were a boy. Although Warbucks was used to being regarded with respect and even awe, he valued Annie's respect. Perhaps it was because he sensed that Annie, although too young to grasp the full extent of Warbucks' wealth and influence, cared little for money or power. It was Warbucks' personal power, his charisma if you like, that earned her appreciation. She liked him because he was himself, not because he was the tycoon Warbucks. For him, it was a refreshing change. He sometimes longed to be a little more relaxed, but he wasn't sure exactly how to go about it.

Warbucks was aware that time was passing very quickly, and that Annie's visit would soon be over. Sometimes he saw that fact reflected in Grace Farrell's eyes when she looked at the little girl, and he thought it was too bad, but there it was. A promise was a promise, a week was a week, and that was all there was to it. It had been a more pleasant and less taxing week than he'd imagined, but all things must come to an end, and Oliver Warbucks was a very busy man.

And, thank heaven, there had been no repetition of that uncomfortable conversation about sliced bread.

CHAPTER SIX

And then it was Annie's last day but one. The time had flown by so quickly, and Annie had soaked up so many wonderful memories that she thought she'd have a life-time to take them all out over and over again to relive them. A born optimist, Annie had accepted most of the burdens of her wretched life with cheerful equanimity, cer-tain that tomorrow would bring something better. Now to-morrow had come and was almost gone, and Annie found it hard to be cheerful. She'd always known it had to end, but now that the end was in sight, the thought of Miss Hannigan and the mean and drab discomforts of the Hud-son Street Home for Girls weighed on her heavily. Cer-tainly, she didn't expect life to be all luxury, as it was here at Warbucks', but here she had received attention, respect, and even love, and it was hard to be going back to kicks and cuffs and the scrubbing brushes and the sewing machines, with only baby Molly to love her. And Sandy, what about Sandy? Annie knew they were committed to each other, never to be parted again. But how was she go-ing to sneak him past Miss Hannigan, who had a contract out on Sandy with the sausage factory?

Do you suppose Miss Farrell would adopt Sandy and give him a home? He'd be real good, and he could live downstairs in the kitchen. No, Mrs. Pugh's cat would never allow that. But, after all, he did help save Mr. War-bucks' life, didn't he? But if Miss Farrell gave Sandy a home, that probably meant that Annie would never see him again.

Or Miss Farrell either. Or Mr. Warbucks. Or the Asp, or dear Punjab. Best not to think of that, 'cause it made Annie feel like crying, and Annie never cried.

But on her last day but one, Annie got up extra early,

even before Annette could come in to wake her. She didn't want to waste one precious minute of the little time she had left. She raced through an early-morning swim, managed to hit three back over the net to Don Budge, rode her pony for an hour in the grounds around the mansion, ate breakfast in the kitchen with Mrs. Pugh, and still arrived at Warbucks' office on the dot of ten.

But today it seemed as though neither Miss Farrell nor Mr. Warbucks had any time for a ten-year-old orphan, even one whose tennis game was improving. The World Situation was worsening, and Warbucks was needed every minute. Frantic telephone calls kept coming in from the major cities of the world, as national leaders were turning to Oliver Warbucks for help. The ticker tape was chattering like an excited chimpanzee. Saying "Sell, sell, sell." Warbucks was on the phone ordering his brokers to buy, buy, buy. The teletype machines were going crazy, spitting out long ribbons of paper on which the news from everywhere appeared as soon as it happened.

So Annie found himself ignored. At first, she kept out of the way, sitting in the big green leather chair in the corner, her large blue eyes watching Mr. Warbucks solve the world's problems by telephone. But after a while even that became boring. Still, she was reluctant to go; she loved it here in the busy, important atmosphere of commerce, industry, and politics. If only she had something to do! Sandy, having eaten too much breakfast, was curled up asleep at her feet, while his digestion carried on without him.

Mr. Warbucks was on two telephones at the same time, and the third phone was ringing off the hook. A brace of typists, hired by the hour, was sitting at a pair of typewriters turning out memos, notes, and letters. Grace Farrell had the Dictaphone headset on and was typing Mr. Warbucks' most secret correspondence. Punjab was on guard at the door. The Asp was off heaven knows where doing heaven knows what in his silent manner. Only Annie had nothing to do.

Suddenly, her eye fell on a small desktop model of Oliver Warbucks' latest enthusiasm, his "autocopter," a plump airship with short wings and a huge gyroscopic rotor on its roof. Warbucks and a man named Igor Ivan

Sikorsky were experimenting with it, and Warbucks intended to put it into production within three months; a factory hidden in Wyoming was tooling up for it even now, and nobody in Europe had seen anything like it. It was a craft that didn't need an airfield or even a landing strip; it lifted straight up, hovered, went backwards or forwards, and could land on a dime by coming straight down. The prototype was sitting even now on Warbucks' roof, and the model was sitting on his desk.

Quick as lightning, Annie had the model in her hand and was playing "aeroplane" with it, silently at first, making *"RRRRRRRRRR"* engine noises under her breath. But she was soon caught up in her game, and flying the 'copter noisily around Warbucks' office, around everybody's head. Punjab watched her with delight for a few minutes, then, he, too, joined in the game. Without leaving his post, he waved one hand in the air, and a World War I fighter plane model took off from its stand and began circling the room, its miniature guns blazing. With a whoop of joy, Annie chased it, the autocopter in her hand. Bedlam broke out. The phones kept ringing, the secretaries typing, the dog snoring, the tiny planes barking bullets at each other.

"Ambassador," Warbucks was shouting into one of the phones, "I'm not prepared to bicker over price! That young lunatic, Hitler, is a real threat, whether you see it or not. I make the best fighter in the air. I would advise you either to pay my price or to learn German!"

He slammed down the phone, and the little fighter plane model zoomed low, narrowly missing Warbucks' bald skull. He scowled in annoyance.

"Don't encourage her, Punjab."

Punjab bowed his head obediently and waved two fingers in the air. At once, the little plane flew to its perch and settled there, its guns silent.

Warbucks snatched up the second phone. "Hello? Who is this?" he demanded. "Oh, Wilhelm. Let me call you back."

Annie was now firing on an aircraft carrier model, making the kind of racket only a ten-year-old in a war game can make. Warbucks rested his elbows on the desk and clasped his head in both hands.

Grace leaped to her feet. "Maybe I could take her out, Mr. Warbucks."

"Good idea," nodded Warbucks vigorously. "Annie, where do you want to go?"

Annie turned a shining, excited face to him.

"To Washington," she said with certainty. "To meet President Roosevelt."

Too late, Annie saw that Warbucks' eyes were cold as gray iron and that his jaw was an angry knot framed by a scowl. Roosevelt! That Man in the White House! Warbucks despised him, considering him a traitor to his class and a know-nothing do-gooder. Annie laughed nervously.

"Sorry, sir."

"How about a movie?" asked Grace quickly.

Annie gasped in excitement. She'd never seen a movie, but she'd heard about the miracle of talking pictures. "Pepper went to a movie once, before she came to the orphanage. She said it was swell. And Miss Hannigan goes all the time."

"Splendid!" Warbucks nodded decisively. "Take her to Radio City Music Hall."

Annie's eyes stung and her lower lip trembled a little.

"I thought *you* were gonna take me," she said to Mr. Warbucks.

Warbucks uttered an indulgent laugh. "Me? Annie, you may think Miss Farrell does all the work around here, but it's not entirely true. I'm a busy man. A very busy man."

Annie's face fell. "I know," she said quietly. "I didn't mean to get in the way, Mr. Warbucks. Nobody has to take me anywhere. I'll go practice my backhand." She turned and headed slowly for the door, Grace biting her lip as she watched Annie go. But she didn't dare say anything.

At the door, Annie stopped and threw them a tiny smile.

"Pepper lies a lot. She probably hasn't been to a movie ever either." Her smiled widened a little as she looked clearly at Mr. Warbucks.

"Actually, I think it's better when you don't know what you're missing," she declared.

Warbucks felt something move inside him. Not pity; Annie never wanted pity. Not even sympathy. It was more like . . . empathy . . . it moved, was gone, leaving him feeling a little empty.

"Punjab!" he shouted suddenly. "Buy out the eight P.M. show. Let's *all* go to the movies!" He felt suddenly rewarded by the grin that appeared like magic on Annie's freckled face, and, oddly enough, by the smile on Grace Farrell's.

Dinner was early that night so they could make the show. Annie could hardly eat for excitement, and she was so overwhelmed by it all that she was almost silent at the table. But her dancing eyes did the talking for her, and Warbucks, watching her, felt younger than he had in years. He couldn't remember the last film he'd seen, probably a Charlie Chaplin silent movie. The talkies were only three years old; he discovered he was eager to see one.

After dinner, Annie went to Grace Farrell's room to watch her get dressed. In her pink silk slip, she looked very different from the prim young woman in the business suit. For one thing, her waist was thinner and her bosom fuller than appeared in her tailored clothing. And, for another, her hair was down.

Annie had never seen such beautiful hair, silky and thick and a soft golden brown with reddish highlights. She yearned to touch it, and begged Miss Farrell to let her brush it for her. Back at the orphanage, she brushed and combed Molly's hair all the time and because this was Annie's last evening, Grace permitted it. She sat down at her dressing table with Annie standing behind her. For a few minutes, nothing was said. The girl brushed the lovely hair with gentle but sure strokes, and the young woman watched her in the mirror, thoughts sadly on the next morning.

At last, Annie had finished, and Grace took up the pretty handfuls and began to roll them up in her usual neat coiffure.

"Ah, leave your hair down," begged Annie. "It's so pretty."

"Annie, I couldn't," protested Grace with an embarrassed laugh, and stuck the pins quickly into her hair, securing it modestly.

"Miss Hannigan says a man don't look at your brains,"

remarked Annie, provoking a blush from Miss Farrell. Together they went through Grace's clothes closet, looking for something to wear. Grace pulled out hanger after hanger, but Annie kept shaking her head in disapproval. Everything Miss Farrell had was either dark gray, dark blue, dark brown, or tweed, and everything was mantailored! At last, Grace found a light silk dress, demure in cut, but of a lovely soft material, in gunmetal gray. Putting her head to one side, Annie regarded it judiciously for a minute, then gave a reluctant nod of approval. She would much rather have had red.

But once the dress was on, Annie uttered a little admiring whistle. The demurely cut little nothing of a dress clung to Miss Farrell's slender shape in all the right places, and the slivery gray color set off the gray of her eyes and the roses that had suddenly appeared in her cheeks. Annie made Miss Farrell take a good long look at herself in the mirror, and both of them liked what they saw.

They stood side by side, looking at their reflections in the glass. There was not the slightest resemblance between them, and yet they looked somehow right together. As if they belonged together, the skinny little redheaded girl and the silvery gray color set off the gray of her eyes and Grace gave Annie's hand an extra squeeze as they left her room and went down to join Oliver Warbucks in the library.

Warbucks was sipping a rare Napoleon brandy and contemplating the pins in the globe as they came in the door, and his startled glance at Miss Farrell gave Annie a stab of pleasure. He was noticing her at last, as a person, not as an efficient piece of office equipment. He was noticing for the first time that Grace Farrell was one very pretty lady, and Annie felt partly responsible. She was very proud; her week here might have some good effects after all.

But now it was magic time, time to go to the movies. The Dusenberg was waiting at the front door with the Asp at the wheel. Punjab was ready to escort them, and even Sandy was wearing a brand-new leather collar. In her red dress and black Mary-Jane shoes, Annie felt quite the lady as Punjab stepped back to let her pass. They all climbed into the car and the Asp stepped on the gas.

It was a beautiful evening, the Dusenberg's convertible

top was down, and before they knew it they were pulling
up to the brand-new Radio City Music Hall, showcase of
the stars and home of the famous stage show featuring the
Rockettes. Or so it said on the marquee, and Annie for
one was ready to believe it. Huge signs posted in the lobby
informed the public that the eight o'clock show was completely sold out. It was now three minutes to eight. The
ticket man accepted their tickets with a bow.

When they stepped into the lobby, Annie's heart did a
little jump of sheer surprise. Even the incredible luxury of
Oliver Warbucks' mansion hadn't prepared her for the
vast sweep of the Radio City Music Hall lobby. It was four
stories high, and totally carpeted in what felt like velvet
underfoot. Across the vast expanse of carpet, a staircase
wound up to the higher floors, but of course there were
elevators to take people as high as they wanted to go, or at
least as high as their tickets entitled them to go. It was all
decorated in the latest style, art moderne, as it was called
then. The pictures on the walls, the huge murals, the mag-
nificence of the chandelier and the other lighting fixtures,
the sweep of the balustrade, all these made Annie gasp in
wonder. Even Warbucks was impressed; they didn't call
this a picture palace for nothing.

A little overawed, Annie slipped her hand into Mr. Warbucks', and he took it in his, marveling to himself how
small and fragile it seemed to be.

An army of ushers and attendants was there to greet
them, wearing magnificent uniforms trimmed in gold braid,
with large gold shoulderboards and shiny gold buttons. As
they were handed their programs, Punjab stepped up to the
candy counter and filled his hands with Raisinets, Good
and Plenty, two boxes of Dots, and Bonomo's Turkish Taffy, all guaranteed to last through the picture and the stage
show.

The head usher, in the uniform of a full colonel in the
Bulgarian cavalry, showed them to their seats in the beam
of his flashlight. They were close to the stage.

Annie looked around. Apart from their party, the vast
movie theater was entirely empty.

"Where is everybody else?" she whispered to Grace Farrell.

"Mr. Warbucks bought out the house," Grace whispered back.

Suddenly, an eerie light began to play and a swell of music came from nowhere. Sandy uttered a hoarse bark of terror, and Annie crouched low in her seat.

The music was coming from the left-hand corner of the stage, and in a moment they saw, to their wonderment, an organ rise majestically out of the pit, with a man at the keyboard. He was playing "Lady of Spain," pulling out all the stops in great quavers and vox humana. After another selection and an encore, an orchestra broke into the *William Tell Overture* as it, too, rose out of the pit, bathed in colored lights. Annie had never even imagined anything like it.

The stage show was heaven, with dancers, clowns, jugglers, Chinese acrobats, a lady on a trampoline, and even a roller-skating bear. There was a dog act in which poodles wearing ruffled clothing walked around on their hind legs balancing things, while Sandy, not too appreciative, growled low in his throat, and Annie wondered if she could get Sandy to jump through a paper hoop with a little American flag in his teeth.

And the Rockettes—what words could Annie use to tell about them back at the orphanage? And how would they ever believe her? Here was an incredible line of fifty of the world's most beautiful women, dressed in daring costumes covered in spangles and sequins, and dancing with the precision of an army drill team, kicking up their legs in perfect unison, and making it appear so very easy! Annie wriggled with joy in her seat, and never wanted them to stop dancing.

But at last the show was over, and it was time for the movie itself to begin. But before that, a cartoon, Annie's very first cartoon, a Mickey Mouse called *Steamboat Willie*. What bliss! And then a newsreel, and a trailer for the next big feature and, at last, the movie! By now, Annie was so exhausted by the entire thrilling experience that her eyes were beginning to shut.

The film was a love story, in which Greta Garbo, surely the most beautiful woman in the world, suffered for love. Her boyfriend, Robert Taylor, surely the most beautiful man in the world, also suffered for love, but in his case it was harder to tell, because his facial expressions didn't change all that much. Annie found the film a little difficult to follow, because there was so much mushy love stuff in it, and after fifteen minutes of "Armand, Armand," and "Marguerite, my adored one," she fell fast asleep in her seat. In the seat next to hers, Sandy had given up during the disasters in the newsreel and was snoring gently.

Had Annie stayed awake, she would have seen something a lot more interesting than what was going on up there on the silver screen. As Marguerite died in the arms of her lover, Grace Farrell, who had been weeping silently during most of the movie, broke out into loud, gasping sobs, and Oliver Warbucks was patting her shoulder and handing her his handkerchief. Not only that, he was looking rather pleased with himself.

When the movie was over, Punjab lifted the sleeping Annie and, cradling her gently in his arms so as not to waken her, carried her out to the car and placed her on the back seat. She slept on, and so did Sandy.

But when they arrived home, Mr. Warbucks would not let Punjab carry her into the house and up the stairs. Instead, he lifted her himself, marveling at how light she was, and, with Grace following, carried her upstairs and into her room.

He helped Grace take off Annie's shoes and socks and, under Grace's expert guidance, managed to get Annie out of her clothes and into her nightdress without waking the child. He noticed as he did so that Annie was still wearing that broken little locket on a chain he'd seen when first he laid eyes on her. Indeed, she'd never had it off. One would think that with all the beautiful new possessions she'd acquired, she'd throw away the useless thing.

"You certainly are efficient," he praised Miss Farrell, who was looking . . . different . . . tonight. "I don't know how you manage to do everything. I don't know anything at all about children; I could never put one to bed."

Grace threw him a ravishing smile.

"Why, Mr. Warbucks, what an odd thing to say. You just did!"

He looked down at Annie. She was still sound asleep, her red curls tumbled on the pillow. The sight of her peaceful little face touched him mightily. He was glad he hadn't swapped her for a boy.

"Why, yes," he said slowly. "I did, didn't I? I put her to bed."

Smiling at each other, they left the room and shut the door quietly behind them. Annie slept on.

CHAPTER SEVEN

Her last day. Today is the day Annie goes back to the Hudson Street Home for Girls, Established 1891. Today is the day she goes back to being cold in the winter, hot in the summer, hungry all year round, unloved and lonely. Today is the day she says good-bye to everything and everybody she has come to care about and is delivered back into the clutches of Miss Hannigan, who hates her. Miss Hannigan has been waiting for one solid week to work out her hostilities and frustrations on the bodies of one small redheaded child and a dog.

Is it any wonder that Annie is sleeping late?

She had planned to get up as early as the day before, to enjoy every last minute of her last day. But when day broke, Annie couldn't face it, and burrowed deeply into her pillow.

And it was a beautiful day, too, with balmy temperatures, soft breezes, sunshine. Oliver Warbucks decided to have his breakfast in the garden, which was something of a departure for him, because he usually didn't notice the weather or his surroundings. But he was still Warbucks, so he ordered the ticker-tape machine brought to his table, and, while the birds sang in the trees and the squirrels packed their cheeks with seeds and berries, Warbucks sipped his scalding black coffee and studied the stock market quotations intently. He might have been in a brokerage office for all he noticed the garden now that he was in it, for the stock market figures were looking particularly black today.

Carrying the silver coffeepot filled with fresh brew, Grace Farrell came into the garden. She matched the flowers with her beauty this morning, for she had left her hair flowing to her shoulders, and had pinned a blooming tea

81

rose on the lapel of her jacket, close to her cheek, where its perfume might reach her nose.

"She's still asleep," she told the scowling Warbucks. "That was a wonderful evening you gave her." She waited for a reply, a nod, a smile, but none of those were forthcoming. Instead, Warbucks muttered something dire at the ticker tape.

This was going to make things a lot more difficult for what Grace intended. But she had made her mind up to speak, after spending a restless night wrestling with the new idea. She took a deep breath.

"Sir, I was wondering—" she began, but Warbucks cut her off without listening.

"I'm going to have to close the factory in Pittsburgh, Grace," he said. It was the first time he'd ever called her by her first name, and she felt a brief thrill of pleasure.

"About Annie—" she began again.

"What about Annie?" asked Warbucks brusquely. He, too, knew what day this was.

"Could we keep her?" She hadn't meant to blurt it out like that, but to lead up to it tactfully. Still, there it was, spoken between them. She looked eagerly into the billionaire's face for some encouragement.

But there was no encouragement there. Warbucks' scowl cut deeper into his face, and he gave an impatient shake of his head.

But Grace wasn't frightened off . . . yet. This was too important to her.

"You haven't seen that horrible orphanage," she pleaded. "I can't bear to send her back there."

"What's come over you, Grace? Get hold of yourself," snapped Warbucks, looking acutely uncomfortable.

"You have plenty of room," she persisted. "The staff adores her. She wouldn't be a bother, I'll look after her. She could live here as . . . well . . . as your ward. Couldn't she?"

Warbucks shook his head irritably. "Absolutely not. I'm a businessman. I love money. I love power. I love capitalism. I do not now and never will love children." It certainly sounded final.

Fighting back tears, Grace stood up. She turned to go, hesitated, then turned back, for a final feeble try.

"Watching you with her last night, I thought maybe . . ." her voice trailed off, and she turned again to go, but Warbucks caught hold of her hand.

"Wait," he begged. He, too, had been remembering last night; how she'd cried at the film, how the two of them had put a sleeping child to bed. And there was something different about her today, something softer. He wasn't sure, but he thought it had something to do with her hair. Annie was right, he never noticed anything. But he could learn, couldn't he?

He drew Grace back into the chair beside him. "I just noticed something," he told her softly. "You're very pretty when you argue with me."

Twin spots of color appeared in Grace's creamy cheeks. "Thank you, sir, but—"

"Oliver."

"Oliver," she whispered, her eyes unable to meet his. Then she looked him full in the face. "Do you really love only money and power and capitalism?" He still had hold of her hand, and now Grace put her other little hand on top of his. "They're never going to love you back."

They were gazing now into each other's eyes, fascinated by what each saw in the other's depths. As with that first Garden at the beginning of recorded time, this one too held a man and a woman who were suddenly and passionately aware of one another.

"Your teeth are crooked," said Oliver in a near whisper.

"I'll have them fixed," blushed Grace.

"I like them crooked."

"I'll leave them."

"Thank you."

Without taking her eyes off his, Grace murmured, "I could get the papers signed this morning."

"Grace?"

"Oliver?"

"It means a great deal to you?"

The girl nodded. "A great deal."

"Then I'll do it myself," he decided. It was an enormous step for him to take, a man whose responsibilities were great but impersonal, a man who involved himself in everything but who was truly involved in nothing. And he never did anything in half measures. If Annie was to be his ward, she would be his to protect and defend and, yes, love.

Because he was coming to care for her a little. He could see her face as though she were standing in front of him this very minute. The eyes, so blue and honest; she was forthright and said exactly what she meant without fear. The red hair, sign of a feisty temper and a pair of fists to be wary of. That incredibly optimistic grin of hers, and the way she never let you see anything but the bright side of her. Why, she was like him in so many ways. And, in the ways they were different from each other, little Annie was the better person of the two, and he could learn from her. Yes, he loved Annie! She had, with her courage, and her independence, and her strength and intelligence, touched something in him that had never been open to touch before, something vital that had been close to dying undiscerned. She held his heart in her two little hands, and she was going to be his little girl.

A great happiness washed over Oliver Warbucks, and no day had ever been sunnier or more beautiful. In a few short moments he had found love, not in one place but two! What man had ever been happier?

"Oh, Mr. Warbucks, I could just kiss you!" cried Grace, and her lips were dangerously close to his. He reached for that kiss, but she'd already jumped up, her face radiant with a joy that matched his own. Never had he imagined she could be so beautiful, but then never had he imagined anything about her at all. It had taken Annie to bring the two of them together. No, it would be the three of them together.

Grace was running toward the house, to wake up Annie.

"Grace!" he called after her, and she stopped and turned, the sunlight illuminating her hair and making it glow.

"Get her a little present!"

"Oh, yes, Oliver!"

He thought for a second. "Something from Tiffany. A new locket."

Her eyes misted at his thoughtfulness. She, too, had been touched by the pathetic quality of the little broken

84

locket Annie refused to take off. She'd buy her one a thousand times better. "Oh, Oliver!" she breathed. Then, as he reached her side, loping up the velvet lawn like a boy, she warned him with mock severity. "And you. Be careful when you go to the orphanage. That woman has claws and fangs."

He threw back his head and laughed, and Grace marveled at the rich sound of it. She realized she'd never heard him laugh before, and she was very grateful to Annie.

And then, surprised, she was in his arms, and being very thoroughly kissed by a billionaire, a mover and shaker of nations' destinies. He kissed exactly like a man.

Miss Hannigan woke up early, with a smile on her face. She'd been having a lovely dream. She dreamed that Annie was back from the Warbucks house, and scrubbing the floor in an evening gown, which was getting more and more dirty and torn the more she scrubbed. She dreamed that Annie had splinters in her fingers and scabs on her knees from the filthy old floor, and that, while the other orphans crowded around for their bowl of midday mush, Annie was forced to clean the chimneys, shinnying up them like a little monkey, and coming down all covered in soot and ashes, gasping, wheezing, and choking. And when she woke up, the smile on Miss Hannigan's face grew broader and brighter. Because the dream was going to come true. Today was the day.

She was so tickled that she was almost nice to some of the orphans today, but she caught herself in time, and forced herself to be extra nasty, to keep in practice for when Annie came back. She rather imagined it would be late in the day, because she was sure that trouble-making brat would stay to the last possible minute. *I know I would,* said Miss Hannigan.

So she was surprised to hear a powerful motor car drive up so early, but she hastened to the door, eager to get her meathooks on Annie in the first possible minute. She expected the Town Car and Miss Farrell, so she almost fainted at the peephole when she laid eyes on the gleaming, sporty Dusenberg and saw Oliver Warbucks step out.

It was unmistakably Oliver Warbucks. Not only had she seen his picture in the Sunday supplements time without number, but who else possessed that powerful posture, that commanding walk, that bald head, that diamond as big as a golf ball in his shirt front, that nine-foot-tall Indian bodyguard?

Nine-foot-tall Indian bodyguard? Was she still dreaming? No, there he was, standing watch on the pavement as Warbucks gave the bell an extra loud ring. There was no sign of Annie.

She flung the door wide.

"Good morning, Miss Hannigan," said Warbucks, brushing past her to step inside.

"Holy Mary, Mother of God, saints preserve us," she whimpered as she caught the aroma of money and power that exuded from Warbucks. She followed after him like a hungry hound as he made his way down the corridors of the orphanage. He was shocked at the conditions that were evident to even a cursory glance, and he made some mental notes for immediate relief.

"I want to talk to you about Annie," he snapped, as he led the way into Miss Hannigan's office.

"You want to return her and forget it or you want to trade up?"

Warbucks opened his crocodile briefcase and pulled out an official-looking sheaf of papers. "I want to adopt her."

Miss Hannigan nodded slightly, and her expression didn't change. "Would you excuse me for just one moment?" she asked politely, and, at Warbucks' nod, she stepped into the supply closet and closed the door behind her. There she let out a blood-curdling scream, a Comanche yell of anger and frustration. Then, wiping her mouth with her pocket handkerchief, she stepped out smiling to confront the bewildered Warbucks.

"Thank you so much. Won't you please sit down?"

Oliver Warbucks placed the papers squarely on the desk in front of Miss Hannigan, then carefully seated himself and took a pen from the pocket of his coat. He looked up to see Miss Hannigan flaring her nostrils at him, her false eyelashes fluttering like moth wings.

"For a Republican you're sinfully handsome. Has anyone ever told you that?" She leaned forward like a snake, and her hands were suddenly all over him, fingering the expensive cloth of his Saville Row suit.

"Miss Hannigan—" began Warbucks in protest, but she was now focusing in on his stickpin, a single flawless diamond the size of a hen's egg.

"Oh, my gawd, is that thing real?" she breathed, regarding the stone with genuine lust.

"Just sign the papers," snapped Warbucks.

"What's it worth to you?"

Warbucks blinked in surprise. Miss Hannigan leaned back in her desk chair, regarding him through slitted eyes. She was breathing hard and beginning to tremble.

Oliver's face hardened. "What exactly do you mean, what's it worth to me?" he demanded coldly.

Miss Hannigan was now making kissing motions with her lips, looking like a carp in heat. "I go positively weak in the knees with men like you," she husked.

"Annie's told me a lot about your operation here."

"Misses me, huh?" sneered Hannigan.

"Clean sheets once a month, no schooling, no meat, no fresh vegetables or fruit," enumerated Warbucks in a voice of steel. "You're breaking every child welfare law on the books—"

"Would you like to see my bedroom?" interrupted Miss Hannigan, caught in the toils of her passion.

"Miss Hannigan—"

"Would you care for a martini, my little billiard ball?" she invited, ignoring his anger and impatience.

Miss Hannigan stood up a bit unsteadily, and Warbucks stood, too, picking up the sheaf of adoption papers and waving them under her nose. She evaded them and danced into her adjacent bedroom, Warbucks one step behind her. She knew that she had the power to drive him mad with lust, if she could only get him to stop talking about that damn adoption! Slinking like a vamp from a silent movie, she made her way toward him, a scarf thrown over her shoulders, only to be met by the barrier of the papers and the pen.

"Sign," he commanded.

"In a moment, *chéri*. First, we have ze little drink, *non?*"

She whirled gracefully (she thought) into her bathroom, and dipped two chipped tumblers into the bathtub, bringing them up brimming. When she popped back through the beaded curtains, he was still holding that pen and those papers, and he waved the gin away in distaste.

"*Sign.*"

"Oh, but, Oliver," she simpered in a Dixie drawl, "surely there are more things for a man and a woman to talk about than silly old papers?"

"*SIGN.*"

Vamp didn't work, French didn't work, and now southern belle didn't work. What was this guy, a pansy? Any red-blooded man would have fallen victim to her passions long ago.

"Miss Hannigan, do you want to keep your job?"

"Not if there's an alternative," she purred with a significant leer.

"The alternative is the streets," he told her coldly, handing her the pen and the papers.

She snatched the pen from his fingers and furiously scribbled her signature on the dotted line. "If that's the way you feel about it, why didn't you say so in the first place?"

Then she made one more try. "Now that I've signed, would you care to celebrate with a little drink?"

But Warbucks was already on his way to the door, the precious adoption papers safe in his briefcase.

Miss Hannigan was so brought down by the events of the morning, which had turned out so differently from her hopes and dreams, that nothing could restore her to her customary wonderful disposition except several tumblers of gin, taken directly from the tub. Thus fortified, she stormed out of her office to exact vengeance from the remaining orphans—and marched straight into the dead mouse that Duffy was dangling. After shrieking her head off for a full minute, Miss Hannigan clutched at her heart and staggered back for another drink. The next time she opened her office door, she did so with extreme caution, one inch at a time. Satisfied that the rodent had vanished (she would find it again, hours later, underneath her pillow), she made her way into the orphans' quarters.

"No lazing about, my little pig droppings, no luxury and idleness for you. Industry! I want to see those drops of sweat flying, or it's kill! kill! kill!"

If she couldn't make Annie pay, she'd take it out of the hides of the others. Most especially, out of the hides of Annie's friends.

CHAPTER EIGHT

When Oliver Warbucks arrived home, he went directly to his gold and black marble bathroom, where he turned the shower on as hot as he could stand it and climbed under. He scrubbed at his skin for more than ten minutes, until he could feel clean again. It seemed to him that the dirt and the stench of the orphanage was still clinging to him, but it was the moral stench he was trying to wash away, the filth of Miss Hannigan's perverted and cruel little mind. He shuddered to think that he had come within a hair's breadth of sending Annie back to that horrible place. How right Grace had been! And how glad he was that today she looked so beautiful and so lovable that he could deny her nothing.

Well, never mind. Annie was soon going to be his daughter; he promised himself to give Grace Farrell a whopping raise and think about marrying her someday, and meanwhile all of them would go on happily together under one roof, as they'd done all week. Must remember to contact the board of orphans about Miss Hannigan. The woman is a monster, he mused, making mental notes. She ought not to be allowed within ten miles of helpless children.

After he dried himself, he selected a fresh set of clothing from the multitudes—all identical—that thronged his dressing room with its custom-built closets. Dressed and feeling somewhat refreshed, he repaired not to the office but to the grandeur of the drawing room, where a fire was lit in the fireplace, and gargantuan bouquets of roses and white lilac stood on the mantel and on the white piano. He sent for Grace, only to be told that she had not yet returned from her errand.

This information set his teeth on edge; he was as jumpy as a cat in a lightning storm. He began to pace the room, a caged animal smoking cigars, until the soles of his shoes had worn discernible ruts in the Axminster carpet's luxurious pile.

"Women!" he snorted to Punjab, who stood on the alert at the side of the fireplace nearest the door. "Does it take this long to get to Tiffany and back? Where is she?"

Punjab remained his usual unflappable self. "I hear the car, sahib," he remarked quietly.

"It's probably not the right car," fumed Warbucks.

"It's the Town Car. Miss Farrell took the Town Car."

A moment later, Grace rushed in, out of breath and looking lovely, a little blue box tied in a white bow conspicuous in her hands.

"What took you so long?" demanded Warbucks. "The Asp was due back with Annie ten minutes ago—" He whirled to Punjab. "Has something happened to *them?*"

The ghost of a smile crossed Punjab's face, but didn't land there. "They are in the kitchen, sahib."

Grace crossed to the fireplace and pulled the bellrope hanging there. A faint tinkle sounded in the kitchen below.

"I told the Asp to wait until I got back with this," she said, holding the Tiffany box out to Oliver.

He snatched it from her fingers. "Why doesn't anyone tell me anything?" he pouted.

"Mr. Warbucks," said Grace, declining to use his Christian name in front of Punjab, "there's no need to be nervous."

"Nervous? Who's nervous?" squeaked Warbucks nervously. "Do I look nervous to you?" he demanded of Punjab. "Do I look nervous to you?" he asked Grace rhetorically. He whirled to confront himself in the mirror. "Do I look nervous? No. Do I look warm and loving? No." His face fell. He thrust the blue box back into Grace's hands. "You give it to her," he pleaded.

But Grace was handing the box back, Grace was shaking her head no.

"It was your idea, sir . . ." she reminded him.

Warbucks pushed the box back at her again. "She likes you better than she likes me."

Grace allowed herself the luxury of a smile. "Oliver, pull yourself together," she admonished him. It tickled

91

her that this man, who was the equal of potentates and princes, who dealt daily with ambassadors, papal legates, and presidents, should come unglued at the thought of giving a little gold locket to a ten-year-old orphan.

It was at that moment that Annie skipped in, followed by the Asp and Sandy, still skidding on the waxed surfaces of the hallway floor. Since nobody had appeared to be around when Annie woke up that day, and nobody had said anything to her about the time she was due back on Hudson Street, Annie had stuck to her usual schedule. This included her karate lesson with the Asp, and she was wearing the pajamalike karate suit when she came running into the living room.

"Oh, Mr. Warbucks! Wanna see what the Asp taught me today?"

Before Oliver could answer, Annie struck out with her left foot, catching Warbucks on the kneecap and sending him hurtling to the ground in agony.

As Punjab and the Asp rushed forward to raise their fallen master, Annie's face went white and she threw herself down beside Warbucks, her features contorted in sorrow.

"Oh, gee, I didn't think it would work!" she gasped.

"To the couch, Punjab, if you don't mind," said Mr. Warbucks through gritted teeth. As Punjab stretched the billionaire out gently, and began to palpate the injured leg, Warbucks called out to the angry and humiliated Asp.

"It's all right, Asp. Now she knows it works. I believe in being able to defend yourself. Even for girls."

"Shall I call the doctor, sahib?" asked Punjab.

"No, fix it yourself," instructed his master. As the Indian giant made some mystical passes in the air over Warbucks' knee, Oliver felt the pain beginning to leave him. After less than a minute, he announced, "The pain is gone. I'm fine now."

Annie and Grace breathed audible sighs of relief. When the Asp and Punjab had rushed to the aid of Warbucks, Grace, knowing that she'd only be in the way and knowing, too, that Annie needed her, had stood close to the little girl, holding her by the shoulders and giving her little hugs for comfort. Now she stepped forward and laid the little blue box on Oliver's chest, next to his hands.

"We'll leave you alone a moment," she said.

Warbucks gave her an imploring look from panicked eyes, but Grace merely nodded to the Asp and Punjab, who followed her out of the room. Annie and Mr. Warbucks were alone.

Feeling like an awkward schoolboy, Oliver slipped the Tiffany box into his pocket and took Annie by the hand. He wasn't sure how to begin, so the two of them sat there for a minute or so in silence. Then Warbucks said, "Annie, I want to talk to you about something very serious."

Annie bit her lip. "You don't want me anymore, right?" she said as cheerfully as she could through the pain in her heart.

This caught Warbucks totally off balance. "On the contrary . . . I *do* . . . good Lord . . ."

They sat for a minute more in silence, Annie searching her memory for something she might have done to offend Mr. Warbucks. It must be serious or he wouldn't be looking so uncomfortable. Or maybe it was just that, because this was to be her last day, Mr. Warbucks wanted to give her a useful little lecture on life to take back with her to the orphanage. Whatever it was, it didn't look as though it was going to be pleasant for either of them.

"Annie, can we have a man-to-man talk?" asked Warbucks at last.

Uh-oh, thought Annie. Out loud, she said, "Sure."

But still he couldn't meet her eyes, or find an appropriate jumping-off point. He didn't want to tell her too much; there was more brimming inside him than Annie needed to deal with, but he didn't want to tell her too little either. He wanted for both of them to live happily ever after, nothing more nor less. And that wasn't going to be as easy as it sounded.

He took a deep breath and went for it. "What I'm proposing would involve a long-term . . . well . . . agreement."

Bewildered, Annie could only stare at him. She hadn't the faintest idea of what he was driving at.

This sitting still was driving Warbucks crazy. He stood up and began pacing back and forth.

"Actually, maybe you should know more about me before you make up your mind," he told her.

"Okay," agreed Annie readily. She still had no idea

what he was talking about, but whatever it was, it was making Mr. Warbucks sweat, and she'd never seen him sweat, not even when he was on the telephone yelling at Mussolini.

"Let's go for a walk," he suggested. What he needed was a breath of air.

"Okay," said Annie, standing up immediately.

As soon as they reached the back garden through the kitchen door, Oliver Warbucks let his breath out in a deep sigh of relief. This was better, much better. He began to tell Annie about himself. "I was born in Liverpool, in a railroad switch house," he began. *Ah,* she thought, *England. That's why he has that strange accent.*

"My brother died of pneumonia because we didn't have the money for medicine. Well, I decided then and there one day I would be rich. Very, very rich."

"Good idea," Annie agreed. But it was difficult for her to picture Oliver Warbucks either as very young or very poor.

The back garden was terraced, and old stone steps, covered in picturesque silvery moss, led down to a small pool, a stone bench and some very old trees. Side by side, they walked down the steps. Warbucks strode with his hands clasped behind his back, and Annie was a step or two behind him, her hands clasped the same way in unconscious imitation of him. Sandy pattered along at his mistress's side, just happy to be out in this beautiful weather with a full belly and Annie by his side. He had achieved canine Nirvana, and wouldn't have traded his lot for that of the most pampered Pekinese lapdog.

"In those days," continued Mr. Warbucks, "America was the land of opportunity. I signed on a ship as cabin boy when I was twelve. By the time I was twenty-one, I'd made my first million. In the next ten years, I turned that into a hundred million." He stopped and turned to Annie, waiting for her reaction.

"Wow!" What else was there to say? Annie could no more conceive of what a hundred million dollars was like than she could flap her wings and take off.

"In those days, that was a lot of money," added Warbucks, and Annie nodded her concurrence. It sure was.

"I was ruthless, hurt a lot of people. But, like the man

says, you don't have to be nice to the people you meet on the way up if you're not coming back down. Making money was all I ever gave a damn about." He paused, then added softly, "Until now." He looked significantly at Annie, but she was still in the dark. Even so, she was enjoying this walk and talk, and she gave Oliver Warbucks a heartfelt smile.

He fingered the little box in his pocket. "Let's go inside," he said abruptly.

"Okay," said Annie agreeably.

Once back in the monumental living room, Warbucks resumed his pacing, while Annie sat in a baronial red-velvet chair, trying to follow what he was saying.

"It's occurred to me that no matter how much money I have, no matter how many houses, how many Rembrandts and Dusenbergs, if I have no one to . . . share it with, well, I might as well be back in Liverpool, broke." He turned to her, stopping in his tracks. "Annie, do you understand what I'm trying to say?" he demanded.

"Sure," said Annie uncertainly. Did it have something to do with Grace Farrell? Annie kind of suspected it might, but then why was Mr. Warbucks talking to *her* and not to Grace?

"Good," said Warbucks, straightening up and letting his breath out.

"Kind of," Annie added, rather timidly for her.

"Kind of?"

"I guess not," she admitted. She was letting Mr. Warbucks down, and she knew it, and it embarrassed her.

"Damn!" Here they were, back on square one. Well, there was only one more thing he could think of to do. He took the little blue box from Tiffany out of his pocket and shoved it into Annie's hands. Taken totally by surprise, she looked up at him, bewildered.

"You've given me so much already, Mr. Warbucks," she protested.

Warbucks beamed at her. "I got the papers signed today. It's official."

Annie was busy untying the ribbon on the box.

"What is?" she asked, and then she saw the locket, and a strange expression came over her face. "It's so pretty, but . . ."

Warbucks, watching her lift the little gold locket out of the cotton-lined box, noticed neither the expression on her face nor the "but." He took it out of her hands and undid the clasp himself.

"Here, let me put it on you," he said gently, but Annie broke away from him and ran, shouting "No!" fiercely.

At her shout, the household staff and Grace, who'd been waiting outside with their congratulations, ran in, concerned.

But Annie and Warbucks didn't even see them; they were staring at each other, pain written on both their faces.

"It's a really swell locket, Mr. Warbucks, but if it's all the same to you, I'll keep my old one." Tears were beginning to form behind her eyes, and she blinked them back ferociously. She could see that she'd hurt Mr. Warbucks, and she could kick herself for that, but it couldn't be helped.

Warbucks was hurt beyond anything Annie could comprehend. He had never for one minute anticipated that the scene could be played this way.

"It's *not* all the same to me," he retorted angrily. "Your old one's broken. This one's engraved. You didn't even look at it." He turned the locket over in his hand and read the pretty script on the back. " 'To Annie, with love from . . ."Daddy" Warbucks.' " He glared at Grace. Daddy? Wasn't that carrying things a bit far?

Didn't anybody understand? Annie looked around her for support, but it was evident that everybody in the room thought she was being ungrateful; their sympathies were with Mr. Warbucks. Suddenly, it burst on her—what all of this was about. What the words on the locket meant. What Mr. Warbucks had been trying to tell her with so much difficulty. He wanted to adopt her, that's what those papers meant. He wanted her to be his little girl. No wonder he was so hurt. But how was he to know? She hadn't told any of them about the Dream.

Now she was going to have to hurt him even more. Because, although she liked him so much . . . no, *loved* him . . . she couldn't be his adopted daughter. Annie drew a deep breath.

"Mr. Warbucks, when my folks left me at the orphanage ten years ago, they left a note saying they'd come back to get me, soon as they could, and that they'd keep the other half of this old locket, so I'd know them when they came."

She paused, and she heard a murmur of astonishment from the staff, spreading like a ripple. Only Mr. Warbucks and Grace Farrell said nothing. Grace kept looking from Annie to Oliver and back again, hurting for both of them at once.

"I'm gonna find them someday, Mr. Warbucks," Annie continued in a softer voice. "I'm gonna have a regular mother and father like a regular kid. I am."

Hearing these words, Oliver Warbucks felt the heart break in his chest, although his anger disappeared. He'd never expected this, that Annie would say no. That she had a reason to say no. He'd had a rosy vision of the four of them walking down life's pathway together, Annie and Warbucks and Grace and even that damn dog of Annie's. And here he was, the richest and most powerful man in the world, savior of nations, on the brink of tears because a little orphan girl had turned him down! He'd had absolutely no idea of how much he'd come to love her until this minute, when she was telling him gently that he couldn't be her "Daddy" because she already had a Daddy somewhere.

And yet, he felt closer to her now than ever before, because he could hear the pain and determination in her words, and they reminded him so much of the boy he'd been, back in England long ago, when he'd vowed that he would be very, very rich.

"I don't mean to hurt your feelings," Annie said, choking back her own tears. "You've been nicer to me than anybody in the whole wide world. But I been dreaming of my folks for as long as I can remember, and I just gotta find them." She stopped, having said everything she could.

It took him a silent minute, but Oliver Warbucks pulled himself together. Then he formed a resolve. By thunder, he wasn't the most powerful man in the world for nothing! If Annie wanted her parents, Annie would get her parents. He, Oliver Warbucks the billionaire, would see to it personally. Now he was on firm ground, on turf that he owned and operated, and he began to bark orders at everybody.

"Well then, I'll help you." He turned to Drake. "Get me J. Edgar Hoover on the phone." To Grace, he said, "Get me Mayor LaGuardia and the chief of police." At the Asp, he growled, "Get me Walter Winchell," and to Punjab, "Get me Lowell Thomas."

Everyone scattered, scurrying off to do his bidding.

They were alone again, Warbucks and Annie. They looked at each other with love, but Warbucks wasn't going to soften again. "And you," he said to the little girl, "when we get all this under way, I'll take *you* to Washington!"

This was more happiness than Annie could hold; it was starting to spill over and roll down her cheeks in the form of tears. To have a mother and a father! She knew Oliver Warbucks well enough to know that if anybody on the face of the planet could find them for her, it was him. And now, to meet the president, her hero. Her *other* hero, she corrected herself. Well, she just wanted to go off somewhere and blubber for joy, with only Sandy to see her. Darting forward, she threw her arms around Oliver Warbucks' neck and gave him a swift, loving hug. Then she ran out, Sandy at her heels, and vanished up to her room.

Warbucks stood looking after Annie. Ironic, he needed her more than she needed him! Who would ever have guessed it? Well, at least he could do this one thing for her. He looked down. In his hand he was still holding the little gold locket from Tiffany. For a moment, his fingers closed around it tightly, as though to crush it, the tangible symbol of his greatest disappointment. Then he sighed, and dropped it into his pocket. No time for wasteful and useless sentimentality. Not when there was work to be done.

CHAPTER NINE

Today, television brings the entire world into your living room, with nightly news to tell you how many disasters have taken place all in one day. In 1933, people had the same dependence on the radio. Radio brought them everything—music, comedy, drama, true stories, mysteries, the news, the weather, and the racing results. In the evenings, people sat around and *watched* radio. It's God's truth. They gathered around the box as though it were some kind of holy temple, and looked at the sounds coming out of it. If you were a big star in the movies or on stage, you went into radio. If you were a top singer, radio was the place for you. More people heard you on the air than ever went out to buy your records.

Walter Winchell was the number-one columnist of his day, but he got bigger when he went on the air to broadcast to "Mr. and Mrs. America and all the ships at sea." Radio reached everybody, rich and poor, black and white, young and old. It even reached the orphans at the Hudson Street Home for Girls, Established 1891. That was no thanks to Miss Hannigan, who owned the only radio in the building, and who was addicted to daytime soap operas (yes, they started on the radio) like "Young Widder Brown," "The Romance of Helen Trent," "Our Gal Sunday," "Mary Noble, Backstage Wife," "Aunt Jenny's Real Life Stories," "Lorenzo Jones," and "Pepper Young's Family."

The orphans had worked out a system for gaining access to the precious radio. The best time was when Miss Hannigan had passed out from gin. (I told you she had her good side.) Then, they simply tiptoed in and snaffled it, carrying it off (it was a table model) to a room with a closed door and playing it very quietly. It was then they learned all the new songs, such as "Oh, You Nasty Man" and "I'll Be Glad When You're Dead, You Rascal You," which they dedicated to Miss Hannigan.

But Miss Hannigan didn't always oblige by passing out, so the orphans sometimes turned to Plan B. This involved taking turns, three at a time, with two girls getting to listen, and one to stand guard. There was a small hole in the wall of Miss Hannigan's bedroom, which led to the outer corridor, and by dint of much scraping, Pepper and Duffy had enlarged the hole enough to be able to hear most of what was being broadcast. Faintly, but it served the purpose. The two lucky girls whose turn it was would bring mops and pails with them, so that if Miss Hannigan emerged suddenly, as was her happy custom, yelling "Kill! kill! kill!" the girl on guard would whistle a warning, and all Miss Hannigan would see were two diligent orphans scrubbing the corridor outside her room.

Miss Hannigan listened to the radio all the time. The romance-dramas and the soaps were her favorites; they always put her in a steamy and inevitably frustrated mood, which she relieved by taking it out on the orphans. But actually, she'd listen to anything, even the Iodent Toothpaste Hour, an awful melange of bad music and bad comedy, therefore everybody's favorite program. The Iodent Toothpaste Hour starred the inevitable M.C., a trio of dreadful girl singers who dressed like triplets, and a comedy team comprising a ventriloquist named McKracky and his dummy, Wacky, very bad imitations of Edgar Bergen and Charlie McCarthy. Miss Hannigan loved the program and never missed it.

She was listening to it tonight, as she added more juniper berries to the brand-new batch of alcohol in her bathtub. Miss Hannigan had fallen on hard times in the last few days. Not only had she been forced to face the prospect of her least favorite orphan, that miserable troublemaker and rotten kid, falling into the gravy boat, but yesterday a couple of unknown little pig droppings had sneaked into her bathroom and pulled the plug out of the tub! Eight bucks' worth of gin, a whole tubful down the drain in one great gurgle! And it was good gin, too; a month's supply. Now she had to start all over from scratch.

Was it any wonder that her only consolation in life was the radio? She had it turned on right now, listening to the Iodent Toothpaste Hour, as most of America was doing.

Bert Healy, the M.C., had promised his listening audience a big surprise, a real-life heartwarming human drama, guaranteed to bring a lump to the throat and a tear to the eye. Miss Hannigan dearly loved a good cry; she was blessed with so tender a heart. So she was listening eagerly when Healy announced, in his oleaginous broadcaster's tones:

"I'd like to introduce a little orphan named Annie."

A little orphan named Annie? Could there be two? Impossible! So Miss Hannigan did the only thing possible in the circumstances. She screamed and fainted.

Well, wouldn't you? She tumbled straight down, and her head hit the bathroom floor hard enough to knock her out. Good thing for her she didn't fall into the bathtub. Not only might she have drowned, but the gin would have tasted just terrible!

The two orphans out in the hall, at the earhole, were Molly and Pepper. When Molly heard Annie's name, she, too, jumped up and screamed, but she didn't faint. She was too eager to find out what was going to happen next.

Just as today the parents of a missing child might go on television to plead for his return, so Oliver Warbucks decided that, to reach the most people in the quickest way, he must take Annie's case to the radio audience in the forty-eight states. Of course, his first idea was the news broadcast. It was timely and above all it was dignified, as befitted a billionaire and something of a newsmaker himself.

But Oliver was soon convinced that nobody listened to the news. On the other hand, just about everybody in America listened to the Iodent Toothpaste Hour, and Annie's real father and mother might very well be among them. Certainly, it was worth a try.

So Warbucks had Grace telephone the head of the Red Network (nothing to do with the Bolsheviks; there were two radio networks in those days, the Red and the Blue, which later evolved into the CBS and NBC we know and revere today). The head of the Red Network notified the sponsors and the sponsors thought it wasn't quite the right thing for Iodent Toothpaste's image. So Oliver Warbucks bought the Iodent Toothpaste Company outright, and didn't have to listen to any more arguments. To the station they all of them went.

The top radio writers in the business had knocked out a quick script. Time was of the essence; once Oliver Warbucks had made his mind up he wanted to see immediate results from the decision. When they arrived at the radio broadcasting studio, they were handed the pages of the script and told where to stand.

Annie was surprised. Here she'd been listening to the Iodent Toothpaste Hour for years, and she'd pictured it very differently. Somehow she'd imagined a big stage and a real show going on. Instead, it was a really small studio, with four floor microphones—one for Bert Healy; one for McKracky and Wacky; one for the girl singers, the Lovely and Famous Moylan Sisters, Tilly, Milly and Agnes; and one for the most important person on the program, the sound effects man. There was a huge clock on the wall with a long sweep second hand, a little sign that lit up and said On the Air when they were on the air, and a soundproof control booth with dials and knobs to twist, in which sat the producer of the program wearing headphones. He communicated with his cast by making menacing faces and threatening gestures through the glass.

Annie and Mr. Warbucks were to share Bert Healy's mike. Oliver had never used a live mike before, although he was quite used to dictating, and had not laid eyes on the script until this very second. Otherwise, they were prepared.

At last the sweep second hand came around to the hour, and the sound man put the opening theme song on the record player. Bert Healy cried with great enthusiasm, "Good evening, ladies and gentlemen, it's the Iodent Toothpaste Hour!" and the sound effects man turned on the applause machine, which simulated a large audience breaking into wild and spontaneous applause. Then the sound man opened a door, and walked two shoes with leather heels over a wooden board. Footsteps. Annie was fascinated.

" 'Say,' " Wacky McKracky, the ventriloquist's dummy,

said into his mike, pretending to read it off the script, " 'who's that who just walked into our Red Network station. Bert Healy?' "

Healy stepped to his mike and read, " 'Wacky. It's none other than the Wall Street tycoon, Oliver Warbucks!' "

More applause, long and loud, from the machine.

Silence from Warbucks, until the assistant director pointed frantically to the place on Warbucks' script where he was supposed to start.

" 'Thank you, Bert Healy,' " read Oliver slowly. " 'It's swell' "—he looked up scowling; "swell?" he queried with disdain—" 'to be on the Iodent Hour.' "

" 'I understand,' " read Healy, picking up the tempo, " 'that you're conducting a coast-to-coast search for Annie's parents.' "

Warbucks nodded, a gesture entirely lost on a radio audience. The assistant director darted forward again, his finger on the script.

" 'Yes. Bert Healy, I am now conducting a coast-to-coast nationwide search for Annie's parents. Drop page.' "

He looked up, mystified. Drop page? Then he noticed the other radio actors dropping their script pages on the studio floor as they finished them, and he understood. Paper rattles, especially in front of a live microphone, so radio people drop their finished pages silently instead of tucking them behind the others.

Oliver nodded and continued. " 'Warbucks,' " he read, once again including the stage directions, " 'Furthermore, tonight I am offering a cash reward to Annie's parents. Fifty thousand dollars. Cash.' "

This was the first time Annie had heard anything of the reward money, and the announcement filled her with excitement. Dropping her script, she ran to Oliver and embraced him, hugging him tightly.

"Are you really? Oh, Mr. Warbucks, you are the wonderfullest man in the whole wide world." And that's how it went out over the air.

Miss Hannigan, unfortunately for her, had come to in time to hear Warbucks' offer and Annie's spontaneous reaction. It almost made her sick; it was a good thing she was already in the bathroom. Her head was beginning

Annie

to ache from the grinding of her molars; God was really picking on her lately. Fifty thousand dollars!

Outside, the orphans had their ears pressed up to the office wall, listening to Bert Healy saying:

" 'So, if you're listening, Annie's parents, contact Oliver Warbucks—' "

" 'Warbucks. Interrupts,' " interrupted Oliver Warbucks, reading off the paper. " 'At my house. 987 Fifth Avenue, New York City.' "

Molly leaped to her feet, her brown eyes huge with excitement. "Annie's gonna find her folks!" she yelled.

Miss Hannigan, hearing the same announcement, winced.

In the studio, Mr. Warbucks was down to his last sheet of script. By now, he was a master at the mike, and spoke with booming confidence, causing the sound-level dials to spin like roulette wheels in the control booth, and the producer to tear his hair out.

" 'Thank you, Bert Healy, and thank you, Iodent Toothpaste, with the all-new miracle ingredient, Y-37, to fight bad breath, for letting me come and talk to you this evening. Good night, Bert Healy, and good night for the Red Network. Drop page.' "

He dropped the page and strode angrily toward the studio exit, furious for allowing himself to be suckered into doing a commercial for bad breath. He made a mental note to buy the Red Network and fire Bert Healy and everybody connected with the Iodent Toothpaste Hour.

Behind him, the sound effects man turned the volume up up up on the applause.

The announcement caused as much joy among the orphans as it did pain to Miss Hannigan. The story spread like wildfire from dormitory to dormitory, until every girl in the Hudson Street Home knew that Annie was going to find her parents, and that Mr. Warbucks, the billionaire, was going to pay out a hundred million dollars to whoever was Annie's mother and father. What a sock in the eye to Hannigan! What a kick in the teeth! What a pain in the you-know-where! And what a boost for the orphans! It would put them on the map, for certain sure. And who knows? Maybe a slew of would-be mothers and fathers would turn up at the Hudson Street Home looking for little girls to adopt, in case some other billionaire might be handing out mazuma.

Miss Hannigan had been dealt some severe body blows one right after the other, but tonight was the knockout punch. Fifty thousand American dollars were to be laid out to find a happy ending for that little redheaded brat, while she, Loretta Louise Mary Margaret Hannigan, was still wearing her lovely feminine fingers down to the bone nursing and caring for an ungrateful, undeserving, undermining passel of low-life orphans, all of whom put together weren't worth fifty American cents. Was there no justice in the world? Up there, somewhere, she could hear the sounds of godly laughter. What fools these Hannigans be! No, by all that was unholy, the ghostly laughter was not from up there, but from out *here*—right outside her door. The final indignity, the straw that put the camel's sacroiliac out of whack! Oh, what she wouldn't give for the mask of Medusa to turn these orphans to stone! Laughing! I'll show them laughing!

She threw open the door, and the orphans froze. They'd seen her mad, they'd seen her drunk, they'd seen her crazy. But they had never seen Miss Hannigan so mad drunk crazy as she was at this very moment in time. It frightened them.

"Did I hear happiness in here?" she shrieked. *"Did I hear sounds of merriment and mirth? Did my ears detect joy?"*

The girls scattered in all directions, fleeing for their lives, while Miss Hannigan's "Kill! kill! kill!" echoed to the skies and the street. And heaven help the laggard orphan who couldn't keep up. Miss Hannigan would have her scrubbing down the attic ceiling at four in the morning.

Like all media events, the story of the orphan girl Annie, as the press called it, was on everybody's lips the following day. Right after the broadcast, the mansion had been besieged by reporters and photographers from the major New York newspapers—the *Daily News*, the *Mirror*, the *Journal*, the *American*, the *Herald-Tribune*, the *Times*, *the Sun* and the *World. Life* and *Judge* and the *Police Gazette* sent photojournalists; the *New Yorker* sent Dorothy Parker; and *Vanity Fair* dispatched Cecil Beaton to take pictures. Adela Rogers St. John came as a free lance. Warbucks received them all graciously, plied them with food and drink, and Annie told her story. With one big omission. Warbucks and Grace had instructed her carefully not to breathe syllable one about which orphanage she came from or about the locket. For, as they explained to her, how was she going to know if they would be her real folks unless she and they were the only ones to know where they'd left her or about the broken locket? Annie saw the reasoning behind it, and kept mum, telling only about the note. And Warbucks reiterated his offer, fifty thousand dollars to the couple who could prove they were Annie's parents.

What they also kept to themselves was the fact that Annie and Warbucks were heading out of town, nor did they tell the press where they were going.

Early the next morning, by prearrangement, Annie and Sandy met Oliver and Grace on the roof of the mansion. There the autocopter was kept, on what Warbucks called laughingly a "helipad." Annie was dressed in a leather coat and goggles, like a miniature fighter pilot. Warbucks had on what he always had on, a three-piece black suit, stiff collar, bow tie, and his outrageous diamond stickpin. He would show That Man how a Republican dressed.

As they climbed into the single seat of the autocopter (license plate NY-3, the Asp at the joystick), Grace ducked low to avoid the downdraft from the rotors, and backed off to wave them good-bye. Annie, who had never been up higher than the third floor, felt her stomach do tricks as the 'copter raised itself straight up, as though by Punjab's magic. The racket from the engine and the blades was terrible, but the view was magnificent. Below her was spread the entire Warbucks estate, and most of upper Fifth Avenue as well. And what was that long snaking line of people doing in front of the house? It was moving, stretching out for blocks down the avenue.

"Mr. Warbucks, look!"

Warbucks looked down. It was exactly as he'd feared. Hundreds and hundreds of couples were down there, lines of them beginning to form, pushing, shoving men and women, all determined to collect that fifty thousand dollars they'd heard about on the radio or read about in the papers. Annie and Warbucks were today's headlines, front-page stuff. And stealing the show was the fifty thousand smackers. And if they had to take in an orphan kid to collect, it made no never mind. How much can a ten-year-old kid eat? The mutt could always go to the pound.

Every couple on the jostling line was shouting out its own claims to be the real article, while deriding the claims of the others. There were couples with real red hair, and couples who'd gotten up extra early for a dye job. There were Irish couples and Spanish couples, Italian couples, Jewish couples, Polish, Ukrainian, even Chinese couples!

Annie, once Warbucks had explained the matter to her, was totally bewildered. She had only one mother and one father, right? That's all anybody ever *could* have for real. So who were all these other people and what did they want?

"Money, I'm afraid, Annie," said Mr. Warbucks as gently as he could.

Annie shook her head. They were willing to tell such a whopping lie for money! For the first time, she realized that finding her parents might not be all that simple and clear-cut. And another thought crept into her mind for the first time. Suppose they *did* turn up. Suppose they were down there right this minute, holding the other half of the broken locket that only she and they knew about? Well, where had they been before this? Why hadn't they come back for her at any time during the last ten years? How could she be sure that it was Annie and not the fifty thousand they were coming to get?

No, that was impossible. Times were bad, everybody knew that. There was a depression on, wasn't there? So it stood to reason that they'd been too poor to come and get her, but now the fifty thousand would enable them to buy her food and give her shelter. They'd be a family again. Mr. Warbucks must have known that would be the case; that's probably why he offered the money. The thought struck her again that he was the kindest person in the world, underneath all that power.

The cityscape had given way to the beaches and pine barrens of New Jersey as the 'copter headed due south to Washington, D.C., but back on upper Fifth Avenue, all was chaos. Punjab had opened the doors, and the line was supposed to proceed a couple at a time, with Grace Farrell asking the questions and taking the notes. But at the first sign of the massive wooden doors beginning to open, the wavering lines broke into a mob and everybody stormed the gates at once. Even Punjab was no match for the howling couples, who pushed their way in, trampling everything and everybody in their path, yelling for Annie and for the fifty thousand fish.

The scenery below the 'copter was spectacular, but Annie hardly saw it. She was thinking hard, and her little brow was knotted. She might be close now to having a family of her own, and it suddenly scared her. What would it be like not to be an orphan anymore? For the first time in many days, she thought about the Dream. What if her parents turned out to be nothing like the dream images she had of them? After all, why should they be? It was only a child's fantasy. Annie suddenly felt very alone. Anxiously, she turned to Oliver Warbucks and shouted over the racket of the 'copter.

"If all your dreams come true, do you die?"

Warbucks gave a shout of laughter and squeezed Annie's shoulder. "Of course not," he yelled in her ear, "you live happily ever after."

Annie laughed, suddenly relieved. She was being silly. Her parents were going to be wonderful, and they *would* live happily ever after. And Mr. Warbucks and Miss Farrell would always be her friends.

And meanwhile, in less than an hour she was going to meet the thirty-second president of the United States, Franklin Delano Roosevelt. And Eleanor, too.

CHAPTER TEN

The thirty-second president of the United States was just as eager to meet Annie as she was to meet him. After all, Annie (and the fifty thousand simoleons) had pushed him and his New Deal right off the front pages of every newspaper in the country. Which gave him at least one day of peace and quiet. FDR (and Eleanor, too) was curious to see the little redheaded orphan who had captured the nation's imagination. Besides, FDR was an extremely shrewd politician, and he knew that his leverage with Annie would be his leverage with Warbucks. It had not escaped the president's notice that this change of mind on Warbucks' part, to visit with him and talk with him, followed *after* Annie had come into the billionaire's life. Before that, Warbucks wouldn't even take his telephone calls.

The thing about politicians is that, no matter how honorable their objectives, no matter how high their moral tone or how outstanding their virtues, there's not one man jack of them who is above using a ten-year-old girl for political purposes if one floats within reach.

And now they were coming, and would stay to tea, and would be here, if the 'copter were on schedule, within the next fifteen minutes. With his handicap, and with the dignity of the highest office in the land, the president (and Eleanor, too) might have sat in state in the White House and waited for Warbucks to be ushered in. But FDR had the mind and heart of a small boy (even if his body had betrayed him) and he had heard a great deal about the potential military uses of the peculiar craft that Warbucks had developed, but had never seen one. He wasn't about to miss out on this opportunity. So, with Eleanor pushing his wheelchair, he set out down the White House lawn to watch the 'copter land.

There it was, right on time, puffing and chugging its lazy way across the sky. The machine still had to go back to the drawing board for speed, but what was outstanding about it was its maneuverability. Now, for instance, the Asp was sizing up the lawn as a place to land, and the 'copter's controls were in "hover." And hover it did, like the fattest hummingbird in the world, and the noisiest. And when it began to set down, it came down in a perfectly vertical approach.

"Marvelous!" laughed FDR, his cigarette holder pointing at the sky. "Aren't Republicans ostentatious?"

"Franklin, behave," his wife chided humorously. "It's astonishing that he's here at all."

The Asp brought the ship down in a perfect one-point landing, and switched off the rotors. But it took the blades time to come to a full stop, and they churned up a fearful wind, enough to snatch the president's yachting cap off his head and send it tumbling and skimming across the White House lawn. Two Secret Service men went barreling after it.

"What do you call this thing, Oliver?" shouted FDR over the wind, after Warbucks and Annie had climbed cautiously out of the craft.

"An autocopter," the billionaire shouted back. "You don't need an airport, just a backyard."

Suddenly shy now that she was really here, Annie ducked behind Oliver Warbucks.

The parties came together, and Warbucks bent to kiss the First Lady's hand with consummate gallantry.

"I appreciate your coming down here," said the president. "It means a great deal—"

"It means nothing," Warbucks interrupted sharply. "It means only that"—he reached around behind him and pulled Annie out—"Annie wanted to meet you."

Laughing, the president leaned forward in his wheelchair—which was an old office chair fitted out with a set of baby buggy tires, Annie was astonished to notice—and took Annie's hand, shaking it with great ceremony.

"It's nice to meet you, Mr. President Roosevelt," said Annie in the smallest voice of which she was capable.

"It's my pleasure, Annie." The president's eyes twinkled into Annie's own. "And thank you for bringing the old goat. We'll make a New Dealer of him yet."

Now it was Oliver Warbucks' turn to laugh. "Inconceivable!"

With his strong hands, the president turned his chair around and headed uphill toward the White House. Feeling a bit more at ease, Annie ran to help push it, smiling shyly at Mrs. Roosevelt, while the two men continued talking.

"If I can change Bernard Baruch's mind, I can change yours," said FDR.

Warbucks shook his head again, this time more firmly. "Never," he said shortly, his Republican hackles rising.

"Don't mind him, Oliver," said Eleanor smoothly, taking his arm. She was often FDR's buffer, and did it graciously.

Annie was surprised to find the White House so modest, but then she was comparing it with the Warbucks mansion. Three decades later, another First Lady, Mrs. John F. Kennedy, would refurbish the old White House and make it sparkle, but on the day Annie visited it it was something on the shabby side, with worn carpets, threadbare furniture, and ancient draperies. Still, there was a sense of history in every room, a feeling of great events having taken place here, of the destinies of nations and peoples having been altered in these halls.

They had tea in the little drawing room outside FDR's office, and it was a pretty room, just like the living room in the Dream, comfortable, with soft places to sit.

They had a simple meal—fruit and cakes, cookies, and cups of tea and tiny sandwiches, and Annie helped pass the plates around. At first, only polite small talk was made, which gave Annie a chance to study the president and the First Lady. They looked very much like their pictures in the magazines and newspaper supplements she'd sneaked a peek at in Miss Hannigan's office back at the orphanage.

FDR had been a vigorous active man, a sailor, a sportsman, when he'd been struck down by a crippling disease, infantile paralysis, the dreaded poliomyelitis. It left him without the use of his legs, a cripple in a wheelchair.

But it hadn't taken away any of his dedication; if anything, it had strengthened his sense of purpose, and he had campaigned for and won the presidency of the United States from a wheelchair, an unheard-of victory. He had been a handsome man at one time; Annie could see the tattered remnants of that beauty still in his face, but the lively eyes were sunken in dark ringed sockets, and the famous jaw, jutting and proud, had wattles under the chin.

As for Anna Eleanor Roosevelt, the president's wife, well, she had never been a beauty to begin with and she wasn't a beauty now. Her face was on the horsey side, and her famous buck teeth had been caricatured by every Republican newspaper cartoonist in the country. But to Annie none of that mattered. She perceived in the First Lady an inner glow that transformed her features when she spoke, gave her an air of majesty. And Mrs. Roosevelt's eyes were truly beautiful, large, clear, warm, and kind. Annie felt at home right away.

But eventually the talk turned inevitably to politics, and there politeness gave ground to conviction.

Oliver Warbucks had been furious when FDR had closed the banks for federal inspection and given them a "holiday." It was against every business principle he held sacred. Even though it did give the banking institutions a short breathing space to recover and even though it forestalled another run on the banks, Warbucks disapproved mightily of the high-handed way that the president interfered in big business, and he'd set up a howl when Congress had voted FDR extraordinary powers.

He set up a howl now, too.

"The New Deal, in my opinion, is badly planned, badly organized, and badly administered. You don't think your programs through, Franklin, you don't think of what they're going to do to the economy in the long run."

"People don't eat in the long run," said the president mildly.

Mrs. Roosevelt put a protective arm around Annie. "Parents can't feed their children," she added.

"The lucky ones end up in orphanages," said FDR shrewdly, an unspoken reference to Annie.

"The older ones are abandoned, to steal, to starve—"

"The business of this country is business," Warbucks interrupted. "You should—"

"I want to put them to work," interrupted FDR in his turn.

Eleanor's lovely eyes were alight with enthusiasm.

"In the national parks, building camps, clearing trails, fighting fires, planting trees—"

"Hold it! Hold it!" protested Oliver, but FDR caught up the refrain.

"I want to feed them and house them and pay them. Not much but enough so they can send a little back to their parents, hold up their heads, and be proud to be Americans!"

Annie's eyes were shining, too. "That's a swell idea," she exclaimed.

Warbucks shot her a look of annoyance. "It isn't a 'swell idea,' Annie, it's impractical foolishness. Goodhearted and empty-headed. Which parks? Which children? How much will it cost? Who's going to organize it? Who's going to run it?"

"I was hoping you would," said Franklin Roosevelt quietly.

Warbucks was shocked into silence. Was this a joke? He looked from Franklin to Eleanor then back to Franklin again. No, the two of them were perfectly serious.

"Me?" Warbucks pointed an incredulous finger at himself.

"And Annie," said FDR with a sly smile, applying the leverage with a vengeance.

"Leapin' lizards!" cried Annie, hardly daring to breathe.

"Out of the question!" snapped Warbucks.

"How could I help?" demanded Annie, thrilled beyond measure.

"Now wait a minute—" began Warbucks, his face turning purple, but FDR, who knew which side his political biscuit was buttered on, had turned his full attention to Annie.

"You could help us recruit the young people," the president told the eagerly nodding child.

"Now hold everything!" Warbucks was on the edge of exploding. He could see how FDR was using Annie, casting a spell over her with his rhetoric and his voice, but he

113

was powerless to stop him. The president's enthusiasm was as catching as a brush fire, and Annie was burning already.

"Many of them have given up hope, Annie," said the president. "They think their government doesn't care if they live or die. You can help us convince them that, with a little effort on their part—"

"I want to say something!" Warbucks shouted, but in vain. It was too late. Annie was recruited as one of the first members of the Civilian Conservation Corps, which would come to be known as the CCC, the president's favorite work-relief program, in which jobless young men between the ages of eighteen and thirty-five were set to renewing the land, restoring forests, digging ditches, building small dams, sleeping out under the stars, eating decent food, and earning thirty dollars a month.

"You'll help us, too, won't you, Oliver?" implored the president.

"Think of the children. Think of Annie!" put in Mrs. Roosevelt, taking Annie's hand and reaching for Warbucks'.

How could he refuse to take the hand of the First Lady when it was offered to him? But, as her soft fingers closed around his hand and pressed it, as he saw Annie's shining face, filled with ideals of a glorious future under the New Deal, Oliver Warbucks shut his eyes. All he could think of was, how the devil am I going to explain this at the next board meeting of the Republican Club?

Miss Hannigan was feeling a whole lot better, pretty good, in fact. After her tantrum, after locking up the orphans and going on a bender for a day and a half, she woke up smiling again. Because Miss Hannigan remembered something, something important. She had forgotten that she was in possession of a piece of information very much relevant to the case of the orphan girl Annie, as the newspapers were calling her. Very relevant. Crucial, in fact. And she, Miss Hannigan herself, was in *exclusive* possession of said information. She had nearly blurted it out the night she heard Warbucks on the radio, blurted it out to the orphans in her anger.

But that would have been a big mistake. That would

have been giving away something valuable for nothing. And this was one valuable nugget, believe you me.

And the beautiful part was this: although the information was hot, there was no need to hurry. It would stay hot. It wasn't going to get cold for a long time, not until Miss Hannigan had figured out a way to make it pay off, and pay off big. She was actually sitting on a gold mine; all she had to do was work out the details and then present the entire thing to Warbucks. He would pay, oh, how he would pay for the evidence and the information Miss Hannigan had been sitting on all these years. She'd been saving it as a present for Annie, for some wonderful day when Annie had been so rotten that she deserved it. A secret weapon, so to speak. Thank God she'd never had to use it. Thank God she'd been patient. Not patient, smart. Because this was her meal ticket, her entry visa into paradise. Miami, here I come! No more Hudson Street winters for you, old girl. No more whining orphans, lying through their teeth: "We love you, Miss Hannigan." No, it would be afternoons on the beach and nights at the casino and tangos without a break, and shenanigans for Hannigan under a big beach umbrella.

So it was with a light heart that she opened the front door of the Hudson Street Home for Girls, Established 1891. But the couple standing on the doorstep brought the frown right back to her face.

They were so *drab*, this middle-aged man and woman; they looked as though they were going to be a real pain in the duff. The man wore glasses, a nondescript fedora as shapeless as his wife, and a raincoat two sizes too large. The dumpy lady with him could only be wifey; no man ran around with a girlfriend who looked like that. Strictly from Nerdsville, the pair of them.

"Excuse me," said the man in a whiny voice. "Are you the lady who runs this establishment?"

"Unfortunately," snapped Miss Hannigan, immediately on her guard.

"Ten years ago," croaked the woman timidly, "we left our little baby girl on the front step—"

"We were starving," the man cut in. "There was a job, managing a hotel in Maine, but only if we had no children—"

"Wrap it up," snarled Miss Hannigan. "I'm listening to Helen Trent." This was the soap opera that proved what so many women longed to prove, that love *can* live in life at thirty-five . . . and even beyond. And, since Miss Hannigan was well "beyond," she needed all the proof she could get.

"We never meant to leave our little Annie," said the woman, tears forming in her drab eyes.

"Annie?" Miss Hannigan's breath began to shorten.

"Now we have a hardware store in New Jersey, and we could take care of her," the man said.

"We've always loved her," the wife put in.

"You're Annie's *parents?*" Miss Hannigan's eyes were popping out of her head, and she was feeling faint. She had a mental picture of her meal ticket with wings on, flying away to Miami without her.

"Our place isn't fancy," said the woman, twisting an old handkerchief in her nervous fingers, "but it's home. We live over the store."

"There's a yard out back," chimed in the husband.

"We have some chickens," said the wife.

"And a *rooster*," cried the man with a laugh, pulling off his glasses and his wig and giving a loud crow. Rooster Hannigan, her shiftless brother. And hiding under a similar wig and a shapeless coat was the shapely body of Miss Lily St. Regis, named for the hotel.

Miss Hannigan stared dumbfounded at the giggling pair.

"Rooster! My God! I never would have recognized you!"

And, in her mind's eye, she saw the meal ticket flying back from Miami, and it had a nice suntan.

CHAPTER ELEVEN

But before Miss Hannigan could figure out a way to use Rooster and Lily in her plans, or even make plans, *they* put the moves on *her*. It turned out that crafty Rooster and curvy Lily had decided to go for the big scam, Warbucks' reward money. That's what the corny getup was all about.

"If we can fool you, sis, we can fool Bigbucks," Rooster told her earnestly, leaning over the desk.

"Fifty thousand smackers," and Lily licked her catlike chops at the mere mention of the words.

Miss Hannigan heard them out and sipped at her gin, saying nothing. But her brain was chugging a mile a minute up the grade. This put a whole new light on things. There were definite possibilities here. Hannigan had only been thinking vaguely of peddling her secret information to Warbucks, but what Rooster had in mind was far more audacious and a lot nastier. She was beginning to like it, but she still sat silent and shook her head. No point in looking too eager. Besides, she had no use for Miss Walbarf-Castoria in the low-cut polkadot blouse, sitting there, draped over Rooster like he was furniture.

"Aw, sis," Rooster turned on his never-fail charm, "this is gonna be the best bunco job ever. All we need is details."

"About Annie. Specifics," the floozy chimed in.

Miss Hannigan leaned back in her chair and eyeballed the pair of them. "What's in it for me?" she asked.

Rooster's grin split his ratty little face right in half. Now she was talking!

"Money. A three-way split of the fifty thou."

Miss Hannigan shook her head uh-uh. "I want half."

"Half!?!" squeaked Lily, all fluffy indignation.

But Rooster knew a bargain when he saw it. "All right, half," he conceded briskly. Besides, promising to pay and actually paying off are two very different things.

"Rooster!" protested Lily, but Rooster waved a shushing hand in her direction.

"It's all right. Twenty-five grand for me and Lil, twenty-five grand for you."

"Let's see what she has first. See if it's worth twenty-five grand," pouted Lily.

Miss Hannigan threw her a look of contempt. With what she herself knew that nobody else did, and Rooster's way with a con game, the money seemed in the bag. Why not? Let Rooster and Lily do the dirty work, lay themselves on the line. Miss Hannigan would sit back quietly and collect. But she resented every penny that would go to Rooster's cuddly little fuzzball, and she longed to drop a cyanide capsule in Lily's Moxie.

"I got specifics on every kid in this dump." She stood up and made her way into the small, crowded storeroom attached to her office. The walls of the storeroom were floor-to-ceiling shelves, and the shelves were crowded with piled-up and dusty boxes, boxes which had sat there unopened for years.

"It's just a question of finding the right box," she said, waving at the shelves. "Now listen to me, and listen good, because what I got is worth a lot more than fifty thousand dollars. Annie's parents are dead, see? Nobody knows that except me. They were killed in a fire, years and years ago. The cops brought me all their junk, and it's in there somewhere. Two boxes full, as I recall.

"I read all the newspaper stories and listened to all the radio reports. There's two things that Warbucks and Annie left out of the story. Which orphanage she came from and why she wears that old broken locket around her neck. Her parents had saved the other half to claim her with. I figure they left those things out on purpose, to make sure the real parents turned up. Well, the real parents aren't *ever* turning up, but only we know that. And, my darling Rooster, if Annie's so-called parents can claim her with that locket, so can we!" She flashed her brother an evil grin of triumph.

Lily drew her breath in. It was beautiful, foolproof!

They were the only ones with the key to all that money; the legit claimants were playing harp duets somewhere above the clouds. Oh, that was worth half the money any day.

"Fifty thousand smackers," she breathed out, her voice caressing the money as though it were in bed with her.

"And the kid we'll drop in the river," chortled Rooster.

"It can't miss," agreed his sister.

Now the only thing Miss Hannigan hadn't taken into her calculations were those miserable orphans. She should have known better. She knew they had ways of learning everything; their wretched little eyes and ears were everywhere. They had cut peepholes and earholes all over the ancient building; why did she keep forgetting that? Also, the building was heated (when it *was* heated, which was never in the winter) by forced hot air, and there were ducts and vents in almost every room, which carried voices clearly. But Miss Hannigan never took that into consideration. She should have known better, but she hated those orphans so, that she pushed them out of her mind whenever she could.

Molly, scrubbing out the upstairs bathroom, heard voices coming out of the vent—Miss Hannigan's and two strangers'—but, being only six years old, she didn't pay much attention to them until she heard Annie's name mentioned. Then she listened as hard as she could, in growing alarm, until Rooster declared he planned to throw Annie in the river. Molly dropped her brush and gave a shrill little squeal of fear.

"Pepper!" she yelled, because Pepper was on bathroom detail with her, "they're gonna do something bad to Annie!"

Pepper gave an elaborate yawn. Annie had never been her favorite, and she was sick to death of hearing about her. Annie This and Annie That and Annie was going to live like a millionaire, and now Annie had stubbed her toe or something stupid like that. "Did you clean out the can?" she ordered.

Molly sniffled, but there was no way that a six-year-old could take on a thirteen-year-old, so she picked up her scrub brush and the pail and got back to work.

Downstairs, the Unholy Three were tearing the supply

closet apart, ripping up the boxes and dumping their contents out on the floor. Litter was everywhere, but so far, no luck. "It was in an envelope, a sealed envelope," Miss Hannigan was saying nervously. She grabbed another stack of boxes off the shelves. "Look in those," she ordered Lily, shoving them at her. "Make yourself useful. It'll have her name on it."

Lily took the boxes and began to look slowly through them. Rooster and Miss Hannigan dug through their stacks frantically, looking for the envelope only, but Lily took her time, examining everything in every box, and tucking away in her cleavage any little pathetic heirloom that caught her rapacious eye. In the fourth box she opened, she came upon a white envelope, creased and bulging. On it was scribbled in pencil a single word: Annie. Teasingly, she held it up in the air and waited for the other two to notice it. When they did, Rooster gave a loud crow, grabbed it away from her, and ripped it open.

There was nothing in it but half a locket.

For a long, awed minute, they crowded around it, looking at their ticket of admission, the cheap little broken trinket that spelled Easy Street.

"We got it," said Lily triumphantly.

"We got it!" yelled Rooster and Lily.

"WE GOT IT!!" the three of them shrieked, then Rooster broke again into his evil cock-crow, a sure sign that something wicked was going to happen.

Upstairs, her ear to the bathroom vent, Molly felt the hair on the back of her neck prickle. Pepper or no Pepper, she had to get out of here and warn Annie. She stood up as quietly as she could, and laid her brush down. She peeked around the corner of the toilet cubicle to see Pepper sitting on the floor, smoking a homemade cigarette and goofing off. Pepper's back was turned. Molly picked up Pepper's mop and swung it with all her little might, clipping Pepper on the ear and putting her temporarily out of business. Then she fled past her into the dormitory, where the rest of them were stealing a break, now that Hannigan was locked up on business downstairs.

"They're gonna do something bad to Annie!" yelled Molly, bursting in. The other girls looked up, startled.

"Who is?" demanded Duffy.

"*They* are!" yelled Molly, pointing at the bathroom. She meant, of course, the people who owned the voices coming out of the hot-air register, but she was too little to get that out right away.

"Who's they?" Kate asked again.

Molly was wriggling all over with frustration. She knew they were wasting time. "Come *on*, you guys," she urged. "We gotta warn her! We gotta hurry!"

One by one the orphans got to their feet. If Molly's words hadn't convinced them, Molly's face and the anxiety in her voice had. It was clear: They had to warn Annie. Of what, they'd find out later. But now that Miss Hannigan was out of the way for a while, it was a good opportunity to hit the trail. They made for the window, which gave onto an old-fashioned iron fire escape. One by one—even Pepper—they climbed on the wrought-iron landing and began to go down the stairs. Orphans to the rescue.

Down in Miss Hannigan's quarters, the conspirators were celebrating, with gin and music and revelry. Having tanked themselves up on the new brew, they'd put on the radio and danced, Miss St. Regis throwing a mean cancan, and Miss Hannigan hopping around on her stork legs imagining she was Isadora Duncan. Easy Street was their new address, and they were planning to move there that very afternoon, right after they picked up Annie and the money, disposing of one and dividing the other.

As Miss Hannigan tilted her bottle back for another healthy swallow, movement caught the corner of her eye. Movement outside her window. "Hey," she said shakily, and staggered over to see. What she saw sobered her. A bunch of those miserable orphans was tiptoeing down the fire escape, right past her very nose, making their escape. Of all the nerve! Sounding her battle cry: "Kill! kill! kill!" she dashed out the door.

As they rounded the corner, the girls could hear Miss Hannigan pounding after them, shrieking. They ran faster, all except Molly, whose stubby little baby legs wouldn't carry her any faster. Molly was falling behind and getting out of breath in the bargain. Suddenly, a bony hand like a falcon's talons clutched the child's shoulder. Miss Hannigan! Caught!

"I got Molly," Miss Hannigan called out tauntingly to the others. Reluctantly, they stopped running, stood there, half a block ahead of her, uncertain of what to do. Annie or Molly? Molly or Annie?

"No!" yelled Molly at the top of her lungs. "Go on! I'm okay! Go *on!*" She struggled in Miss Hannigan's strong arms, trying to find an opening to kick the woman's shins, or even to step on her toe. But Hannigan promptly clapped a hand over the child's mouth, and held her wriggling body at arm's length, tantalizingly, so that the orphans could see it. And it worked.

One by one, the girls straggled back, defeated. Miss Hannigan collected them with a triumphant cackle and marched them back inside. Then she dragged them up to the top floor and locked them into a tiny, airless closet, which was littered with boxes and mouse droppings, and threw away the key.

"All right," said Pepper into the darkness. "Whose rotten idea was this?"

987 Fifth Avenue was a shambles; it bore little resemblance to the stately mansion it had been this morning. Rather, it looked like a village after a horde of insane elephants had thundered through it on a rampage. Precious Ming vases lay in shards. Pictures hung askew; the walls were covered with grimy fingermarks and the lustrous marble floors were covered by a scuffed mantle of footprints. Cigarette butts were everywhere—on the mantels, in the potted palms, stubbed out in priceless bibelots.

Grace Farrell sighed and put down her pencil. In front of her on the card table was a mountain of questionnaires, hours' worth of paperwork and discouragement. Around her, she could see the servants tackling the mess with mops and pails, vacuum cleaners and polishes. They were as angry and depressed as she was. It would take hours to make a dent in this mess, and days before the extent of the damage could be assessed. And most of the damaged things were priceless, therefore uninsurable, therefore uninsured.

Yet these were, in the last analysis, only *things.* But how to face Annie? How to tell Annie that among all the hundreds and hundreds of people who came clamoring for the money none of them had emerged as her true parents? Miss Farrell sighed again.

Outside and above the house, the noise of the autocopter was at first faint, barely discernible, like the buzzing of a faraway hive of bees. But it grew closer and louder; they were coming back from Washington.

Oh, dear, thought Miss Farrell. If only they'd stayed longer! Given the servants a few more hours to get this mess straightened out. Mr. Warbucks . . . Oliver . . . would be furious!

And it was true. When Warbucks walked into the room with Annie and the Asp, Punjab following, the look of astonishment on his face turned to a deep scowl of displeasure. But Annie didn't notice a thing. Her face was lit up by excitement, and she was chattering to Punjab.

"Maybe they brought me a sister and a brother. Maybe they—"

Punjab put a gentle hand on Annie's curly head. "Buddha says that man who counts his chickens before they're hatched is a scrambled egg," he told her gently. But Annie wasn't paying attention. Spotting Grace, she ran over to her at once, eyes questioning.

"Is my mother pretty? Is my father tall? What are they like? What do they do? Are they the grandest people you ever met?" she demanded all in one breath.

Miss Farrell bit her lips and exchanged glances with Mr. Warbucks. Drake, noticing this, signaled silently to the other servants. "We'll finish later." And the maids and footmen filed out swiftly.

Grace, looking with sympathy at the excited child, decided that the most direct way was the kindest. "We haven't found them, Annie."

Annie paled, and the excitement drained out of her face, leaving it without color or life. She seemed to grow shorter and younger, and a weak little smile trembled on her lips before it disappeared entirely.

Grace's heart ached for her, and she turned to Oliver Warbucks with tears in her eyes.

"I've interviewed eight hundred and sixty-five couples," she said, indicating the card table piled high with papers. "None of them knew about the locket. I never realized

123

how many dishonest people there were in New York." Discouragement was written all over her pretty features.

Warbucks sighed, and his hand touched Annie's hair briefly and gently. He, too, felt deeply for the child's pain, but he was more experienced and more cynical than Grace, and his disappointment wasn't aggravated by disillusion, as was hers.

Annie suddenly needed to be alone, very alone. She ducked out from under Oliver Warbucks' hand and made a bolt for the stairs, Sandy bounding along after her. Grace uttered a small cry and started after her, but Warbucks laid a restraining hand on her arm.

"I'll go," he said quietly, and he mounted the stairs to Annie's bedroom.

The child was sitting forlornly on the windowseat of her room, her dog in her arms. She had evidently been fighting a losing battle with her tears, for Sandy was busily licking the salt from his little mistress's face.

The look on Annie's face caught Mr. Warbucks in the solar plexus, like a blow. Until this moment, he'd not realized how important her optimism, her enthusiasm for everything, was to him. She represented his lost youth, his vanished ideals. Making her happy was like making some long-hidden part of himself happy, too. And seeing her so unhappy was like having that hidden part of him die a little. And he felt so damn helpless, that was the worst part of it! He loved her, and he could do nothing for her.

"Annie," he said gently from the doorway.

She didn't look up at him, but stared straight ahead of her. "I guess they're dead," she said without emphasis, her voice lifeless. "I guess I've known that deep down for a long time."

"I'm not giving up!" Warbucks told her stoutly. "Don't you give up."

But Annie shook her head sadly. "I didn't want to be just another orphan, Mr. Warbucks," she told him. "I wanted to believe I was special—"

Crossing the room in two swift bounds, Warbucks caught hold of Annie's shoulders and turned her to face him.

"You *are* special," he said fiercely. "Don't ever stop believing that! You are special to me, special to all of us and special to yourself. It's the most important weapon you have in the fight! Do you believe that? Annie, look at me! Do you believe that?" His eyes probed deeply into hers, forcing her to meet his gaze.

Without a word, Annie burst into tears and threw her arms around Oliver Warbucks' neck, clinging to him and crying bitterly. Sandy set up a furor of barking and licking, trying to get at Annie's face to comfort it.

Warbucks sat holding the little girl he had come to love so much, rocking her in his arms, patting and stroking her shoulders, and feeling very, very much like "Daddy." After a while, the great sobs became tears and the tears sniffles, and at last the crying ended. Annie sat up and dried her eyes on Mr. Warbucks' clean linen handkerchief, and blew her nose, and smiled a little, and patted Sandy, and felt a whole lot better. Crying does that sometimes, especially if you're not much of a crier.

"Well!" said Warbucks brightly, standing up. "Shall we go downstairs?"

Annie nodded.

Downstairs, there was a ring at the doorbell. Punjab opened the front door and looked down from his enormous height onto a small, rather dim-looking couple. The woman was clutching the man's arm fearfully, and the man himself bore a striking resemblance to Casper Milquetoast, the Timid Soul of the funny papers. Yet, small and unprepossessing as the couple was, Punjab felt a warning prickle under his turban.

"Is this the Warbucks home?" asked the man.

"It is," said Punjab distantly.

"We've come for our little girl," said the woman. "We've come for Annie."

"This way, please," and he led them into the living room, where Grace looked up annoyed. Another pair of deceivers, for she couldn't imagine them to be anything else. A couple of deadbeats who came out of the woodwork to exploit a poor little orphan child for gain. Her thoughts surprised her, but Grace Farrell had had a rough morning, and it was late in the day and she was weary. If nothing else, today had been a bitter educational experience.

They started on their tale of woe immediately, and it was the same one she'd heard over and over today, a young couple down on their luck, unable to care for their one and only child. This one had a variation too boring to talk about, a job in Maine somewhere, but no children allowed. She wasn't buying word one of the tale.

"We were starving, ma'am," Rooster whined pathetically. "We needed the job, even though it meant—"

Grace had heard all she cared to. "Punjab," she called, so that the giant could escort the pair to the front door.

"—leaving our baby girl," continued Rooster.

"—wrapped in a newspaper—" contributed Lily.

"—on the steps of the Hudson Street orphanage," Rooster finished all in one breath.

An immediate and heavy silence fell, in which Punjab and Grace exchanged glances of consternation. Could it be possible? There was something so obviously fishy about this couple, and yet they had said the magic words; they knew the name of Annie's orphanage. What to do next?

Annie and Warbucks were coming down the marble stairway, followed by Sandy.

"What's this?" asked Warbucks as he came into the living room, scowling.

Grace consulted her notes. "Ralph and Shirley Mudge, Mr. Warbucks. From Hoboken, New Jersey."

Sandy growled. His instincts were all telling him that something here was smelling funny. Mr. Warbucks didn't care for the look of them either, but he shook the limp hand that "Ralph Mudge" was holding out to him.

There was a soft commotion, as "Shirley Mudge" caught sight of Annie and began to flutter around her husband.

"Oh, Ralph," she pointed breathlessly. "Do you think that's our Annie? Our very own little girl?"

Purposefully, Miss Farrell picked up a handful of paper.

"If you'll just fill out this questionnaire—" she began, but the Mudges weren't paying attention.

"Oh, Ralph, look!" cried Lily sweetly. "She still has the locket!" While Grace and Oliver stood by in shock, Lily St. Regis trotted over to Annie, dug in her purse, and came out with the other half. She held it up to the locket around Annie's neck, and the two halves fitted perfectly together. Then she smiled breathlessly into Annie's face.

"We've finally found you!"

Annie gave a sharp cry. But instead of throwing herself into her mother's arms, as she'd dreamed of doing for so many years, she turned and buried her face in Oliver Warbucks' waistcoat.

CHAPTER TWELVE

What else was there to do? Ralph and Shirley Mudge might not have looked like much, but they certainly satisfied the requirements. Not only did they know where Annie had been abandoned, but they had produced the missing half of the locket. Ergo, they must be Annie's parents, Q.E.D.

Annie Mudge. She tried it out in her mind, but it had a funny sound and an even funnier feeling. This was all so different from what Annie had imagined. In her mind, her mother had always been beautiful and sweet-looking, like Grace Farrell, and lately her mental image of her father had worn a commanding air and a bald head.

But she didn't mean to be ungrateful. These were her real parents, and they couldn't help how they looked. Annie had never been one to place good looks above everything that counted; if she had, she never would have picked up Sandy. But it was more than only their looks, or the fact that their manners were crude. Annie knew she must come from very poor folks; why else would they have left their baby at an orphanage? Poverty was no crime, and neither was lack of education or culture. *I'm spoiled; that's what's wrong with me,* thought Annie. *Spoiled and ungrateful. It's just that I've waited for this day to come for so long, and now that it's here . . . it's so . . . different from what I'd imagined.*

And yet . . . and yet . . . there was something else, something she couldn't put her finger on. But Sandy was still growling, and Punjab had that look on his face, and Grace looked so unhappy, and Mr. Warbucks was scowling like a thundercloud.

Oliver Warbucks had done a lot of business with a lot of shady types and had developed an instinct for spotting them that didn't take a back seat to Sandy's. He knew these two were shady, but unfortunately they were Annie's parents and his hands were tied. It wasn't that he thought they were lying about who they were; didn't they have the only proof? No, what Warbucks believed was that they had come to claim their little girl only because of the fifty thousand reward. If there had been no money, they would have left Annie to rot in the orphanage.

And these were the people he was supposed to entrust his precious little Annie to! The thought cut him like a knife, and evidently others were of the same opinion, because Grace was positively suffering, and Punjab looked unhappy, and Sandy was down on his belly with his neck hairs raised, and only the Asp was inscrutable, as usual.

Still, he had no choice. Alarmed as Warbucks was for Annie's safety and well-being, what legal recourse had he against the child's natural parents?

"I suppose you heard about the reward on the radio?" he asked Mr. Mudge.

Rooster forced his face to look surprised. "There's a reward?"

"We don't have a radio," "Shirley" put in meekly.

"You saw the newspapers, then."

"Papers? What papers?" asked Rooster innocently.

"How did you know that Annie was here?" asked Grace.

"Some dame at the orphanage told us," said Rooster.

Lily dug around in her shabby pocketbook, coming up with a worn and folded piece of paper, which she handed to Warbucks.

"Here's her birth certificate. I've kept it next to my heart all these years," she said. Actually, she'd found it in the same shoebox with the locket only a few hours before.

Unfolding it carefully, Oliver read aloud, " 'Ann Marie Mudge. Born October 18, 1922.' "

Now Annie spoke up for the first time. "I'll go pack," she said quietly, and started out of the room.

"Want me to help, baby?" cooed Lily.

Annie stopped. "No, thanks. Mom," she added. The word sounded strange on her tongue. Slowly, she headed for the stairs.

Oliver Warbucks led the way into his library, where he opened the top drawer of a massive desk and took out a scrap of paper, holding it so that Ralph Mudge and his wife could see it clearly.

"A certified check?" Rooster's eyebrows lifted. "Sir, we're just so thrilled to have found Annie, we don't need any money," he simpered piously.

Bushwah, thought Warbucks, but all he said was, "Then I'll take it back."

Before the words were out of his mouth, Lily's soft little hand had snaked out and fastened over the check.

"Of course, we are poor people. It would help us a lot. We could buy Annie milk and a warm blanket—"

Spare me, thought Warbucks. *Don't insult my intelligence.* Out loud he said, "Put it in your pocket, Mrs. Mudge."

The check vanished like a snowflake on a sizzling stove top, and there was nothing left to say. In silence, they waited for Annie to come down, Warbucks and Grace lost in gloomy thoughts, Rooster and Lily trying to keep their glee from showing on their faces. The scam had gone off without a hitch! Easy Street, here we come!

The orphanage had been quiet for hours. It must be very late, but to the unhappy girls sandwiched into the uncomfortable supply closet, the hours had dragged by like years. They had no idea what time it was, or even if it was the very same day. Molly had told them everything she'd learned from the bathroom vent, and they'd pieced the rest of the story together, and it was obvious that Annie was in very bad trouble indeed. Molly was right. They *had* to warn her. But what if it was already too late? They couldn't think about that. They had to get out.

But how? Miss Hannigan had locked them in tightly, and that door was the only way in or out. It looked hopeless.

Suddenly, Pepper cried, "Look!" and pointed up. They followed her finger. There was a kind of trapdoor on the ceiling of the closet, and it probably led to the roof. But how to reach it? The closet was narrow but high; these old buildings had tall rooms, and there was no ladder.

Unless . . . they agreed. The largest and strongest on the bottom, the smallest on top. That meant that Pepper took the firmest stance she could and braced herself. July, the next largest, climbed up onto Pepper's shoulders and wavered there. Kate climbed up over Pepper and July, and stationed herself. Duffy, who was small but wiry, scrambled up over the human ladder and tried to open the trapdoor. It hadn't been opened in years, and it wouldn't budge. It was dark and stuffy at the top of the closet, and what little air there was was choked with cobwebs and dust, and that didn't help Duffy's struggles any. Under her, the girls were beginning to groan and wobble and call advice up to her.

"Put your back into it!" yelled Pepper.

"Hurry up!" pleaded Kate. "I can't take much more of this."

"I'm doing the best I can," Duffy shouted down. "This is no picnic, y'know."

The dust was getting to her, filling her nose and eyes with terrible itchings. Duffy opened her mouth to sneeze, shut it again, opened it, and out issued a sneeze like the roar of a lion. The human ladder wobbled and almost fell, but Duffy shot upward on the force of the sneeze. Her hard little head struck the edge of the trapdoor in just exactly the right spot, and the hatch flew open!

Duffy scrambled through it and found herself on the roof, just as they'd hoped.

"It's all right," she called back down. "C'mon up."

Molly was sent up first, as the smallest, then Tessie, who was murmuring, "Oh, my goodness, oh, my goodness," as usual. Kate climbed through the opening, then they reached down and pulled July through.

That left only Pepper, and she had an uncomfortable climb up a hot-water pipe before she, too, popped like a cork out of the trapdoor and onto the roof. Now they were there, but where were they? They ran to the edge of the roof and looked down.

The late-summer sun had set less than an hour ago, and it was that strange hour between the sunset and the moonrise that is called twilight and has a special radiance all its own. There was still some light to see by, but it was fast fading. Below them, three stories down, they could see the street, and the alleyways, and a handful of people who'd had their supper (the orphans, of course, hadn't) and were out again in the warm evening.

In order to get off the roof, they'd have to climb down

the drainpipe; there was no other way. It was perilous and terrifying, but these were no ordinary girls. These were orphans who'd never known decent treatment; they had developed a certain amount of toughness, independence, and courage. They were scared, sure, but what choice did they have? One after the other, they set out on the long road down, sliding down the rough iron drainpipe, grabbing at a clothesline to swing over, dropping to the next roof, from that roof down to a metal awning and from the awning, down to the street. Pepper led the way; Annie might not have been her favorite person, but now that she was in danger, it was up to the orphans to take care of their own. The girls took turns handing Molly down until, as though by a miracle, they all stood safe and sound on the sidewalk.

Now all they had to do was find Annie.

The radio had given the address of Oliver Warbucks' mansion, and they knew in a vague way that it was up-town on the east side and they were downtown on the west. Without carfare for the trolley, all they could do was walk. As it was going to be a long, long walk, they'd better not waste time. And so they set out, six ragged little girls with one sense of purpose and, they hoped, a decent sense of direction.

"I'll go see what's keeping Annie," volunteered Grace, glad to leave the unspoken tension of the situation. Up-stairs, she found Annie putting the last of her things into her suitcase and trying to put a brave face on things.

"We're still going to be friends, aren't we, Miss Farrell?"

"Of course, Annie, we'll always be friends."

"And now that I'll have a home of my own, I can have you come to visit, you and Mr. Warbucks. Will you come?"

"We'd love to." Grace tried hard to smile; she owed Annie that, at least. Not to break down in front of her.

"It's gonna be all right, you'll see. They're real nice folks, I can tell. I'm gonna love living in New Jersey."

"Of course you are, darling. Who wouldn't love living in New Jersey?"

* * *

They'd been walking for what seemed like hours, and it was starting to rain, one of those swift, ferocious, merciless summer rains that come pelting at you from a suddenly angry sky, driven by gusting winds and punctuated by green and blue lightning. There was a park ahead of them and an arch, and they huddled under it unhappily, waiting for the rain to stop. They waited a very long time before it was safe to come out, but finally creeping from their insufficient shelter they made their way across the street and onto a broad boulevard that seemed to begin right there.

"Oh, my goodness," said Tessie for the seven hundredth time.

"We're never gonna make it," predicted Pepper dourly.

But Duffy had spotted a street sign and was trying to read it with some difficulty. It was dark, the sign was wet with rain, and she couldn't read all that well, anyway. But at last it clicked into place, the letters held a meaning.

"We've found Fifth Avenue!" she turned to the others and exulted.

Pepper looked at the house number on the nearest building's canopy. "Number One, Fifth Avenue," she read. "We gotta get to *Nine Hundred and Eighty-seven!*"

They groaned and plodded on.

The moment was here, and it couldn't be put off any longer. Annie's bag was packed, she was dressed to go, and go they must. When they walked out the front door and Annie saw the battered 1929 Ford pickup truck sitting between the proud Town Car and the haughty Dusenberg, she felt a pang of disappointment, followed by anger at herself for her snobbery. Didn't she know there was a depression on?

Mr. and Mrs. Mudge bundled Sandy into the open part of the truck, and Rooster slid behind the wheel. Lily gestured for Annie to slide in after her, then she climbed into the cab next to Rooster and snuggled close. Annie felt mighty left out of things, and desperately sad as she took last looks at Grace, Punjab, and the Asp. Mr. Warbucks was nowhere to be seen; he had made his good-byes inside, and wished to be alone with his grief. But he was watching, from the balcony outside his office, as the old pickup began to drive away, and there was a suspicious wetness in his eyes.

But they didn't go far, only around the corner, where Rooster stepped on the brake and the pickup came to a stop. An old lady with a shopping bag came hobbling out of the shadows and climbed onto the running board with surprising agility. She yanked the truck door open and slid in next to Annie, who was now squeezed between her and Lily, and getting more and more bewildered, especially as her "mother" and "father" began to peel pieces of their disguise off. "Mom" snatched off her dowdy hat and wig, revealing a head of blonde hair, while "Dad" threw off his eyeglasses and his beady little eyes glittered.

"Did you get it, Rooster?" screeched the bag lady, in a voice so unmistakable that Annie's blood froze in her veins. Miss Hannigan! No two ways about it, that's gotta be Miss Hannigan's voice!

The woman who had posed as Annie's mother was waving the certified check under the bag lady's nose. Miss Hannigan snatched it.

"*I'll* hold it. For safe keeping."

The younger woman, quick as a hungry cat on a plump mouse, snatched it back.

"Over my dead body."

"Over anything," snarled Miss Hannigan, grabbing the check again.

Sensing that this might be her only chance, Annie made a leap across Miss Hannigan and grabbed the handle of the truck door, but the woman was too fast and too strong, and grabbed her tight.

"Help! Mr. Warbucks! Help me!" yelled Annie, shouting as loud as she could. Miss Hannigan's hand clamped over her mouth.

Rooster jammed the truck into gear and they took off into the night, swift as a bat.

Oh, thought Annie. *Oh, no, no. Where are they taking me? What are they going to do with me?*

They had come about three miles, two of them up Fifth Avenue, and they were exhausted. Hungry, cold, stiff, and totally worn out, their feet aching, bodies begging for sleep. Yet they were only as far uptown as Forty-second Street, and they still had nearly two more miles to go. When they reached the broad steps of the New York Public Library's main building, the orphans simply collapsed, sprawling on the marble stairs, unable to go on. Maybe this expedition had been crazy in the first place; they were too tired to trust their judgment. It seemed to them that they would never reach Oliver Warbucks' house, never be able to warn Annie in time. It was probably too late by now anyway.

Annie watched horrified as Lily and Rooster and Miss Hannigan discarded what was left of their disguises. Two of the three she had never seen before, but if they were only half as bad as Miss Hannigan, Annie's goose was cooked. They sat jammed together in the front seat, and Annie was scared and uncomfortable, and unable to think. Sandy was in the back . . . she hoped . . . but she hadn't seen him or heard him in a long while. Anything might have happened. She felt very small and very alone.

Merriment was rising all around her, as the conspirators began to realize that they'd really pulled it off, really gotten away with the fifty thousand bucks. Now all they had to do was figure out how to spend it.

"I wanna get me one of them little gold lamé numbers," said the cheap little blonde who had called herself Shirley Mudge.

"If they sell them in Atlantic City. We're not stopping until we get to Atlantic City," laughed the skinny little ferret of a man Miss Hannigan had called Rooster.

Atlantic City! What am I gonna do in Atlantic City? moaned Annie silently. She wasn't even sure where Atlantic City was. She wasn't even sure where they were right this minute.

Where they were was Fifth Avenue at Forty-second Street, heading downtown past the library. As a matter of fact, they were driving right on by the orphans at this moment, but they couldn't see Annie because she was jammed between the others on the front seat, and she couldn't see them for the same reason. But Sandy saw them, and he began to whine.

*　　*　　*

"I say we go back," said Pepper gloomily.

"We *can't*," came from Molly.

"We been walking for a hundred years," Kate sighed.

"Yeah, and we're never gonna get there," Pepper stated vehemently, bringing the others way down.

"We *have* to!" Molly was still keeping the faith.

"Let's take a vote," suggested Duffy.

"All those in favor of calling it quits," said Pepper, raising her own hand. Kate voted with her, then nervous little Tessie, and finally a reluctant July raised her grubby hand. Four to two, with Duffy and Molly outvoted. They'd go back. It was probably too late to do anything for Annie anyway. They never saw the pickup truck passing by, or the whining dog inside the back.

As the distance grew between him and the orphans, Sandy made up his mind. He wanted with all his doggy heart to stay with Annie, especially since he knew she was surrounded by danger. Those were bad people with her; he could sense it. Miss Hannigan he knew of old, but as soon as he'd laid eyes on Rooster and Lily, back there in Mr. Warbucks' home, he'd known they were not good guys. Annie needed him now more than ever.

But when he saw the orphans outside the library, sprawled on the steps, he sensed that Annie's only salvation lay in bringing help. It was the conflict inside him that caused him to scratch and whine, and it was the resolution of that conflict that caused him to leap out of the pickup truck and run the four blocks back to the library.

"It's Sandy! Look, everybody, it's Sandy."

And he was jumping up and licking faces and barking loudly.

"He wants something," said Duffy.

Sandy would run a few steps off, then turn and bark furiously, then run back, then run off again barking.

"He wants us to follow him!" Molly cried.

"Then what are we waiting for? Let's go!" yelled Pepper, who a moment ago had been all for returning to the orphanage. But that was forgotten now, as they followed Sandy at a run. He raced up Fifth Avenue, north, as the truck holding Annie prisoner headed south.

It was a long run, but the little girls had their second

wind now, and, with Molly on Kate's back, they managed to keep up pretty well with the dog. Whenever he got too far ahead of them, he'd turn and wait, barking at the orphans to please hurry.

Eventually they got there, to Oliver Warbucks' mansion, to the high iron gates and the thick stone wall. But nothing stopped Sandy. Squeezing in between the bars of the gates, he ran around the huge pillars and up to the front portico. The orphans, one by one, did the same. Ahead of them was the massive wooden door, and Sandy, on his hind legs, was scratching and barking at it.

Now that they were finally here, the little girls were terrified. What would Mr. Warbucks say? What would they dare to say to him? They stared at one another in panic, until Pepper, the oldest, hiked up her skirt and marched up to the front door and rang the bell hard.

"Now what?" scowled Oliver Warbucks. He really wanted to be alone tonight; he had no patience with anything or anybody. Annie was gone, and he would have to pick up the pieces of his life tomorrow. As for tonight, just let him alone.

Punjab and the Asp went to the door together, and Punjab pulled it open. There was Sandy, barking furiously, and Punjab knew he'd been right. The little Princess was in trouble somewhere. But where? Behind Sandy, he could see a little group of anxious faces, six raggedy little orphans, staring at him in terror. Nobody had told them there would be a man as big as a mountain and all black. Did he eat little girls? They just stood there trembling, with their mouths hanging open, much as Annie herself had done when she'd first laid eyes on Punjab.

Suddenly, Oliver Warbucks appeared in the doorway at Punjab's side. The man they'd come to see, and now they were too scared to speak to him.

"Sandy!" Warbucks exclaimed. "What are you doing here?"

"Sir . . ." began Molly in a tiny little voice.

Kate jabbed her in the ribs. "I think he's a Highness," she whispered.

"Your Highness," Molly whispered.

"We're friends of Annie's," said Duffy bravely.

Warbucks frowned deeply, and the lines around his

mouth tugged the corners down. "She's gone," he said flatly. "Her parents came and got her. They—"

"That wasn't her parents, mister!" Molly cut in excitedly. "They was bad peoples." She saw Oliver Warbucks' eyes open wide, and then the giant had her by the shoulders and was glaring into her face, willing her to say more. He *did* eat little girls. Molly fainted dead away.

Punjab lifted her gently and carried the tiny girl into the house, with the other orphans trailing behind him and the Asp.

As for Oliver Warbucks, he was running for the stairs, shouting for Grace, shouting for the servants, the police, the army, navy, and marine corps. The entire house was galvanized into action.

Because Rooster was the strongest of them, it was decided that he should keep hold of Annie, and so he and Lily changed places, Lily taking the wheel, while Rooster sat jammed close to Annie, his hands digging roughly into the flesh of the little girl's arms. The truck was way downtown now, where the office buildings yield their places to docks, piers, and warehouses, totally deserted at night, except for rats of the rodent and human kind.

"Rooster, honey," whined Lily, squirming in her seat. "It's so cramped in here, my dress is getting all sweaty. Let's get rid of the kid and make some room."

"Okey-dokey," chortled Rooster.

Lily put on the brake and the truck rumbled to a stop in a totally empty street filled with vacant lots and chainlink fences. Rooster opened the door, and Annie, sensing that her final hour might be at hand, began to fight like a tiger, flailing out with her tiny fists, and kicking and squirming.

"Mr. Warbucks is gonna knock your lights out!" she hollered. "Mr. Warbucks is gonna rearrange your teeth. Mr. Warbucks is gonna cut off your—"

Suddenly, she saw her chance. Miss Hannigan was holding the check as she, too, struggled with Annie, and Annie reached up and snatched it out of her surprised hand, pushed her aside, and leaped down from the truck. She ran, pounding hard, down the old cobbled street that hurt her shoes and twisted her ankles. She dodged around fences and darted through an alley, her breath coming fast and her sides aching. But she was getting away! She was getting away!

Annie ran around a corner and smack into Rooster Hannigan, who was waiting for her with a twisted smile on his ugly face. He grabbed her roughly and bent her arm up her back until she yelled in pain. Then he marched her back to the truck, and his evil chuckle made Annie's blood run cold in her veins. Oh, she was trapped all right!

CHAPTER THIRTEEN

The orphans were quickly and efficiently debriefed by Warbucks and Grace, and now Oliver Warbucks knew everything they knew. The culprits were Miss Hannigan and another pair, the couple posing as Annie's parents. The truck had last been seen heading south on Fifth Avenue, a few blocks down from Forty-second Street. The orphans were wrapped in blankets and taken down to the kitchen for Mrs. Pugh to feed from the huge steaming pots of good things she kept on the stove.

Warbucks swung into action. It was his element, action, and he felt almost happy. At least he was doing something, barking commands into the telephone, using his clout, exercising his power. He felt almost elated, larger than life. Annie—*his* Annie, because she wasn't anybody else's—was in danger, and by God he'd get her out of it if it cost him his last million dollars. Mobilization, that was the ticket. All units operating and in communication.

"You take the autocopter, I'll take the car," Warbucks commanded Punjab as he held the phone for J. Edgar Hoover, head of the Federal Bureau of Investigation. Hoover came on the wire. "Yes, J. Edgar, Warbucks here. The orphan, Annie, has been kidnapped. I want every G-man east of the Mississippi on this case in the next twenty minutes. Yes? Good."

The coast guard was assigned to all ports of exit; the New York mounted police to do a block by block search south of Forty-second Street, while squad cars of New York's Finest set up roadblocks. The train stations and bus terminals were covered. So the criminals couldn't escape. But that was only the mop-up operation under way, to prevent them from getting away with the money. But something could be happening to Annie this very minute, and who knew where they might be? *If anything happens to Annie. I'll never forgive myself*, thought Warbucks. *I never should have let her leave with those two; I knew they were fishy characters as soon as I laid eyes on them! I might have signed Annie's death warrant. We* must *find her!*

Grace had the Dusenberg's engine running, waiting for Warbucks to come out. When he did, she stepped on the gas and the powerful automobile roared out of the driveway and into the streets, speeding downtown. Above their heads, the autocopter whirred, the Asp at the controls, and Punjab in direct radio communication with the Dusenberg. Around them, sirens shrieked as police squad cars flanked them and fanned out to take other avenues downtown.

Punjab had a pair of powerful binoculars with him, Swiss-made, with which he was scanning the city below, looking out for the 1929 Ford pickup, one lone needle in the haystack of a city of five million people.

"Punjab," Warbucks barked into the radio transmitter. "The bridges to New Jersey first!"

The autocopter turned in obedience to the command.

"He's got her now," remarked Lily as she saw Rooster coming back with Annie. He was still twisting her arm cruelly, forcing her to march double-time. "Well, we'll soon be rid of the brat. Good riddance to bad rubbish, I say."

"Where are we gonna dump her?" asked Miss Hannigan.

"In the river, of course."

Miss Hannigan's brow creased in a frown. "But she might drown!"

"Might drown!" hooted Lily derisively. "Get you! Might drown. Of *course* she'll drown. That's the plan, ain't it?"

"You mean Rooster is gonna *kill* her?" Miss Hannigan couldn't quite get that through her head.

"Well, I sure hope so," pouted Lily.

"*Kill* her? Really *kill* her?" She had never taken this into consideration as a possibility, and she obviously was having problems with the concept.

"Will you look at who called who dumb," snorted Miss St. Regis scornfully.

"He *can't!*"

"Ha! Watch him."

The bridges were a false lead, not one of them, or any of the ferry stations either, showing so much as a taillight of the pickup. But near the southern tip of Manhattan, where the trucking depots and warehouses are, near to the river, Punjab spotted something. He gestured for the Asp to fly lower, and the craft descended and hovered while Punjab fiddled with the fine adjustment on the binoculars. That looked like . . . it might be . . . it was!

"Sahib," Punjab spoke into his transmitter, "the truck is on Canal Street, heading south. Repeat, the truck is on Canal Street heading south."

"I read you, Punjab, loud and clear. Pursue and take whatever action is necessary. We are on course." Warbucks turned to Grace. "Floor it," he said tersely. The Dusenberg shot forward like the mechanical rabbit on a dog track. The needle on the speedometer went crazy. 80 . . . 85 . . . 95 . . . 100 miles an hour. Around him, sirens wailed as the New York Police Department and the G-men stepped up the chase.

They were all back in the pickup, heading south to the Battery, where the riptides could carry a body far out to sea and never bring it back. Miss Hannigan sat strangely silent, and this frightened Annie even more than Rooster's punishing grip on her arm. Her mind was racing; there must be a way out. There must!

They were in the most neglected part of the city. Nothing but old freight-train tracks and railroad bridges. Because there were virtually no cars here even in daylight, the roads had been permitted to fall into ruins, and the streets were a mess of potholes, bone-jarring bumps.

The pickup, with Lily at the wheel, jounced over the holes, throwing them around in the front seat, and slamming them up against the doors and the dashboard.

"Next time, Rooster," complained Miss Hannigan sarcastically, "find a hotel that can drive."

"Zip your lip, stringbean!" snarled Lily. Her arms were getting sick and tired of jockeying this behemoth around, and she was anxious to be on the boardwalk at Atlantic City, someplace warm and wonderful, sitting in a deck chair sipping champagne and wearing sunglasses.

Annie held her breath. An idea was forming in her mind, a last-chance idea that might possibly work. She began to squirm around in her seat.

"Excuse me, mister," she said to Rooster in a little-girl whine. "Can we stop a second? I gotta go." As Rooster didn't even bother to reply, Annie turned to Miss Hannigan. "I really gotta *go*, Miss Hannigan." Then, to Lily, "I mean it, lady, you're asking for it!"

Rooster, no mean con artist himself, and you can't con a conner, grabbed Annie by the front of her dress and, growling, shook her like a rag doll.

"Miss Hannigan!" yelled Annie, pressing her knees together as though an accident was imminent.

But Miss Hannigan was shaking her head. "It's a con. She's housebroken."

Nevertheless, Lily slammed on the brakes.

"Drive, dammit!" Rooster shouted.

But Lily was climbing down out of the cab.

"To Atlantic City? In a puddle? Not this little honey."

Annie saw her chance, the cab door was open. With a single jerk, she pulled herself out of Rooster's clutches and vaulted out of the truck. The check flew from Miss Hannigan's fingers, and sailed out on the draft that Annie had created. Grabbing it in midair, Annie made a dash for it, sprinting as fast as she could.

"Grab her, Rooster!" Miss Hannigan yelled needlessly. "She's got the check!"

"This is news?" snarled Rooster as he pelted after Annie.

Annie ran through the dark tangle of the tracks, feeling the rough ties cutting into her feet. She had no idea where she was going; this place was a jungle of railroad tracks and sheds. But up ahead of her was a bridge of some kind, reached by a perpendicular ladder. At least a truck couldn't follow her up the ladder, so she made for it.

Behind her, Rooster came running fast and low, murder in his heart. He had expected to throw the brat in the ocean long before they reached Atlantic City, but never mind that now; this place would do as well. He'd had it with her. The sooner the kid was dead, the better off they'd all be.

A steep and rocky right of way led to the ladder, and Annie scrambled up on her hands and knees, the sharp stones cutting into her tender flesh. She could hear Rooster gaining on her, getting closer with every second.

Lily drove the pickup as close to the bridge as she could. The two women peered into the darkness, seeing Annie and Rooster silhouetted against the sky, caught in the glare of the bridge lights.

"That's it," said Lily. "He's almost got his hands on her and when he does, bye, bye, Annie."

Without a word, Miss Hannigan climbed down from the truck and started after Rooster.

Annie was climbing the railroad bridge ladder now, making for the top. Below her Rooster's fingers had closed around the bottom rung. But she mustn't look down. She must look up to the top of the . . . oh, no!

What Annie had mistaken for a closed bridge was actually a drawbridge, the kind that splits open to let ships pass through underneath. And this unused bridge was locked open permanently. What seemed to be a ladder was actually railroad ties, upended. So, beneath her was a man who wanted to kill her, while ahead of her was . . . nothing. A void. Empty space. Climb to the top and there was nowhere to go but thin air, more than two stories up. She turned and looked down; Rooster was very close, she could see his ferrety eyes glinting with malice, and she knew that he'd show her no mercy. Once he caught up with her, Annie was done for.

No, there was nowhere to go but up, and fast. As she scrambled up the perpendicular section of track, she felt Rooster's hand grabbing for her ankle, missing, grabbing again, then it closed around Annie's ankle and clung. She was caught.

But then the hand fell away, and Annie looked down.

To her amazement she saw Miss Hannigan tugging at her brother's sleeve, pulling his arm down, freeing Annie.

"A loathsome child, no doubt about it," Miss Hannigan was saying, "a monumentally irritating, horrible, dreadful, obnoxious child, but that's not enough to kill her, Rooster, that's not enough to kill her."

Rooster turned around savagely and beat his sister's hands away from him. Then, with one punch, he knocked Miss Hannigan cold, and took off after Annie again.

The brief tussle had given Annie time to climb nearly to the top. She could feel the cold wind of the void rushing past her face, and she knew there was nowhere to run, nowhere to hide; she was doomed.

Yet she kept climbing, to the narrow top, to the thin edge of the span where the bridge yawned wide. It was only a matter of seconds before Rooster would be upon her, his hands would be around her throat, choking the life out of her. And yet she kept going, crawling out to the lip of the bridge, hanging on there, clutching tightly.

Above her, in the night, a faint noise grew louder. And louder. And nearer. She recognized the sound. It was the autocopter. *It was the autocopter!*

But how could they save her? All Punjab and the Asp could do was hover helplessly as Rooster caught up with her, grabbed her, reached for her throat. Even if Punjab used weapons, even if he had a gun with him, he would not dare to shoot for fear of hitting Annie. And he had no gun, only the pair of binoculars through which he watched the life and death battle going on below. Annie was kicking and struggling, the two of them were moving around dangerously close to the narrow edge where the bridge ended in midair, and Rooster was pushing, pushing. A body hurtled through the air as Punjab watched in horror. It was Annie.

She fell about eight feet. A steel bar was projecting from the bridge eight feet down, and Annie managed to catch hold of it. Now she was dangling precariously from the inner face of the bridge, her feet swinging over empty air and the river. And now she was more vulnerable than ever, right where Rooster could pick her off easily.

He scrambled down the ties until he was parallel with Annie, looking into her eyes. He had a ladder below him, while Annie had only empty space. She heard Rooster's snarling laugh, looked into his mean little eyes, and knew her last hour had struck.

Now Punjab had an idea, a risky one, but it just might work. Everything depended on the tensile strength of precious Indian silk, the stuff of which Punjab's turban was made. Hundreds of feet of it, woven lovingly by master craftsmen, and wound around and around, fastened with a ruby. Swiftly Punjab pinned the ruby to his tunic. Swiftly he freed the end of the turban and wrapped it many times around the passenger seat of the 'copter, tying it tightly. Now he opened the 'copter door and, holding tightly to the silk as a lifeline, began to lower himself into the air. The Asp maneuvered the craft so that it hovered as close to the bridge as he could come without crashing into it.

Today, helicopter rescues are commonplace, but then there were no precedents. Nobody had ever attempted this before, possibly because this was the first 'copter in existence. On the other hand, nobody today would be fool enough to lower a nine-foot, 400-pound man on a thin makeshift rope of turban silk.

Rooster reached his hands through the ties and found Annie's hands, still clinging to the steel bar. If he could force her fingers free, she'd plummet straight down, a hundred feet into the river. He began to tug at her small hands with his powerful ones. Annie felt her grip beginning to loosen.

"Hang on, Annie!" a voice shouted below her. It was Oliver Warbucks, who had arrived escorted by screaming sirens. "Hang on! Bring a net," he yelled to the police.

The turban silk that Punjab was clinging to stretched thinner and thinner. Above him the 'copter was being pulled off balance by his weight, with the Asp struggling to regain control of the craft.

There was no way that Punjab would reach her in time. Rooster was prying Annie's fingers loose from the bar, one by one and . . . there! One hand had come free, and now Annie was swinging over the river by only her other hand, panting with fear and exertion, dangling, dangling, the seconds of her life ticking away. Rooster's malicious fingers began working on hand number two.

But just as Annie was done for, Rooster was jerked off balance. It was Miss Hannigan, pulling from below. Furious, he kicked out at her, but that was a mistake, a bad one. The kick destroyed his balance completely, and he fell, screaming, into the net the police were holding at the base of the bridge. They slapped the cuffs on him, and threw Rooster into the paddy wagon, next to Lily.

But Annie was still in mortal danger. Her arm had been nearly pulled from its socket by her weight, and she was dangling so perilously that she couldn't bring her other hand up to share the weight. More than that, the air currents were twisting her around like a puppet on a string.

On the ground, Oliver and Grace watched helplessly, Grace sobbing openly, twisting her hands in fear. Warbucks' hands were knotted fists; his face was pale, and the muscles in his jaw stood out like clenched knots.

Annie's hand was slipping. It was all over.

But Punjab had reached her now. Punjab's arm was around her plucking her from the bar, holding her tightly.

"Oh, Punjab," Annie murmured, and let herself go limp in his arms, fainting.

"Do not sleep yet, Princess," said Punjab softly.

Annie's eyes were drifting shut. "I can't help it. I'm so tired . . . so very tired."

They hung by a gossamer thread of silk, over the river, over the city. It was so beautiful, to drift like this, in the safety of Punjab's arm.

But they were far from safe. At any moment the silk of the turban might snap, the threads parting, and plunge them both to a watery death.

"To pull us to safety, I need both hands. You must hold onto me," warned Punjab.

"I can't," whispered Annie. Every ounce of her strength had been used up in her ordeal with Rooster.

"Buddha says a child without courage is like a night without stars," said Punjab.

The words roused her. Never, never would Annie be called a child without courage. She rallied and managed to wind her arms around Punjab's neck and cling to him.

Hand over hand, inch by inch, the Indian giant climbed back up the silken rope and into the safety of the 'copter.

It was over. It was finally over. Annie was too dazed to believe it. It was only when she stepped out of the 'copter and into Oliver Warbucks' waiting arms that she began to feel safe, to feel loved, to feel as though she really, truly had a home.

CHAPTER FOURTEEN

I'm not sure you want to read about this part, because there are no villains, and there's no danger, no daring rescues out of the sky, no valiant orphans or nick-of-time warnings. There's only love and friendship and good times and—let's face it—that can be pretty dull to read about.

But if you like parties, well, you should have gone to the blowout Warbucks threw for Annie when the official adoption papers were finally signed, and Oliver Warbucks became "Daddy" Warbucks at last. That party was like the circus, the ballet, Radio City Music Hall, and Christmas all rolled into one. The New York Philharmonic played. Even the Rockettes came, after the last show at the Music Hall, and high-kicked and strutted to Annie's delight. There were elephants and clowns and monkeys, and Sandy wore a red-and-white ribbon around his neck and ate so much he got sick later.

There were fireworks that spelled out A*N*N*I*E in the sky in red, white, and blue letters, and FDR and Eleanor sent a telegram; they couldn't come because Eleanor was inspecting a coal mine and FDR was busy signing more bills into laws. But the president sent his chief aide, Harry Hopkins, and Mayor LaGuardia came himself.

Grace looked beautiful in a dress of sky blue that changed the color of her eyes, and a diamond ring on her left hand that sparkled nearly as brightly as her smile. And as busy as she was with the party, and as popular as she was with the guests, she would come over frequently to wherever Annie and "Daddy" were and hug them both.

Punjab and the Asp were heroes, and everyone wanted to hear about the daring rescue from the air, especially Miss Hannigan, who had heard it many times, and besides, she'd been there, hadn't she? But there was something about the way that Punjab told it that made her heart go flutter-flutter and, besides, she *loved* tall men. Miss Hannigan was at the party? Oh, yes, didn't I mention that? See, she was forgiven for everything because she really did help a lot in saving Annie's life, and that was the best recommendation to Mr. Warbucks' good graces. And it was decided that Miss Hannigan wouldn't be all that terrible if she had a job that wouldn't put her into contact with little girls. Ever. So they were working something out. Meanwhile, Miss Hannigan was living in a furnished room nearby, listening to her radio and drinking store-bought gin, but less of it than before.

Oh, and Pepper, Molly, Duffy, Tessie, Kate, and July never did go back to the Hudson Street Home for Girls, Established 1891. But you knew that already. You also knew that a new and enlightened director was appointed, and that the girls who remained behind were now well fed, well clothed, and learning French and tap-dancing. As for "our" orphans, they were all going to be adopted into rich homes by friends of Oliver's who wanted to be in on the latest thing. And if any of them got left out, Mr. Warbucks promised to adopt them himself.

Annie wore a dress of red velvet with a white collar, in the style she loved best, and danced with everybody who asked her. But most of all, she stayed by her new "Daddy's" side, holding tightly to his hand and dizzy with happiness. Around her neck she was wearing the golden locket he'd bought for her at Tiffany; and when he hung it around her neck the music played, the bells rang out and photographers snapped their pictures for the front pages of the newspapers.

Not that they were ever to live a quiet life. Oh, no, they would have many adventures over the years, and Annie would be brave and resourceful, just as you'd expect, and Sandy would always be by her side, and Punjab and the Asp somewhere nearby, in case the going got too rough for a little kid to handle. But they always had fun, good times or bad.

And it was some party.

After all the guests were gone and Annie had been tucked into the canopy bed in her room, Sandy curled up at her feet, she couldn't sleep. Too much excitement, probably. She lay there in the darkness, pleasantly weary, listening to the murmur of voices outside her door. She could make out some of the words . . . "she" and "Annie," and she knew that "Daddy" Warbucks and Grace Farrell were planning for her future.

And a little later, the door opened and she saw two people come in. She could smell a sweet perfume, and see a bald head gleaming in the light coming in from the corridor. A soft, fragrant hand touched her brow to see if she had a night fever (she didn't), and a man's hand touched her on the shoulder and pulled her blanket more tightly around her.

And Annie reached out with both her hands and caught the two hands in hers and held them.

And this time the Dream didn't dissolve.